RED
TEMPEST
BROTHER

H. M.
LONG

TITAN BOOKS

Red Tempests Brother
Print edition ISBN: 9781835411377
E-book edition ISBN: 9781835413548

Published by Titan Books
A division of Titan Publishing Group Ltd
144 Southwark Street, London SE1 0UP
www.titanbooks.com

First edition: July 2025
10 9 8 7 6 5 4 3 2 1

A CIP catalogue record for this title is available from the British
Library.

EU RP (for authorities only)
eucomply OÜ, Pärnu mnt. 139b-14, 11317 Tallinn, Estonia
hello@eucompliancepartner.com, +3375690241

Printed and bound by CPI Group (UK) Ltd, Croydon, CR0 4YY.

For Marco

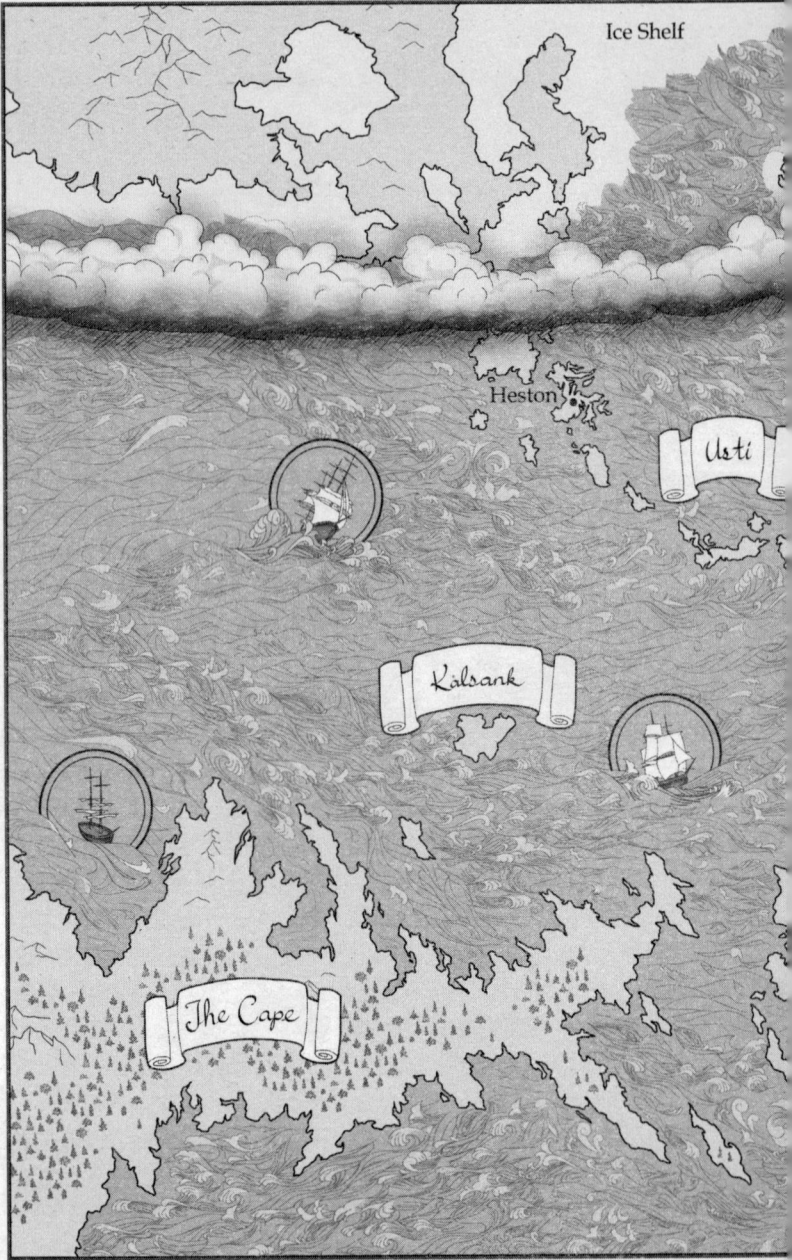

Ice Shelf

Heston

Usti

Kälsank

The Cape

Northern
Mereish
Isles

The Storm Wall

Aeadine

Tithe

Ghistwold

Whallum

Aeadine
Anchorage

Maase

Ostchen

Mere

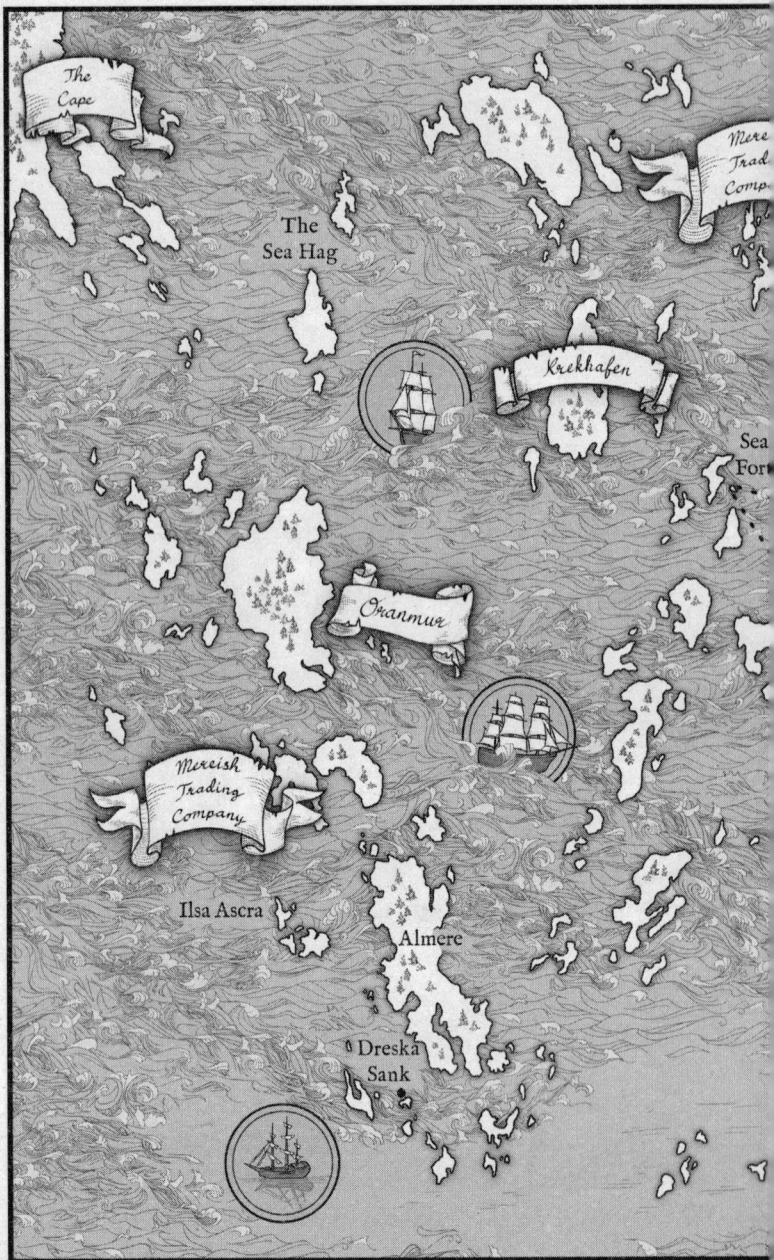

The Cape

Mere
Trad
Comp

The
Sea Hag

Krekhafen

Sea
For

Oranmur

Mereish
Trading
Company

Ilsa Ascra

Almere

Dreska
Sank

Port Sen

Indry

doldrums

MEREISH SOUTH ISLES —*Comprised of some three thousand islands south of Mere and the Cape, the Mereish South Isles officially fall under the rule of Mere. In practicality, however, the islands are broken up under the governance of dozens of local warlords, monarchs, trade companies and rulers of other distinctions. These rulers are everything from pirates to royal exiles, hailing from across the Winter Sea and beyond, and are united under the banner of a so-called Unified Council of Lords. See also* MERE, MEREISH, MEREISH NORTHERN ISLES, MEREISH-CAPESH ALLIANCE.

—FROM THE WORDBOOK ALPHABETICA:
A NEW WORDBOOK OF THE AEADINES

ONE

The Burning of Port Sen

BENEDICT

Sometime between learning of the Usti spy's escape and returning to the docks, my temper snapped. I knocked a lantern into a pile of refuse, glass cracking, oil spilling. My crew began to enact similar vandalisms with willful abandon, the invisible threads of my Magni power compelling their minds to vengeance and their hands to destruction.

Naturally, there were attempts to stop us. A musketball skimmed past my ear, loosed by one of the port's converging guards, so I turned my power upon them. As I strode out onto the sprawling docks, the guards, then civilians, took up our task with startled, frightened and ravenous urgency. A little girl hurled rocks through windows, burning hay scattered about her small feet. Fishwives set fires, cart drivers knocked aside the poles of the market stalls and laborers began to dump goods into the South Sea by crate and barrel and upended basket.

The Port Mistress survived only by her honesty.

"South," she said when I stood in her door, the streets a riot behind me. "The last ship was headed south."

There was only one dock fit for a vessel as deep and grand as my *Red Tempest*, and it was to the end of this long, barnacle-crusted arm we strode as the fires spread. My influence followed me like the billows of smoke that drifted across the bay, wrapping about the other ships and prompting men and women to load cannons, swivel guns and small arms. Then they, as I willed, turned the lot of them upon the shore.

The Red Tempest did not participate in the bombardment of Port Sen. We sailed out long before the Port Mistress's mansion toppled from its stilts and the battery at the harbor mouth exploded. I observed the chaos from *Tempest*'s deck, listening to the thunder of the guns and watching the inhabitants of the port scatter like rats, leaping into the water, fleeing into the hills and putting themselves out in boats.

The smoke trailed us out of the bay. I felt the sphere of my influence slip from the last of the anchored ships, and my world narrowed once more. The deck beneath my boots. Blood on my hands, though I could not recall how it came to be there. Hot breath raking from my lungs. The taste of sweat and smoke on my lips. The chanting, rolling, rumbling voice of my Stormsinger, summoning the winds that swept us away and prevented pursuit.

"Benedict."

I turned, squinting smoke-burned eyes. Charles Grant considered me from a pace away, one restless hand on the hilt of his smallsword.

My attention caught on him like fingers on a crumbling slope. I corralled myself and straightened.

"No need for that," I said, glancing back towards the port. Something stirred in me at the scene, a lightness that might have been excitement, or shock, or unease. I could ill define the sensation, but I was swiftly learning that reflection was arduous and uncomfortable. Particularly with the stink of smoke and gunpowder in my nostrils.

I pulled my baldric over my head, taking my sword and brace of spent pistols with it, and tossed it to Grant. He caught it, then coughed a protest as my soiled coat followed the weapons.

"Am I your fucking valet?" the former highwayman demanded, shaking his blond hair out from beneath the coat.

I ignored him, heading for the companionway.

"Ms. Olles," I called to my first officer, a black-haired woman in her mid-thirties. "What is the nearest port?"

"Aside from the one he just burned," Charles interjected, following me with my coat draped over his shoulder and my weapons in his arms. His tone was dry but I recognized his disapproval.

"To the south," I clarified.

Olles shot Charles a quelling look. She was a good-natured woman, evidenced by the crinkles around her eyes and the laugh lines on her cheeks, but she had little patience for interruptions. Or Charles. "I'd need to see the charts, sir."

"Fine, I will do it myself," I said. "Send Faucher to my cabin."

"Yessir."

A few more paces and Charles and I were swallowed by the shadows of the first gun deck. We made for the stern, where the grand cabin lay, passing row upon row of nestled guns and sea chests in the close, brine-scented gloom.

In the cabin, Charles dumped my coat and weapons on a chair and moved to the stern windows, where he peered out at the shrinking, smoke-blurred visage of Port Sen.

"There will be repercussions for this," he commented.

"One enemy among a thousand islands and a hundred lords," I said, pouring water into a bowl on the central table then beginning to work the blood from around my nails. "Port Sen is irrelevant. Once we find Alamay, I will be the only one with true power in these seas."

Charles sank down in a chair on the other side of the table. "I am still unclear as to how a stack of unverified documents will satisfy your megalomania."

"You need not know."

"Ah, now, see," Charles raised a finger. "That is where you are wrong. Friends share their minds, Ben. I know you have very little experience in these matters, so you will simply have to believe me. Unless I *am* a prisoner, in which case, perhaps you would consider a villain's illuminatory ramble?"

I shook pink water from my fingers. "Handkerchief."

Charles fished one from his pocket and tossed it over. I proceeded to dry my hands, only to slow when I saw the embroidery around the cloth's edges. "What are these? Nooses?"

"Yes, and there I am, hanging in the corner," Charles replied, leaning forward to point. "Mary made it for me. Try not to stain it."

"Mary," I muttered, disliking the reminder of my brother and his… whatever they defined themselves as nowadays. The thought of them stirred a host of feeling and, admittedly, conflict, that did not bear contemplation.

I had left them behind, and for good reason. They had done enough for me. And to me. It was time to part ways and carve our own destinies.

The blood around my nails refused to come clean. I frowned at it and scrubbed, much too hard.

A knock came at the door and Jessin Faucher strode in, shadowed by two crewmen who remained in the hall. We were nearly of an age, he marginally shorter than I and dressed in a simple shirt, breeches, stockings and a straight-cut Mereish waistcoat.

He closed the door on the guards without a word and joined Charles and I at the table.

Charles, reclaiming his handkerchief, sighed at its condition and tucked it away again.

"You know these isles," I said to Faucher. "I need you to determine where Enisca Alamay is most likely to try to sell those documents. We cannot chase her like blind dogs—we must get ahead of her."

"So, she did escape," Faucher clarified, leaning back to cross one knee over the other. His Mereish accent was marked but not burdensome, and he spoke Aeadine for my benefit. "I heard a commotion from my quarters, but my... escort... was unforthcoming."

"Kapper saw her board a ship leaving harbor. There was no time to get word to *Tempest* to stop her, and as I cannot fucking fly, there was nothing I could do."

"Ah. And we have no notion of where she went?"

"South."

"Nearly everything in the isles is south of our position. That is vastly unhelpful."

"She may not intend to sell them," Charles pointed out with an air of weary repetition. It was not the first time he had waged this battle. "She is more likely intent on some Usti stronghold where she can disappear or find aid. Send the papers home."

Faucher shrugged. "You know her better than I. But I know the isles, yes. And I am glad to share that knowledge in return for greater freedoms."

"I am not releasing you," I stated.

"Freedoms," the Mereish man repeated. "I have no interest in leaving my ship."

I held his gaze, a reminder that *The Red Tempest* was now my ship poised on my tongue. But he knew that well enough, and I would not rise to his provocation.

He would, naturally, attempt to retake the vessel if the opportunity arose. I would have thought less of him otherwise.

"Give me a location to begin and we can discuss these freedoms," I countered. "Particularly if you can tell me where to hire a Sooth."

Faucher thought for an instant, tilting his head back to stare up at the beams of the ceiling. Then he sat forward and rested his elbows on the table. "I agree with Charles. If I were her, I would make for Usti waters. That likely means the Sea Hag, the Indry or Krekhafen. We can hire or buy a Sooth in any of them."

"The Sea Hag," Charles repeated with a snort. "Did she give herself that title?"

"Actually, yes," Faucher's lips turned in a small, dry smile. "Which tells you something of her nature."

I had heard of the Indry, but neither of the others. I did not, however, admit my ignorance. "Which is the closest?"

"Krekhafen," Faucher replied. "It is ruled by exiled Usti royals, from a dispossessed line. There are more than a few of them down here, vaguely allied with, and casually hostile to, one another and everyone else. All distant relations of the current queen. Krekhafen in particular would both be an easy place for an Usti to blend in, and a very, very good place to sell secrets that might overturn the current crown. If they so desired."

"Very good. Where is Krekhafen? South, I presume."

"In a manner of speaking. One must go south to get there." Faucher moved to one of the bulkheads, where numerous charts were pegged. "This is Port Sen."

"Was," Charles corrected.

Faucher cleared his throat and moved his finger across the heavy paper. "This is Krekhafen, here, in the west. In between, here, is this arc of islands. This is under the control of the Mereish Trading Company, and thus the Mereish Navy. They have multiple strongholds throughout the islands, do be aware of that. I do not recommend catching the attention of either the Company or the Navy, particularly as they will have stronger ties to the Ess Noti and their augmented magecrafts. Also, the events at the Anchorage and the fate of my ship may be known already. The war will bleed south."

"Company waters might provide an opportunity for your rescue," Charles pointed out. He considered the other man dubiously, then looked at me. "Are you bewitching him?"

I felt a flicker of offense. "I need not always enthrall everyone in my company. You bear with me."

"Our bond, as established, has been forged through great travail. And abduction," Charles pointed out, a little distractedly.

Faucher laughed without humor. "As I said before, I have no desire to leave my ship. I, too, wish to find Enisca Alamay and those documents before they land in the wrong hands."

The conversation continued for some time, including further discussion of charts and courses. Regardless, the first order of business remained to find a Sooth, so I sent Charles above with the word to make for Krekhafen. Faucher I banished back to his quarters, trailed by his guards, and I was finally left alone.

I remained at the table, where the bloodied bowl of water sloshed. It was more brown than pink now and made my stomach turn.

Or, perhaps, it was not the blood that made me ill. Perhaps it was the memories flickering through the back of my mind, glimpses of burning buildings, of people throwing themselves from the docks. Of a little girl, mindlessly throwing a rock at a window as flaming hay scattered around her skirts.

Another time, I might have cut that imagining off. But I found that I was drained, my mask of indomitability slipping. My discomfort grew.

I leaned forward and a Sooth's talisman, warm from my skin and tarnished from constant wear, swung out over the table.

In a flash, I saw another little girl. Her face was vague, a mix of the infant I had once seen and the shadow of my mother. My eyes peered out of her small face as she became the girl from Port Sen, in my thrall, throwing stones and unaware of the fire around her, the danger on every side. Then she was elsewhere—tucked into a shadow. Beneath a bed? Behind a door?

I shoved the talisman back under my shirt, scrubbed bloody water across my face with brusque hands, and walked away.

TWO

Fire in the Fog

MARY

After surviving the greatest naval battle in a century and carving my name among the most powerful Stormsingers in history, being outwitted by pirates barely a day into the Mereish South Isles was, mildly put, demoralizing.

I considered the depth of my misfortune in a bleary, half-feeling way as I lay like a starfish on the sand, staring up at cool drifts of fog. The wind smelled of brine and rotting seaweed, but also cedar and greenery, and the rich damp of deadfall. The latter, I suspected, was entirely my imagination. I had just been blown overboard, half drowned, and taken a solid knock to the head—it was only natural that my mind would retreat to where I felt the safest. A Wold in the mist, tucked at the feet of slate grey hills.

Something pinched me. I rolled my head to see an oddly opalescent, and rather gigantic, crab plucking at my sodden shirtsleeve. I squinted at it, still not quite rooted in reality, but the second pinch—or rather, the creature's attempt to pull my flesh from my bones with one long, serrated claw—set me right.

I shot up, blacked out, and woke up again with the creature hauling me into the surf by the ankle. I shrieked, flailing and kicking, only to receive a mouthful of water and sand for my struggle.

My hands moved without my prompting, jerking a knife from

my belt and twisting. I stabbed the blade down at the joint below the claw once, twice. My knife deflected, striking only sand and water. I writhed like a cat on a string and shouted my horror and defiance.

A third stab. I felt the blade dig into a chitinous limb.

The claw released. I flipped, crawling then stumbling back onto the shore. Just out of reach of the lapping waves I collapsed against a rock, hip high and oddly flat on top, then proceeded to gasp and curse and spit water, gritty sand between my teeth. My ankle bled freely, stinging with salt, but I had eyes only for the waves. I stared to and fro, sure at any moment the giant crab would come back to snap off my feet and crush my skull.

The waves simply lapped, smoothing away the signs of my struggle into a flat, pale beach.

"We should have stabbed out its eyes," I rasped, but instead of sounding fierce I put myself into a fit of coughing. I set the knife down and braced on the rock, retching seawater and bile.

In its defense, you did look dead, Tane's voice replied in the confines of my mind.

Hush.

Still coughing, I assessed my condition. I wore sodden trousers, belted, a torn shirt and stays. There was a swollen gash on my forehead—the source of the blood—and only one shoe had survived my swim. My hat was nowhere in sight, nor were my pistols, and the twists of powder and shot in a pouch at my belt were soaked.

I pulled off my useless shoe and set it beside my knife on the flat rock, still eyeing the waves.

"One shoe, a knife and five bits of wet shot," I summarized. "Samuel had best find me soon. I am ill-equipped."

The ghisting in my bones did not reply, but I knew her thoughts. They spun back to Samuel, *Hart,* and the battle I had been so abruptly removed from, tossed overboard by a cunning gust of wind as we fended off petty local pirates and their surprisingly deft Stormsinger.

My stomach began to turn. I could not fear for *Hart,* I told myself, not truly. He had survived far greater foes.

Then why could I not hear cannons, or bells, or voices? The engagement had been within sight of shore, at least before the fog had rolled in.

I surveyed my surroundings more intently. I stood at the center of a circle of stones on a flat expanse of sand, all of them knee-high and surrounded by the sea fog. The stones were narrow, weathered by centuries of exposure. The larger rock I leaned against was different, however: broad and flat, dark with damp and rimed with salt in the muffled light. It looked, oddly, like an altar.

No, it *was* an altar, complete with carved trenches for blood and wave-worn symbols.

That felt like a bad sign.

I snatched up my shoe and knife and limped from the circle.

I stared out at the veiled, disconsolate sea as I fled. It was growing darker and the water was cold, even this far south. I whistled to the wind and the fog shifted, granting me a clearer view. Inland, the sand continued as tidal flats, interrupted here and there by sheer shoulders of rock and sea stacks twice my height. These were capped by dense forest, blurs of green leaves and reddish bark. A few toppled trees lay here and there upon the sand, smoothed by time and the waves, and bleached by the sun.

There was no sign of *Hart.* No sign of Samuel. No sign that any human had trodden this shore, save the macabre stone circle.

We need to see further.

I began to hum, swaying slightly as I eased the weight on my clawed ankle.

New tendrils of wind stirred the mist into eddies about my sodden form. They brought a host of information, glimpses and sensations. Salt. The wash of waves on sand, their crash against rock, the slop of seaweed and debris. The dart of little birds in and out of crags in the sea stacks. The whispering of the forest and the distant cries of gulls.

Voices. Voices shouting.

An explosion.

I took off at a stumbling run.

Smoke gusted past me as I staggered around the foot of a rocky peninsula. Beyond, the miasma dissipated into scattered banks, dragged across a tidal flat surrounded by rocky coastline, smooth beaches and lush, temperate forests of cedar, hemlock and spruce. Further out to sea the smoke relented to natural, wispy fog, revealing dozens of scattered islets.

My stomach lurched. There, on a barren tidal flat between rivers and listless pools, lay *Hart*. Beached by the tide and toppled against one of the rock towers, his wounds were laid bare: a toppled mast, another visibly cracked and threatening to split, and a shattered section of hull spewing fire and flotsam. The ship's grand figurehead of a rampant hart was half-buried, rammed into ridges of sand. Indigo ghisten light flickered across the wreck, spasming, trying and failing to heal wounds that could not be closed.

Nausea overcame me and I doubled over. My mind felt numb, my ears ringing. Surely, this was not real. I was delirious, dreaming, still adrift in the waves.

But the horror continued. The crew were little more than specks at this distance, but the wind brought me their cries of coordination, panic and pain. Ripples of musket fire and the deep boom of cannons sounded again and again. The latter echoed through the stone towers and muffled in the fog as I sighted its source—a small, swift sloop anchored before an islet, masts separating from the blur of conifers that clustered its shores.

The mouths of long guns flashed again, echoing across the sands as I saw a second vessel, twin to the first. This one was much nearer, nosing along what must have been a steep drop in the seafloor. A flag rippled lazily from her maintop, bearing the empty-eyed profile of a wolf skull, stuck through with a vertical, thick-bladed machete. The field behind the head was yellow and blue—Capesh colors.

I hobbled into the shelter of the nearest sea stack and took a moment to calm my thundering heart.

"So much for petty pirates," I muttered, my voice thick, my mind numb. "Why are they still firing? They'll destroy *Hart*."

Perhaps that is their intention.

Another volley of cannons made me peer around the stack just in time to see an explosion of sand near *Hart*. The moving specks that were the crew—my crew—scattered with more shouts and screams.

I had to act. I edged back out into sight, marking the position of our enemies as I dragged ragged air into my lungs and began to sing a chanting song. *"And the coming wind did roar more loud, and the sails did sigh like sedge…"*

The winds came, weaving, then rushing, then roaring. They whipped damp shanks of hair into my face and snatched up the sea fog, driving it into a protective barrier between *Hart* and the pirates. Other winds lashed out, sending the enemy ships creaking and rocking. Shouts and cries came from them now, along with the song of their Stormsinger.

I kept close to the stack. *"And the rain poured down from one black cloud, the moon was at its edge."*

My fear and anxiety began to disperse into the wind, borne away and replaced with a grim exhilaration. It bloomed in my chest, pushing my shoulders back, making me a wind-harried shadow on the sand. I edged further out into the open, keeping my prey within sight as I reveled in the feeling. This was retribution. This was salvation. This was power—

A cannonball slammed into the stack behind me. Stone

exploded, peppering me with fragments as my song turned into a shriek and I cowered away. Another, then another ball hurtled past me and I had no choice but to take off at a tottering, flailing sprint, barefooted as a billy goat but not a fraction as deft. My head ached. My ankle throbbed. The whistles of the shots gave me only momentary warning, particularly when those whistles turned into the deadly shrieking of canister shot. Rogue threads of wind blasted sand into my eyes before my own winds could stop them, and I flailed on in blindness.

I toppled behind a barnacle-covered boulder as shrapnel and musketballs peppered the area around me. Breathless, I cobbled together a few more lines of song. Fog immediately shrouded me and when more shots came, they were further afield.

That was foolish, Tane observed.

I realized I was still carrying my useless shoe and hurled it aside with disgust.

Gathering my courage I set off again, keeping low and pulling the fog around myself. I sprint-hobbled across an open expanse of tidal sands, leaving a drunkard's path of dry-edged footprints in my wake. I splashed through pools and creeks rather than taking the time to circumvent them. Spurts of water from subterranean clams chased me as I navigated a rocky patch, darted around more sea stacks and squished over seaweed.

I saw the first body tangled in that seaweed, half-hidden by the fog. She lay face-down, more of the massive crabs converging on her spilled intestines in a pool of pink water.

I couldn't tell who it was. I couldn't look closer, could not afford to break down. I coughed back a surge of bile and carried on, giving her and the crabs a wide berth.

I passed other debris now, tangles of rope, pieces of hull— some from *Hart*, new and raw, others old and wave-battered and smooth—signaling we were not the only vessel to run afoul of this bay, or the machinations of the pirates who had driven us here.

I was just beginning to fear I had bypassed *Hart* entirely when figures burst around a massive sea stack, helping one another towards shore.

"Mr. Keo!" I shouted, as loud as I dared.

"Ms. Firth!" he called back. "They are coming ashore!"

My beleaguered heart slammed in my chest. "Where is Sam?"

"Gone for the ghisting with the Uknaras!"

Relief that Samuel, Olsa and Illya were alive collided with numb understanding. The ghisting in question was undoubtedly Hart himself, the spectral creature who inhabited the figurehead of our ship, guided and guarded it. But if they had gone back to the ship *for* the ghisting, that meant only one thing.

Hart, the vessel that had granted me freedom, where Samuel had found his redemption and where we had begun to build new lives, could not be saved. And, in fulfillment of a captain's last duty to his vessel, Samuel would try to salvage the ship's ghisting— even while the enemy advanced and the ship burned.

"Send us what hands you can!" I shouted to Keo. As far as the chain of command went, I wasn't part of it, but he nodded his affirmation.

I took off again, following their footprints and cursing my ankle. I wanted to sprint, to fly, to already be at Samuel's side.

My impatience, however, was unnecessary. With a swirl of fog the hulk of *Hart* loomed before me, figurehead tilted to one side, the great stag's open, baying mouth soundless in the haze. My heart wrenched but I carried on, picking my way over broken sections of hull and fallen yards and spars.

"Sam!" I shouted as another explosion shook *Hart*. Fire plumed. Heat buffeted me, light blinded me, and all at once I was in another place, another time. Standing over another blaze, with Silvanus Lirr's hand on my back.

I stumbled over a body, still twitching in a tangle of lines and torn sailcloth. I instinctively reached out to steady myself on a pile of debris, noticing too late that it was a cannon—hot and steaming and embossed with depictions of conquerors astride armored horses. I jerked back a scalded hand.

I froze in place, eyes pinned closed. I counted a handful of breaths, each one pummeled by the hammering of my heart.

Then, slowly, I forced my eyes open again.

The fire remained, but there was no Lirr. No frozen Ghistwold. No flames rushing over my skin.

Just the dying ship, the billowing fog, and Samuel Rosser.

THREE

The Liberation of the Hart

MARY

Samuel emerged from the murk like a specter. He was tall, his well-formed frame clad in a blood-stained shirt and his brown hair a tangle about his face. My relief at seeing him was tempered by the firelight that spilled around him, casting harsh shadows across his face, and glinting off the axe in his hands.

He didn't appear to have seen or heard me, my calls drowned by the roar of the flames. Grim with determination, he mounted the wave of sand towards the figurehead's great, baying head. Then, backed by smoke and fog and encroaching firelight, he began to hack.

"Mary." I startled as Olsa Uknara appeared, followed by the larger figure of her husband, Illya. "You lost your shoes."

"I have," I huffed, and it felt like a sob. I clutched the wrist of my scalded hand, though Tane had mitigated the pain. "I'm glad you're alive. Both of you."

Illya saluted in reply, making for Samuel. As he joined the other man he hefted another axe, weighty and sharp, and spoke to our captain.

Sam turned, finally catching sight of me. Hart's neck gaped open above him, chipped wood raw, and the creature's great antlers spreading like the branches of the tree the ghisting had once inhabited.

"Mary," Samuel panted. For an instant he was still, gaze flicking between me and the miasma around us, then he hefted the axe again. "Give us cover? They will soon be—*Down*!"

Olsa hauled me into the shadow of the hull.

My startled protest was lost in a cacophony of booming cannons and shrieking shot. Canister shot raked the wreck, lead balls slamming into wood, shards of metal tearing into sand. I saw the body I had tripped over twitch with impact—one of the bosun's mates, I dimly recalled, and gagged.

"Thank you," I panted to Olsa, pressing my back into the hull, then jolting away. The hull was hot, not to mention sharp with barnacles. They plucked at my clothes and the stink of green, briny growth assaulted me, along with the hiss and whine of heating wood.

This had to stop. I felt half mad, assaulted by threat and discomfort on every side. Sweat and seawater made my clothes cling to my body, sticky and hot. The fog felt like a weight in my lungs, too thick, and growing thicker with trapped smoke.

The thudding of the men's axes resumed, faster than before.

"There's no chance of saving the ship?" I asked Olsa as she took a knee, unslinging her rifle and beginning to load it.

"No. Just the ghisting." She shoved a ramrod down the barrel of her gun and deftly clicked it back into place. She nodded out towards the enemy. "Which is all the Capesh care about."

I looked up at *Hart* again, eyes burning with more than smoke. Suddenly, it made sense. The Capesh and Mereish were allies, largely due to the fact that the Capesh had no Ghistwold and relied upon the Mereish for their ghistings.

To a people with no Ghistwold, Hart would be the greatest treasure.

A protective instinct—Tane's or mine, I could not tell—made me reach out. I rested my fingers on a bare, hot portion of hull between cracking barnacles and melting oakum. Light skittered across the wood in response. Another light wreathed my fingers as Tane began to whisper to Hart, their words susurrating back and forth in a language of imagery and emotion too fast for me to follow. But I felt Hart's distress, his rage, his drive to protect his ship. So too I felt Tane's need to save him—the desperation and determination of a Mother Ghisting.

Child, she soothed, before her will rushed through me like a gale. *Sing, Mary.*

"Samuel!" I shouted over the noise, backing away from the ship—lingering strings of luminescent ghisten flesh stretching between my fingers and the wood. My eyes stung, but I blinked the smoke and tears away. "I intend to sink them! Are you opposed?"

Wood exploded somewhere above and the ghisten light skittered away from me and back to the figurehead, casting Sam and Illya's laboring forms into cavorting silhouettes.

"Leave one, destroy the other," Sam bellowed in return. "They took my ship from me. I will fucking take theirs!"

The rage in his voice was enough to make me pause. For half a breath I stared at the fury in his half-lit face and the taut lines of his body. I hardly recognized him—or rather, I recognized someone else. Benedict. Wrathful. Unchecked. And even as my blood rose, my own rage boiling in sympathy, I was uneasy.

"Now," Olsa urged. Her eyes had a distant quality, one that told me she looked beyond this tidal plain, into the Other. "They are nearly here."

I shifted my shoulders purposefully, pushing away the image of vengeful Sam, my worry for Hart and our own lives. Remaining in the shelter of his beached hulk, I began to sing again.

"About, about, in reel and rout, the Death-fires danced at night."

The first wind came swift and cold, dispersing the fog between me and the enemy vessels. I saw their forms as shadows in the deepening twilight, their lanterns extinguished. There were figures on the sand between those ships and I, advancing at a jog. Muzzles flashed again, this time smaller and closer—rifles and muskets.

"The water, like a witch's oils, burnt green and blue and white."

Another wind came, arching over the islands and seastacks with a great rocking of trees. It swept what was left of the fog and smoke out to sea, momentarily suspending us in a genuine, windy twilight, cold and brisk and tasting of salt.

Clouds rippled out across the newly visible sky like a shaken cloak, and the hail began. It rushed past us in pelting arms, pummeling the sand and converging on our enemies.

"And some in dreams assured were, of the spirit that plagued us so," I sang.

Another voice began to clash with my own, equal parts breathless and urgent. The enemy Stormsinger, here, on the sand.

I squinted through the growing murk, searching for my counterpart. That figure? No, that was a man. That one? No, she could hardly sing so steadily at a run. She must be further back, sheltering behind her crew. Hiding.

"Come wind and sleet and woe..." Her words snatched at the wind and tossed it back upon us. Smoke wafted into my face, hammering hail advanced upon us, and my song stifled in a fit of coughing.

"Mary!" That was Illya. "Stop them!"

"Nine fathom deep he had followed us," I rasped. By now flames had completely engulfed *Hart*, its light blinding and the heat rolling out in great, sickening streams over our heads. *"From the land of mist and snow."*

Figures burst into view—but not from the direction of our enemies.

"Captain!" shouted the familiar form of Mr. Penn, his bald head streaked with blood and soot.

A dozen crewmembers led by Mr. Penn joined us beside the wreck, bearing muskets and a torn section of sailcloth. Some immediately sheltered behind piles of debris and trained muskets on our attackers, cracking off shots at will. Others joined Samuel, our helmsman spotting him out with the heavy axe.

"*About, about, in reel and rout, the Death-fires danced at night,*" I cried again. I flung the wind back at the enemy, blood racing, my face flushed with frustration and exertion.

The hailstorm swirled, now trapped between the wills of two Stormsingers.

Samuel stepped down beside me, his face slick with sweat, his shirt sodden and singed. He accepted a musket from Penn with one hand and snagged mine with the other, squeezing my fingers. It was a momentary contact, a flicker in my awareness, before he shouldered the weapon again. He stepped partially in front of me and knelt, facing our attackers.

Short as it was, his touch pulled me back into myself. I summoned the winds and crouched behind him, resuming my previous song but shifting it into a more ominous, more haunting key. The weather responded in kind, adopting my mood.

Inspired by the banners of flame overhead, I held the hail at bay while I sent a subtler wind to blow, gently and steadily, across *Hart*. It snatched sparks and embers and bore them across the tidal sand like a thousand fae dragonflies. Then, in a glistening stream, I hurled them not down upon our attackers—as the Stormsinger would expect—but on their distant, vulnerable ships.

I did not have time to see if those sparks found tinder. Samuel's musket cracked, the taste of gunpowder bit at my nostrils, and with a fateful thud, *Hart's* severed head tumbled onto the sand.

I couldn't help but stare, even as enemies sprinted towards us, as the fire raged and the other Stormsinger's voice rose. The hart's baying head settled, frantically pulsating with ghisten light. It became brighter and brighter as the flames picked up, taking advantage of the ghisting's impending departure to devour the ship more freely.

Within my bones, Tane roiled. I had rarely felt her this agitated, this close to the edge of her own, seemingly endless control. Ghisten light rippled across my skin as she threatened to manifest, her drive to go to Hart nearly overwhelming her need to stay with me and keep us alive.

So long as we remained in contact, we were nearly immortal. But caught separate? I would be another body on the sand, and Tane would cease to exist.

"Stay down and take this!" Samuel thrust his rifle into my arms and bolted for the fallen figurehead, shouting as he went. More crewfolk joined him and together, they rolled Hart's head into a bundle of canvas and rope.

Another musketball skimmed past my arm. Tane surged to the surface, her ghisten flesh now sheathing my flushed, baking skin. I did not raise Sam's rifle—I barely remembered it was there, slack at my thighs. Instead I hummed, catching up a fresh wind and, lastly, casting fire from the blazing ship lower across the sand like crackling war pennants.

Oncoming enemies shied, granting me enough time to watch as the ghisting Hart finally, irrevocably, fled the ship's crumbling wood.

He poured into the half-shrouded head in a thousand visible threads of ghisten flesh. The threads came faster and faster, converging on the figurehead until, at once, the ship was devoid of light and Hart resided entirely in that single, salvaged chunk of wood. Then it too extinguished, save for a thin sheen over the weathered surface.

"Mr. Penn, see Hart into the forest! Guard him!" Samuel called over the roar of the flames. "The rest of you, with me!"

FOUR

Reckoning

SAMUEL

Water splashed around my ankles. Something low and hulking scuttled from my path—a massive crab, of all things—and I hit the sand once more, boots gouging, muscles burning. Despite the cool of the wind my skin felt hot, seared by the fire. Sweat stung my eyes and a ringing persisted on the edge of my hearing.

These discomforts, however, were distant things.

Pirates burst into sight, shadows and swirls and flashing muzzles.

"Beware!" I roared and ducked, easily avoiding a peppering of shots aimed in my direction. I already knew the path of each, just as I knew which of the figures was the pirate's captain.

He hovered at the rear of his charging crew, a woman at his back. His Stormsinger. The very one that had blown Mary overboard, forced us into the inlet, and ensured the destruction of *Hart*. Of my ship. Of my home. Now, they would kill us, capture us, and take Hart for themselves.

I would not let that happen.

Mary joined me and we skirted a deep pool, rimed with seaweed and detritus, then nipped into the shelter of a seastack.

I paused just long enough to squeeze her hand. It was cold, her skin gritty with sand. "Take the Stormsinger, I have the captain. Ms. Skarrow! Give us some cover!"

The chief gunner Skarrow joined us, along with the dark-skinned Ms. Vin. Both set to reloading their rifles with admirable efficiency, Vin flicking one of her dozens of tight, thick braids out of her amber eyes. I reloaded, then peered out from behind our shelter as Mary began to sing.

At Mary's word, hail surged across the sand in a vicious, hammering whip. It struck the enemy with sand-churning force, followed by a bank of fog as thick as the smoke that billowed from *Hart*.

There was a breath of quiet. The long glint of the barrel stretched before me as a single figure flitted across my sight—or rather, the empty space where my Dreamer's Knowing told me the enemy captain would soon be.

I fired. A figure dropped and shouts and warnings exploded in the night. The enemy, rather than retreating as their captain hit the sand, rallied. There was a recklessness to their cries, a mindless desperation that chilled me and recalled me to other battles—of the armadas clashing at the Aeadine Anchorage, and the shrieks of drowning sailors. Of my own crew over the past hours as we were harried, run aground and battered to pieces. Of seeing Mary swallowed by the waves, and the thud of Hart's head hitting the sand.

My rage returned in a flash of heat, then a rush of cold. I reached for another twist of powder and shot in my pocket.

I found none.

The enemy was paces away now, drawing swords, raising pistols. I flipped my rifle around, stepped from the shelter of the stack and swung it like a club.

I took a man full across the side of the head with a crack. He crumpled into the seastack as I seized his sword and sidestepped a musketball, which cracked off the rock in a peppering of shards.

"Your captain is dead!" I shouted. "Surrender!"

A moment of reprieve, another uncanny hush. Mary hovered at my side, hair and skirts rustling in a wind I could not feel.

A pistol cracked.

I seized Mary around the waist and pulled her from the path of the shot. I felt a rush past my ear, a spark of pain, then someone bowled us over.

We hit the ground. Mary gave a squawking shriek that I would have, under any other circumstances, been forced to mock. But just then our attacker decided to strangle me.

I clutched at the arm locked around my throat and with one hand reached back to grab their collar. I hurled them over my head and slammed them into a shallow, tidal creek. They twisted. A foot connected with my jaw.

I reeled into blackness. Then there was water in my nose and mouth, a great slap of cold on my hot skin. I rolled onto my hands and knees and staggered upright, spitting blood and sand and feeling, for all the world, like a monstrous, shadow of a man.

Like Benedict. Like Benedict had been.

That realization struck me like another, colder wave and I swayed on my feet.

Calm. Steady. Calculated. That was what I needed to be, for my crew, for Mary. For Hart.

Fog began to flee on a gentle breeze. The tide was coming in again, a gentle spreading of creeks and pools and an onset of waves. Bodies lay here and there. Someone was shouting in Capesh, repeating themselves over and over again—"Mercy! Mercy!"—and gradually, pirates began to surrender.

They were thrust to their knees by my victorious, bloodied crew. Mary was among them, soaking wet from our tumble and assisting Mr. Keo in gagging the enemy Stormsinger with a kerchief. The woman, pale blonde and not much older than Mary herself, still struggled.

"Surrender!" I called across the sand, my voice chasing down the last, far-flung figures. My mouth tasted of iron and I could feel blood in my beard, clotted with sweat and sand. "Surrender and live, or fight and die. The choice is yours!"

The last of the enemies dropped their weapons and the Stormsinger relented. The fog fully retreated, and we were granted a full view of the bay, the seastacks, the cliffs and the damp green of clinging trees. One of the enemy ships blazed, billowing smoke and flame and already half sunken in the shadow of an island as the remains of her crew staggered ashore. The other lay at anchor, longboats bobbing along a swiftly vanishing shoreline.

Water crept across the sands towards the smoldering remains of *Hart*. The tide was coming in.

"Bind and bring them," I ordered my crew, trying to shed the shadow of my brother as I did. However hot my blood still ran, however angry I was, I could not lose control.

I turned from *Hart's* wreckage and focused on the remaining pirate vessel. "I want to see my new ship."

∞

The Capesh vessel *Ata Lapa*—roughly translated to *Sun Sparrow*—was a serviceable but small ship, intended for darting between islands rather than the rigors of open sea. She had no ghisting, as anticipated, nor even a common figurehead, and her crew was a surly, unhappy lot. I could hear them chanting vengeance from the hold as I lingered on the deck, watching the sun rise.

If we were ever to return north, I reflected, I would need a new ship. If I *could* go back north. In that moment, the entirety of my future seemed grim, scarred by failure and loss.

I had been offered a Naval commission and rejected it. We had broken contract with the Usti, made ourselves personal enemies of the Mereish, and turned our backs on the Aeadine. My Letter of Marque and Mary's contract had burned with the ship. We had no credentials, no protections and no accessible funds.

My thoughts dulled as dawn broke in a haze of orange and pink cloud, cast over a horizon of brooding red. Gold struck the waves as the tide, once more on the wane, withdrew from the islands, the seastacks and the charred remains of my ship.

Every scrap of wood was blackened, desiccated and crumbling, unfit to host ghisten life. Cannons jutted here and there, and the sand was cast with wave-washed rimes of debris. There was nothing living, save the crabs who preyed upon the dead.

A rifle cracked and my attention shifted to several of my crew, wading through the receding water. One of the great crabs ceased its attempts to tear the limbs from a corpse and scuttled away. The crewmembers converged on the body, hefting what was left onto a makeshift litter. At this distance, I could not see who it was. It did not matter who it was, perhaps. They were one of my crew, and I had not been able to save them.

I dug my nails into the rail of my commandeered ship until my forearms ached and my fingers felt like they would crack. The pain, however, was grounding.

"Take the longboat, fetch Penn's crew and the figurehead," I heard Mr. Keo direct the crew. "Ms. Skarrow?"

"Gone, sir."

Ms. Skarrow was dead? When? I recalled the last moment I had seen her, but could not pinpoint the moment of her death.

There was a moment of silence. I released my breath slowly, steadily, and pushed the dead woman's memory from my mind.

Keo went on. "Simina, divide the remaining able-bodied between getting this tub ready for open sea and joining Severn in the search for bodies."

"Sir."

More conversation and orders passed, ringing out of my comprehension, then I felt a presence at my side.

"The prisoners need to be set ashore," Mary said, lowly. Beneath us, the stomp and chanting of the Capesh pirates continued, backing her words. "This ship isn't big enough for all of us. And we should also rename it quickly. The prisoners insist they've friends who will come for them, so we need to disappear."

"Agreed." I looked at her, searching for… something. She wore a coat that was not her own, had one hand bandaged, and she favored her left foot. Her eyes were rimmed with fatigue, her hair in a careless knot at the nape of her neck.

I took the side of her windburned face in one hand and, my lips a breath from hers, looked into her eyes.

She stared back, startlement twining with worry. "Sam?"

"I am searching for an anchor."

She was quiet for a moment, her gaze gentling. "Have you found it?"

I kissed her, gentle and lingering. Her lips were dry and tasted of salt, but the feel of her, the scent of her skin beneath the seawater and smoke, dispelled my doldrums.

"Yes." I began to lower my hand, but she snared it between both of hers—her skin finally warm, though rough with bandages—and held it close.

"We are alive," she told me, intuiting, somehow, what I needed to hear. "We are alive, as is a good portion of the crew. We have a ship, and we did not lose Hart himself. All we need to do is reach Demery, and we can… We can mourn. And decide what to do next."

I nodded. "Are you well?"

"One of the crabs tried to eat me, but otherwise, yes," she said with a humorless smile.

I returned it, hard-edged and grim, then glanced about the deck. "I suppose my charts are lost? We will need to locate the nearest port, preferably one which is not governed by pirates, though I realize that may be too much to ask."

"Port Sen," she said promptly. "Poverly saved the charts. I've already looked them over."

"That is something," I admitted, glad in the same breath to know that the steward's girl was alive. Without real hope I ventured to ask, "Was anything else saved?"

Mary rubbed at her face. "No."

A moment of strained silence.

"Tell me of Port Sen," I said, pushing the disappointment aside.

"It's an open port—a pirate port—but well organized and affiliated with the Council of Lords."

"That does not mean it is safe."

"No, but it is our only option. I don't suppose they would have a proper inn? With a hot bath?"

"If they do, I will gladly help you into it."

She smiled again, but this time with feeling. The shadows around her eyes, however, could not be completely dispelled. "Sam… Demery's island is ten days away. *Hart* barely lasted one in the South Isles."

"We were still damaged from the Anchorage," I admitted. "Ill-prepared, and that negligence is mine to bear. We should have made port sooner."

Mary prodded me in rebuke. "Where? The Mereish mainland? We had no choice. Now, decide what to name our new ship."

I eyed her. "That hardly matters."

"Name it."

"Nothing comes to mind. You do it."

"*Reckoning*," she said with a light to her eyes that, while harkening to the lawless side of her I had always rebuked, stirred me. The inclination was one to hide in, a heat and want that momentarily erased the weight of loss in my chest.

"That is… theatrical," I observed, watching her eyes, her lips.

She met my gaze. "It's fitting."

"Then *Reckoning* she shall be."

FIVE

The Red Company

BENEDICT

My first challenge, after enlisting a company of miscreants to help me steal *The Red Tempest* from beneath the eyes of the Aeadine Royal Navy and establishing myself as captain, had been to choose my officers.

My options had been sparse. The majority of the original Mereish crew were uncooperative, and I elected to maroon them on a passing cay. That left me with the embittered Aeadine Naval dregs I had found in an Anchorage tavern and convinced to join my piratical enterprise—formerly pressed men and women eager for escape, and a smattering of habitual renegades who had nothing better to do. They were a rough lot, but I was, if nothing else, persuasive.

Now, I surveyed my assembled officers at the table in the main cabin. My first officer, the former Aeadine fourth lieutenant Ms. Olles, sat by my side. She was as northern as they came, having been born within a stone's throw of the Stormwall. She had the weathered brown skin to prove it, eyes deeply lined from smiling, and an accent that bordered on Mereish.

My second officer had died in a brawl not a week after his election, and his replacement was one Mr. Wuthy. Wuthy was a small man, pale-skinned and graced with the passive, companionable disposition of an aged dog. There was little danger of him following his predecessor's example, but he was experienced, and well trusted among the crew.

There were others, of course—the bosun, carpenter, gunner and so forth. In total a dozen men and women sat with me over a meal of fish, potatoes and a sauce with a remarkable lack of flavor. Grant and Jessin Faucher were present too, the latter sitting at the opposite end of the table and eating with reserve and gentility.

"We need a cook," Olles informed me, shoving her empty plate away from her and sitting back. "A Sooth and a cook."

"And musicians," said Wuthy, stabbing a slice of potato and popping it into his mouth.

"What happened to the Mereish musicians?" The gunner, pale blond and clean-shaven Hashaw, demanded. "Thought we kept those."

Wuthy shook his head. "We kept the fiddler, but she's in poor spirits and poorer health."

"A Sooth and a cook are of far greater priority," Olles interjected.

"Your people killed my cook," Faucher informed us, taking a piece of fish onto his fork. "He was excellent."

I ignored the exchange and forced myself to eat without reaction, though I too wished my countryfolk had been more discriminate with their musketballs.

"Musicians are vital," Wuthy pressed. "For morale, for dancing, for the constitution. Neglect these, and we'll have mutiny on our hands, mark me."

"Mutiny is no concern," I said, sitting straighter in my chair and taking a sip of wine. "And if the crew thinks to, they will learn what it is to sail under a Magni Captain."

There was a span of quiet, into which Ms. Olles finally gave an unconvincing nod and drained her cup.

"Why this concern?" I asked, glancing between the bosun and Wuthy, both of whom spent a great deal of their time playing cards below decks. "The crew have the prospect of ample prize moneys; they are fed and free of the Navy. Why such concern?"

Wuthy twisted his mouth about in thought and sucked his teeth with an audible *snick*. "They are restless, unsure of you and their future. They have yet to see prize money, while if they'd remained behind, they'd certainly have seen a cut from the battle by now. They speak of time ashore."

"Both will come," I frowned. I had been tactful with my Magni influence upon the crew thus far, other than that momentary loss of control in Port Sen. Perhaps I should have been more attentive.

"Several crew went missing in Sen," the bosun, Kapper, said. He was a former pressed Navy man, and had a perpetually sullen squint to his eyes. "We cannot afford to lose more. We've a hundred guns and not enough hands to use them."

"We could sell some guns," Grant offered. "Buy better wine."

Faucher gave him a cold look. "Do not sell my guns."

Kapper ignored the pair of them, pointedly continuing, "Perhaps they were left behind, perhaps they ran. Hard to say."

My discontent deepened. I recalled the rush of power I had summoned, the hum and spread and blossom of awareness as it seeped into the blood of my crew. I had not *felt* myself lose anyone.

"Who?" I wanted to know.

Kapper produced several names I did not know, and my interest waned.

"Then they made their choice," I determined. "Or had no choice."

Ms. Olles considered me steadily. Her blatant regard plucked at my patience, but I sensed what she did not say. It was what Samuel would have said.

I was being callous.

I was, however, saved from meaningless placations by the arrival of the steward. She peered her head in the main door, looking first at Wuthy, then me, as if she was unsure who to address. "A problem, sirs."

A chorus of shouts reverberated through the ship behind her.

"Best make haste," she urged.

I rose to my feet and strode out into the companionway, then out onto the gun deck with Olles and several others in tow.

I heard more shouts, thuds and shrieks as we flowed onto the uppermost gun deck. There, half a dozen crewfolk were engaged in enthusiastically beating one another. It looked like the entire ship's complement of four hundred were crammed onto the deck, hovered about whooping and cheering or otherwise taking in the entertainment.

I subdued the offenders with a wave of Magni power. Grips loosened, eyes blinked in sudden lethargy and confusion, and the knot gave way.

"Mr. Wuthy," I prompted.

"Moody," Mr. Wuthy said, stepping up to my side and nodding his chin to a nearby woman, arms crossed over her chest and a distinctly withdrawn air about her. "What happened here?"

"These lot." She pointed to several bloodied figures, then a crumpled man on the deck. "Had a disagreement with him."

The him in question proved to be my Stormsinger, Alfwin, identified as he slowly raised his head and squinted back at us. The young man had been soundly beaten, his face already beginning to swell, blood streaming from a split lip and a gash across his brow.

"Why?" I demanded. "What possible reason could you have to damage our greatest asset?"

There was no response. Unconsciously, I sent a wave of power out.

"Bloody Mereish bastard," one of the attackers declared. She looked horrified at her own words, and clamped her mouth shut.

"He is Aeadine," I corrected. "However, where he was born is irrelevant. He is not Mereish or Aeadine or Capesh. He is a Stormsinger. He is *ours*."

At my words, something passed over Alfwin. A pinch of the brows. A tightening of the lips. A slight caving of the chest and hunkering of the shoulders. I recognized the hallmarks of a deep sadness, even the subtlety of defeatedness, but why eluded me. I had reaffirmed his place among the crew, his belonging. That should have soothed him and resolved the conflict in the eyes of the crew.

"He's loyal to the Mereish, sir," another of the aggressors said, this time of his own will. "To Jessin Faucher."

"They were paying insults on the former captain," Moody translated. "Crude and base insults, too unimaginative to repeat. The Stormsinger took offense."

One of the brawlers glared at her, insulted.

"Unimaginative and false," Alfwin said with a spark of renewed ire. "I'm loyal to my captain, sir, and that's you. But such disrespect—"

"Is uncalled for," I affirmed. "Jessin Faucher was a competent captain and remains worthy of your deference, even in defeat. That is the civilized way."

There was a mutter among the crew.

I eyed the assembly, the row upon row of still unfamiliar faces. I recalled Wuthy's words over dinner. A restless crew would find outlets for their aggression, and Magni influence could not solve that—not constantly, in any case. There were limits to my reach and the broader my power was spread, the thinner it would be.

My power, still drifting through the room, tightened. Silence fell again and I raised my voice.

"But we no longer bow the knee to civility, to outside laws and decorum," I clarified. There was another murmur, this one a little lower, a little more eager. "We, *The Red Tempest*, the Red Company, shall be a law unto ourselves."

I heard mutters of outright agreement now—genuine agreement, no construct of my Magni influence. It was an exhilarating thing, and I warmed to my topic.

"Tomorrow, we shall finish writing up our articles, agree upon them, and sign our names. Tonight, each mess head will report to Mr. Wuthy and make their desires known."

Mr. Wuthy nodded and Ms. Olles looked, passingly, content at the declaration.

"Now, no brawling," I stated. "Particularly not with our Stormsinger. He is to be guarded, not abused."

Alfwin's face was unreadable.

I went on, "I understand you are restless. We will make port in Krekhafen, and you will have shore leave."

"Shore leave will be naught but trouble with empty pockets. Pardon me, captain, but where's our prize?" The woman who Wuthy had addressed, Moody, spoke up. "We attacked Port Sen and saw not a penny for it."

I looked at her for one quiet moment, turning over the impulse to snap back or overpower her with magecraft.

No. I wanted peace and loyalty. Violence and force would not necessarily establish that.

"Respect, Ms. Moody," Mr. Wuthy reprimanded.

"Beggin' your pardon, sir," Moody added without feeling.

"A valid question, if poorly presented," I said. I held my hands behind my back, fingers twitching with suppressed power. "Port Sen did not welcome us, did not *respect* us, and so it burned. That was a matter of justice, a statement, an establishing of our name and reputation. Now as we carry on and take proper prizes, our reputation will precede us—none shall cross us."

There was a stir at that, once again genuine and unensorcelled, and I felt an echoing stir in my chest. Was this the feeling Samuel had always chased? The weight of eyes, the hushed anticipation. They hung on my next words.

"As to your pockets, I promise you, they will be full," I went on. "Keep watch on the horizon, inform me of every sail. As to you," I looked at the brawlers again, and Alfwin still on the deck. "Witch,

I want to see you in my cabin. The three of you—a night in the hold, no rations for two days."

As glad as I was to claim the crew's regard naturally, I still chose to send a brush of power with my words. After all, if I did not, what influence I had gained might fade.

But I did not instigate fear. Rather, I prodded a fear of disappointment into their hearts, ever so subtly—the distress of a child who has failed a beloved parent. It was a subtle thing, a feeling which surpassed base emotion and would linger long after I was out of sight.

"Mr. Wuthy," I said, turning to leave. "I leave this matter in your capable hands. Send the surgeon to my cabin. Alfwin, with me. Now."

The mage staggered to his feet and followed me through the press.

Back in my cabin, I gestured for him to sit at the table, which he did gingerly.

I closed the door. "Do you require protection?"

Alfwin reached up to rub the back of his neck, forcing a smile. Given how bloodied and swollen his face was, it looked pathetic. "No, sir. I can manage the situation myself. I've a habit of speakin' out of turn."

"Then you had best break that habit," I said. "I need a Stormsinger."

Alfwin's forced cheer slipped and for half a breath his gaze grew guarded. Mary flitted through my mind, her eyes a mirror of Alfwin's, and something inside me shifted.

To be a Stormsinger aboard any ship was a vulnerable position. Most captain–Stormsinger relationships were fraught with abuses, and it occurred to me to wonder which of them Alfwin feared. Those fears could be utilized, after all.

I contemplated this briefly, then discarded it. I discarded the last of my power too, passively meandering though the air around us, and softened my expression into impassivity.

"Come to me immediately if you are mistreated."

"Yes, sir."

There was a knock at the door and the surgeon entered. With a nod, I left him to his work and went out on deck.

At the fore of the ship, in the cool of the breeze and the sight of the horizon, I rested a hand on the rail.

A hum passed through the wood as the ship's ghisting stirred. *Miaghis.* Mereish for Red Tempest, the creature was one of the most reclusive ship's ghistings I had ever encountered. Rarely did he leave his figurehead, a tentacled monstrosity wrapped about the beakhead, bowsprit and forecastle. Even more rarely did he visibly manifest.

But just then, a whisper of teal ghisten light passed beneath my hand.

"Did you hear my pretty speech?" I asked the creature aloud, but low enough so that the nearby crew would not hear me. "I require loyalty."

The light slowed, coiling. I could not hear ghistings, but the movement struck me as recalcitrant.

"I am your captain now," I reprimanded. "Not him."

The light lingered on the rail, momentarily gaining texture—suckers and glistening flesh, like a tentacle—then it was gone.

∽

The following evening, I ordered the crew gathered above decks, in the waist of the ship. All the lanterns were lit, the sea was gentle and the wind curtailed by Alfwin's steady humming at the stern.

I stood at the quarterdeck rail, surveying the assembly as Mr. Wuthy read our newly inscribed articles. My power was manifest, drifting through the crew, but I exerted no influence. Instead, I monitored them. The rhythm of their breaths. The rush of their blood. The shift and brush of their limbs.

The articles were standard, as far as the accords of pirates went. But to the ears of formerly pressed sailors, they were control. Autonomy. Protection. A taste of democracy, however misleading that taste might be.

They needed no prompting to sign when the table and heavy book were laid out. Most did so with gravity, some with jesting and nudging of one another, and the remainder with their expressions too complex for me to analyze.

The expressions and moods of those around me had grown easier to read since my healing, but I still, evidently, had room to learn.

At last, I descended the stairs. I took up the pen, as they had, and dipped it into the ink as they looked on.

I could not resist a push of power over them, then, a nudge towards awe that made my skin prickle and my muscles relax, as if I stood under a warm sun instead of a cool, starlit night.

I signed my name at the top of the articles, bold and clear between the Aeadine name *The Red Tempest* and the date, *The 2nd Day of the First Turning of the Sweet Moons, in the 22nd Year of Queen Edith of the Aeadine.*

Benedict Reginald Rosser, Captain

I laid down the quill and straightened.

"We are a company," I declared. "A bold company, a free company. The Navy left their coins in our cups, stole our service and our years. No longer. Our riches shall be our own, as shall our destinies. We are a unified company. We stand united by this accord, a law unto ourselves. And we are a red company."

I smiled with a polite, predatory calm. "Our reputations shall precede us. They will yield to us. They will whisper of us. They will fear our sails on the horizon."

At this, two sailors stepped up to the quarterdeck rail and unfurled the flag I had commissioned from the bosun's mate. A simple, grinning skull upon a red field.

There were murmurs of approval, ripples of whispered commentary.

Not loud enough.

I added a nudge of Magni power.

They roared my name.

There is much to be said concerning the Council of Lords. Comprised of some one hundred seats, it is populated by the richest thieves, brigands, traitors and exiles to seek refuge in the Isles. Most seats are bound to ports or islands of significance, and can only be claimed through the purchase or conquest of those islands. (Notable exceptions include the Drifting Queen and the Seasonal Isles, as detailed in the second volume of these observations: ISLANDS, CAYS AND STRONGHOLDS.) Despite the frequently nefarious origins of its members, the Council abides strictly by its laws, though these laws may fall outside the moral codes of the seas at large.

—FROM EXILES AND PIRATES: A SUMMONER'S OBSERVATIONS IN THE SOUTH MEREISH ISLES, VOLUME III, BY SAMUEL I. ROSSER

SIX

Voskin

SAMUEL

I smelled char, gunpowder and the sickly sweetness of rot, all backed by the salt rush of the sea.

Port Sen was a burned and blasted shell of a town, its chaotic rows of wooden homes, shops and warehouses marred by fire and peppered with holes from cannon fire. Shattered ships bobbed in the harbor—broken spars, listing hulks.

The haggard, soot-smeared faces of the townsfolk barely turned as our longboat bumped alongside what remained of the wharf. The only person to approach us was a boy, who grabbed the rope Mr. Penn tossed to him. He efficiently tied it to a post and stuck out his hand to Penn, speaking in rapid Mereish.

Penn looked to me and asked in Aeadine, "What's he sayin'?"

"Half dette for the knot," I translated, climbing up onto the docks and digging my own hand into my pocket.

"Some fancy knot," Penn muttered.

I produced a handful of coins and appraised them with no little regret. A smattering of Usti marks. Half an Aeadine solem, clipped straight down the matronly Queen Edith's profile. My Mereish talisman marked with snakes entwined, worked from years of worrying. Mary and I had other funds, but it was either hidden or banked in Usti. All well beyond our reach.

I moved to give the boy one of the Usti marks, which was near ten times what he had asked for. He seized it eagerly, but I held on to the coin.

"What happened here?" I asked in Mereish.

"A Magni," the boy said, still clutching the coin, which I did not relinquish. "All anyone can agree on. That and it was a Mereish ship he came off."

Mary put a foot on the gunnel and stepped up after me. "How could one ship do all this?"

The boy gave her a derisive look. "They didn't. The Magni made everyone else do it."

"Ah," I said with grim understanding. Such powerful Magni were rare, but after the Mereish's recent advances in magecraft, I suspected they would become less so. "I see. Were they pirates?"

"Must be. But this fellow was looking for his woman, I heard." The boy tugged at the coin and glared when I kept hold of it.

"Poor woman," Mary commented. The rest of our party had joined us on the docks now, Mr. Penn and three other crewmembers, all discretely armed. "Did he find her?"

The boy shrugged. "No idea. Just offed with his big ship."

I considered pressing further, but I had larger concerns—namely, whether there would be any provisions worth buying in Port Sen.

"Where is the Port Mistress?" I asked.

"Bottom of the bay," the boy replied. "Whole office fell right in, in the barrage. Rats didn't even make it out."

"That is regrettable. Then who can I speak to about provisioning my ship?"

The boy gave me a high-browed look. "How should I know?"

I tugged the coin.

"Voskin," the boy tossed out. "Just go see Voskin and give me my money."

Mary's lips quirked in something close to a smile, though her gaze remained appropriately stern. "Where would he be?"

The boy looked ready to cut his losses and walk away. He sighed with profound weariness. "Stone house on the hill."

I finally released the coin. He left, glaring back at us before he vanished into the crowd. A crowd which, I realized, had begun to rapidly disperse.

I watched the patterns of the locals' movements and noted several figures surreptitiously prodding people away. One woman whispered to another, watching me as if I were a ghisting manifest, then the pair of them fled. A man rested his hand on the hilt of a sidesword, gathering several children to his side and ushering them down an alleyway.

Another woman opened her coat to show a pistol jammed through her belt, staring us down.

"Cautious of outsiders?" Mary observed.

A prescient tingle chased up the back of my neck. "We should return to the ship."

"How dare you come back here!" someone screamed. A woman started towards us, eyes swollen from exhaustion and her finger outstretched in tremulous accusation. "Go on, go! Make me do it again, you bastard! Try!"

Several other townsfolk lunged after her, grabbing her by the arms and dragging her back. This cleared the way for a new group to approach, armed and led by a burly man with short-cropped grey hair and a trim beard.

"Benedict Rosser!" he called in challenge. The woman's furious shrieks faded and, with a last scuffle, the quay was empty, save the newcomer and his companions.

I heard the name, comprehended it, but had no time to respond. In my mind's eye, I saw him level a pistol. I saw the burst of light as he fired, muted in the noonday sun. I saw the shot tear into my cheek, shattering bone and spraying blood across Mary's shocked face.

I nudged Mary in one direction and stepped in the other. The pistol cracked and a lead ball passed harmlessly between us.

My crew's reaction was only marginally slower. Mary snapped a word I did not catch, harsh and ending in a melodic crack. Wind blasted the strangers, sweeping up water and ash and cold embers. We drew weapons with clicks and scrapes and closed into a half-circle, but there was nowhere for us to go save the water and the open, bobbing longboat.

"I am not Benedict Rosser!" I shouted. A sickening dread sat in my stomach, my Sooth's senses meeting with the scene before me in creeping, unwanted clarity. "Let us put down our arms and speak like gentlemen!"

Another shot tore past us, clipping Penn in the shoulder. The man flinched but did not move until I grabbed him and stepped out front of our little knot, raising empty hands.

Mary came with me, humming lowly. The winds continued to harass our attackers, but with less vehemence.

The grey-haired man raised a hand in signal and his company lowered their weapons.

Mary eased the wind a fraction further.

"Do not think to overpower me, Magni," the man said, tapping at the center of his chest. I sensed, rather than saw, a talisman beneath his shirt and jacket. "I am not so easily influenced. Nor are my companions."

"If he has a talisman, he may be connected to the Ess Noti," Mary warned in a whisper.

I nodded.

"I am no Magni," I said to the stranger. "How do you know of Benedict Rosser?"

The man laughed without humor. "What mad fuckery is this? Do you honestly believe you could come back here and *not* be recognized? We drank together." He stabbed a finger at me. "Even then, enough of my people saw your face as you enthralled them."

"If you and Benedict drank together, give me the opportunity

to prove I am not him," I stated, lowering my hands. "I am Samuel
Rosser. Benedict is my brother. My twin."

The man's eyebrows rose so high, I thought they might vanish.
He seemed to choke for a moment, only for me to realize he was
laughing again—a strangled, incredulous bark of a laugh. His
armsmen mirrored him, their expressions ranging from bewilderment to outrage.

"Well now," he said, rubbing at his forehead with the back of
one hand, pistol still in hand. "Let me speculate for a moment,
you mad Magni dog. Old Lapa got the best of you, ran that great
man-o'-war aground or caught you unawares, as he is wont to do,
so you took his ship and came back here to, what? Finish razing
my port to the ground? Find yourself a better ship before that little
isle skipper is swamped by the next swell?"

I thought quickly. "Do you have a Sooth? Have them verify I
am no Magni."

"He has taken off his talisman, Voskin," a woman said to
the man, speaking of me—of Benedict, rather—as if I were not
present. She had a rifle cradled in her arms, her expression taciturn.
"I can see his aura now, sullied, but crimson. A Magni Adjacent."

Mary gave me the barest flick of a glance, obviously as startled
as I was by this assessment.

"He is a Sooth. They are twins," she retorted. "Of course there
is bleed between their powers."

The leader of the company, evidently Voskin, had had enough
of the conversation.

"Seize all of them and bring their ship in," he ordered his
companions. "Shoot them if they struggle. Lock the crew in the
hold of their ship, throw Rosser in the pit and bring the weatherwitch to the stone house."

He continued with a wave of his pistol at Penn and the others.
"If you try to escape, one of these three dies. If you harm one of
my people or try to influence them, one of them dies. If they are

all dead, I move on to the rest of your crew. And if you are the heartless son of a bitch I believe you to be and that is not persuasive enough—every time you step out of line, I will break one of your bones. Understood?"

"If I was Benedict Rosser, you would already be dead," I snapped, my rage at him, Ben and the situation at large approaching unmanageable intensity. It was a familiar feeling, at least in regards to my brother, and I was beyond weary of it.

I wished Olsa were here, instead of back aboard the ship with Illya, but Voskin would hardly have trusted her word as a Sooth.

"If your Sooth is too weak to identify the variances between Adepts," I stated, "you had best find a better one."

Voskin raised his pistol and, without another word, fired.

Penn's head jerked back with a crack and spray, and he toppled into the water.

For an instant I stood frozen, unable to believe what had happened, that I had not foreseen it, that I could not stop it.

Then I surged forward, jerking my sword from its scabbard. Mary screamed some vengeful, wordless cry and the rest of the crew broke into motion around us.

The second gunshot sent one of my rowers to his knees. Another would have taken me in the shoulder had I not seen it a moment in advance. I sidestepped, ducked a thrusting sword and, in a vision so strong it stopped me in my tracks, I saw Ben.

My brother, face twisted with rage, stalked through swaths of smoke and running figures. He moved through this street, across these docks. He was almost unrecognizable, his expression thick with both wrath and elation, his eyes a hollow well of unfettered, untamed—and, I knew, unfamiliar—emotion. He looked trapped, and ecstatic.

"James Elijah Demery!" Mary's voice shouted, slicing through my vision and returning me to the moment—to a regiment of rifles and the knowledge that Mr. Penn, my trusted ally and companion, was dead in the water behind me. "Lord James Demery can confirm who we are!"

Voskin considered her, and the amusement on his face was more chilling than any glare. "If Demery is any friend of yours, he would have warned you not to speak his name on my island."

SEVEN

The Fleetbreaker's Daughter

MARY

"The Fleetbreaker's daughter, you say?"

The grey-haired man from the docks, Voskin, moved behind a large desk. We were in a study on the top floor of a three-storied stone house in the heart of Port Sen. It had narrow windows, built to withstand the wind, and had massive beams and lintels that reminded me of Tithe.

No ghistings, however, lived in these beams. Tane was the only Otherborn being present, beyond the dragonflies in a lantern fastened to the wall. They slowly pulsed, gold and plum in their sleep.

I stood quietly before the desk as one of Voskin's people untied the gag around my mouth.

"Cause any trouble, and you will suffer," the guard murmured in my ear.

Even without the deadly calm in her voice, I had no doubt that was true. I thought of Mr. Penn, of how sharply his head had been thrown back, of how limp he was as he had toppled into the bay. Of how half his face had vanished in one cracking blow.

Bile crawled up my throat and my eyes burned.

"Quite a mother to claim," Voskin went on, riffling through a stack of papers and selecting one, which he put on the desk before me and spun about. He added a quill and inkpot, at the side. "Sign this."

I flicked my gaze from him to the paper. It was written in Mereish, momentarily jumbled before my eyes until Tane translated. "A forfeiture of freedoms? What is that?"

"An indenture, entitling me to your service for a specified period of time. If you do not sign by the time Osso there opens the door and steps into the hallway, another member of your crew dies."

"Why would I sign that?" I asked, suddenly confused. Stormsingers were commodities for trade—giving written consent for my servitude was unnecessary. Ridiculous.

"Find the youngest member of their crew," Voskin said to the guard, Osso. "Go kill them and bring us their head."

The guard reached for the door handle.

That would be Poverly. "Wait!" I cried, snapping up the pen. I wanted to ask more, to rage and resist and throw the paper in Voskin's face, but my signature was not worth Poverly's life, nor any more of my companions.

Poor, poor Mr. Penn.

"I'll sign," I insisted. But despite my words, and the very viable threat, I still hesitated as I put quill to paper.

Poverly. The Uknaras. Mr. Maren, the talisman maker. Willoughby and Keo.

Voskin watched me in a silence so thick with threat, I felt it might choke me.

I scribbled my name in uncaring, hasty script and tossed the pen back down. Whatever scheme Voskin had in mind, papers, as Jessin Faucher had once warned, could burn.

And they had. My contract with the *Hart*, making me the first contracted Stormsinger in a century, had burned with the ship, along with our Letter of Marque. We had nothing to prove who we were, or our status in the world.

But Demery would come for us. My mother would come for us.

"Good." Voskin tossed drying sand over my signature and, turning, puffed it out the open window. Shaking out the paper he surveyed it for a moment, then put it in a drawer. "Hardly need Uma Idriss coming down on my head, do I?"

"Who?"

Voskin settled in his chair and laced his fingers over his stomach. "Do you know nothing of the Isles, woman?"

I surveyed him, warring within myself. On one side was grief and despair, but on the other determination and injustice. I chose the latter.

There was another chair against the wall. I dragged it over and sat across from him, forcing myself to sit straight-backed and dignified.

"I know James Demery is one of the richest lords here, and my mother will wash what's left of your port into the sea if you harm me or my captain," I stated.

Voskin didn't look the least bit intimidated. "How do you know Demery?"

"We sailed together, north of the Stormwall. We were allies against Silvanus Lirr. And he is expecting us within the month." The last was a lie, but I delivered it as seamlessly as the preceding truths.

That silenced the man and for the first time, I saw something like doubt flicker through his gaze. Or perhaps it was not doubt, but calculation.

He took out the paper I had signed again, and looked at my signature. "Mary Firth. Daughter of Anne Firth?"

"Yes. Have you heard of *Hart*?"

"I have not."

I pinched my lips momentarily, sifting through my thoughts and conferring with Tane.

Let me, Mary. She said in the quiet of my mind.

I drew a deep breath, and relinquished control.

I—Tane—leaned back in the chair and folded my hands in my lap. "I am hungry."

Voskin blinked at me. "Pardon me?"

"Feed me a good meal, and I shall tell you a story," Tane said. There had been a shift in my voice, but Voskin appeared not to notice. "The story of James Demery, the Firths, the Rossers, and the death of Silvanus Lirr. The story of the Battle at the Aeadine Anchorage, and the theft of *The Red Tempest*."

"Were you present at Lirr's death?"

"I helped kill him."

That brought a wave of silence and I sensed, with a thud of my heart, that this fact might not be the boast we intended.

Voskin glanced at Osso and something unspoken passed between them.

"Fascinating," Voskin said at length.

"Samuel and Benedict Rosser are different men," Tane stated, willing the certainty in our words to persuade him and distract from our misstep. "We came because our ship was lost and this was the closest port. We came for help and provisions. That is all."

Voskin drew a huffing laugh and, mirroring me on the other side of the desk, he lowered his gaze to meet mine.

I thought, then, that we had gained ground. I thought, as crow's feet spread from the corners of his amused eyes, that we had at least won his curiosity. I could foresee how we would persuade him, how we would convince him that Sam was not Ben and that whatever he intended to do with us was both unjust and unwise.

"You are entertaining," Voskin said, his voice low. "And your loyalty to your captain... it is inspiring, if perplexing, since he is not here to enthrall you. Perhaps I might even believe your story, if I had not seen your captain with my own eyes, in this very room, demanding I help him find that little tart. Yes, it seems all heights of stupidity for him to come back here, but here he is, and here he was, and that truth trumps the mystery. My people deserve vengeance."

"Who?" I demanded, shifting back into control. The transition was fluid, a gentle nudge, with Tane's will remaining present and reassuring in my mind. "Who was he looking for?"

Voskin gave me a withering look. "The Usti woman."

I was taken aback. My mind immediately leapt to Olsa Uknara, but that made no sense. Enisca Alamay, then, or whatever her true name was? She had vanished during the battle at the Aeadine Anchorage—either lost to the Other, or to the sea. How, then, had she gotten to the Mereish South Isles?

And why is Benedict pursuing her with enough vehemence to burn an entire port? Tane wondered.

These were questions I could not answer, and the very need to ask them was both unsettling and heartbreaking. Benedict had been healed of his corruption, through great trial and effort. Had that healing not taken? Had he relapsed? Or was he simply so accustomed to entertaining his base instincts that he had lost control?

"If you hurt us, Demery will destroy you," Tane said. I was not sure that was precisely true, my relationship with Demery being rather more complicated than that. But if Sam died on this island—Saint, I could barely fathom the thought—I would call on everyone I knew to destroy Voskin, including the former pirate. "If the real Benedict Rosser does not do it first. He may be a villain, but he loves his brother. And I am his future sister-in-law."

"Now you and your captain are betrothed? You are reaching," Voskin chided, reaching across the desk to pat my hand before he rose to his feet. "Your life is not under threat here, Ms... well, I suppose I can call you Firth. You are too valuable, not only for your skills but your connection to Lirr. And in that indenture, you have bound yourself to me. You are *mine*. Demery cannot change that, for Demery bows to the council and the laws of these islands."

Something edged into his tone as he said that, and I sensed he did not precisely approve of those laws—though he was clearly willing to use them to his advantage.

That frightened me, naturally, but I found just then that my frustration was stronger than my fear.

I wasn't sure whether it was Tane or I speaking as we said, "Of course. Of course, I am. Then chain me to a mast, see how long you manage to keep me. I shall be gone by morning."

Voskin looked at the guards and gestured to me, "Can you believe this woman?"

"A good beating would put her to rights," the woman Osso commented.

Voskin blew out his cheeks. "Gibbet her. She will be more malleable after a few days of exposure."

"A Stormsinger's mask, sir?" The other guard asked.

My heart slammed against my ribs.

I will not be gagged again, I silently hissed to Tane.

Then we change tack.

"Osso, see her to the guest room," Voskin was saying, oblivious to our silent communication.

The guardswoman narrowed her eyes at me, but she nodded. "Sir."

Voskin rounded the table and looked down at me, hands in the pocket of his coat. "Do not betray my trust. One step out of line, and I will cut off your feet."

"Then someone will have to carry me everywhere," I pointed out.

Voskin grinned, and this time it was full and genuine. I held his gaze, locking away the thunder of my heart and part of me that warned I could not keep this up, that my courage would crumble and my plan would fail. Then the crew, Sam and myself would suffer all the more for it.

Voskin slapped Osso on the shoulder and strode out of the room.

EIGHT

Vachon

BENEDICT

I ducked my head as I entered the Port Mistress's office in the stone and plaster town of Krekhafen, narrowly avoiding a low beam dented by the unwary heads of previous visitors.

Judging by the thud that followed me, Charles did not.

The highwayman groaned. "Saint's bones."

"Duck," I offered.

Charles fell to muttering and slumped onto a bench beside the door as I surveyed the room. It looked something like a tavern and perhaps once had been, with a long counter to one side and an array of tables and chairs. The Mistress's apprentices sat at these tables, all surrounded by bookish accoutrements and many meeting with the various locals and visitors.

Upon seeing me, a thin man approached and inquired something in a dialect of Mereish I could not decipher.

"I am Aeadine," I stated. "Speak Aeadine."

The man paused, considered me with escalating eyebrows, then repeated himself.

"He is asking what you want," Charles translated, still holding his forehead and looking like a kicked dog.

I furrowed my brows at his condition and glanced at the offending beam, but did not remark upon it.

"I want to see the Port Mistress," I said to the thin man in

Aeadine, stating the obvious. Almost without thought, I accompanied my words with a push of Magni power. "Port. Mistress."

The man promptly turned and vanished through a door. As he left my line of sight my hold over him weakened, but I could still feel him—the pulse of blood, the whisper of breath, the indecipherable hum of thought. There was an intoxication to that feeling, like the scent of a woman's skin in the dark, and I stretched my neck in unexpected discomfort.

I took a seat next to Charles, arms crossed loosely over my chest, the scabbard of my sidesword tapping between us. I eyed the apprentices as Charles complained eloquently about Mereish–Usti architecture—a conjunction that he, apparently, did not condone.

I noted one woman in particular, and was in the midst of trying to decide whether or not she qualified as attractive, when the thin man returned with an older, grey-haired woman.

I rose to meet the Port Mistress. The impulse to lay aside my Magni influence for the meeting and to see how pliable she would be without it arose, but I let it recede once more. Efficiency was of the highest order today.

I allowed a small push of my power to slip into the air between us, just enough to make her amenable. Or, at least, not hostile.

"Madam," I said.

"Aead," she replied without warmth. Her eyes flicked to Charles, who wearily tipped his hat, before she continued in Usti, "If you wish to register your ship and pay the port tax, one of my apprentices would better serve you."

I opened my mouth to reply in the same language, but the words refused to come together on my tongue. With a flicker of irritation, I increased the weight of my influence and continued in Aeadine, "My steward has already done so. I intend to hire a Sooth."

"No one will work for an Aead," she replied, still cold, but this time she had switched into my language.

"I was told the Isles are both liberal and welcoming."

"The Isles are not immune to the conflicts in the north," she said, unmoved by my flattery. "Nor are we ignorant of them."

They had heard of the war's escalation, then, and perhaps the Anchorage.

"Then where can I buy one?" I asked.

"There is no slavery here," she replied, her tone growing even icier. "But you may be able to purchase an indenture."

"Ah, my apologies, there is such a vast difference, I know. Where?"

She nodded vaguely deeper into the island. "The prison."

"I hate prisons," Charles muttered.

I hated them far more, enough that the mere mention made my fingers twitch. But I kept my back straight and my expression cold.

I took the particulars from the Mistress, then gestured Grant towards the door. He had a visible welt on his head now, and I found my amusement culled by a niggling sense of injustice.

I looked at the Mistress one more time, sending the strongest pulse of power I had since our arrival with my words. "You must do something about that beam."

"Yes," she said in her wintery way, nodding as if the idea were her own. "I will."

❧

The jailer squatted and banged his cudgel on the bars implanted in the ground. Around us spread a broad square of earth and smooth rock, surrounded by a palisade wall on three sides and the sea on the last.

The prison was, to my undeniable relief, no high-walled fortress, stinking and damp and dark and frigid. Instead, it was a natural cave beneath Krekhafen, its mouth barred with iron.

"Vachon!" the jailer yelled.

I crouched next to him, the tails of my coat fluttering in the breeze, and shaded my eyes against the harsh sunlight. Through the bars, in a pool of barred light, figures clustered. Dirty faces. Sunken eyes.

My memory provided a glimpse of other eyes, other faces. A Stormsinger with her lips sewn shut. Her eyes blinded. Bloody fingers on vertical bars.

Mary standing in the center of that cold chamber, staring directly at me.

"I'm Vachon!" a voice called in Usti.

"No, you're fucking not!" an Aeadine voice replied.

"Vachon, Vachon!" another voice caroled madly from the shadows, and descended off into cackling.

"Sir." This level, respectful reply came from a woman of about thirty. She hovered on the edge of the light, the sun igniting her short auburn hair in a halo of crimson.

The jailer bellowed, first in Mereish, then Usti. Between the two languages, I could piece together an understanding: "Anyone else tries to climb up, I'll bash your skull in, understood?"

With a clatter and the grating of iron, the bars were raised and a wooden ladder lowered into the pit. The Sooth called Vachon ascended slowly, painstakingly.

When she reached the top, I offered her a hand. My fingers were stiff, however, and something about the world seemed to have... shrunk.

I could smell the captivity on her, cold sweat and damp iron. I saw the shadows both around her eyes and behind them. Her caution and mistrust.

I understood all of it. I felt it, viscerally, in a way I had never felt another human being's emotions before.

As such I was not surprised when she glanced warily from my hand to my face, and stepped up on her own. She straightened to her full height—an ill-fitting phrase, considering she was remarkably short. Her hips were broad, evident even beneath her loose shirt and trousers, though her other assets escaped the eyes.

Save her face. Her skin was sallow from imprisonment, but dusted with freckles and possessing, at least, the potential of beauty. Great beauty, even. Beauty enough to eke at my thoughts of prisons and shadows, and draw me back to the windswept rock.

I dropped my hand back down to my side, aware of Charles watching me.

"Do you speak Aeadine?" I asked the Sooth.

Vachon shook her head. "Little," she said in Mereish. "Usti, yes. Capesh. Ismani."

Inwardly, I frowned. My Usti was little better than my Mereish, and neither Capesh nor Ismani had been included in my education.

"Then you will have to learn," I informed her, and looked at the jailer. "How much is her contract of indenture?"

"Three thousand dette or the equivalent days of service, equal to one and one half dette per day," the jailer replied in Usti and scattered Aeadine, producing a fold of parchment and holding it out to me. He eyed me, then added, "Indentures are registered with the Council of Lords. If you have any issue, take it up with them. Not my problem."

I dismissed that and met Charles's gaze, gauging his response to the price. He gave a subtle shrug, clearly no more versed in the prices of indentures than I was.

"I see. Take this," I pulled a pouch from my pocket and, opening it casually, pulled out a gold ring crusted with emeralds. "I assume that will be equivalent?"

The jailer visibly startled. His hand shot out, but I pulled the ring back and nodded off to the side. He skulked after me as we took up position some ways away from Vachon, Charles and the guards. The sea breeze rushed across the yard and, up on the wall, two guards casually conversed against a backdrop of droll grey.

I held out the ring again. The jailer's hand closed around it, but I still did not let go.

"Are there any other mages in that pit?" I asked, lowly and accompanying my words with power in case the meaning of my Aeadine evaded him.

The man shook his head. "No, sir."

I released the ring and, turning on my heel, shoved my hands into my pockets. As I did I pushed aside all lingering thoughts of prisons, of Sooths and Magni and Stormsingers in the dark. I had a task ahead, a world to overturn, and a Sooth clothed in rags and the stench of captivity to see to.

I started back towards the town, calling back to Charles and Vachon, "Charlie! Red! Let's be off."

NINE

The Convict's Good Counsel

SAMUEL

I squinted dust from my eyes as the grate slammed above me and the silhouettes of the jailer and guards departed. I was left in a barred pool of light on straw-strewn rock and puddles, the darkness to all sides impenetrable.

I retreated from the light and let my eyes adjust. The blackness was not as complete as I originally expected, alleviated here and there by fissures in the rock. In this scant illumination, I picked out multiple figures gathered on a ledge, out of the water.

Several more skulked towards me, their postures predatory.

"I want no trouble," I said in Mereish, raising my hands.

A rock sailed past my head. I dodged, started to issue a warning, and was promptly assaulted from behind. Dirty, moist arms clamped around my head, overwhelming me with the stench of sweat and piss. I shouted and seized an arm, to no avail.

Gnarly feet dug into the backs of my knees. I dropped like a stone and my attacker crowed, the sound like a drunken wood frog.

"Give it to me!" A wiry, fierce woman, old enough to be my mother, tried to rip my coat from my shoulders. She descended into a stream of colorful curses and insults, half of which were lost to her southern Mereish dialect. "Die! Die and give it to me!"

"Captain!" another voice roared.

I had no time to see my unexpected ally before water crashed over my head. I twisted, barely breaking through the surface for a salty, choking gasp. "Stop! Woman—*STOP*!"

She did not stop. Fetid, stinking seawater flooded my mouth and I realized, with an odd kind of detachment, that I had two choices—fight an old woman or drown.

Mercifully, I was saved from such a decision. Someone stepped over me, the hands pummeling me tore free, and I thrust myself out of the water.

I staggered upright, fists clenched, chin up, braced for another attack. Sure enough a new, burly figure flew at me and I punched. I heard a satisfying crack at the same time as my knuckles split in an explosion of pain.

"Anyone else tries it and I'll pop your bloody damn eyes!" someone shouted from right behind me.

I spun. I had stumbled back into the light from the grating, and a woman in her mid-twenties stood with me in the barred pool of light. She was lean and muscular, with pale Southern Aeadine coloring, white-blonde hair and a split, bleeding lip.

"Captain," she said, flicking me a glance. "Pardon me, sir, but—" She abruptly cut herself off and screamed into the shadows, "Back you fish-fucking Mereish bitch, you impling-spawned clot of shit! Anyone comes after this one, I'll be your end, you hear me?"

Her voice echoed in a sudden, sloshing quiet. I, too, found myself at a loss for words. I had never seen this woman before, but she clearly knew me. Or thought she did.

The answer unfurled in my mind, affirmed by Sooth precognition. She was one of Benedict's crew, left behind in the attack.

And she appeared to be shockingly, genuinely, loyal.

"Is anyone else with you?" I asked.

She shook her head, back partially to mine, eyes pinned on the shadows. "No, sir. Geoffries was, they killed him first night. Pallo died on his own, drowned in the tidewater. Found him this morning." Her voice grew tighter as she spoke, stress showing through her rage and bravado. "Right glad you're here, Captain. You'll see us through this, I know."

"I will," I vowed. Admitting I was not Benedict seemed unwise, uncomfortable and provoking as that was. If my fellow inmates were this violent, I would need an ally. "But we will need somewhere more defensible, for the time being."

"I've a ledge," my companion said, nodding into the shadows. "With me, sir."

I trailed her beyond the light, braced for an attack which did not come. We sloshed into a natural alcove of sorts, elevated, dry, and still within sight of the grating and its shaft of illumination.

"How many others are in here?" I asked quietly.

"At least twenty," she answered, gesturing for me to sit on a salt-eaten reed mat.

I sat, eyeing her as she sat a respectful distance away on the stone. I would have insisted she join me on the mat, but Benedict would not.

"Is there any other way out or in?" I inquired, lowering my voice further.

She hesitated. "Yes. Spaces where the tidewater comes in. Too far to swim, though—it's suicide. One of the other prisoners, he told me it's the way in the Isles. You can stay in prison or give your life to the sea. You have a choice."

"I cannot decide whether that is merciful or macabre."

She shrugged and, reaching forward, scooped up some seawater and rubbed it over her bloodied lip. She hissed softly in pain and did not meet my eyes. "That's how Pallo died. His body's all swollen up like a cork now, stuffed into a crevice over there."

She nodded to the far side of the caves.

"A pity," I said, feeling a prickle of regret for a man I did not know. "This other prisoner, would he be of aid?"

She touched her lip again. "Mayhap."

"Then please fetch him."

Soon after, a dark-skinned Capesh man settled down across from me. He was younger than I expected, barely beyond twenty, with a crown of tightly curled hair and a short, wild beard.

"Atello," he introduced himself, leaning forward casually to offer me a hand. His accent was warm and rounded, a storyteller's voice that I found instantly agreeable.

I shook his hand, firm and short in Benedict's way. "Rosser. You have already met my companion."

Atello nodded to the woman. "Brid."

Brid. Good, my ally had a name now.

I fell to business. "What can you tell me? The port, Voskin, this prison, anything that might be of use. In return, I will take you with me upon my escape or rescue."

"You are very confident," the Capesh man observed.

"Have you better prospects?" I asked curtly. Slipping into Benedict's persona was, I found, chillingly easy in my current state of mind.

"No."

"Then talk."

Brid watched, her expression obscured by the shadows as Atello outlined Port Sen's position and influence, Voskin's person and connections, and his own tale of imprisonment. He spoke low but his voice carried, amplified by the water. So too did the scuffing and muttering of our fellow inmates, making the cave seem far smaller than it was.

"A month," the Capesh man admitted when I asked him how long he had been in the prison. "I demanded a full council trial, but had the foolish notion to do it in private, and Voskin appears to have ignored my claim."

"If he had not?" I asked.

"He would have been forced to bring me to face the full council at the Sea Fort."

I marked this for later reference. "What were you arrested for?"

"He's a fucking spy!" Someone shouted from off in the cave.

Atello let out a long, irritated breath. "Not a spy," he called, raising his voice. Speaking more quietly again he continued, "But I was accused as one. You didn't happen to see a Capesh oar galley in the harbor?"

I shook my head.

"Prolly burned it," someone else interjected.

"Oi!" Brid bellowed back, her temper snapping like a strained line. "This is a private conversation!"

A few mocking comments drifted back towards us, but they lacked volume or enthusiasm.

Atello eyed Brid. "You've made a mark, lamb."

"I'll make more," she replied, possibly meaning it as a threat or flirtation.

Atello smiled briefly, then returned to the previous line of conversation. "Well, I could not expect my ship to wait for me."

"What was its purpose?"

Atello shrugged. "We're merchants."

My dreamer's sense told me that was far from the truth, but not whether the truth would be helpful. Escape had to remain the priority, and I judged Atello to be a useful partner.

"Very well," I said, sitting back with Benedict's broad, self-assured posture. "Chin up. For now, we wait. I have a woman on the outside."

TEN

Otherwalker

MARY

O sso and I watched one another as I ate my dinner. She had her boots up on a chair to one side, while I methodically worked my way through a surprisingly full plate.

The 'guest room' was illuminated by a dragonfly lantern, though there was little enough to see. A narrow cot, a table, several chairs and a bucket. It was cool, fully below ground, and had only one door.

In short, it was a cellar.

Clearly Voskin is not fond of guests, Tane observed.

Osso shifted, dropping her feet to the floor and glancing at the door. Light caught at the pistols in her sash and the hilt of her cutlass, carried high at the ribs. There was a length of rope on the table, another warning against my good behavior.

"Eat faster," she said.

"You needn't stay," I offered. I held up a chicken leg, "I can hardly turn this into a weapon."

Osso only grunted in reply, as if she agreed but had little choice in the matter, and silence stretched long and uncomfortable once more.

All I wanted was for her to leave. Then I could leave and find Sam and get us the hell out of here. But while we were forced to endure one another's company, I could make a play for information. Maybe. Osso did not look particularly forthcoming.

"Voskin has a Magni talisman," I stated. "Did he acquire that from the Ess Noti?"

Osso gave me a long, arch look.

"The Mereish secret-keepers," I filled in the quiet space, just in case she genuinely didn't know what I was talking about. "I was at the battle at the Aeadine Anchorage. The Aeadine Navy had conscripted me, and I nearly died a dozen times for it. But I saw the Mereish talismans. I've felt their ensorcelled shot. I've heard talk of the Ess Noti."

"Shut up and eat," Osso snapped. There was something in her eyes, though, and I suspected she had at least *heard* of the Ess Noti.

I cleaned my hands on my skirt and leaned back with my arms folded over my belly. "What do you want to know about Benedict Rosser?"

Osso's eyes narrowed a fraction. "Are you proposing an exchange of information?"

I nodded.

"How can I trust anything you say?"

"Maybe wait until I say it, and decide if it sounds like the truth."

Osso leaned forward to consider me from a handspan away. Her breath smelled like hunger and the edge of drink. "Why would you trust anything *I* say?"

"Because I have to. I am, it seems, indentured to your master. I would like to know what kind of man I serve and arm myself with knowledge. If I cannot be free, I will need to be invaluable."

She examined my face for another moment, then sat back. I sensed I still had not won, though.

"I'll start," I volunteered. "Benedict Rosser is a Black Tide Son, taken as a child and tortured by the Black Tide Cult in Aeadine. This amplified his Magni power, but left him corrupt in return."

I did not mention his healing, nor Samuel's relationship to the matter. The healing opened far too many questions. Besides, they were determined to believe Samuel was Benedict, and I did not want to distract from the issue.

I went on, "Does Voskin have dealings with the Ess Noti?"

"We trade heavily with the Mereish mainland," Osso replied vaguely.

"That is hardly surprising. What do you trade?"

Osso cocked an eyebrow.

"Benedict Rosser was trained at the Naval Academy in Aeadine, but was recently disgraced and left the service."

A greedy lightness crept around Osso's eyes. I could well imagine what she was thinking, how Voskin would reward her if this intelligence proved true and useful.

"We trade in anything and everything," she said, "But our most lucrative cargo—which you will no doubt sing safely up north— are dyes and ore."

I furrowed my brow. "Ore? Like iron? Oh, Benedict Rosser is the nephew of Admiral Rosser, Admiral of the North Fleet."

My choice to share that particular information was tactful. Illustrious connections meant that Benedict—and Samuel—had value. Perhaps that value could be extracted. Or perhaps, it would simply muddy the waters and prevent an immediate execution.

My throat tightened at the thought.

Osso sat back, hands folded in her lap now to match mine. "Admiral of the North Fleet?"

"Yes. I have met him. Chin like a shovel."

Osso opened her mouth to press further, but caught herself. With something that might almost have been described as a smile, she said, "Not iron, no. Nothing so common. An ore called gianeo, found only in the Isles."

That sounded dull indeed, but the fact that I had never heard the name before might indicate a certain secretive importance among the Mereish.

My questions were coming at a swift knot now, piling up against my tongue. But I was running out of facts to safely convey.

"Benedict stole *The Red Tempest* in retribution for his discharge and has turned his back on his country," I said.

"That's obvious."

I thought a moment. "Benedict Rosser was imprisoned in Mere this past spring, at a fortress on the northern coast. What is gianeo used for?"

Osso shrugged. "That, I don't know."

"Does it go to the Ess Noti?"

"More information, witch."

"You didn't answer my last question."

She frowned at me and fingered the pistol at her belt. "I could beat these answers out of you," she offered coolly.

"This is so much more pleasant, though," I countered, hoping my smile was not as brittle as it felt. "Much less work for you, too."

"The ore is bought by a trader, just as everything else is," Osso said, but her words were a little more distracted, and I began to worry she actually *was* considering beating the truth out of me.

I weighed my options. It was a silent conversation with Tane, a rapid exchange of pros, cons and possible outcomes.

It really was unfortunate that circumstances such as these, when I most needed to be sharp and clearheaded, were also the times when stress and fear and pain and fatigue made that the most difficult.

But Tane, bless her, had a possible solution.

"Benedict Rosser does indeed have a twin brother," I said, willing her to hear the sincerity in my voice. What I said next felt thick in my throat. It felt like betrayal, though it also felt like the right thing to do—even if I was not sure it was true. "If you want Benedict, simply make it known that you have Samuel. He will come for him."

"Your Samuel may be dead by then."

I pretended not to hear that. "You believe me?"

Osso shrugged. "The creature who destroyed my home could be called many things, but he did not seem so idiotic as to come back pretending to be someone else. Voskin may even believe you. A little. But someone needs to hang." She shrugged. "Double the brothers, double the revenge."

I let out a long, slow breath to smother the anger her words caused.

"Your people deserve justice," I agreed. I felt a pain of genuine sympathy in my chest, though I could not decide how much of it was sympathy for the burned port, for Samuel and his dashed hopes of a healed brother, or even for Benedict himself, perhaps still victim of his corruption. "I'm sorry."

My guard's upper lip twitched in a suppressed snarl. "No. You don't say that to me. You don't get to speak like that."

I fell silent, a rabbit in the brush. There was a new expression in Osso's eyes—a hollow, aching threat. Had she lost someone? Or had Ben made her do something?

"I know what it is," I added softly, "To be under his control."

Osso abruptly smacked my plate from the table. With the other hand she pressed her pistol to my forehead, shoving my head back so fast and so hard that my neck cracked. I would have toppled right out of my chair if she hadn't grabbed my shoulder as well, pinning me in place.

"Don't try to commiserate," she hissed. "Do not try to be my friend. You're a witch. A prisoner. So fucking act like one."

She looked as though she would say more. Instead, she let go of me so suddenly that my chair toppled.

I hit the ground. Winded, I managed to roll onto my side, somewhere between protecting myself and trying to get back up.

The lantern swung, the door slammed, and I heard the thud of a bar being rammed into place.

For an instant I stared into the sudden, unyielding dark. I was alone. My heart hammered, my skull was void of thoughts, and my forehead ached with the impression of the pistol mouth.

I rubbed at it slowly as I listened to a further clatter and scrape outside. Footsteps retreated.

You went too far, Tane observed. She partially manifested, sheathing my skin in a muted glow.

I did not expect sympathy to be so dangerous, I returned.

I meant concerning Benedict and the Ess Noti. The last thing we need is them following us to the Isles.

Then why didn't you stop me?

Disapproving silence was my only reply. Frustrated, sore and now properly uncertain, I pushed myself upright and went to the door. I pressed my ear to the barrier, listening for another, longer moment.

Can you tell if it's night yet? I asked Tane.

Her glow slipped into the wood of the door, then the frame. It skittered off through the walls, leaving only a spectral umbilical between her and I that, while whole, connected and protected us.

She returned a heartbeat later, converging in the wooden door before me.

Night has fallen and the way is clear.

My cell filled with a wash of teal ghisten light, and I saw the other side of the barrier with her eyes. An empty stone corridor. Several more doors, only one of which was closed. A staircase on one end.

No sign of Osso. No sign of a guard. Not even a servant at work.

Then let's go, I said. *We escape, we find the prison, we release Samuel, and get back to the ship. We've faced worse odds.*

Unfortunately, Tane muttered.

I took a deep breath and slipped into the Dark Water.

Unlike a Sooth, who entered the Other in spirit alone, my ghisting-saturated flesh wholly left the mortal world. The room vanished, the door vanished, and I stood ankle-deep in black, glistening water. Lights sparked to life all around, marking ghistings and implings and every other imaginable creature. There were mages too, or, at least, their shadows. Other Stormsingers in blue, Magni in red, and Sooths in green, all scattered across Port Sen and the ships in her harbor.

Can you see Samuel? I asked Tane.

I felt a nudge in response and my eyes locked on a forest green light. It was close: shockingly close. Good. Perhaps my luck was turning.

I stepped back into the human world in the hallway. There was a chair and a small table here, presumably set up for a guard. A lantern sat on it, dragonflies pulsing in their sleep, along with a stack of cards and a dirty cup.

I passed it by and ascended the stairs softly. A landing lay at the top and my path divided between a servant's stair leading up to the next floor and a hallway. Down the latter, I caught the mutter of voices, including Osso's in a low, steady rant.

I chose neither direction. Instead, I stepped back into the Other and right through the outer wall.

I dropped into a divide between the main building and separate kitchens, full of the scent of bread and the moss on the walls.

Fortune remained with me. I saw only a pair of distracted washerwomen as I straightened my shoulders and, ramming my courage down my spine, strode past the kitchens and away down a dark street.

No one shouted. No one chased. Still, it was everything I could do not to break into a run.

This way, Tane directed.

The fires had not reached this region of the town. Beyond the largely open space in which Voskin's fine house sat, the port closed into tight streets of high, tall houses. Narrow canals ran here and there, weaving under hefty bridges and the chaotic conjunction of streets and alleys.

It was at one of these junctures that I found the prison. A walled square and squat tower sat between Voskin's house and the sea, perhaps once a watchtower that had been swallowed by the sprawl of the settlement.

There was a light in the tower and guards at the gates. I was not so fortunate to find them distracted, but there was plenty of wall out of their line of sight.

I found an alleyway that ran beside the wall and lingered in its darkness. Tane's light was a risk here—the common folk of Sen might mark it, even if the guards did not. But we had to take that risk.

I rested my hand on the wall and waited as Tane examined the prison beyond. The courtyard was empty save for the supports of ramparts, which sheltered several miscellaneous buildings and stocks of firewood. A grating lay in the middle, perhaps access to the canals—an odd asset for a prison. The tower itself had a hefty door and elevated windows, some of which were illuminated.

I saw no sign of prisoners and assumed they must be housed in the tower. That was, until a low, keening wail reverberated through the night.

It came from the grating.

There was no space for hesitation, no second-guessing or fear. Tane pulled us wholly into the Other and through the wall. In a breath I ran across the courtyard, and fell to my knees beside the grating. I grabbed the bars—wood, hard and weathered and unyielding.

But not to a ghisting. Tane surged into the bars, her light temporarily, traitorously bright.

A creak. A crackling, rippling hiss. The grating collapsed into itself in a dusty cloud of shards.

Mutters of surprise filtered from below.

"Quiet!" I hissed down. "This is a rescue!"

Someone cackled. Someone else cheered. Someone else called in Usti, "A ladder, woman!"

Tane pulled my gaze to the side, where a ladder rested against the ramparts. I sprinted for it.

The guards finally noticed me.

"Stop!" Someone bellowed. I heard a door slam, and, flicking a glance over my shoulder, saw the door of the tower was open. Three figures were already sprinting towards me, and the courtyard suddenly felt far, far too small.

I seized the ladder and whirled. The ladder struck the closest guard with a crack and I charged back towards the grating, ladder bumping and juddering as I went.

"Sam!" I shouted. I shoved the end of the ladder into the pit, letting go just as I was grabbed from behind. "Sam—"

The first figures left the pit in a rush. One was immediately knocked backwards by a guard, but more prisoners came. Some bolted. The others attacked the guards with reckless abandon.

I, meanwhile, flailed and tried to pry off my assailant. No one elected to help me, their valiant savior who was, currently, being strangled.

A warning bell began to ring. My assailant promptly dropped me and fled, howling something indistinguishable as he went and laying about him with a club.

I rolled out of the way. One old woman tried to grab my coat, but I slapped her off and she skittered away, shrieking her way to the still-closed gate as more guards flowed out of the tower.

Samuel unfolded from the pit. I made a choked sound that would have embarrassed me any other time and seized him in an embrace. He buried his face in my hair for half a breath, then took in the scene.

"Atello! Brid!" he called.

A younger man with short black hair clambered from the hole, followed moments later by a muscular woman. She had an odd look in her eye, a hard-edged kind of confusion. This only deepened when she saw Sam grab my hand.

But then we were running, and there was no time for questions or introductions.

We raced more guards to the gate, where two lonely figures tried to form up, bayonet leveled. A dead prisoner already lay at their feet, blood spilling across the ground.

Tane manifested before us, sprinting in a trailing, half-human form and a blinding wash of ghisten light. The guards shied, shocked and bewildered, as she burst through them and into the gate.

The wood shattered.

"The guard!" Samuel shouted in my ear. "Get his sword!"

We came upon one of the overwhelmed guards. The poor fellow had already had his rifle confiscated and hadn't had the presence of mind to draw his sword for close quarters. Samuel delivered him the straight punch of a pugilist, following it up with an arm across the throat, pinning him to one of the rampart posts as I darted in and drew his sword. I snatched up his cudgel too.

"Ma'am," the woman with Samuel held out a hand for the cudgel. Something about the look of her told me she would be more useful than I with the weapon, and I handed it over.

She immediately turned, shouting a stream of profanity at two approaching guards.

"Brid, with us!" Samuel shouted.

If the escape from the courtyard had been chaotic, the journey from prison to docks was an absolute melee. Between the prison bell, the shouts of the guards and the flood of prisoners tearing through the streets, the port stirred like a kicked hornet's nest.

After their encounter with Benedict, the locals seemingly had no intention of allowing their supposed villain to escape a second time.

A piece of charred brick narrowly missed Sam's head. We

stumbled through half-cleared streets in the burned quarter as guards chased us and the good people of Sen converged from all sides. There was the flash of blades, the pop and crack of muskets, and a growing, stomach-turning roar.

"Sam!" I stumbled into him as the rubble of a fallen building blocked our path. He grabbed me across the chest and pushed me behind him as a horde of locals closed in.

Brid, in turn, stood between us and the throng. She screamed, laying about her with the cudgel until the crowd backed off.

But they did not disperse. They thickened, trapping the three of us in place.

Three. I glanced around for Samuel's other companion, the young man, but he was nowhere to be seen.

Well, he had escaped or was dead, and either way was not my concern.

"Rosser!" Voskin shouldered his way through the crowd, wearing his nightshirt stuffed into trousers. But rather than leaving him looking disheveled, it brought his bear-like physique into focus. He was thick and broad and generously hairy, not at all the frame of a desk-dwelling bureaucrat. "Saints, I am sick of you. Someone give me a gun!"

A woman in a banyan shouldered up next to him, finished loading a pistol, and handed it to him.

He faced us, pistol pointed to the sky. Brid stood directly in front of Sam, as if she intended to take the shot for him.

I remembered Mr. Penn in a stomach-dropping flash.

"We demand a fair trial before the Council of Lords!" Sam bellowed.

Whatever this meant, it was enough to give Voskin pause. I glanced around, searching the faces in the crowd. There was not a kind expression in the entire mob.

Except for Osso. She approached Voskin, her face closed, and murmured something in his ear.

All around us, there was a ripple of unrest from the crowd. It seemed that they, too, recognized the weight of Samuel's request.

"Run if they come for us," Sam muttered to me, jarring me from my thoughts. "Do not hesitate, please."

"I'm not leaving you," I said stubbornly. "He won't kill me anyway."

He muttered something under his breath that might have included "stubborn woman" and raised his voice to shout again, "We demand a *fair trial* before the Council of Lords!"

Osso said one final thing in Voskin's ear, her eyes alighting on me, then she stepped back.

"Then before the council you will stand," Voskin spat. "And when I drag you back here in a few weeks' time? I'll tie your noose myself."

ELEVEN

Usti-Aeadine Relations

BENEDICT

Vachon and Charles trailed me through Krekhafen's market on the way back to the ship, Charles heading up a polite conversation in Mereish. I understood little of it, particularly in the bustle and clamor of the crowd, and it soured my mood.

I approached a stall selling clothing, myriad items from a wildly eclectic range of backgrounds draped on lines and stick mannequins. The stallkeeper approached as I began to pull down random garments—anything roughly Vachon's size.

"Sir?" The stallkeeper asked, trying to catch my eye. He spoke Mereish, but I hardly needed to be fluent in the language to understand a run-of-the-mill "Can I help you?"

"Ben! Ben, let me," Grant intervened, pulling the clothing from my hands as Vachon watched with vaguely arched brows.

Grant offered the stallkeeper an apologetic smile and set the clothes on a nearby table, launching off into Mereish. I caught apologies, a request for something green, and gave up.

I went to stand next to Vachon, stuffing my hands into my pockets again. She glanced at me but continued to watch Grant work.

The silence, which I normally would have preferred, began to strain.

"For you," I said in Aeadine, waving a finger at her and then the stall. "Clothes."

She nodded politely, the look in her eyes clearly communicating that she was humoring me.

That bothered me. I began to cobble together Mereish words, an instruction of her role aboard my ship and what I needed her for. But the grammar, the structure of the language continued to elude me.

I resorted to silence again. I sucked my teeth and rocked back into my heels, eyeing the crowd for threats, until a thought occurred to me.

"You can choose," I said in Aeadine, moving to prod her forward. I stopped myself just before my fingers touched her back and waved instead. "Go."

She looked at me again, more slowly this time, and I had the unpleasant sensation of being appraised. Then she went to join Grant, speaking in rapid Mereish and indicating a profoundly practical dress of brown and black that would, no doubt, fit like a sack.

Grant alternated between trying to dissuade Vachon from the sack and flirting with the stallkeeper, who was soon properly charmed.

I watched the other man, trying to memorize the way he held himself, the tone of his voice, the length of his eye contact, even how often he made the stallkeeper—and Vachon—laugh.

I had never been able to do that. At least, not without a tactful use of Magni sorcery.

I had been healed, though. Supposedly. Surely genuine charm was a skill I could learn, a face I could add to my masks. It would not only be satisfying to win a stranger over with something other than Magni force, but a necessary skill in a world increasingly infiltrated with sorcery-killing talismans.

I was still contemplating this when Vachon and Grant rejoined me, Grant gallantly bearing a twine-wrapped bundle while Vachon set about wrapping a scarf around her head. Her curls flashed bronze and russet under the sun, full of light and demanding to be admired.

I instinctively began to push at her will, slowing her hands and making her reconsider hiding her hair away.

I caught myself. What had I just decided?

Vachon finished her task and settled her shoulders, seeming to breathe more easily.

"You look lovely," Grant informed her, the meaning of his Mereish made further evident by the crinkle about his eyes.

Never mind. He looked like a simpleton, and I was not about to stoop that low.

Vachon, too, cocked one brow skeptically at him.

"What else does she need?" I asked the highwayman. "Aside from a bathhouse, which we will find before we return to the ship."

Charles translated, and we spent the next half hour finding a bathhouse and wandering the market, Vachon selecting a few modest items she would need while I lightened my purse as little as possible, thanks to Charles's charm and my power.

And everywhere we went, Charles put out the word, "The captain of *The Red Tempest* will pay one hundred dette for news of a blonde Usti woman called Enisca Alamay."

∽

Rumors began to filter in as night fell, various men and women coming to the end of the gangplank and spinning stories about pale-haired Usti women. Most of them were nonsense, but two stuck out.

One was a sailor who claimed Alamay had been aboard his ship out of Port Sen. The other was a scullery maid from a disreputable inn. I was inclined to discard her upon sight—she was unattractive, her clothing worn, her apron stained, and her fingers swollen and red from work. But she described Alamay perfectly, right down to the fact that she was a low-level Magni.

"She is at your inn?" I clarified, standing on the docks with my new informant. "Now?"

The maid nodded and spoke in rapid Usti. I was fairly certain I caught her meaning but looked at Charles for a translation.

"She says Alamay has been sleeping for most of the afternoon, rarely leaves her room. For another hundred dette, this woman will lock her in, let us in the back door and point out the window of Alamay's room, so we can block it," Charles said, looking impressed. "I, er, have a sense she has done this before. We should move quickly."

"Agreed. Give her fifty more after Alamay is captured," I said and gestured for Charles to pay the woman. I was already striding back up the gangplank.

∽

I stood with Charles, Vachon and three crewmembers in the shadow of the alleyway behind the inn. Already I could see two more crewmembers situating themselves outside Alamay's window several stories above. Both were experienced topmen: they moved with the surety of a lifetime in the rigging. Not a scuff gave them away.

"There is a low Magni in the room. They do not move," Vachon murmured in Mereish. She had a distant quality to her gaze I knew well from Sam. She might be physically next to me, but her spirit was in the Dark Water.

There, every mage and Otherborn beast in the city was a beacon to her. Including Alamay.

The back door opened and the maid squinted out at us. As soon as she recognized me, she stuck out her hand.

"Another hundred," she said in thickly accented Aeadine.

Time was too short, my focus too narrow. I sent a wave of

power out at the same time as I shouldered inside. The woman staggered back and went eerily still, eyes pinned wide as my associates poured in after me.

The image of the inanimate woman cooled my temper, but only marginally. I could still feel the rush of her blood, the intoxication of my superiority of will. It was heady as wine and potent as poison.

Wrapped in my will, the maid dutifully led us up a narrow servant's stair. We moved soundlessly into a hallway, around a corner and into another staircase. We spied several other figures on the way, but my power raced ahead of us like invisible curls of crimson smoke.

Breath. Murmured words. The warmth of blood. A press of will, of distraction.

Not one of them looked our way.

The maid indicated a door on the third floor, handed over a key and retreated, still enthralled.

I took position outside the door, signaling Grant to stay with Vachon and for two of my pirates—including the no-nonsense woman Moody—to join me.

I pushed my power through the door. I felt Alamay immediately in the rhythm of deep breathing. I slowed, easing into the sensation. I felt her flickers of feeling and emotion, passing through a sleeping mind.

The sleeping mind was the most vulnerable, but meddling with another Magni, even a low one like Alamay, was no simple thing. I carefully began to sift my will deeper into her mind, urging her into an unwaking slumber.

Something clattered in the hall. The door to another room opened and someone peered out curiously.

Grant grabbed the door and pulled it shut in the person's face.

"She wakes!" Vachon hissed in Mereish.

My power stuttered at the same time as I heard movement

in Alamay's room. I did not take the time to turn the key in the lock—I slammed the door open with a shoulder.

And took a fist directly to the face. I bellowed and bent double, blinded by pain. I could taste iron, too, and I felt a thick, warm slick of blood on my upper lip.

Someone, Moody by her voice, shoved past me with a cry of challenge. Alamay shouted in return, her own, lesser Magni influence berating us.

I heard a scuffle and squinted up. Moody was in the midst of reeling, Alamay trying to lunge past me. She shed my power like water—this was more than a Magni-to-Magni conflict of wills.

I shoved her into the wall and jerked at the collar of her shirt, sparks still dancing through the edges of my blurred vision.

Alamay's expression turned from unadulterated anger to caution, her gaze flicking from her open shirt to where the two talismans lay against her skin. Two Ess Noti talismans, one of which, I had little doubt, was preventing me from overpowering her.

I grabbed them and pulled them over her head. "Grant!"

The highwayman hazed into the corner of my vision and took the items from my hand.

"You are bleeding, Ben," he noted.

"I am aware." The taste of iron in my mouth was overpowering, as was the stomach-flipping ache of my damaged nose. But with the departure of the talismans I could *feel* Alamay again, and that tempered my pain.

Alamay stilled, staring at me with hateful eyes. I pulled at my influence, but while the heights of her walls had toppled, a barrier yet remained. A barrier of Magni power that, while not as powerful as my own, was fiercely stubborn.

"Where are the documents?" I asked. Blood. Bone. Breath. My will, a tightening noose. Her will flexed and strained but did not yield. "Moody, Grant, search the room."

The two immediately went to work.

I kept my gaze on Alamay.

"Not. Here," she hissed, releasing each word like an angry wasp.

I felt the honesty in her words, along with her hate and exhaustion. And despite the determination that had borne me thus far, the combination of them sat oddly in my chest, like stale bread I could not manage to swallow.

I pulled Alamay off the wall and shoved her into the hallway. She immediately moved to run, then stilled as my pirates closed in.

"Fine," I said. "Then you will take me to them."

"I do not have them! I gave them to someone for safe keeping," Alamay shot back, not bothering to be quiet. I tightened my will and managed to marginally lower her voice as she added, "I have no idea where they went."

"Who are *they*?"

Alamay stared. My power was in full bloom again, angry and red at the corners of my vision. But so was hers.

Another nearby door opened and someone shouted, angry and groggy. The sound of more stirring patrons came to us.

I also noted that the maid who had brought us here was gone.

"Back to the ship, then," I decided. "But first, Vachon, come here. Quickly."

The Sooth came forward slowly, eyeing the other woman with a mixture of caution and sympathy.

She startled as I took her hand and pressed it to Alamay's face. My grip was hard, but Vachon's touch was soft, and the other woman stilled under her palm.

"There," I said, releasing Vachon's hand. The warmth of her skin remained on mine, and I resisted the urge to brush it on my coat. "My Sooth has your scent now. Do not think to run."

Alamay spoke again. I expected threats or defenses, anger and resentment, but her tone was more shocked, more disappointed, than anything else.

"I helped save you," she said. "You are healed, Rosser. Why are you doing this?"

It took me several moments to realize everyone present was staring at me.

There was an empty hum in my mind, like a deserted corridor or a stagnant well. I was trapped in it, in that immuring silence. I had answers, of course. I had my grievances and my decisions and my vengeance, primed and ready to execute. But all of them might as well have been in a foreign language.

"Move," I strode past the concerned-looking Grant, the staring Vachon, and back down the stairs.

It was not until we were halfway back to the ship that Vachon caught up and took my arm. I nearly ignored her, anticipating some comment on my earlier lapse, but she tugged insistently.

I slowed, tilting an ear as she murmured something in Mereish. Her proximity was a pleasant distraction, but I could not understand her beyond a perplexing "I saw a man with faces."

"Grant," I snapped, and the former highwayman joined us.

Vachon repeated herself and Grant translated.

"When she touched Vachon she saw, or summoned, several visions. Alamay with another person, a lover. Miscellaneous moments. But, most importantly, she saw Enisca Alamay with the documents and in the same vision, she saw a dark-haired man, and a ghisting with many faces."

"These documents, the man and the ghisting are connected?"

Vachon shrugged at the question and picked up her pace, putting a span of distance between us once more. I watched her go, briefly resenting that she had chosen clothes which in no way flattered her figure.

"I am unclear whether that was helpful," I muttered to Grant.

He tilted his head to one side and made a non-committal sound. "Ben... did you ever *see* Harpy? James Demery's resident ghisting."

"I did not."

"She has many faces. Many. And Demery is a dark-haired man."

"You are suggesting that she entrusted the documents to Demery?"

Grant nodded. "He is here, in the Isles, living as a Lord. He is deeply—and quietly—connected to the Usti crown. It is no stretch to believe he would have an interest in the documents and their repercussions."

I mulled this over. Anticipation was building inside of me, but I blocked it out for the time being. I had given my feckless emotions enough rein tonight.

"If that is the case, he is likely to either destroy the documents or hand them back to Queen Inara—who will also destroy them."

"Perhaps," Grant cautioned. "Demery's loyalty is more nuanced than that."

"Then we had best find him quickly."

SOOTH PRIMARY —*A Sooth Primary is a division of Adjacent Mage which, naturally, originates in the abilities of a Sooth. Thereafter through sorcerous interventions or happenstance of birth, that original power is augmented to include a secondary power. When Sooth is augmented by Magni, a Summoner is often produced. When Sooth is augmented with Stormsinger, the outcomes are far more varied, and exceedingly rare.*

—FROM A DEFINITIVE STUDY OF THE BLESSED;
MAGES AND MAGECRAFT OF THE MEREISH ISLES,
TRANSLATED INTO AEADINE BY SAMUEL I. ROSSER

TWELVE

The Council of Lords

SAMUEL

A lantern swung out of sight, releasing the shadows from their corners and casting Mary, Brid and I into darkness.

I shifted, manacles cold against my skin. The ship rocked gently around us and voices and footsteps reverberated through the wood as Voskin's crew prepared the vessel to leave port.

"You're not Benedict Rosser," Brid said quietly. She hadn't spoken since our standoff with Voskin, nor through the march to the docks and our temporary captivity on deck, in the wind and the cool of the night.

Now, as the tide shifted and our departure drew close, we sat crammed together with our legs manacled side by side and our hands pulled over our heads. I could feel both women pressed into me, though Brid had made what meager space she could, shoulders hunched and knees pressed together. For her part Mary sat somewhat listlessly, neither leaning into me nor leaning away. Simply quiet. It was concerning, but there was little I could do, or perhaps even say, with Brid next to us.

"I am not," I acknowledged. "Forgive me. I took no pleasure in deceiving you."

I felt her shrug. "Suppose I should be grateful you're not. Your brother left me behind to die. You made sure I'll get a fair trial."

I closed my eyes in the darkness. "I am sorry. For his abandoning you."

The deck rumbled as the anchor was raised, accompanied by the rhythmic stomp and chant of men at the capstan. Ghisten light rippled through the hull as the ship's ghisting prepared to help guide the vessel away from dock and out of harbor.

"Brid," I said when the light had vanished, the anchor had come home with a thud, and the chanting had stopped. "What is your full name?"

"Bridget Deeds."

"Deeds. Eastlander?"

"As we are." A smile touched her voice. "How'd you know?"

"There are great many Deeds at sea, and all of them hail from the East. That coast makes for good sailors."

"Aye, you've the right of it."

"You seemed very devoted to my brother, in the prison. Can I ask why?"

She did not speak for a moment, seeming to choose her words. "I thought you'd—he'd—come back for me. And I suppose... It's hard not to feel loyal, when he took us out of the Anchorage like that, stealing a bloody second-rater from right under the Admiralty's feet. We felt unstoppable."

"You were aware he was a Magni, back then?"

"Aye, but didn't much care. Had one before. Don't mind a little courage and contentment here and there, and there's something to be said for *knowing* your captain's orders, in a scrap. Just didn't realize how... didn't know anyone could do what he did." She did not need to specify what she meant. "Didn't realize I'd be a puppet. Didn't realize I already was, from the moment I saw him."

"I know what that feels like," Mary said from my other side. "I'm glad you're with us, now."

"Same," Brid said, stoutly. "Mary?"

"Mary."

Brid shifted, seeming more comfortable. "Did either of you see where Atello got to?"

"He ran, and I am glad of it," I said.

Brid made an affirming sound, though I sensed a little disappointment in it. "Suppose he'll find his way home. I hope we all will."

Mary made a small sound, a little, sad breath of a laugh that I almost ascribed to the sounds of the ship.

"Home," she murmured, still so quietly I almost didn't hear. "Some of us can never go home."

∞

Hours passed before Brid fell asleep, and Mary nudged me with her elbow. "Are you awake?"

"I am," I added, trying not to sound as grim as I felt, "Though my arms are not."

She made a sympathetic sound. "Shall I break us out, and we take the ship?" There was humor in her voice, a forced dryness, but there was seriousness too. She spoke in earnest, even though she knew there was little hope of success.

I turned to regard her fondly, but it was too dark to see, and I ended up with a face full of my own bicep anyways. "There is no need. Demery will verify who we are, the council will acquit us and *Reckoning* will be released."

"The council is made up of pirates and exiles," Mary pointed out. "Voskin has power and influence, and ties to the Ess Noti. I'm afraid he might pull too many strings."

"Ties to the Ess Noti?" I asked. "What do you mean by that?"

Mary briefly and thoroughly informed me of her meeting with Voskin and her conversation with Osso. As enlightening and critical as the information was, it was also disheartening.

"Demery has power and influence of his own," I pointed out, trying to stem the tide of my own demoralization. "Also, let us be honest with ourselves, chances are Benedict has committed another atrocity in the last few days, and someone at this Sea Fort will have heard of it. Obviously I cannot be blamed, so there may be no trial at all. This indenture of yours… that we will have annulled. You signed under duress."

"Aren't all documents like that signed under duress?" Mary asked. "But sure, Demery may be able to help, and as we well know, documents can burn."

"As can Voskin."

"As can Voskin," she repeated. There was a span of quiet and I waited, sensing she had more to say. "Why did Ben do it, Sam? Before he left the Anchorage, he seemed better."

"He was," I affirmed, resting my head back against the bulkhead. "Perhaps Ben simply has the option to be better now, but does not know how. A muscle atrophied."

"He burned a whole port," she reminded me soberly. "He turned hundreds of people against their own home, all at once. Some died. He's more powerful than he ever was, and if he's unmoored…"

I took a moment to put my words together, something to reassure her, but she kept talking.

"Or it worked for a time," she suggested, "And now it's failing."

I read between the lines. "I am fine, Mary. I am here with you, more firmly than ever. My aura has changed slightly, but not for the worse, I am sure."

"Truly?" she pressed. I felt her turn and heard the clink of irons. "You haven't felt yourself slipping?"

"Not at all."

She seemed to settle, quiet in the darkness. "Then there remains the question of why Benedict is tracking an Usti woman. Do you think he's looking for Enisca Alamay?"

"Enisca is likely dead," I cautioned. "Though the documents she stole would be a powerful motivator for anyone to verify that."

Another quiet stretch, then: "If this woman is Enisca and the documents are at play... Should we tell Demery?"

"No," I said instinctually, then slowed to consider how visceral my response had been. "No, I do not believe we should. He is too connected to the Usti queen."

"Maybe that's why we should tell him. Give him the responsibility. Whatever Ben intends to do with world-changing secrets cannot be good, and I want nothing to do with it. We came to the Isles to rest. And be married, or do you not intend to keep that promise?"

"Of course I do," I returned, shocked and marginally offended. "Why would I not?"

"Ben," she stated. "Because you will either try to save him or stop him, and whether or not I come with you, he will tear apart our lives again."

A boulder settled on my chest. I gathered myself to contradict her, to assure her it was not true and that Ben's fate was his own.

Then I remembered the wreckage of Port Sen, the hollow hatred and fear in its people's eyes, and my conscience roiled.

"I love you, Mary," I said quietly.

She did not speak, and for a few heartbeats, I feared she would not. Waves rushed against the hull and, above, a bell tolled the change of watch.

Finally her reply came, soft and a little defeated. "I love you too, Samuel."

∽

Three days after we sailed from Port Sen, we arrived at the Sea Fort. The island was a stone fortress, centuries old but in perfect repair. There were no natural landings, no beaches or shoulders of rock, only meticulously hewn stone walls, breakwaters, and a quay to which multiple deep docks were affixed. Towers thrust into the sky, both on the Fort and as outer watchtowers, their bases berated by waves and skirted with barnacles. Ships of all kinds packed the artificial harbor while boats moved between them, ferrying people to and from shore.

I observed all this from the deck of Voskin's *Dominion* as the ship tied up at the docks. Mary, Brid and I stood together with our wrists chained before us and a row of armed guards at our backs.

"I do not see *Harpy*," Mary murmured to me, naming Demery's ship. "Tane can't sense her."

Brid glanced at the two of us, but after three days of captivity together, she knew of Tane and our history with Demery. Her hope relied on him too.

I brushed my senses across the divide between realms, searching for James Demery's ship. A shadow passed over the world before me, the Dark Water overlaying the human world in a clamor of lights and a wash of black, pure water about our ankles.

"There are too many ghisten ships," I surmised, squinting back into the bright, salt-laden air of the human world. "We cannot know for sure."

Mary looked more and more uncertain. "We should have tried to take the ship," she mumbled. She cast her eyes across the harbor and sucked her teeth thoughtfully. "But we do have a lot more options, now. As far as ships go."

"Just give the word," Brid put in. She shifted her hands with a clink of iron, and I noticed her clench and unclench her fists. The woman had enough courage—and violent capacity—for all three of us. "I'm with you."

A gangplank was fitted and we proceeded onto the docks. Voskin strode far ahead, but I caught a flash as he pulled a medallion from under his shirt at the gate. The guards allowed him through and we followed into the long, echoing shadows of a tunnel. Intermittent dragonfly lanterns barely illuminated an ascending walkway. The sound of running water echoed in the gutters to either side and we clattered over a three-meter span of criss-crossing iron, the slosh, slop and yawn of waves marking yet another layer of the island's defenses.

We emerged into a bright courtyard. I blinked, not just from the shift in light, but from the alteration of setting. The courtyard was large enough for several thousand people to congregate, and paved with time-worn stones. These yielded for the roots of five great trees, placed evenly throughout the space. Archways of mixed, patterned stone lined the edges of the courtyard, leading to high buildings and one of the great towers. Banners fluttered in the archways themselves, alternately concealing and revealing various people as they went about their daily activities.

"Those are ghisten," Mary murmured in my ear, her eyes fixed on the trees. I followed her gaze to a gnarled, bowed pine, its branches descending from an ancient trunk like spider limbs. "But not natural. Grown from old figureheads, like the trees in Tithe. Tane suspects they're wardens."

"Will they know what you are?" I asked.

"Unlikely." The voice that replied was a little more distant, a little deeper. Tane. "Not unless we touch them."

We fell silent as, up ahead, Voskin stopped to speak with a woman. She was ebony-skinned and clad in a gown vaguely reminiscent of the Aeadine style, but with a narrower silhouette and loose, voluminous sleeves covered with heavy embroidery. Her thick, braided hair was swept up under a stiff, three-pointed kerchief.

They spoke briefly then, without casting us a glance, Voskin followed the woman through a doorway and out of sight. My companions and I were passed off to new guards, their vaguely conical helmets glinting under the sun, and led in another direction.

We were brought down a staircase and into, predictably, a dungeon. It was not the worst of dungeons, however, relatively dry, and devoid of the sounds of suffering. Lanterns were permanently affixed to the walls and the cells we passed contained an assortment of prisoners, from gentlemen and ladies to urchins. Some played cards at tables. Others slept. Others watched us, and one woman in a worn military uniform saluted in solidarity.

Mary, Brid and I were directed into a cell at the end. Narrow, tight bunks lined one wall and there was a table with several stools.

"Full council convenes in two days," one of the guards informed us with professional detachment as one of his companions locked our cell door. "When your advocate arrives, they will be brought to see you. Your accuser retains the right to interview you at any time."

With that, the guards left.

I leaned against the bars, watching them go and assessing the nearby prisoners, while Brid went over to pick up one of the chairs and test its weight as a weapon—an eventuality which the Sea Fort was, evidently, not concerned about.

Mary looked over the bunks and picked something up with a "Hah!" She turned to deliver us a half-hearted grin and waved a stack of cards, neatly tied with string.

"Our predecessors were kind souls," she decided. "Who's up for a game?"

❧

Two days passed, and Demery did not come. Mary and Brid played a great deal of cards, and spoke of Aeadine and shipboard life and other things besides. I attempted to speak to the nearest prisoners, but the guards always intervened, banging on the bars with clubs and warnings of "No conspiring."

Advocates came to see the other prisoners. Voskin appeared twice, once to simply stare at us, the other to point us out to several companions, one of which was a young woman who watched Mary with soulless, glacier-hearted eyes. When I stepped in the path of her glare, sheltering Mary, she simply transitioned her gaze to me and smiled a knowing, wolfish smile.

The second night I sat up alone, watching Mary sleep. Brid had taken the topmost bunk and was almost completely hidden from sight. But Mary was on the bottommost, curled beneath both of our coats.

I brushed at the stack of worn Mereish cards. They had once been a fine deck, lavishly decorated with pattern and color and depicting Mereish saints at what I supposed must be their signature activities—sailing, battling, weaving, tending sheep. Having been to the Mereish mainland and met one such ghisten saint, several repeating motifs did not escape me. Branches. Roots. Leaves. Reminders that many Mereish saints were, in fact, living ghistings.

The position of ghistings within Mere was shockingly varied. Some, worshipped. Most, enslaved.

That naturally brought my thoughts to Hart and the loss of his ship. Our ship. I imagined his pain in those final moments, as I hacked and sweated and my muscles and skin seared.

Had Hart hoped for freedom, in the coals of that blaze, and a slow transition back to the Other? Or had he been glad of my rescue, glad to stay with me and our crew?

The immense weight of responsibility, both to him and my crew, settled on me again. Now, Voskin had them all, along with Olsa and Illya and Mr. Maren, with all his Mereish secrets.

And I sat in prison with a crewwoman my brother had abandoned and my would-be wife, whose hard-won freedom Voskin intended to erase.

I would not let that happen. I would right all of it, though the righting of some matters was more clear-cut than others.

I sank into the Dark Water. The transition was instinctual, as were the selection of lights I searched for among the haze of other, unfamiliar illuminations.

I found Olsa and Illya Uknara, along with Hart. They sat in the north, vague with distance. Mary's light was close enough to touch, though still somehow obscured by the sheer intensity of ghistings and mages collected at the Sea Fort. I could not sense James Demery or Athe Kohlan, but they were simply *ghiseau*, not mages, and their lights could easily be missed or disguised.

I could not find Ben's light. I had a sense of him, of his existence, but it was so vague and indistinct I could not place it.

He still wore a Sooth's talisman, then. He was still blocking me out, even though the world insisted on dragging us together. Had he any notion of what he had brought upon us?

Would he care if he did?

∞

The hum of conversation swelled as we were led into an immense council chamber. A circular table stood at its center, set with the hundred seats of the Council of Lords. All were level with one another, save one section of three chairs, where the woman with the three-pointed cap and an Aeadine man I did not recognize had already taken their seats. Another, younger woman hovered by them, speaking in a low voice. Her sun-warmed brown skin, loose dark hair and the embroidered sash across her hips identified her as full Sunjani, and likely of a powerful bloodline. She wore loose trousers below the sash, while her upper body was clad in a fur-lined wrap and her feet in high, warm boots.

Our guards led us through a gap in the arms of the table and left us alone on an expanse of slate floor.

"It's Demery," Mary hissed.

I quickly followed her gaze, searching faces. "Where?"

"No, not here. On the wall."

I lifted my eyes, as did Brid, silent beside us. Row upon row of portraits lined the walls, each frame containing a placard and a name. Lords, ladies, and their predecessors. One face was none other than Lord James Elijah Demery, clad in regal, nearly royal clothing, and backed by a selection of drapes.

"His breeches are rather tight," Brid commented wryly.

Mary bit her lip in the shadow of a laugh, but her mirth faded quickly. "Look above him, four portraits further on."

Steel-grey eyes. A fine jaw. A face that was not attractive but arresting, even in death.

"Who is that?" Brid asked.

Mary did not answer, so I did. "Silvanus Lirr."

A whisper of knowing drew my gaze from that portrait and over to the table, to the hundred seats and their occupants, and to the face of a woman. A face which, despite feminine contours and a jaded brand of youth, clearly echoed that portrait of Lirr.

It was the young woman Voskin had brought to view us in prison, the one who had looked at Mary with those glacial eyes. She sat at ease among the lords, her finely tailored jacket of deep plum visible above the table, with a high collar and suggestions of lace at both it and her cuffs. Her presence was a remarkable thing—and I knew then, without question, that she was Lirr's daughter.

I voiced this to Mary, adding, "And she is heir to his council seat, it seems."

"A daughter of Lirr," Mary murmured in reply. The quality of her voice changed, and I heard Tane behind her words as she added, "There will be many. But *she* is also host to a ghisting."

Mary and I did not look at one another, but we both stood a little closer together.

"Gentle folk, exiles and rogues, let us resume." Julana, the black-skinned woman at the high table, overrode the general hubbub. Quiet descended and people took their seats, leaving only a scattering of servants rushing about, filling cups and passing notes with the stealth of mice.

The Sunjani woman who had been at the head chairs retreated to the wall and, notably, did not sit at the table. For a moment she eyed an open seat, then its owner sat, and she turned her attention back to Julana.

Voskin, too, took his seat—directly next to Lirr's daughter. They exchanged some pleasantry and Lirr's daughter sat back in her chair, revealing the glint of an ornamental sword at her hip.

Voskin's attention returned to the head councillors. He had barely perched in his chair, clearly impatient to air his grievances.

Julana continued, "Our first order of business stands before you. Let us speak of *The Red Tempest* and Captain Benedict Rosser. He has been brought to us by Lord Voskin, along with his Stormsinger and a member of his crew."

"Tempest is an apt name, considering the state of Port Sen." The Aeadine man at Julana's side commented. His accent and his appearance were staunchly Northern Aeadine, with their characteristic mild brown skin and lilting accent. It was his wig, however, a trim white sack-backed with gold ribbon, that finally allowed me to recall who he was. Howell. Grand Duke Howell Esmond, banished from Aeadine some twenty years ago after involvement in an unsuccessful coup. Those twenty years in the warm south seemed to have been little burden, however, and he looked a full decade short of his sixty years. "Lord Voskin, you have brought the charge. Is the accused's advocate present? Lord Demery?"

Mary leaned forward, peering around the room. I turned my own head, scanning the many faces, but Demery was not among them.

Howell conferred briefly with Julana, then waved a hand at Voskin. "We cannot wait. State your case."

"Two weeks ago," Voskin began, chest out, chin raised. "This man landed in Port Sen and came to me, searching for an Usti woman. He would not speak of why, but I surmised that she had stolen something from him. The woman was present in my port and I gave him leave to apprehend her; however she evaded him. Upon learning this, he used his Magni influence to turn my own people upon their home, along with allowing his crew, including this woman"—he indicated Brid—"to run wild in the streets. Fifty souls perished that day, and Port Sen remains in ruins.

"My people deserve justice. Yet this villain and his companions claimed right to be heard by this council, so in the name of that justice, I have brought them here," Voskin's chin was high, his hands braced on the table before him. "Give me leave to execute Benedict Rosser, as he deserves."

A chill poured down my spine and at my side, Mary shifted, her expression taut with frustration. I caught her hand and held it, tightly.

"Speak, man," Howell now challenged, holding my gaze. "Justify, if you can, your actions. And do not think to persuade this council through your magecraft—we have mages aplenty, and your efforts will not go unnoticed. Do you understand?"

"I do, sir. However, I cannot and would not persuade you though sorcery," I replied. "I am no Magni, and I am not Benedict Rosser. He is my brother. I am Samuel Rosser, Sooth, and captain of the *Hart*, a privateer under the Usti crown. Your Sooths can verify my claim."

"My Sooth has already affirmed he is a Magni Adjacent," Voskin stated.

"He is an Adjacent, yes," an elderly woman spoke from her chair to one side. She had a distant look to her eyes that I recognized—she, too, was a Sooth. "But a Sooth Primary, with Magni influence. Likely a Summoner."

Voskin's expression twitched. "A Magni, then."

The elderly Sooth shook her head. "No, he is not. A Magni influence does not a true Magni make. This man does not have the power to have overridden Port Sen. I would hazard that no one does, but I digress."

"As I said, Benedict is my twin," I went on, encouraged. I spoke levelly and respectfully, determined to show as much contrast to Benedict's character as I could. "As I understand it our magecrafts are intertwined, and not only due to the nature of our births. We are Black Tide Sons."

A murmur rippled through the assembly.

Julana looked at the elderly Sooth for further confirmation. The elder nodded, but there was fresh caution in her eyes at mention of the Black Tide cult.

Lirr's daughter leaned forward now, scrutinizing me the way she had watched Mary, down in the cells.

Mary seemed unable to contain herself any longer. "This is all ridiculous. James Demery will confirm Samuel's identity, as will my mother, Anne Firth, and any of their associates." She slid her gaze to Voskin. "As we told *him* many times."

"I am unclear," Howell boomed. "Is this Captain Rosser on trial, or his windwife?"

"A moment, please," a female voice interrupted. The Sunjani woman I had marked earlier had drawn up to the table, forcing two seated councillors to lean aside, indignantly. "The Stormsinger falls under my protection."

Across the room Voskin produced a sheet of paper and, handing it to a page, waited for it to be delivered to the head chairs. "As you will see here, the Stormsinger Mary Firth forfeited her rights to the protection of the Stormsinger's Enclave and indentured herself to me."

I glanced at Mary sharply. All color had leeched from her face as she turned on Voskin. "I signed that under duress!"

Voskin shook his head, unruffled. "I explicitly stated your life was not under threat, Ms. Firth. My Lady Julana, here is a statement affirmed by two witnesses."

"What witnesses? Your guards?" Mary shouted. "You conniving piece of shit!"

"What is this?" The question barely cut over the hubbub, and had to be repeated, followed by a "Bleeding Saint."

A man strode across the floor, looking distinctly displeased. His sun-lightened brown hair was shot with grey and contained in a short, smooth braid, tied with a black ribbon. His formerly clean-shaven face was now adorned with a trim beard and mustache, and his skin was a mild, far northern brown. Between that and his handsome features, he could have hailed from Usti, Aeadine or Mere.

"That is Demery," I said to Brid with a relieved smile.

More figures filed into the hall behind Demery, too many to pick out from the crowd, but I recognized the admirable height of Athe Kohlan.

Demery waved dismissively at the guards, who granted him space to pass through into the circle and approach us.

"I've no clue who *you* are, but given your company and predicament, I feel I should apologize," Demery said to Brid, then laid a hand on Mary's shoulder.

The touch was momentary, less than a heartbeat, but I saw a flicker in Mary's eyes. Demery, the more experienced *ghiseau*, showed no change whatsoever, but I knew they were exchanging silent communication. Even in such a brief touch, Mary—or Tane, rather—would communicate months', even years' worth of information to Harpy, Demery's resident ghisting.

Demery now knew all he needed to.

"Who is this man?" Howell asked Demery. He had risen to his feet, and pointed to me with one long arm.

"This is Captain Samuel Rosser of *Hart*, privateer under Queen Inara, last I heard," Demery said, squinting at me. "He looked much better last I saw him. You have let yourself go, good man."

I smiled mirthlessly, hoping no one could see the depth of my relief. "Captain."

"Lord," he corrected mildly, and turned his attention back to the council. "So, what say you? Did you anticipate another answer? Lord Voskin, you are looking peevish today."

"Then who is this woman?" Voskin demanded, pointing to Mary.

Demery pretended not to understand and looked at Brid. "I haven't a clue. James Demery, madam."

"Bridget Deeds."

"Ah, an Easterner."

Brid grinned.

"The other woman," Howell said, though not without amusement.

"That is Mary Grey, also called Firth," a woman's voice carried over the crowd, strident and accompanied by a rustle of wind. Anne Firth stepped up to the table, contained behind several council members. "My daughter."

Her last two words came with a chill and weight of warning that no occupant of the room seemed to miss. Guards stiffened, hands discretely reached under the tables, and Julana rose to her feet to stand next to Howell.

Mary twisted to stare at her mother, her eyes touched with child-like relief.

The memory of my own mother, untrustworthy and mad, flitted through my mind and was gone.

"And do you affirm, as a member of this council, that this man has a Magni twin, Benedict Rosser?" Julana asked.

"Saint, is that bastard still alive?" Demery let out an exasperated breath, feigning shock—though from Mary's communication, he knew the situation already. "Yes, yes. Mirror twins. I doubt their own mother could tell them apart."

Murmurs rippled around the chamber until Julana silenced them with a raised hand.

"Samuel Rosser," she said, addressing me, and I felt relief at my name. "You now have the opportunity to plead your case."

I did. I spoke of our intention to visit Demery, of the pirate's attack, *Hart's* destruction and our quest for aid, then of Voskin's accusation and Mary's and my imprisonment, and the threat over our crew.

"Furthermore," I added, an ache of anger and loss in my chest. "One, and possibly more, of my crewmembers were murdered at Lord Voskin's command. My ship was taken, and my crew and ghisting remain in his possession. I, too, demand justice."

Voskin looked as though he might leap the table, but at his side, Lirr's daughter reached up to put a hand on his sleeve. Grudgingly, he leaned down, and she spoke in his ear.

My attention was diverted as Demery spoke up and deliberations deepened, leaving my hands entirely. Voskin spoke again, still unwilling to admit defeat, issuing speculation as to bribes, intellectual failings and other thinly veiled insults.

Demery, who spoke mildly and blithely, continued in our defense, eventually taking a chair beside us and crossing one ankle over the opposite knee.

"Has anyone else encountered this *Red Tempest*?" Demery asked at one point.

"We sighted a ship with red sails sailing for the Trade Strait," someone said.

"That could have been any Mereish warship," Voskin countered.

"She flew no colors," the person added. "And gave no signal." Julana turned to Howell and spoke lowly.

"We have heard enough," Julana declared. "Cast the vote."

Servants began to scuttle about with buckets, delivering white and black tiles and gathering the votes. Demery continued to watch, picking at his nails and studying Voskin.

"Voskin, your petition of execution is denied," Idriss declared.

"Samuel Rosser, you and your crew are acquitted. The matter is now closed."

Voskin, looking as though he were about to suffer a bout of apoplexy, made a strangled sound. "You cannot! My port is in ruins! Is there no justice in this council?"

"Sit down, man," Howell ordered him.

"The Stormsinger!" Voskin shouted. "My indenture holds!"

My heart stopped. Mary froze and turned, staring across the floor at Voskin with an incredulous expression.

"It does. The Stormsinger is yours," Julana said dismissively. Her gaze turned to Brid, narrowing as if she could not remember why the other woman was present. "What of this common sailor? How is she worth this council's time?"

"She is not. However, she is as much a victim as the citizens of Port Sen," Demery said gravely. "I would suggest a general fine for piracy and, as her advocate, request she be remanded into my care."

"Pirates fining pirates for piracy," Mary hissed. "What the hell is this place?"

Julana glanced at Howell, who shrugged, and Julana waved. "A fine, to be decided by the petty court. Lady Wight! You may bring your petition now."

Brid blinked, looking more than a little lost, and I leaned into whisper, "I will see your fine paid."

She appeared not to believe me, but nodded as the four of us left the circle.

"Now shut up and do not make matters worse," Demery said to the lot of us. "Wait in the entryway. Do not try to leave, do not cause a scene; otherwise there will be violence and my influence only goes so far. We will settle this matter once council closes."

THIRTEEN

Sister

MARY

I sat on a bench under the glare of Osso, who had stalked out of the council hall in our wake with more of Voskin's henchfolk. But they, I quickly realized, were the least of my concerns.

My mother eased herself down next to me and finished unbuttoning her coat, letting it fall to the sides of an obviously pregnant belly. I stared, my mind suddenly blank enough even to forget Voskin and my forced indenture.

Samuel and Brid arrived at my other side but did not sit. They watched Osso silently. Sam noted my mother's condition but did not comment on it.

Athe, meanwhile, sat on the other end of the bench and waved down a passing servant. They spoke quietly, and the servant hurried off.

"Well," I finally said, rubbing at my eyes and looking into my mother's expectant face. "Who did that?"

"A handsome rogue," my mother said mildly, lacing her fingers atop her belly.

I started to *tsk*, about to restate my question, when her belly shuddered of its own accord. "Did that... Did the baby just move?"

"Yes. I've a month or two left, give or take, and your sibling doesn't take well to confinement." She smiled, despite the situation, and I noted the pleasant roundness of her cheeks. I didn't think it simply a result of her pregnancy. She looked well-fed and collected, no longer gaunt and haunted as she had been. She did not even seem particularly ruffled by the looming presence of Voskin's people.

But then, my mother had spent over a decade as a captive of Silvanus Lirr.

The thought of him, and his cold-eyed daughter, soured my stomach.

"Stay calm," she advised, unhelpfully. "The council will last another few hours, then we will be back aboard *Harpy*."

Osso made a sound of disagreement, but she and her companions seemed of a similar mind. Before long, they pulled over stools and dealt a deck of cards. The servant Athe had sent brought over wine and food and a table, and the tension decreased. Marginally. Samuel still refused to sit and had taken up station with Athe, the two of them conversing quietly. Brid hovered, ever slightly on the outside.

"Who is the father, then?" I asked my mother. "Not Demery."

My mother laughed, genuine affection in her expression. "No. No, you've not met him. His name is Emre. Emre Solla. He is Capesh, a good man, good family. Very good family."

I eyed her. "What does that mean?"

"He is no pirate, if that's what you're after."

I wasn't sure that *was* what I was after, but I put aside the topic for the time being. "Congratulations, Mama. I'm very happy for you."

She offered me a reserved smile and patted my thigh. "I'll introduce you. You will stay with us in Oranmur for some time, I assume?"

"That was the intention," I admitted. I glanced from her to Sam, then back to her. "Samuel has offered to marry me."

My mother looked taken aback. "You don't sound... over-wrought with anticipation."

I laughed, a little bitterly. "This *is* my second engagement."

"So you may not be happy?"

"It's not that," I couldn't quite articulate my feelings on that matter. "We can speak of betrothals later."

The hours passed tensely. Every so often someone would pass by, eyeing us, hands hovering over weapons as if they expected us to attack one another at any moment. But, whether by the servants' steady supply of food, coffee and wine, or a surprising show of honor, there was no violence. Athe even fell to playing cards with Osso's companions, while Samuel finally consented to sit between Brid and me.

"I believe I hate the Mereish South Isles," Samuel said.

"I hated them first," Brid put in.

I buried my face in a cup of wine.

Finally, the council finished. People flooded out of the doors in a cacophony of footsteps and voices. Sam and I rose, spying Demery as he fell into step with Voskin. They exchanged terse words, but by the time they arrived had settled into stony silence.

"Come," Demery said, nodding down the entryway. "Let us speak somewhere more private."

We moved into a smaller chamber, equipped with a long table and a fireplace large enough to sleep in—or push Voskin into. Sadly, the hearth was cold.

"I will be brief," Voskin said, arranging himself self-importantly in the center of the floor. "By law, the Stormsinger is mine until her indenture is paid in full. I will not sell the indenture for anything less than the head of Benedict Rosser. If such a person does exist, and the council is not victim of your lies and conspiracy."

"Unacceptable," Samuel stated.

I touched his arm to quiet him. "Voskin, your paper is worthless. I will escape, as I did before. There is nothing you can do to hold me."

Voskin rolled his eyes. "Must we do this again? The indenture is valid, and the council will uphold it within these Isles."

The reply *Then I will leave the Isles* died on my tongue. Where would I go? Not back north, not so soon. I would be forced out into a world I had no knowledge of, a world of strangers and unknown threats. Once, that might have thrilled me. Just then, it left me unspeakably tired.

At the same time, my gaze dragged to my mother, the swell of her belly and the lines of her face, familiar and yet still somehow unfamiliar. I had spent most of my life separated from her, but that made the thought of leaving her again harder to swallow, not easier. There was a future there, perhaps beside her and that child, that I could not easily set aside.

"There is also the matter of your ship, crew and the ghisting," Voskin said, his voice far too mild.

"You will release them," Samuel said, stepping forward. My hand slipped from his arm. "As you have no right to hold them."

"Perhaps," Voskin shrugged. There was such polite vengeance in him, such cold intensity. "But Old Lapa's people would dearly love to reclaim their ship and have that ghisting. And they, I dare say, are hungry for blood. Matters may... slip out of my hands."

Demery glowered. "I will not let this stand, Voskin."

Voskin shrugged. "You may try to intervene, but who can say what will transpire? Ah, Talys, glad you could join us."

We all turned as a young woman entered the room. Lirr's daughter, walking with the calm reserve of a woman three times her age.

"Voskin," she said, and her voice, too, was not that of the young woman she appeared to be. It was smooth, self-assured and unhurried.

Tane shuddered. There was little else I could describe the feeling as: a ripple in my marrow, through every inch of muscle I possessed.

She is more ghisting than human, Tane whispered. *I cannot say how much of Talys even remains.*

Is she a mage?

No, but that should not console us, Tane cautioned. *This creature is not right.*

"This is Talys Lirr, daughter of Silvanus Lirr, who I believe died at the hands of... well, *you*," he said, encompassing Demery, my mother, Athe and myself in that word. "Talys has inquired about purchasing Ms. Firth's indenture."

The bottom dropped out of my stomach. My mother grabbed my arm and Samuel's jaw clenched so hard as to crack.

"I have yet to agree, of course, matters still being as unsettled as they are," Voskin said airily. He was the happiest I had yet seen him, practically radiating triumph. "Ms. Firth, you will try to escape your indenture, I am sure. You may even flee to the Far Seas, and perhaps find a place to hide among strangers, under another sun. But see, friends and enemies, none of this need happen. Give me Benedict and I will burn the indenture. I will ensure your ship, crew and ghisting are safely returned. We can put this all behind us."

"I will kill you," Samuel informed him. It was no wrathful vow, nor an idle threat. It was a statement of fact, as solid as stone.

"You are emotional, I see that," Voskin said to him with false sympathy. "I understand the pair of you are betrothed? Such feelings are natural. However, your nuptials will have to wait until I no longer own your wife."

Samuel moved for Voskin, but Demery grabbed him by the collar and held him back.

Talys watched it all with eerie stillness.

"Saint, man," Demery reprimanded Sam, "No wonder you've been mistaken for your brother. Be *calm*."

"A duel," Samuel tossed at Voskin. "We close this matter, you and I."

Voskin suppressed a smirk and looked at Demery. "Did you not warn him?"

I grabbed Sam's arm. Demery, noting me, let the younger man go.

"Stop this," I hissed, pulling him back a step.

"I will not let him do this to you."

I gripped his arm as tightly as I could. My mind felt as though it might rupture under the weight of all that was happening, but one thing was clear to me. "If you get yourself killed, nothing else matters. Nothing. Do you understand me?"

Sam nearly replied, but Demery and Voskin were still speaking.

"I do not need *money*," Voskin was saying, throwing out the word like a refuse. "I need justice. Benedict. Rosser's. Head. Or I sell the Stormsinger to the daughter of a man she murdered. Or, perhaps, I keep her for myself, with all the privileges therein. Saints, perhaps I shall even put a bounty on Rosser myself. Five thousand dette? Ten thousand? Enough to bring every fiend and rogue from here to Hesten down on him."

Samuel's arm was iron under my hands. I felt the same tension in myself, along with an inevitable, edgeless kind of dread.

Even when he tried to strike out on his own, Benedict threatened to destroy us.

There was more to the matter, of course. The documents, and Enisca Alamay. The balance of power on the Winter Sea. The freedom of our crew and friends and Hart. My mother.

My sibling.

I closed my eyes. Too much. It was all too much.

"I'll find him," I heard Athe say. "I've managed the bastard before, I'll do it again. But I want the bounty for myself."

Voskin shrugged. "Naturally."

Demery rubbed at his forehead. "Perhaps it is the simplest route."

I opened my eyes to stare at him. Even my mother looked at him quizzically.

"I have your word, then?" Voskin asked the pair of them. "You will see to Rosser?"

"So long as Ms. Firth is paroled into my keeping," Demery replied.

"No," was Voskin's unyielding response. "Do you think me a fool?"

"You already have his ship and crew," Demery said. "And a ghisting. A powerful one, very valuable. Keep them as collateral."

I covered my face with my hands. The impulse to simply submit to Voskin was growing inside me, like the pressure of the ocean depths on a sinking body.

I could not let so many suffer on my behalf. I could not be the crux of this conflict.

But I was not, was I? Benedict was.

There had to be another solution. There *would* be another solution. We just needed time, and to get out of the Sea Fort alive.

Then, just when I had begun to calm, my mother stepped forward. "Voskin, if I may."

Voskin stepped aside with my mother. I hated to see them in proximity, and was even further unsettled by the thought of what they might be saying, what deal my mother might cut.

After a brief exchange, Voskin turned back to us.

"It is settled, then," he said. "Take the Stormsinger with you, for now. Your ghisting Hart, your ship and crew will be held as collateral for the Stormsinger. If I do not have Benedict Rosser's head by the end of summer, they will all be mine."

❦

Stepping back aboard *Harpy* was a homecoming. It came with both familiarity and an uncanny disconnect, as if I walked within my own memory. So much was the same, and yet much had changed. Almost every member of the crew was new, *Harpy's* former complement having scattered to riches and retirement. The great cabin now had a distinct Sunjani lean thanks to Athe as captain, with a lavish carpet on the deck and the table arranged to one side, leaving the space with a more open feel. My former cabin, off the great cabin, was now my mother's.

My mother who, with a weary sigh, eased herself into what had been my customary seat at the table, closest to the gallery windows. She was forced to sit sideways, making room for her belly.

Demery pulled off his hat and cast it on the table. "What did you do, Anne?"

"That is none of your concern," my mother replied, lacing her hands over her belly.

"Saint, you vex me. Athe, where is my wine?"

"*My* wine," the taller woman corrected, striding across the cabin and opening a cupboard as the rest of the company filed in, took seats and settled in.

The Sunjani woman from the council came last. She offered us a tight smile, nodded to Athe and Demery, and took a seat at the table next to my mother.

"Anne," she greeted her, and flicked her eyes down at her stomach. "How is the fetal witch?"

"Digging her heels into her mother's lungs so that she cannot sing," Anne inclined her head. "Idriss, is there truly nothing you can do about the indenture?"

"Not under the law I have fought to establish, no," Idriss replied. "They are a double-edged blade, these indentures. But it is a rung on the ladder to freedom."

"How long has the law been in place?" Sam asked.

Idriss settled deeper into her chair. "Less than a year. You are aware that Silvanus Lirr had numerous Stormsingers in captivity here in the Isles. His witches. His concubines. I was one of them."

My mother did not flinch at the mention of Lirr.

"Talys is one of their children?" I asked.

Idriss nodded. "One of many. When word came that Lirr was dead, we Stormsingers took his island and resources, and now I rule Isla Ascra in his place."

I blinked at her, speechless. There was a delicious justice to the news, along with a host of more vague possibilities and repercussions. An island of Stormsingers, ruling themselves? It was unheard of. It was momentous.

It was also unspeakably dangerous. The island would be a target like none other.

"But you did not take his seat," I said, recalling that Idriss had not sat at the council.

"No," my mother replied. "Talys claimed his council seat and would gladly reclaim the island, too."

Idriss nodded. "Isla Ascra is as much of a prize as we are in the eyes of the Isles. But we will not be so easily overthrown."

"How many of you are there?" Samuel asked.

"Stormsingers? We number seventy-seven. Children of Silvanus Lirr? Twenty, of which a handful found their father's favor and were made *ghiseau*. Talys is the second eldest, of that group."

"Her ghisting, however, is the oldest and most dangerous," Anne added.

"Talys will not be an issue," Demery said dismissively. "We will deal with Benedict and be done with it. But first, we will return to Oranmur."

Idriss nodded again. "I wish you well. If you've ever need of a safe harbor, Isla Ascra is open to you."

FOURTEEN

The Oranmur Spur

SAMUEL

The island where James Elijah Demery had taken up residence lay in the western region of the Isles. It was a lofty bit of land, graced with rolling, rocky hills and forests, the latter of which grew denser and lusher the further inland they stretched. A series of jagged spurs added to the island's silhouette against the late afternoon horizon, one of which lorded directly over the singular settlement of Oranmur like a natural fortress of weatherworn rock. It descended sharply into the sea, where the waves had pounded and shaped it into something of a sheltering arm, buttressed by man-made breakwaters and a watchtower that significantly predated Demery's occupation.

Harpy nosed alongside a private dock. From my position midship, sheltered from sight and the wind, I could see Mary on the quarterdeck with her mother. For a moment, memory assailed me—the days when Mary had been Demery's Stormsinger and I had tried, and failed, to convince her to join *Hart*.

An ache settled in the back of my throat, not only for my ship. I had already begun to fall for her back then, tracking her light on the horizon and trying to unravel her connection to Silvanus Lirr. Now, she had agreed not only to be my Stormsinger, but my wife. She was mine. But Lirr's shadow still stretched long, and the mire we now found ourselves in seemed, if I was honest with myself, insurmountable.

But I would not admit that to her.

"Capesh galley," Demery commented, situating himself beside me. "It seems I have company."

I followed his gaze to an anchored vessel, noting the skirt of oar blades and her long, low construction, with two masts and a fore-and-aft rig. Her colors were nowhere to be seen but her make was undoubtedly Capesh, marked out by high, decorative prow and stern.

"An oargalley," I noted. "That is not something one sees in the north."

Demery nodded. We had settled at the dock and a gangplank was being lowered, but he lingered with me. "Indeed. They rarely have ghistings, or Stormsingers. Though, that one does. Occasionally."

I glanced at him, sensing he had more to say on that topic.

"Anne. That ship belongs to the father of her child. Who, it seems, you will also soon call family."

"I see." I surveyed Mary and Anne again. They stood close, conferring rapidly, and from the way Mary looked at the Capesh ship, they spoke along similar lines. "And? What kind of man is he?"

"Very interesting, Saints be praised," Demery said, slipping his hands into his pockets and starting to leave. "I never understood Anne's infatuation with Mary's father. He was too common a man for such a remarkable woman, but she was young, and we were all very stupid, so I suppose such things may be excused. I will ask him to table, this evening. I have a question, however."

"Ask it."

"Your woman Brid. Or rather, Ben's crewwoman. Do you trust her?"

"With my life," I said with honesty.

"Then she may prove useful. I'll see her well appointed, set up at an inn in town. Athe may even have a position for her, if she is amenable."

"That is very kind."

"I am an excellent host," Demery said with a wink, and left me to my thoughts.

Soon after, I joined Mary and Anne on the docks. The port was quiet in the cool of the breeze and the warmth of the sun, aside from a scattering of hawkers and stallkeepers who, rather than shout their wares, socialized in the shade of awnings with cups in hand and children underfoot. Many of the awnings connected to a tall, thick stone wall which divided the docks from the town proper, though there was no gate in its archway. A single guard, meandering along the top of the wall, had her head on the shoulder of a man in a frock coat.

There was a peace to the place, a summer contentedness that seemed deeper than the sun on the stones. Despite everything, I felt some of my tension unravel.

Mary slipped an arm through mine. The movement was casual, but her grip on my bicep was tight.

"I will have a sibling within the next couple months," she said to me. "Half-Capesh and quite likely a Stormsinger."

"How do you feel about that?"

Mary wore a distracted, burdened expression I had rarely seen. "Her—the child's—future weighs upon me. Here I am, denied freedom at every turn, no matter where I go. I don't want that for her."

I did not speak, waiting for her to go on. We passed through the town now, its buildings clean and well built, streets broad and full of air and light. It was built up a slope and intersected with several creeks, each funneled into stone channels that rushed down towards the bay and provided a constant, pleasant rush of water to complement the sea breeze. The air smelled of warm stone, hearthsmoke and the sweet, elusive scent of blossoms on the trees that overshadowed our path.

Mary finally continued, her fingers tightening. "Sam... What if *we* have children? A daughter? A Stormsinger?"

The thought was like a fist, an impact of emotion and instinct so sudden and so forceful that it left me winded. The thought of a child, of Mary carrying that child, of hope and love and fresh vulnerability, and the inescapable threats to that tiny, fragile being.

"We would protect her," I stated. "By whatever means."

"Sam, we can barely protect ourselves."

I turned her to face me, lowering my face to look into her eyes. "I will find a way out of this," I vowed. "For you and I, and the crew and Hart. Then we can look to the future again."

She stared back at me for the longest moment, flickers of hope and fear and something more complex in her grey-rimmed irises. "What way? Turning over your own brother to die? We were better off with the Usti."

I opened my mouth to make another vow, but her final sentence stole my words. She needed more than will and intention.

"First, we will rest," I said, softening my grip to gently brush her upper arms. "We eat, sleep. Bathe." I resisted the urge to further illustrate the possibilities of that last event. "Then we shall sit down with your mother and Demery and lay out a plan."

She glanced ahead to where Demery and Anne had stopped, half to allow Anne to rest, and half to wait for us.

"She won't tell me what she said to Voskin," Mary admitted. She did not look as consoled as I had hoped. "What she promised him."

"Perhaps she did not promise him anything," I suggested. "Perhaps she threatened him."

Mary tried to smile. "Maybe. My mother is… I know her very little, Sam. We had my childhood, and the summer last year. I thought we would have time, now, to get to know one another better. But here she is, beginning a new family, and I am… Saint, I am pathetic."

I saw the brightness of tears prickle at the corners of her eyes. Dismayed, I took her hand in mine. "You are the furthest thing."

She forced a smile onto her face and squeezed my hand in return. "Food and rest," she said, repeating my earlier words. "Then a plan."

I nodded. "Then a plan."

Ghisten vows, usually extracted during the carving of figureheads, are the singular most powerful bond which can be forged. Ghistings cannot break their word unless the secondary party, in most cases a human captain or Forester, do so first. In this manner is the ghisting's loyalty to their captain and ship secured.

—FROM A HISTORY OF GHISTLORE
AND THE BLESSED; THOSE BOUND TO THE
OTHER WORLD AND THE POWER THEREIN,
*TRANSLATED INTO AEADINE
BY SAMUEL I. ROSSER*

FIFTEEN

A Trusted Advisor

BENEDICT

The Krekhafen night was warm and still. I prowled the deck, working off a restless, dissatisfied energy as the sounds of port drifted across calm waters.

James Demery loomed at the forefront of my mind. Did I trust Vachon's vision enough to go up against the retired pirate? I had underestimated him before and ended up a prisoner for my trouble. That was, until my skills had been needed in the fight against Silvanus Lirr. Then we had fought together in an uncanny summer in an arctic Wold, by the light of a blazing bonfire and Otherworldly orange light.

I had stood over Lirr's body in the moss, back on that strange night. He had looked like nothing more than a corpse, but my power had prickled at the echo, the remnant, of his. A Magni. A Sooth. A *ghiseau*. An enviable combination.

I realized I had stopped walking and stood looking blankly out over the water. One of the anchor watch, a small man with black skin and an open jacket, watched me over the top of a book from not two paces away.

"Captain," he said, touching his forehead. "Need something, sir?"

"A long drink," I replied humorlessly.

The crewman nodded out across the water. "Plenty of those

ashore, if you don't mind me sayin'. Captain needs his rest, same as the rest of us."

My eyes tightened a fraction in suspicion. Why would any member of my crew encourage me to leave the ship, if not to conduct nefarious activities in my absence?

But the man's expression was open and, I felt, genuine.

"Perhaps you are correct. What is your name?"

"Barrat, sir."

I marked the name and left the deck.

I entered my cabin to find Charles Grant sitting with his feet up on the table. He was smoking a pipe, a habit he had recently adopted.

He looked at me narrowly as I closed the door.

"Boots down," I said. "Go get Faucher."

He exhaled a stream of smoke in my direction and made no move to rise. "Faucher is a problem. You should be rid of him."

I knocked his boots off the table. Grant rocked forward with an *oof*, a burst of smoke and a fit of coughing.

"He is no threat to me," I said dismissively. "His crew is gone. He has made it clear that he has no desire to escape, and his knowledge is useful. Which is why you will fetch him right now."

"He has no desire to escape because he holds hope of retaking the ship. His ghisting is still loyal," Grant explained. He coughed again, sniffed, and sat back in his chair, composed once more. "My companion has seen fit to warn you of the latter point."

"Your ghisting?" I plucked the pipe from his fingers and took a draw. "Is it not still a child? What does it know? It cannot even keep form."

At my words, ghisten light ignited. Charles's resident Otherborn beast manifested beside him in the form of a large dog, but its posture was not quite right, too human and too at ease, and its eyes were exceptionally intelligent.

"He has taken offense," Charles informed me.

I let the smoke sit in my lungs for a long moment before I greeted the beast with a drift of smoke, "Nosewise."

The ghisting cocked his head at me, too-intelligent eyes sharper still.

"Also, he dislikes that name," Grant said.

"He insists on manifesting as a dog, and that is a dog's name."

Nosewise shifted at that. I met the creature's sea-glass gaze unwaveringly.

"Ben," Grant leaned forward, elbows on the table, as Nosewise continued to stare at me. The ghisting had gotten larger, and could look over the table with ease. "I truly am trying to warn you. Miaghis is loyal to Faucher. As is the Stormsinger. Give me my pipe back."

I did, though slowly. "Alfwin and I have spoken. I am not concerned about him."

"Fine, but Miaghis *is* hostile," Grant stated. "He will not accept you as captain until Faucher is gone. His binding word is to the captain of this vessel, and he does not recognize you as such with Faucher still aboard."

I made a conscious effort to slow my mind and give Grant's words weight. "It would be a pity to kill him. No one else knows the Isles as he does."

"Do not *kill* him, Ben, Saint's teeth. Just put him ashore. And give your crew a good prize. They anticipated a lot more galivanting and whoring and throwing about gold, less boredom and wandering around port penniless. And hire some musicians. Proper ones."

"Musicians, again?" My mood, already dark, grew fouler. "You have a great deal of advice for me today."

Grant made a high-browed, huffing expression, evidently unconcerned at further provoking me.

"Charles, would you like to be captain?" I asked.

Grant paused. Smoke drifted between us and we stared one another down for a long, weighty moment.

Nosewise continued to grow larger. He was now the same size as his human counterpart, his big shaggy head level with Grant's.

"Too much responsibility," Grant decided, pinning the pipe back between his teeth and leaning back in his chair. There was a studied lightness to his voice. "I prefer the role of comfortably appointed and highly valued advisor."

"I see," I said, lacing my arms loosely across my chest. "Then conduct yourself as such."

Grant shrugged. The movement was sharp and I realized that he was genuinely irritated with me. Or, perhaps unsettled. "I have yet to be comfortably appointed, Benny."

"Do not call me Benny."

"You may call me Charlie."

"I have no desire to call you Charlie," I said, but the corner of my mouth tugged.

Grant made a scoffing sound, eyes crinkling. He puffed on his pipe again, then passed it to me. "Perhaps for the best. I had a dog named Charlie, but he—"

"Got run over by a cart," I recalled.

"Aw, you remember. You do listen to me."

"Occasionally."

For a moment we sat, smoking in silence, and let the conflict pass. Nosewise finally ceased to grow, and my mind drifted back to the night's task. Alamay in the hold. Demery to track down. Faucher to consult and possibly rid myself of.

"I still want you to go fetch Faucher," I said. "I need to speak with him regarding the politics of the South Isles."

Grant's eyebrows rose. "Oh?"

"Particularly in relation to James Demery."

Grant gave me an odd look. "Ben, you do realize I lived with him, in Oranmur."

I was, admittedly, taken aback. "Pardon me?"

"I take it back, you do not listen to me," he said, exasperated. "Why do I bother speaking at all?"

"I am listening now," I said. "Tell me, can we take Oranmur by force?"

Grant choked, eyes moon-round, and fell into another fit of coughing.

"Perhaps not by force, then," I observed. I leaned forward and, in a gesture that surprised even myself, patted him on the back with more comradery than force. "There, there, Mr. Grant. You needn't come ashore. But I do need you to gather yourself, now. Then we will plot how to outwit James Elijah Demery and sack Oranmur. I shall find my documents and give the crew a prize at the same time."

Grant made an overwhelmed sound. "I no longer desire to advise you. Put me off the ship with Faucher, please."

Taking the pipe, I refilled the bowl as I added, "No, enough of that. You are mine now, Charles."

SIXTEEN

Ties of Spirit and Flesh

MARY

Demery's house was three-storied and solidly built of red stone, with cream painted doors and shutters. It had little adornment itself, but the surrounding grounds were well tended, a mixture of rustling, mature trees and simple gardens between sections of bare rock. These eventually gave way to snakes of forest, which grew denser and damper the deeper into the island they traveled.

I stood at the window of the room I'd been ushered into, squinting out through exhausted eyes and trying to decide whether to collapse into the bed or prowl off in search of food. My hair was damp and tangled but I lacked the will to brush it.

I had just clambered into bed when Tane manifested, parting from my skin and returning to the window. She stood a little taller than I, a little sharper in her features, and a little older in her appearance.

She resumed standing vigil, as I had moments before. And for once, I could not read her thoughts in the hum of my own.

Tane? I asked.

She rested a hand on the wood of the lintel, ghisten flesh seeping into the wood and skittering off the walls, the beams, until the entire house was mapped out in her—our—mind. The presences of other ghistings welled—Harpy, and Athe's ghisting Medved.

It reminded me of Olsa and Illya's absences because, somehow, I had forgotten, just for a moment. Guilt assailed me.

We must free them.

We will. For now rest. Tane urged. A feeling came with her words, a need that I had rarely sensed from her before. A need for solitude.

That unsettled me, though I understood it. Bound as we were, there were few moments where we were each to our own.

I was too tired to dwell on it for long. But as I drifted off to sleep, the edges of Tane's communication with Harpy and Medved threaded through my mind, merging with the first echoes of dreams.

I saw Hart manifest upon tidal sands, alone and abandoned before the wreck of his ship. I felt Tane's ache of responsibility, Harpy's rage at his unjust imprisonment by Voskin, and Medved's vows of reprisal.

It all awoke a strange, intense feeling, one that blurred into a dream of violence and snow, and recalled to me the feel, the scent, and the presence of the Dark Water.

Sister, Harpy whispered.

Vengeance, Medved vowed.

∽

"Emre Solla," the father of my mother's child said, clasping my hand and smiling at me with genuine warmth. He was older than my mother by perhaps a decade, at ease in Demery's dining room, his coat discarded on the back of a chair to reveal a loose linen shirt with silver buttons and no cravat. His skin was more olive than a Northern Aeadine, his grey-touched black hair thick and smooth and bound into a knot at the back of his head. He wore a short beard, perfectly trimmed and a little greyer than the hair on his head.

He was also shockingly handsome, with black-lashed brown eyes that took me in with interest, without being invasive.

We settled into dinner, I sitting beside Samuel, across from my mother and Emre. Sleep had done me a world of good, but a shadow lingered at the back of my mind, one that crept to the forefront as the conversation meandered from pleasantries to the story of how we had come here.

I remembered my half-dream of Hart, the stag alone upon the twilit sand.

"My ship has no ghisting, no," Emre was saying to Samuel.

My attention leapt back to the conversation.

"Nor Stormsinger." Emre looked to my mother, a smile touching his eyes, "Though this past year, your mother was kind enough to sail with us."

"Yes, and see how that turned out," Athe observed, nodding to my mother's belly.

Emre grinned and my mother smiled like a satisfied cat.

I cleared my throat. "But my mother will not be returning to sea for some time, now. Will you hire a Stormsinger from Idriss?"

"Yes, I may need to, once the summer wanes," Emre said. There was something in his tone that plucked at my attention, a hint of something unsaid, but perhaps I was wrong.

"You are an ambassador?" Samuel asked. His fingers brushed my thigh under the table, providing a welcome distraction.

Emre nodded. "I am the Capesh eye in the South Isles. I make my appearances, island to island, and am called upon to serve as mediator in matters concerning Capesh citizens and Capesh interests. In short, I sail about being fed good food, drinking fine wine and ensuring my people retain distinction from the Mereish in the eyes of the Lords."

A certain hardness entered his voice at the last, and I glimpsed another side of the man—a spine of iron beneath the warm smile.

"I am surprised you were not granted a ghisting, in that case," Samuel said.

"Not yet," Emre gave him a wry smile.

Anne lifted his glass in a toast, "To bureaucracy," she said in a tone that implied she hoped to end this particular discussion.

"And the heavy hand of the Mereish," added Emre, over the rim of his glass.

※

Cool air drifted through the unshuttered window as I sat on the edge of the bed, watching Samuel close the door and pull off his borrowed coat, then roll up his shirtsleeves and loosen the laces of his shirt. I still found a great deal of novelty in the sight of him at his ease, in the privacy of candle-lit darkness. But my head was still too full to appreciate the way the light ran up the muscle and sinew of his forearms, or how his artful fingers moved at his buttons.

Even the mangled knot of fresh, pink flesh where he had been shot by Inis Hae, rival Summoner and servant of the Ess Noti, could not distract me.

"I believe Emre Solla is more of a spy than a diplomat," Samuel said in a low voice. He hung his coat on the back of the chair, ensuring it draped just so. "Or rather, I *know* there is more to his purpose in the Isles, but I would need time in the Other to learn more. And it is, I realize, not the foremost of our concerns."

A weight settled in my stomach. "Not at all. Are we not going to tell Demery about Alamay and the documents? Or what the Usti are doing?"

He came to sit beside me on the bed. This was a weighted topic: one we had dared not broach in the close quarters aboard ship. "Tane did not tell him then, when the two of you communicated at the council?"

"No."

"Good." Samuel thought for a moment. "I believe that at the moment, we need not muddy the waters. Let us see how matters progress."

I nodded tiredly. "I suppose we must. Saint... I would give

anything for a scrap of certainty. About something. Anything."

Sam's arms came around me. I sat stiffly for half a breath, then relented, leaning into him and closing my eyes.

He was quiet for a long while, but I could veritably feel him thinking, feel the pattern of his thoughts in the subtle shifts of his body, the ripples of tension and conscious gentling of his hold.

"Mary," he asked softly. "What do *you* want to do? Right now?"

"Run," I replied, equally soft. "But I can't. I won't. Not with Hart and the Uknaras and everyone in the balance. And I don't want to give up. I don't want to live running from place to place. I'm a Stormsinger. I will always be hunted. At some point, I suppose I must stand my ground."

"Then I need to find Benedict, one last time. I will see our people free and Hart restored. After that... if you want to stay here, I will stay with you. And if you decide you want the horizon? I will give it to you."

"You are too good," I murmured into his shoulder. I added without resentment, "It's vexing."

"I am glad you still think me good," he replied. "Because I feel less 'good' by the day. Though... perhaps goodness is not what I believed it to be."

I stayed quiet, sensing he had more to say.

"I believed it was lawfulness and honor, and that if I upheld those, the world would consider me fairly. But it has not. Laws... laws are dictated by power and money, the same forces that keep our world at war and would see you in chains. And honor? It is nothing of substance, nothing I can hold." He buried his face in my hair and delivered his final words in a brush of warm breath and gentle lips. "Not like I can hold you."

Something inside me wrenched. I had no words for that feeling, no way of bearing it. All I could do was capture Samuel's face between my hands, stare into the warm depths of his eyes for a wordless moment, and kiss him.

SEVENTEEN

The Way of the World

SAMUEL

After Mary fell asleep, I found Demery at his desk in a large, well-equipped study. Thick rugs, wood paneling and extensive bookcases dominated the space, backed by walls that, while clad in decorative paper, also hosted an array of paintings and memorabilia. A massive grey wig sat on the bust of a regal, hook-nosed man on one windowsill, a sideboard was well-stocked with liquor, and an easel occupied one corner.

I eyed the latter, wondering what half-finished painting lay beneath the drape, and better noted the paintings on the walls. Pastoral scenes of meadow, mountain and sea, with gentle colors and a misty quality. Various objects in various qualities of light. Suggestions of a woman's form—a gentle hand, the curve of a hip, long hair cast over a pillow while, beyond the window a ship vanishing over a golden horizon.

"We need to talk," I said, prying my eyes from the image.

"Then pour me more brandy," Demery said, barely glancing up from an unfolded letter. "I have little doubt I will need it."

A bottle sat on the table before us, along with an empty glass. I took it and poured him another knuckle as he finished his reading and set the letter aside.

"Can Voskin be bribed?" I asked.

"No. He has taken this matter very personally. Not that I blame him, with his port in shambles and his reputation on the line. The council may look civilized, but they are a pack of ravening wolves, and his weakness may lose him his island *and* his seat."

"Blackmail?"

"That entirely depends on your leverage."

"And if he was to simply die?"

A smile touched Demery's face, but it did not quite reach his eyes. He was assessing me, but whatever he decided, he did not share it.

"A Council Lord does not simply die," he said instead. "There would be an inquisition, and you are too poor to come out well."

"I am hardly poor," I replied. "Mary and I went over the Stormwall, same as you."

"Those funds are in Aeadine and Usti, are they not? Months away."

I conceded with a nod. "Who are Voskin's allies, and his enemies?"

"Talys Lirr, heir and scion of the departed villain," Demery said. "She took his seat, but cannot retake his island, thank the Saint."

"Isla Ascra, the island Idriss holds?"

"Yes. It would require defeating an enclave of one hundred and fifty Stormsingers and other mages, a fair portion of whom share Talys's blood, but not her affection for her father."

I stared past Demery, mulling this over. "Then Idriss *is* a powerful ally."

"Yes, but as you may have noticed, Idriss's focus is internal—she fights for Stormsingers, and cares little for the broader politics of the isles. Which is one reason why she is continually denied a seat, each time one opens. That and the fact that she *is* a Stormsinger, and half the council thinks she should be chained to a mast. The other half also believes this, but she has so effectively annexed Stormsinger services that they dare not go against her. All of this is rather fresh, obviously, Lirr being hardly in the grave. But here we are."

We spoke for some time on such matters, Demery eventually pulling out a map of the Isles and guiding me through the alliances and feuds, politics and petty grievances of the Council of Lords.

"The position of Port Sen is Voskin's greatest asset," Demery eventually concluded. "He is one of the first ports in the north. His trade network is extensive, as he has managed to keep the peace with the Mereish Trading Company. His ties to the Mereish mainland, also, are firm."

"Trading in dyes and ore, Mary was told."

"Ore?" Demery repeated. "Interesting."

I reached for Demery's glass, looking at him promptingly.

"Go ahead," he said, and I filled and drained the glass myself. "Mr. Rosser, I will speak frankly with you."

"I hope for nothing less."

"The world is not yours to change. So, find a way to live within its boundaries."

"Pardon me?"

"Mary will always be sought after. I know what you and she attempted to do with her Usti contract. It is the same thing Idriss is attempting. But this is a lost cause.

"I am a pragmatist," Demery continued at the expression on my face. "Do you know why Anne is safe here with me? I, a council lord, hold an indenture for her services, drawn up by Idriss. It means nothing to Anne, nor I. It is merely paper. But to the council, it is an unyielding truth, a law of nature. It is a placation. It is simply what we had to do to live in relative peace."

"You are suggesting that I give in to Voskin," I clarified.

"No," Demery affirmed, leaning forward, elbows on the table. "Anne's indenture is a façade. Mary's would be, too, once in our hands. What I am suggesting is rather... a trick of the eye."

I set the glass down again and sat back in my chair, arms on the rests. "Go on."

"Let me state, before I continue, that I am retired, and any action I am taking on my part is a sacrifice of the highest order. So, do appreciate me."

"You are appreciated, my lord," I said with a twitch of a smile.

"Good. Now, I will help you find Benedict. We sail out aboard *Harpy*, together. Either your brother agrees to leave the Mereish Isles and find other waters to conduct his business in, or we indeed turn him over to Voskin."

I felt a spark of… not quite hope, but something close. "How would him leaving satisfy Voskin?"

"Because he will take a new name, a new identity, and we will falsify his death. He will have a clean start, a new beginning. As will you and Mary."

I began to shake my head. Not only was Demery's notion of a clean start for Mary and I clearly different than ours, but Benedict would never agree. Not if he was after Enisca Alamay and the Mereish papers, and likely some grand concept of vengeance.

"What would you gain from all this?" I asked. "There must be something."

Demery glanced at the darkened window for a moment, head tilted to one side as he thought. "Enraging Voskin. Throwing a grenade into the half of the council that is against me. Do not mistake me, I enjoy retirement. But more power and influence secures my peace. And perhaps I am a trifle bored… Saint, is that it? Am I simply bored?"

He poured more brandy and downed it with a world-weary frown.

"I cannot believe you would act out of boredom, sir."

"Well. Regardless. I am your ally, Mr. Rosser. You have considerably inconvenienced me, but an ally I am, largely out of loyalty to Anne and Tane. And Mary, I will admit, has claimed some measure of my affection. So, take my offer. It is the only one I will give. I will not give you a ship, not unless I am on it, ensuring you do not further disrupt my life."

As if on cue, a boom reverberated in the night.

We converged on the window, where he threw the shutters back. Cool air struck our faces and my Sooth's senses bloomed, reaching, stretching, brushing against the Dark Water.

I saw waves against a hull, a ghisting's reaching, twining tentacles. I saw my own face in the flash of powder and the swing of lanterns.

Another boom. Down in the town, warning bells began to ring and dogs to bark.

Demery regarded me, ghisting light creeping into the corners of his eyes. His hands rested on the wooden windowsill, sheathed in the softest illumination.

"Sooth?" Demery asked. "Who is it?"

Fists pounded at the door in the hallway. Brid burst in, her eyes wild and her breath ragged.

"Captain Rosser—he's already ashore!"

∞

There was an eerie, oppressive stillness as Demery and I stepped out into the cool of the night, followed by Brid. Demery passed Brid a cutlass and me a pistol as we went. I primed the weapon methodically, noting the changes in our surroundings with equal precision.

The house behind us was being rapidly roused by the servants. *The Red Tempest* was visible in the mouth of the inlet below, draped in the pale violet of a moon-bright night. Her deck was flooded with lantern light and her every gunport was open, watching over the town of Oranmur as screams and shouts filled the streets. Doors were flung open, muskets fired, dogs barked and children cried.

Up on the hill, at the battery on the spur, guns boomed wildly. Not a defense, by any means. A celebration.

At my side, Demery began to transform. It was a subtle shift, a change of posture, a setting aside of one mantle and the taking up of another. It culminated in a predatory calm that I felt reflected in myself.

Benedict topped the road up from town and stopped a dozen paces away, surrounded by fifty armed pirates and Athe, who had the mouth of a rifle in her back and a stony expression on her face.

Ben looked the picture of a pirate, just then—a cutlass at his hip, a brace of pistols and wooden cartridges across his chest. His tricorn hat sat on his natural hair, bound in a short braid, and he wore the beginning of a beard. He wore a brown frock coat over a loose shirt with no waistcoat and no cravat.

The beard and his lack of uniform made us look all the more alike. But Ben was thinner than I, sharper and harder—the legacy of his captivity in Mere and our subsequent flight.

That hardness, however, faltered as he spotted me. Genuine shock flickered through his dark-rimmed eyes and something less familiar, more vulnerable. Doubt.

It was gone in a flash.

Ben gestured at his crew and they nudged Athe forward. The woman strode over the no-man's-land between the two parties, in the shadow of the house, and took up position next to Demery.

"They took the battery on the hill, as you can hear," Athe said quietly. "By the time the ship itself was sighted, they were already in the port. They've a dozen hostages on the docks."

"How many of them are there?"

"At least two hundred ashore. A quarter of that you see now. The people are surrendering."

Demery's lips twitch in suppressed rage, but he gave a sharp nod. "Good. So long as they survive."

"Lord Demery. Samuel." Benedict began with a slow smile. He did not so much as look at Brid, let alone appear to recognize her, and I felt the woman shift into my shadow.

The door to the house opened behind us and Mary, Anne and Emre appeared—Mary in a hastily donned jacket and trousers, while Anne and Emre were as put together and alert as they had been at dinner.

"Mary, dear Mary," Ben said. "And your mother! Well, this is quite the reunion."

"You have blockaded my port and terrorized my people," Demery replied coolly, but he stuck out his hand and shook Ben's. "What is your business?"

"Invite me in, and no blood need be shed," Benedict said, dropping his hand back to his belt, little finger brushing his cutlass.

"They remain outside," I stated, pointing to his crew.

"I will bring only my favorites," he vowed.

Demery stepped back and gestured up the stairs into the house. "Come with me, Captain Rosser."

EIGHTEEN

Correspondences

MARY

"I will not waste either of our time with threats," Ben said to Demery as he closed the study door with a weighty click. Six of his crewmembers, armed and quiet, fanned out to either side with hands on their weapons. The rest remained outside, as promised.

Charles Grant, I noted, was not among them. Had he escaped Ben, then? Or simply been left aboard ship, either because Ben feared that very thing, or out of a desire not to confront Demery?

"I have come for the documents from Enisca Alamay."

Samuel and I exchanged a look so sharp my neck twinged.

We had been right.

Demery shot Benedict an incredulous look. "What, from whom?"

Benedict watched him narrowly. "The documents smuggled to you by the Usti spy, Enisca Alamay."

Demery exchanged a look with Anne and Athe, his expression unfolding into a disbelieving laugh. But as his gaze slid past me, something sharper lurked there. Did he suspect

Mary and I had not been entirely forthcoming about Ben's goals?

"Then you have very much wasted your time," Demery informed Ben. "I haven't the faintest notion what you mean. And if you do not believe me, compel me to truthfulness. I have nothing to hide."

As they spoke, Anne sunk down in a chair.

"Mother, please leave," I whispered, looking at Emre for support.

"No one leaves," Benedict snapped without looking at me. "Or speaks."

Anne gave me a forced smile and set herself to staring down the guards at the door. Emre and I exchanged a look of mutual unhappiness and solidarity, and he situated himself beside her.

Ben faced Demery from the center of the room. I felt his magic rise like wind through a still forest—first a distant whisper, then a nearing rush. I felt power buffet me, just enough to show its strength and remind me, I was sure, of his perceived supremacy. Then that power focused on Demery.

"Where are the documents?" Benedict asked.

"I do not have them."

Another buffet of power. "That is not what I asked."

"I do not have them, nor do I know where they are or what they are."

Benedict approached him, looking him over closely. "Are you wearing a talisman?"

Demery's brow furrowed. "The new Mereish talismans? No, I am not."

Benedict leaned back in his heels and crossed his arms, staring the other man down. "My Sooth saw your connection to Alamay."

"Then your Sooth was mistaken," Demery said. "I will admit to brushing shoulders with some figures in my youth who might have been called spies, but that was a long time ago."

"Perhaps the vision was misinterpreted," Samuel interjected. "What did she see?"

"'A ghisting with many faces,'" Benedict quoted, still staring Demery down. "And a dark-haired man. Harpy's many faces are difficult to forget. You are also entangled with the Usti crown and, therefore, would have an interest in the documents."

"I see," Demery leaned back on his desk now. "But Harpy, like many ghistings, modeled herself after a figure in the wider world. In this case, Yissik Ocho, the many-faced trickster saint of the Usti. He is also patron saint of the house of Arat, a dispossessed arm of the Usti royal family who happen to be prolific here in the South Isles."

Benedict's expression twitched. The old Ben was in his eyes, the one I'd learned both to fear and despise. "You truly know nothing?"

"Regarding documents and an Usti spy? Yes, I am wholly ignorant," Demery affirmed. "Where is your Sooth? Perhaps they can illuminate us further."

"You must be lying, but I cannot fathom how."

Demery shrugged. "I am not. Did you search my correspondences? I was away for several weeks, and as you can see, I have not had time to read all my mail."

"Give them to me."

Demery stepped aside, gesturing at the desk and stacks of waiting letters and scrolls.

Benedict immediately closed on the desk and began to open everything in sight, discarding papers onto the floor as he went. Seals cracked, paper tore and fluttered. His crewfolk shifted on their feet, toying with weapons. My mother leaned back in her chair, hands on her belly, and exchanged a weighty glance with Emre.

Athe folded her arms over her chest and leaned against the far wall.

"Where is Enisca?" I asked Ben. "Is she your prisoner?"

Ben ignored me, tossing more letters onto the floor. One skittered under the easel. Another drifted under the desk.

"She is aboard his ship," Samuel stated with conviction. "But he cannot make her talk. She's not a strong Magni, but she is strong enough. Charles Grant is there, I see. Did he refuse to join you against Demery? Ah, and you have a Sooth. Her aura is significant. Where did you find her?"

Ben's gaze flicked up and the paper in his hands tore. "There are other methods of eliciting information," he said, ignoring my mention of Grant and the question about his Sooth. He scanned the letter he had torn and dropped it back onto the table. Its broken seal tapped on the wood.

"Benedict," Samuel began again, and his tone made all of us look his way. "Voskin, the ruler of the port you burned, tried to have me executed in your place. He forced Mary to sign a contract of indenture. He took my ghisting, my crew, and the Uknaras."

Ben did not look up. "How unfortunate."

Samuel's expression grew so dark I thought he might erupt.

His twin went on, "But you and Mary are alive and free now, I see. Is that not all that matters?" His question seemed genuine, but he answered it himself a breath later, "No, it would not be enough for you."

His gaze darted to me for half a breath and I felt a twist of his power, nudging my emotions, communicating with me without words.

No, his power seemed to say, our perceived 'freedom' was not enough for Sam. My 'freedom' was not enough. His love, his effort, his devotion would always be divided between me and the greater good.

I tightened my resolve, standing against the current of his power. Because where Ben saw Sam's ideals as a flaw, a wedge that could be driven between us, I saw another reason to love him.

Didn't I?

I pushed back harder, glaring at my intended brother-in-law. "Ben. I am not free. The council recognized the indenture, and if I run, I am a fugitive."

"We're all fugitives somewhere. Go back north," Sam's twin replied, turning to the mail again. He sniffed at one, gave Demery an amused glance, and tossed it his way. "Perfume."

Demery caught it and secreted it away into his coat.

"I am a fugitive in *every* corner of the Winter Sea," I said, realizing as I spoke just how true that was, and how profound and unsettling. "My Usti contract burned with *Hart*. Everything we had burned with *Hart*."

Ben finally discarded the letters to gaze between Samuel and me. For a moment I thought he would ask for the whole story, that he might even care that we had lost our ship and now faced an increasingly uncertain future.

He only he shook his head. "Well, you have interesting lives, and not many can say the same. Demery, who else might have the documents? These Usti exiles, the Artans?"

Samuel cut in: "Ben. Voskin is holding Hart, our crew and Mary's freedom against our bringing him your head. That includes the Uknaras and Mr. Maren—people who risked themselves to heal you."

That gave Benedict pause. At the door, his guards stood straighter. One drew her cutlass in a slow, measured shush of steel.

After a fraught moment, Ben pointedly scattered the remainder of Demery's correspondences on the desk.

"Well, here I am, here is my head," he tilted his chin up, letting the light run down the side of his handsome face, over his short beard, and curve down his vulnerable neck. "Take it or leave me be."

My anger erupted. "Why are you doing this? Why did you burn Port Sen? Why can't you *stop*?"

"I burned Port Sen because I wanted to," Ben said, and with that all my hopes for him, that his healing had changed him, crumbled. "I took *The Red Tempest* because I wanted to. And I will find those documents, unveil the Usti's treachery to the world, shame every fucking power on the waves. They call me a criminal? They are nothing but puppets on a string."

"You *are* a criminal," Samuel said lowly.

It was Ben's turn to snap. From one moment to the next what

remained of his civility fled and his power bloomed, rippling throughout the room and concentrating on his crewmembers.

Everyone moved at once. Ben pulled a pistol and shot Demery in the chest. Harpy burst into sight, a whirlwind of ghisten flesh and rage left behind as Demery crumpled behind the desk. I lunged in front of my mother. Sam spun, sword bared and leveled at Benedict's pirates along the back wall.

Or, where they had been along the back wall. They had burst apart, making for Athe, Emre, myself and Sam.

Someone swung a chair at me like a bat. I shouted in startled outrage and threw up an arm. The chair shattered an instant before it hit me—Tane's ghisten light rendering it to pieces—but the impact still knocked me over.

The next thing I saw was from the floor, a swaying, blurring view as I tried to regain my feet. Athe slammed one of the other crewmembers into a wall, knocking another pistol to the ground before they could do the same to her. Emre went down, wrestling an attacker and punching without reserve.

One of Ben's crew put a knife to Anne's throat. Tight to her throat.

I stilled, halfway back to my feet. My mother froze. A knife dropped from her own hand to the floor and her gaze flicked to me, to the crumpled Demery, then to Benedict.

The air began to leave the room. I felt it go before I heard the hiss from between my mother's teeth—all the sound she needed to suffocate everyone present.

The knife tightened. Blood began to stream down, soaking her collar, and Magni power locked over her.

The hiss ceased. The air relaxed, and the study settled into tense silence.

I could have taken up my mother's efforts, but Benedict had turned his newly primed flintlock on Samuel, though he looked straight at me. And as I looked into the midwinter fury of his face,

I could not help but believe he *would* pull the trigger. Perhaps not to kill, not intentionally. But certainly to harm.

Samuel turned slowly on his brother.

"Benedict," he said in the deadliest of voices. "You have not fallen this low."

Benedict walked to the door. He strode right past Samuel, pistol still leveled.

"Release her," Samuel said.

"Bring her along," Benedict countered.

The man holding my mother nudged her forward, after Ben. I was too shocked, to horrified, to move. The rest of Ben's crewfolk gravitated towards him, too. Only the woman Athe had taken down, crumpled on the floor, failed to move.

Ben paused at the door, surrounded by his ensorcelled loyalists.

"I am leaving now. Try to stop me and I will start killing, beginning with Anne. Oranmur need not go the way of Port Sen, but I will not hesitate."

With that he strode from the room, taking his people and my mother with him.

∞

Benedict and *The Red Tempest* sacked Oranmur. I had never known such prolonged rage, such helplessness, as watching them sweep through the town and back to their ship.

No one intervened. No townsfolk. No guards. Not Athe, Emre nor Sam and me. No one dared, not when Ben's power was so sweeping, so absolute.

Not when Demery, already under the ministrations of a local surgeon, ordered everyone to stand down. And certainly not when a line of pirates stood on the quay with knives and cutlasses tight to the throats of hapless prisoners.

My pregnant mother. A young boy, no older than twelve. An old man, a middle-aged woman, a young woman, and so on. They were a tactful selection from the common folk of Oranmur, and one that ensured any action against them was extinguished.

When the pirates left, they took the prisoners with them as far as the ship. Then they were left in a bobbing, overburdened boat, which was rescued by the Emre's folk as *The Red Tempest's* lights extinguished, one by one, and they vanished into the night.

All that remained was the snap of canvas and the sweep of the wind through the silent, horrified port. And the low, deep voice of a male Stormsinger, all the more eerie for its uniqueness.

I saw my mother to a room in Demery's house and lingered briefly, but Emre was large in the small space, his voice calm and capable, while I could barely speak for my lingering shock and distraction.

"Fetch me if you need anything," I said as I made my excuses and slipped away.

Harpy waited for me in the hallway. The array of masks dangling at her hip swayed in a wind that was not there and her head was cocked, her face an eerie mix of an owl and a small-mouthed woman.

Come, she said.

As much as my head ached and my body longed for rest, Tane and I followed.

Another door, slightly ajar. An oil lamp, burning on a bedside table. Demery sat in the bed itself, his chest bandaged and his body clad in a rather worn banyan. His posture was stiff, but as Harpy returned to him he visibly strengthened.

"You and I need to have a frank discussion," he said.

In answer, I sank into a chair next to the bed.

"What did Benedict mean by Usti treachery?"

"The Usti have been provoking conflict between Aeadine and Mere," I replied. "The documents Ben's looking for prove it."

Demery's gaze was hard. "You knew this was what he was after?"

"We suspected. But the spy, Enisca, went missing in the battle at the Anchorage. We didn't even know if she was alive, let alone had the documents."

"That may be. Still, you should have told me."

"Samuel was not sure we could trust you," I scratched absently at the arm of my chair, following the swirls and loops of a carved pattern. "But. As you said, you and I need to speak frankly now."

I held out my hand to Demery, palm up. Tane's light skittered across my skin, promising the speed and fluidity of ghisten communication.

Harpy's light responded in kind as Demery took my hand in his larger, rougher one. The contact was momentary, the communication brief. But when he released me, his posture was calmer and his expression set.

"I suppose I knew better than to believe I could retire in peace," he said, leaning back into his pillows and frowning across the room. "Our best course of action is to find these documents before Benedict does and allow him to come to us, or perhaps encounter him along the way. Regardless. I know where to begin."

"Exiled Usti royals?" I suggested.

Demery gave a wry little nod. "Exiled Usti royals. Now, go fetch me Athe. We have plans to lay."

NINETEEN

A Knife in the Dark

BENEDICT

The ship was full of laughter. I could hear it through the deck, interspersed with singing and the singular strains of a fiddle. Two decks and the muffled rush of waves against the hull all around barely cut the noise, nor did the creak of timbers.

Enisca Alamay sat on the deck, her wrists bound before her.

"So it has come to this," she observed, leaning her head back against the bulwark and surveying me through tired, dark-rimmed eyes. "A knife in the dark."

The knife was in my hand, a short dagger I had confiscated from the spoils of Oranmur. It was an ornate thing, too ornate for grisly tasks, but it was sharp and well-made.

My jaw felt like stone, my vision dull. An image of Anne Firth flashed through my mind, a similar knife to her throat. Her clearly pregnant belly, the flat expression in her eyes. The horrified disgust in Samuel's face, over the mouth of my pistol. The wild, disbelieving rage in Mary's.

Voskin is holding Hart, our crew and Mary's freedom against our bringing him your head.

Saint, *had* I really fallen so low? Charles had refused to join me, and now my own brother was hunting me with possibly murderous intent. Could I blame them, *him*, with Mary's liberty on the line and the fact that, apparently, I now threatened the lives

158 H. M. LONG

of pregnant women and unborn children?

A line of prisoners on a windy dockside.

I realized that my hands were shaking, though my mind refused to translate why.

"Moody," I said. The woman stepped forward and I passed her the knife. If she saw my hand tremor, she did not flinch. "I will be in my cabin. Find me when she is ready to tell us who has the documents and where they are bound."

Though I did not look at her, I felt Alamay's blood begin to race, her muscles priming for flight. Her breath, however, grew deeper and more deliberate, catching herself on the edge of panic.

That did not bode well. Alamay was too well trained, and the lengths Moody would have to go to too far.

But I had little choice left, and if Alamay continued to resist, the pain was her own doing. I had to end this quickly, before Samuel and Mary caught up.

Before I was forced to do something worse than burn Sen and threaten Anne Firth.

Before I *wanted* to do something worse.

Alamay *tsk*ed. "You will not even hold the knife?"

"I lack the skills," I replied coolly. "I am far more likely to kill you accidentally, and that would be counterproductive."

The prisoner looked up at Moody. "So you are the expert?"

Moody shrugged and I started to move away, forcing my legs into steady, unbothered strides.

But inside, I wanted to run.

∞

Later that night, I moved through the darkness of the gun deck, which was packed with hammocks, brushing against one another in the roll of the ship like cigars in a box.

Vachon's was at the far end. Grant lolled out of the closest, between her and the rest of the crew. One of his pale arms hung down, tanned only at the hand, and his face was buried in a pillow of bundled clothes.

Before I stopped beside her, Vachon grabbed the beam above to still the rocking of her hammock. She looked at me, our eyes at level, and asked in blunt Aeadine, "What?"

I pressed my tongue against the back of my teeth, glancing at Grant. I could wake him to translate, but this was not a topic I wanted to speak of, even to him.

There was also something about the way Vachon gazed at me that made me want to preserve our solitude.

"What do you see, when you look upon me in the Other?" I asked in carefully constructed Mereish. As I did, I reached beneath my shirt and pulled out the talisman that hid my aura from Soothsight.

As soon as it left my skin I felt a shift, a rushing roar at the edge of my hearing. The feeling was new, strange and unsettling, and only reinforced my need for an answer.

"How do I appear?"

Vachon's brows flicked at my use of her language and she glanced at the talisman, dangling free in the air, but she did not comment on either. Instead, her eyes took on the distant cast of a Sooth looking into the Other world.

There was a moment of rope-creaking, snoring silence in which I took in every flicker of her expression.

"You..." she said in Mereish, and as she continued, plucked words from both it and Aeadine. "Are two. Magni, but there is Sooth. *Dimaugia*. A mage of two."

"Adjacent?" I clarified. "I do not simply appear as a Magni? My red aura—is it not clear?"

She shook her head, sitting up a little more, her bronze hair brushing the beam. "You are Magni. You are Sooth."

The rushing sound that had accompanied my removing the talisman grew in intensity. "How strong is my Sooth's aura?"

"Strong."

I took a moment to reflect upon this, forcing my thoughts into order. This had not been the case last time I saw Samuel. He and I had discussed the changes between us, albeit briefly, and he had described the variations in our auras as a gentle twining of our powers—his with a thread of red, mine a thread of green. According to Olsa Uknara, this was not unexpected between mirror twins of different magecrafts.

"There is nothing else?" I asked. "No... corruption?"

She squinted at the word.

"You see nothing bad?"

"No, no," Vachon still looked perplexed, but there was total honesty to her confusion.

I closed my hand around the talisman. The rush at the edge of my mind faded, and I took a deeper, freer breath.

I remained uncorrupted. I could remove that concern from my shoulders, though it left me with the reality that the intensity of emotion, the fits of violence and endless conflict I now endured were wholly natural.

Was that worse?

"Go back to sleep," I told Vachon in Aeadine.

She gave a cocky little salute, so casual it broke me from my thoughts. I raised my brows at her, compiling a dry comment about insubordination.

Abruptly, her face changed. I thought I had been the cause, and felt a spike of... Saint, was that disappointment? At the change of a woman's facial expression? Forget Samuel's influence as a Sooth, I was becoming vapid.

"A ship. They make..." she started, looked visibly frustrated, then rattled off into Mereish. She reached out and smacked repeatedly Charles's hammock. "Charlie!"

He made a disgruntled sound.

"Charles," I said with a push of will.

Charles sat up grudgingly and Vachon repeated herself as I struggled to follow.

"There is a ship in the lee of the next island," Charles said, rubbing his eyes.

"Pirates?" I asked.

Vachon shook her head and said something that included a Mereish phrase I recognized. She moved as she did, starting to climb out of her hammock.

I backed off a step, giving her space. "The Company?"

"The Mereish Trading Company," Charles translated, dropping from his hammock. He seamlessly reached forward, helping Vachon down from hers with a gallant practicality, his hands easy on her waist. "Or so she believes. Whoever they are, they intend to board us."

I stepped into the distraction with gratitude, my shoulders leveling, my mind turning to the task at hand.

"Why would they attack?" I pondered. "Do they make a habit of antagonizing hundred-gun warships? The Company are not pirates, and we are no merchant prize."

"Boarding may not mean an attack. The Company claims large sections of the Isles and reserves the right to search every ship. That is all this may be."

"The fuck they will search my ship."

"And thus the impending violence," Charles concluded.

As we spoke, my power moved, and the crew awoke. Hammock after hammock, line after line, the entire company of *The Red Tempest* roused as one.

Minds, sharpening. Hearts, pounding. Blood rushing. The exhilaration of our connection flowed cyclically, feeding me, feeding them. Urgent voices rose, rousing one another, questioning. Feet hit the deck in a ripple of thunder.

"Beat to quarters!" I called, the satisfying boom and rumble of command in my chest. "We've a prize tonight!"

The crew roared.

TWENTY

The Perils of Notoriety

BENEDICT

I could not say where the crew's nervous anticipation ended and mine began. I stood on the quarterdeck with Grant, Vachon, Alfwin and Mr. Wuthy as the crew organized to action in the light of half-veiled lanterns. They moved quickly and efficiently. There was no shouting, no chanting or singing. Even below deck, Hashaw and his gunners worked in near silence, disrupted only occasionally by the rumble of cannons or the ripple of feet as runners ferried powder and shot to the guns.

Ahead, the hulk of an island lay between sea and sky. I noted Vachon staring at it fixedly, likely watching the other ship in the Dark Water. I had put my Sooth talisman back on, lying warm and heavy against the skin of my chest. If I took it off and stepped into the Other with her, would I be able to see that other ship, too? Would I see visions of the battle to come?

Presuming, of course, I could unravel how to cross into the Other.

"Do they have any mages, Vachon?" I asked, pushing the line of thought aside.

Grant translated and Vachon's gaze took on an even more distant expression.

"It is a ghisten ship," she said with a furrow of distracted concentration. "A Stormsinger. A low Magni. No Sooth."

"Noted." I looked to Alfwin. "Turn the wind against us. Do not allow your voice to carry."

Alfwin's low voice began to rumble across the deck, kept from drifting across the water by a twist of wind.

Time grew taut and stretched into a tense eternity. Under normal circumstances, I despised these long moments, these endless hours—and occasionally, even days—of waiting between sighting an enemy and engaging them.

But that night, I welcomed it. The tension was a pleasurable thing, the hum of blood in my veins made my mind sharp and clear and pushed aside my many concerns. The sword at my hip was sharp, my pistols cleaned and glistening and ready for action.

And action I would have.

Soon, Vachon murmured to Grant. He translated for the quarterdeck to hear, "They are coming."

I spied movement in the lee of the island and brought my spyglass to bear. Our prey's details were obscured with the distance, but from her shape, masts and rigging spoke volumes.

"Perhaps twenty guns," I concluded.

"Despite appearances, we too have roughly twenty functional guns," Charles pointed out dubiously. "That will become obvious if we engage."

"Yes, however we have—"

I cut myself off. There, upon the sea to our starboard, a new shadow appeared—already within cannon range and entirely too large. As large as *The Red Tempest*.

There were two ships.

Both enemies unveiled lanterns in smooth succession. Gunports opened in a ripple and shouts reverberated across the waves.

A flag of the Mereish Navy rippled out from the mizzenmast of the larger ship.

"Vachon," I said lowly. "Did you lie to me?"

Her gaze flicked from me to the first ship, then she twisted to regard the second. "No," she said, seeming more startled than afraid. She gestured to the Navy ship, fingers splayed in a distinctly emphatic, Mereish gesture. Her accented Aeadine was so thick as to be unintelligible. "This ship, I cannot see."

"Even in the Other?"

She replied in Mereish, but the shaking of her head was enough of a response.

A ship with no signature in the Other. That meant it either had no ghisting or mages—a vast unlikelihood—or the vessel was entirely concealed from Vachon's Sight. Like a talisman.

A Stormsinger's voice rose, light and lilting, feminine and eerie. It was a voice made for drifting down mountain passes and across sea ice, for luring wanderers and sailors to their doom.

If the revelation that we faced the Company, the Mereish Navy, *and* the latter had learned how to hide entire ships in the Other had not been enough to chill me, her voice certainly did.

Alfwin's rumbling tones replied to the other Stormsinger, merging and harmonizing—mirroring one another as they vied for the attention of the winds. The melding of their voices was remarkable, powerful to the point of distraction.

"I would ask if we should fight or run," Grant said. "But I believe that opportunity has passed."

The wind abruptly died. Alfwin stood braced, windblown and breathing heavily as a speaking horn cut through the hush. The speaker used Mereish, which I did not catch.

"Ms. Olles," I called.

Ms. Olles appeared at my side with alacrity and handed me a speaking horn of our own.

I promptly passed to Grant. "You will speak for me and trans-late. Hurry."

Grant gave the speaking horn a quick, nervous look but complied.

"One Captain Achron sends his regards and demands we

submit to inspection," he relayed, speaking fast to catch up. "They know *The Red Tempest* was captured by the Aeadine and also wish to know if Jessin Faucher is still alive."

That gave me a moment's pause. Faucher's father was a powerful man, the head of the Ess Noti. The Ess Noti, who pioneered all of Mere's magecraft. If anyone could hide a ship in the Other, it was them.

I sent a long look up to the yards and wondered, in passing, if I should simply string myself from one of them.

Abruptly Vachon took the speaking horn from Grant and shouted something across the waves. Judging from her posture and tone and several words I vaguely recognized, it was not polite. Or helpful.

Grant wrestled the horn back, but her outburst had been damaging. The Mereish Stormsinger began to sing again, low and warning and soft—the shush of snow against a hood, the scratch of morgories against a hull.

Miaghis's light rippled across the deck in displeasure and the crew shifted with obvious anxiety.

"Enough." I reached for my Magni power without conscious thought. Vachon stood down and the crew fell to order.

I looked to Ms. Olles. "Go get Faucher. Mr. Grant, inform them we have Faucher aboard and are bringing him out. No threats for the moment, simply the fact."

Grant and the Mereish officer began to speak again as Ms. Olles vanished below. I remained at the former highwayman's side, shoulders set and wrist clasped behind my back as the enemy ships drifted alongside us in the murky night.

"They wish to come aboard to negotiate." Grant's brows drew close together. "They believe we are Aeadine Royal Navy, Ben. Incognito, but Navy. The war has reached the South Isles."

Now that was useful. The pieces of a plan, until now a collection of violent vagaries, began to form up in my mind.

Grant continued, "We are to stand down our guns and send our mages below decks. You are to offer your sword in surrender."

I felt the smile twitch on my lips. "As any honorable Naval captain would." I slid my gaze to Grant's. "Pity for them I never was."

Rather than look pleased and impressed, Grant took my arm and pulled us slightly away from Vachon, Alfwin and the helmsmen at the wheel.

"What are you doing?" He leaned close. "I am no naval tactician, but that warship has twice the crew we do, not to mention equal guns. And the Company ship. We should surrender in truth. Anything else is suicide."

"No, you are no tactician. You are not so much as a sailor." I squinted over the scant two inches between his nose and mine. "Trust me, Mr. Grant."

"Then be trustworthy," he retorted.

I briefly considered locking him up with Alamay. Yet he was not wrong in his assessment of the situation.

He simply had neglected a factor.

Me.

"Captain," Ms. Olles interrupted. She led a curious Faucher, who in turn was followed by two armed sailors. "What are we doing?"

"Remain calm, Ms. Olles. I have a plan. Mr. Faucher, do you recognize that ship?"

"If you've a play you'd best share it, sir," Ms. Olles said, shooting me a look so hard, it bordered on insubordinate.

Faucher, whose initially inquisitive expression rapidly shifted to concerned, squinted at the Navy vessel. "The ship? Oh, yes I do. That is *Semora*, in Aeadine, *Fortitude*. Captain Mardan, prior to the Battle at the Anchorage."

"Captain Archon, now," I informed him.

Faucher's expression became unreadable. I nudged him with Magni power and he explained, "Archon is my cousin. The Navy must be in a state if he is in command."

"What should I know about him?"

Faucher frowned, upper lip turning and clean-shaven chin wrinkled with the depth of his disgust. "He is a pompous smear of shit and I have no desire to be 'rescued' by him. Saints. What an embarrassing thought."

A flick of humor tugged at my lips.

"Prepare to be boarded, Ms. Olles," I said, turning to my first officer. "With all ceremony. And have Kapper ready to fire."

∞

I felt them. The pulse of blood. The rush of breath. The longboat containing Captain Archon and his boarding party crossed the waves under the protective eyes of his ship and that of the Company vessel, gunports open, cannon mouths yawning.

Only Grant, Faucher, Ms. Olles and two lines of sailors remained on deck with me.

I allowed my eyes to flutter closed. Reaching beyond the longboat to the enemy ships, I sensed over a thousand souls. I could not control them all, particularly with the distance and the fact that I could not see my targets. I also had little doubt that many, particularly the officers, would possess Magni talismans.

But I did not need to control everyone.

At my side, the blood and bone that was Ms. Olles bounced almost imperceptibly on the balls of her feet.

The longboat was almost to the ship. I opened my eyes, stepped up to the rail, and removed my hat. I held it to my chest in faux deference and narrowed my focus to the warship. To one of its oil lanterns, and the figure closest to it.

Slowly, they turned. Reached.

Fire spilled across the deck. It took an instant for the flames to be noticed, then crewfolk converged with buckets and startled cries.

Like a marksman, I sighted another target. A cannon misfired.
A powder cartridge exploded in the center of the quarterdeck
with a burst of light, scattering officers and the helmsman and
destroying the ship's wheel.

Shouts and screams echoed across the waves. In the longboat,
the boarding party turned to point, the little vessel rocking as
some rose to their feet.

Then I took hold of my true target. My blood sang, light and
hot in my veins as I crept my will down the line of guns upon the
main deck, found a cluster of vulnerable minds, and took them.
I guided them, carefully, to readjust the aim and angle of a long
gun. Then I took a second gun crew. And a third. The act required
nearly all my concentration—guiding specific, individual actions
took more effort than inspiring fear or rage or adoration.

When I was ready, I spoke calmly to Ms. Olles. "Now."

"Quarters!" she bellowed.

A cannon flashed across the water. The hatches on *The Red
Tempest*'s deck slammed open and my crew lunged for our guns,
while others scrambled up into the rigging. Marksmen leveled
long Usti rifles. Two crewmen rushed Faucher below, and Alfwin
replaced him at my side.

The longboat, halfway between the ships, shattered under the
barrage of their own ship's guns. Wood and bodies were flung
onto the waves, their screams drowned by the thunder of cannons.

Thus we embarked upon a proper engagement—the crack of
guns and the laments of Stormsingers, the twisting of ensorcelled
wind. We began to move, the piping of the bosun's whistle and
the boom of the filling sails backing the chaos as Alfwin battled.
Miaghis rippled through the wood of the ship in dozens of lashing,
lacing tendrils.

I was in the thick of it, but felt little. My focus still slipped
among the enemy, plucking at hapless minds and guiding
unwilling hands. Fires. Explosions. Misaimed guns.

That was, until their marksman finally identified me as the source of the tampering. Blood bloomed across my thigh and two more shots slammed into the deck.

A fourth shot struck a sailor running past. She toppled into me, taking us both down in a flail of limbs and a gush of blood. Saint—there was a fountain of it, spouting into my face, my eyes, my mouth. The woman clawed at me, grabbing at my collar, my arms, grasping or searching or simply spasming, I could not tell.

I coughed and thrust the woman off me at the same time as Grant grabbed her, more gently than I, and pulled her aside. Her chin sagged onto her blood-soaked chest, limp as a doll, and she ceased to respond.

My mind felt oddly blank as I watched Grant lift her head. Her throat was a mess of meat, sinew and blood. She was clearly dying. Her blood no longer fountained and her eyes, as they stared past me through red-matted lashes, were lost in a dazed sort of confusion.

Grant looked stricken.

Then I saw neither him, nor the woman, nor the blood. My vision filled with a new perspective—one of the deck from above, of myself and the woman and Grant as a cannonball tore through the starboard rail and punched through my chest.

I came back to myself just in time to grab Grant's arm and lunge out of the way. I saw the rail as I did, currently illuminated with ghisten light. I heard the whistle of the coming cannonball.

For one instant, I thought Miaghis would reinforce the rail and guard us from the impact.

But just as the cannonball struck, his light vanished.

The rail exploded, knocking Grant and I down the quarterdeck stairs. I barely kept my feet, glancing back as the blast angled over our heads.

"Did that ghisting just try to kill me?" I yelled, despite a spike of pain and a tide of blood about my teeth. There was a splinter through my cheek. I dropped Grant, whose groan affirmed he was not dead, then jerked the splinter out and spat blood.

Did I foresee it?

I put a hand to my throat. The talisman was gone, not simply fallen out of my clothing. But it was *gone*.

"He certainly had no intention of saving you," Grant panted, then noticed a thick splinter in his arm and looked as though he were about to be sick.

I spat blood again and reached for him, intent on pulling the splinter out.

"She's in the water! The Usti is in the water!"

I abandoned Grant, sprinting across the deck and shoving through a cluster of figures at the larboard rail. All looked down as Enisca Alamay pushed off the hull of *The Red Tempest* and struck out for the nearest Mereish ship.

A musketball struck the rail next to me and I cursed. I knew my control was fraying—both of myself and of the battle. A red haze entered the corners of my vision.

This was Port Sen all over again. Or it would be, if I did not take action.

"You and you," I snapped to two nearby crewmembers. "Take ropes, overboard, now. Retrieve her. You, your rifle."

A brush of power ensured there were no questions, no delays. I sighted down the length of the rifle as the crewfolk leapt into the water after the Usti woman, ropes trailing behind them. She swam faster. Wind berated me, and I was distantly aware that we were moving now, Alfwin's witchery and Miaghis's influence propelling us forward.

I sighted Alamay, following her as the distance between us yawned, musketballs rushed overhead, Alfwin's winds condensed into a raging storm, and cannons boomed.

I fired.

TWENTY-ONE

Adrift

SAMUEL

A storm blew in our second night out of Oranmur. I roused at the change in movement of the ship and reached out to find Mary's hammock, suspended in our small cabin, already empty.

I dressed and went above. A gusty wind plucked at my coat and hair, the coldest I had felt since we entered the isles, and a frigid rain pattered down. I was overcome with memory—memories of winter and the north, of arctic winds down the coast of Aeadine and drifts of sea ice, layered on the shore. It was not an unpleasant reminder. Rather, it came with a wash of unexpected nostalgia, as if my heart did not expect to see it again.

"*Come as the winds come, when forests are rended,*" Mary's voice lilted as I joined her on the quarterdeck. She wore a borrowed boatcloak, and her tricorn hat dripped with rain. "*Come as the waves come, when Navies are stranded.*"

The rain lessened and the wind began to steady, no longer gusting. The crew moved about us, adjusting the sails under Athe's command.

"*Come as the winds come, come as the winds come,*" Mary continued, soothing now, encouraging the change.

A final rain squall passed over us and moved on over the waves. Mary glanced up at me and smiled briefly, then returned her gaze up the line of the ship towards the bowsprit and the horizon.

As the rain departed, so did much of the murk of night, and I realized it was nearly dawn. A bruised half-light surrounded us above the line of the sea, backing the silhouettes of small islands.

"Samuel, do you see that?"

I peered after her pointing finger, taking advantage of the moment to stand closer. She leaned back into me, but only slightly, her attention fixed ahead.

"I see nothing," I murmured.

"There," she pointed. "Something on the water."

At the same time, a voice rose from the maintop. "Sail!"

The following moments were a flurry of activity, then a stretch of anxious waiting while we angled towards the vessel. It was indeed a small boat, its sail alternating between flapping uselessly and threatening to tip the craft.

"Ho the ship!" a weary female voice called in Mereish. In the light of the lanterns held by several crewmembers, I made out the middle-aged speaker and a canvas awning, clearly rigged in haste. "Bring us aboard and you will be much rewarded!"

"How many are you?" Athe inquired.

"Three. I fear we were separated from the remainder of our crew," the woman replied. "Have you happened across any other vessels?"

"We have not," Athe said.

I felt a presentiment tingle up the back of my neck. "Rather low in the water for so few passengers," I observed.

"Rig a hoist," Athe instructed. "Bring the craft aboard, entire."

Soon after, ropes creaked and swung. Draining water from multiple fractures in its hull, the little vessel clattered wetly into a hastily rigged cradle, assisted by a dozen crewmembers. Athe's surgeon stood by as the three foundlings disembarked, though the last, the woman who had spoken, appeared reluctant to abandon her craft. Her arm was evidently broken, and she looked battered besides.

I could just make out the embroidery on her collar through a stain of blood—she had a high merchant ranking, though lacked a captain's higher, stiffer collar. An officer, then.

"They're Mereish Trading Company," I murmured to Mary.

The officer spoke to one of her companions, an able-bodied man with dark curls, and he took up a discrete guard position over their boat. The last, a young woman with a broad face and loose trousers tucked into high stockings, took up position behind the officer and eyed Demery's curious crew dubiously.

"Captain," the rescued officer said. "You have my sincerest thanks. May we speak privately?"

Demery nodded graciously and gestured her away, along with her quiet guard. Demery's crew grudgingly dispersed under Athe's resounding direction. The ship's carpenter approached the Mereish boat to assess the damage, only to find himself warded away by the guard. The two fell into heated, stilted discussion, with no common language between them.

"There's a ghisting in the boat," Mary said quietly. She began to move slowly, weaving through Demery's crewmembers until she stood between the rescued boat and *Harpy's* rail, hidden from the guard by a slice of shadow. I trailed her, eyeing the watchman and carpenter.

Mary climbed up onto the cradle, giving me a prompting look. I set my feet on the wet deck and put a hand to her waist, bolstering her as she peered over the side. I could just see over the small boat's rail myself, to a sodden bundle of canvas no larger than a man.

Mary stared at the bundle first in suspicion, then unease, her eyes threaded with ghisten light.

Hart passed through my mind, briefly, painfully. From what I could see, the Mereish officer had done as I had, performing their final duty to their vessel and saving the ship's ghisting.

I understood that, and I respected it. Though given the

circumstances, I could not help but wonder how many crewmembers had drowned for such weighty salvage.

"Sam!" My attention snapped back to Mary. She teetered over the rail, about to fall headlong into the boat. I grabbed her legs to balance her out and glanced towards the guardsman. He was still distracted.

Mary lifted a corner of the canvas, and together we gazed upon a young man frozen in the act of carrying some great burden—the bowsprit of his intended ship, no doubt.

But the figurehead was still half-carved, his front shaped and his back unhewn. The carved wood was fresh and raw, hardly weathered, while the rest was in a state of semi-petrification. Grey crept around the suggestion of muscular shoulders and biceps and had begun to entwine his throat and jaw, which bulged under the strain of upward force.

"That figurehead is not recent salvage. It is not even finished," I whispered.

"And it's sick," Mary hissed back.

I summoned the Dark Water, sinking my boots into its shallow black wash, and saw more. I saw the ghisting within the wood, a formless blue light knotted in the chest of the half-carved man. And around the petrification, I saw something subtler, something dimmer—a shadow in the dusk, its edges becoming less distinct the longer I searched for them. It obscured the light of the ghisting itself, choking its connection to the Dark Water.

"Do not touch that!"

I abandoned the Other and tugged Mary down, setting her on her feet as the irate guardsman descended upon us.

He came up short against a wall of *Harpy's* crew. Brid and a big man, a helmsman called Brison, faced him chin-to-beard.

"You'd best calm yourself, jack," Brid said.

"That is the property of the Mereish Trading Company," the guard snapped, glaring over the helmsman's shoulder to Mary and me. Despite his disheveled appearance and subservient role, his voice was cultured. No common sailor, then. He added in finger-stabbing threat, "Touch it and you *will* be in violation of trade law."

"Where was this ghisting harvested?" Mary asked. Tane's tones were in her words, though I doubted anyone else would notice.

From across the deck, beyond the edge of hearing, Demery turned to look at her.

"That is not your concern," the guard shot back.

"Your ship is gone. We've pulled you from the sea. You've no allies or weapons." Mary pointed out each fact. Her Mereish was broader than his, an amalgamation of vocabulary and intonation picked up by Tane over her many years of service, but it was excellent. "Answer me and mayhap you'll find an ally in us. Or shall we just take your ghisting?"

"These are Company waters," the guard spluttered. "We are under the protection of the Mereish Navy. You would not dare."

Mary made a derisive little sound and looked around at the ocean. "Some good all that did you. Scuttled by a common storm?"

"It was no common storm!" The guard made to close on her, but the wall of Demery's crew did not yield. The guard let out a hiss of unvented rage. "The worst passed some hours ago. Blew up out of nowhere, a damned witch's tempest fit to sink anything in its path."

My Sooth's intuition fixed on that. "Someone set this upon you intentionally?"

"How should I know?"

"What of your Stormsinger?" Mary asked.

The guardsman snorted. "Took injury, useless bitch. I assume she's dead now."

Mary looked fit to fight. I gently but pointedly took her arm and pulled her behind me—less to stop her from attacking, and more to ensure I could do it myself.

"Enough, Baro," the Mereish officer returned and waved off her companion. "Do not antagonize our rescuers."

Space opened between the guardsman, Brid and Brison, but neither backed down.

I turned my focus to the Mereish commander. "Do you believe someone set this storm upon you intentionally?"

"No. We were caught in the aftermath of someone else's battle, I estimate. When Stormsingers clash, there are repercussions, particularly in seas this populated," her gaze scanned to Mary. "You would do well to remember that."

Mary made a disgusted sound.

The Mereish woman carried on, "We were simply unfortunate enough to sail into it without a serviceable Stormsinger. I doubt we were the only ones, this close to South Ostchen."

I noted Demery speaking lowly to Athe in the background, and now Athe turned to address her crew. "All right. Unload the ghisting, give these three a day's provisions and set them adrift."

The Mereish exploded in a clamor of rageful protest, which Demery overrode. "Calm, calm. Yes, we are keeping your ghisting. But you have your lives! Consider this an exercise in gratitude."

"This will not be forgotten!" The Mereish officer shouted as he and her people were hauled away. "James Demery!"

∞

Athe and I watched, side by side, as Mary and Demery crouched next to the half-petrified ghisting. It had been carefully maneuvered into the hold and unwrapped, and it now stood, half-shadowed and strikingly melancholy in the lanternlight.

"What are they saying?" I asked Athe quietly, not for the first time begrudging my inability to hear ghisten conversations.

"Patience," she chided.

"I see a Wold beneath the sea," Mary said. Her eyes were round and her attention inwards. "But it's not right. I can't describe it, neither can the ghisting. He is not awake, young and half-grown."

"Can Tane rouse him?" I inquired.

Mary exchanged a look with Demery and I sensed further, silent, conversation.

Tane manifested. She gusted from Mary's skin like smoke upon an unseen wind and took shape over the sleeping ghisting, her head tilted to one side, her sea-glass eyes written with maternal concern.

No one spoke as she grew taller, more ethereal, until her height matched that of the half-hewn figurehead. Then she took the creature's carved cheeks between her hands and leaned intimately close.

She exhaled into the other ghisting's wooden mouth in a tendril of light. Briefly the wood ignited, so soft it was almost imperceptible. Then only the lanternlight remained.

We waited, still and soundless. I hovered on the edge of the Dark Water, alert for any change. A vision passed by me, ethereal and vague—a figure standing upon a vast mirror beneath a sunlit sky—then it was gone.

The ghisting stirred. Its light rippled. The grey stone of its petrification began to crack and flake away and the wood flushed with a sudden, healthful hue—that of freshly harvested wood, not its formerly dry, petrified aspect. A scent between cedar and rosemary drifted to me and in the Dark Water, the ghisting's aura began to blaze.

The young ghisting did not manifest outside its host, however. Given my experience with Grant and his immature ghisting, I did not expect it to.

But I expected Demery's next words even less. He looked to Athe and I, his expression as startled and solemn as I had ever seen it. "This ghisting was harvested here, in the Isles. Only weeks ago."

"There is no Ghistwold in the South Isles," Athe stated.

We all looked at one another, Mary, Demery, Athe and I and the manifest Tane.

Tane's voice came from Mary's lips, low and weighty. "There is now."

Ghistwolds, it can be observed, sprout and root in a variety of locations within the human world, their only consistent factor being that of a healthy and fluid border with the Other. It is believed, then, that the locals in which natural Ghistwolds flourish are determined by factors in the Dark Water, rather than environmental or geographical features. This has led to several notable locations of Wolds, including the Mereish mainland Wold, which according to legend, first sprouted overnight in the salted fields surrounding the Old Imperium's capital of Eritasta.

—FROM A HISTORY OF GHISTLORE
AND THE BLESSED; THOSE BOUND TO THE
OTHER WORLD AND THE POWER THEREIN,
TRANSLATED INTO AEADINE
BY SAMUEL I. ROSSER

TWENTY-TWO

The Cartographer's Mark

BENEDICT

It took us over a day to lose the Mereish Navy vessel *Semora*. I did not sleep during that time and left the deck only once.

Alamay lay on a pallet on the deck of a small cabin that had been conscripted from Hashaw and his mates. Her midsection was heavily bandaged, marking where the musketball had been crudely removed from her back. Even now blood soaked through her shirt, and the reality that she might yet die did not escape me.

I sat on a stool, watching her laudanum-induced sleep. My own eyes burned with fatigue and I felt as though my vision was stumbling, every beat of my heart a falter in my awareness.

I needed to rest, but my mind would not slow. I felt the lives of our Mereish attackers once more, so many gentle pulses under my thumb. I saw the boarding party, scattered across the waves by cannon fire. I saw the woman who had been shot in front of me, and tasted her blood in my mouth.

And I saw Alamay, now. Had I killed her? Did I care if I had, beyond the fact that the location of the documents would die with her?

Then where would I be? Adrift in a starless sea without purpose, without a compass.

I looked down at her, considering her pallid face and blood-stained shirt.

Interrogation had not worked. Vachon's vision had proved fruitless. My power had not been enough to extricate the truth from her, not trained as she was.

But right now, she was helpless.

I put a hand to my temple, teeth grinding in my skull. Why was this, this small act, this singular violation in the dark, harder to execute than the burning of an entire port? Yet an innate sense of wrongness plagued me. To stand here over an unconscious captive, preparing to do what I was about to do. Discomfort cinched, like rope around a winch.

This would become another moment to relive, a memory to scar across my mind. Yet I felt I had no choice.

I forced my eyes closed, pushed a deep breath from my lungs, and sank into my power.

It needed no direction, no conscious will. It wrapped about the sleeping, helpless figure, and, slowly, her heartbeat changed. It came to mirror mine, as did her breathing.

It was an eerie feeling, but intoxicating nonetheless.

I drew a deep breath. Despite her bandages, Alamay did the same.

"Where did you send the documents, Enisca?" I asked, my voice low in her ear, gentle and smooth. I did not sound as though I was riddled with conflict, and that sharpened my resolve.

Her lips parted and she spoke so softly, I had to lean closer.

"Dreska Sank," she whispered.

∞

I pulled out every map and chart in the main cabin and spread them on the table, pinning corners with random objects and hanging a lantern low from the beam. Outside the gallery windows, a steady rain had begun to fall.

I poured over them as the rain drummed down. The bulk were in Mereish, however, and before long I grew so frustrated with their archaic, swirling script that I tore one in half.

"Moody!" I bellowed.

The door of my cabin opened and the woman poked her head in.

"Get Faucher."

She looked from me to the table to the torn charts, wisely kept her expression neutral, and vanished.

Faucher sauntered into the cabin soon after, while Moody situated herself inside the door and yawned expansively.

"Where is Dreska Sank?" I demanded of my captive, gesturing at the charts. "Your people's script is untenable. What even is this character?" I snatched up one of the charts and pointed to a looping knot in one corner.

"The cartographer's mark," Faucher said with barely veiled amusement. He glanced over the scattered maps. "Dreska Sank, you say? That is one of the Southern Isles, and it is not Mereish. 'Sank' is an Usti term for port, if you recall."

He took up a thick piece of paper and tilted it towards the light, squinting. "That region lies outside council control, the purview of exiled Usti royals and the worst sort of pirates—those so foul, even the council cannot stomach them."

I squinted at the map in his hands. "Which island is it?"

"Oh, this map is Kalsank," Faucher said dismissively, putting the paper aside. "I do not have a chart of that region of the isles."

I glared at him.

"They are difficult to procure and, as you may recall, *The Red Tempest* is a northern vessel. I had no need of them."

"You could have mentioned your charts were lacking."

Faucher arched a brow. "I am a prisoner, Mr. Rosser. I have been amply cooperative, considering my situation. Surely you cannot expect me to also anticipate your needs."

The same inclination that had led to me tearing the chart made my eyes flick down to Faucher's throat.

"There have been suggestions that I should simply kill you and be done with it," I informed him. "I believed you useful, but perhaps I miscalculated."

Faucher did not speak for a long moment. At the door, Moody watched the exchange from under her lashes and tapped a finger on her cutlass.

"I suggest sailing south, make port here," Faucher indicated a large island. He spoke calmly, giving no sign of awareness that his life hinged on his next words. "Buy the charts you require there."

"Good. Also," I said, "the *Semora*. How is it that she has no signature in the Other? Your father is head of the Ess Noti. I will not believe that a development so massive did not pass through him."

Faucher rubbed at his jaw. "It was a goal of his, a possible application of the talisman magecraft. But it was incomplete prior to the Black Tides and the invasion, and I have no intelligence after that point. For obvious reasons."

"Is there a way around it?"

Faucher slowly shook his head, his gaze cast up to the ceiling in thought. "Not that I know of. The greatest challenge to its application was simply the size of the object—ship—it needed to affect. The focus of the concealment was the ship's ghisting, of course, but perhaps a mage at the stern of a vessel might leak through? One could watch for a lonely mage upon the waves. Or perhaps a moving gap in the lights of the Other. However, this is only speculation."

Speculation yes, but useful. Particularly if I could learn how to access the Other as Sam did, and no longer rely upon Vachon. Though it seemed she had been honest with me about *Semora,* and had not led us into a trap.

That was a relief on more than one level.

"Are there any other advancements you would care to alert me to?" I asked.

Faucher shook his head. "Not at the moment, no. But I will give this some thought."

Catching Moody's gaze, I nodded to Faucher again. She opened the door pointedly.

Faucher did not speak as she led him away, but as the door closed, I saw ghisten light skitter across the doorway. There was something protective about the movement, and I recalled the way that light had vanished from the rail before the cannonball struck, during the battle.

I let out a long, gust of a breath. As useful as the man was, I could not trust him. And Grant, it seemed, had been correct. Miaghis remained loyal to his former captain and would happily let me die.

I was going to have to kill Faucher.

TWENTY-THREE

Whispers from the Cape

BENEDICT

"Well, this looks lively," Charles commented.

We stood together on the quarterdeck as the crew clustered midships, eager to catch a glimpse of our next port of call—an island whose Mereish name translated to Salvage.

Salvage was spread down a low shoreline and out onto numerous small cays and islets, a sprawl of docks and buildings, ships and boats. The sun was bright that day and the air warm, teasing out the stench of seaweed and woodrot beneath drifts of cooking food, smoke and a dozen other scents I did not care to identify. And the sound of it—there was noise without end, bells and shouts and clatters and baying, barking and laughter and hammering.

It was exhilarating.

There was no free dock deep enough for *Tempest*, so we dropped anchor and I took the first longboat ashore, accompanied by Olles, Grant, Moody and Faucher.

"Do I need to leash you?" I asked Faucher as we strode down the dockside and prepared to merge with the press of the crowds. "Or will you behave?"

"Once again, I have no intention of escaping," Faucher said. "I will find you your map and return to my ship."

I accepted this with a nod, though his use of 'my ship' was beginning to irk. "Ms. Olles, see to the Port Mistress?"

Olles touched her forehead and split away, weaving deftly through the crowd.

I prodded Faucher ahead of Grant and I. "Now, maps. Move."

We found a mapseller in a region marked by intensely narrow streets and small, thin buildings, like books on shelves. They were not high, none over two stories, and in predictable Mereish fashion they were painted and scrawled with psalms and patterns. So many signs hung above our heads as to render one another useless, but Faucher secured directions from locals while Grant smiled and charmed, and Moody strode after us with a steady, loose gate. She slapped a pickpocket away at one point, and I found myself cutting her an approving grin. She returned it with a crooked smile of her own and a salute.

The mapseller was pinched between a bookseller and a purveyor of inks, paints and dyes. He was a round, intense man who immediately began riffling through the hundreds of shallow-drawered cases along one wall of his narrow shop.

"Ensure Faucher does nothing untoward," I instructed Grant as Faucher and the mapseller spoke. Light from the high windows cut between us, sunlight filled with drifts of dust. The air smelled of it too, along with some sour brand of ink. "Buy *anything* you think might be useful. We will need all the help we can get. Faucher will not be returning with us to the ship."

Grant's brows twitched up. "Because he is going to become… lost?"

I waved for him to return to Faucher's side. He complied and a warm hush settled in, broken only by steady Mereish chatter, which I understood little enough to ignore.

Then, the door to the shop opened and a woman entered.

She wore a long frock coat with smooth lines and trousers loose at the thigh, tucked into high boots. Despite the cut of her clothes, there was no disguising a truly admirable figure beneath. And her face was… striking was not the word. Nor was beautiful.

Words were useless things.

She noted my open stare and smiled, so briefly and so fractionally it might have been a trick of the light.

On one side of the door, Moody rolled her eyes at me.

"You are in my way," the newcomer told me in perfect Aeadine.

I stepped from her path, but the building was narrow enough that I still caught the scent of her as she passed. She was seasalt and rain and the barest undertone of warm, feminine sweat.

I did not even notice my Magni power bloom until it hazed the air between us, chasing but not yet touching.

I tugged it back, breaking myself from my leering and refocusing on Grant and Faucher, who stood before the mapseller as he rolled our purchases into a waxed leather tube.

My reprieve was short-lived. The woman again invaded my senses as she spoke to the bookseller in Mereish, her voice low and light. I hadn't the presence of mind to decipher her words, but I did register when the bookseller nodded to Faucher, Grant and our maps.

The woman turned to them, then twisted to look back at me. The movement had a dramatic effect on her already dramatic figure, and my blood ran hot.

She spoke to Grant, who nodded her back towards me.

The stranger returned to me, stopping out of arm's reach. "Sir, you have selfishly purchased every map of the southern region of the isles. What must I do to persuade you to part with them?"

I had an answer, which I retained enough wit not to share.

"We cannot," Grant intervened, popping up beside me. "My apologies."

Faucher, for his part, was looking at her rather strangely.

"We ought to go," Grant pressed. "Small shop, we are in the way. Very rude and all."

I allowed him to propel the lot of us through the door but

paused in the street outside. I felt an inconvenient reluctance to let the woman out of my sight, but Faucher's reaction to her had caught my attention.

"What is it?" I demanded of the man. "Did you know her?"

"I believe I did," Faucher said. He glanced at the shop again then strode quickly up the street a few paces, out of its line of sight. We followed. "That was Wesna Forbara. She served a term in the Mereish Navy, as many Capesh officers must."

"She is Capesh," I clarified.

"Yes," Faucher said, as if this should be self-evident.

"Well? What is the issue?" I pressed.

"Because she is dead," Faucher said simply. "That is why I recall her. The ship she served upon reported her death, years ago."

"Ah, she faked it to escape the Mereish." This conclusion came, surprisingly, from Moody. We all turned to regard her and the woman looked taken aback. "What? I'd have done it, given the chance, and I can't see a Cape being happier with the Mere than I was with the Navy. Besides, people come to the Isles to hide."

"You may be correct," I acknowledged.

"All intriguing, to be sure," Grant interjected. "But an unnecessary distraction. Faucher, the books?"

Faucher nodded and, casting the windows of the mapseller one last look, headed into the bookshop. Moody followed him without prompting, giving me a little salute as she vanished inside.

"The mapseller suggested his colleague might have something useful for us," Grant informed me, grabbed my arm and pulled me closer to the wall. He held the leather container of maps tightly beneath one arm.

"What has gotten into you?" I demanded. "If this is over Faucher, I have decided not to kill him. You have made me irreparably soft."

At that moment Forbara exited the bookseller and vanished down the street in the opposite direction to us, moving purposefully.

Grant tried to edge between us, as if to keep me from noticing.

I regarded him coolly. "What are you doing?"

"Keeping you from distractions."

I read—*intuited*—something more from his expression. "You are protecting her. From me."

Grant held my gaze. The noise and jostling of the street battered us, but neither of us looked away.

"I am protecting you from yourself," he replied.

"Are you suggesting I lack self-control?"

"I think that you frequently manipulate the wills and intentions of everyone around you, sometimes without even knowing that you do. And yes, if you truly want something, someone, I fear what you would do to have them."

I scoffed, but the rage I felt at his words was far, far deeper than such a light gesture conveyed. Images of violence darted through my skull, a silent riot of impulses.

Impulses I could, and would, control.

"I was there, that night, if you recall," Grant said, and I had the sense this was something he had been wanting to say for a long time. "That night with Mary in the gardens, in Hesten."

"Liberating someone from their inhibitions is hardly a crime."

Grant's eyes grew flinty, the reserve he usually maintained with me flaking away. "Is that what you call it?"

"I no longer find satisfaction in such encounters," I said, surprising myself at my own admission. I was angry with Grant, taut with offense—I was not confiding in him. Yet I spoke again, possessed by an unfamiliar need to... what? Be thought well of? "And there is no need, regardless. The world is full of whores who require no sorcery to endure me."

"No, they simply require payment." Grant still studied me, long past the point of discomfort. "Benedict. Have you ever had a relationship, of any nature, *not* manipulated by your power?"

"Have you ever had one not manipulated by your charm?"

He nearly smiled at that. "I am rather charming. But that is different."

"I do not see why," I stated, though the words lacked conviction. There was a difference, at least in the way *I* wielded my power. "I tire of this. We will not sail until morning, so if we do not kill Faucher we should at least leave him senseless. Otherwise he will find his way back to us before we leave."

"So you did intend to kill him."

"When we left the ship, yes. But I have decided otherwise."

Grant adjusted the roll of maps and finally looked away from me, scanning the street and letting out a short, weary breath. "I will take care of matters with Faucher, if you trust me to do it."

I considered this. Suspicion, always a shadow of mine, prodded at me. "Will you disappear with him?"

Grant smiled wryly. "If I wished to leave, I would have done so in Oranmur, when I might have exchanged you for Mary. Saint, I miss that woman, and our cards. I have not fleeced a tavern full of halfwits in months."

I nodded to the port around us. "Take Faucher out tonight, then. Play your cards. And do not bring him back with you to the ship. Take Moody and do not get stabbed."

Grant nodded slowly. "I could do that. But what will you do?"

"With my nursemaid absent? Raid the kitchen and track mud across the floors," I said dryly. I puffed out a breath and stared up at the sky, blue and patchworked with clouds. It was so clean compared to the port: the contrast was jarring.

"I," I said at length, shoving my hands into my pockets and cutting Grant a soulless smile, "intend to find a whorehouse."

∞

I sat on the edge of an overly lavish bed as a belltower tolled the first hour of the new day. A pair of balcony doors lay open before me with a view of the masts in the harbor and a sickle moon in the sky, but the night breeze did little to cool my sweaty skin.

"Will you visit me again tomorrow?" a gentle voice asked in accented Aeadine. A nose nudged at my cheek, accompanied by warm breath and the brush of a bare breast against my shoulder. A fall of disheveled, reddish curls concealed most of her face. Shadows hid the rest.

I did not look at her. "No."

A moment of silence from the whore, then I was evicted with a soft-spoken, "I will fetch your clothes."

I descended into the common room of the brothel not long after. Clusters of men gathered at the tables, playing cards and dice and drinking while they awaited the attentions of the working girls.

I passed through their pipesmoke and rumble, and exited onto the street. I set my course back towards the ship, hardly noting where my feet took me.

It was as I waited to hire a longboat to take me back to *Tempest* that a voice came from the dark: "Captain."

I turned to see the woman from the mapseller's approaching. She had her hands in her pockets, her hair uncovered to the night.

Despite my fatigue, the sight of her still gave me pause. "Wesna Forbara."

"Ah, have you been making inquiries about me? I certainly have about you."

I looked down a handspan to her dark-lashed eyes. "To what end? If you are after a lover, I am not opposed."

"You are bold," she laughed. "I prefer women."

"Prefer? So you are not wholly opposed to men?"

"I try not to limit myself," she replied. "But I am not looking for a partner. Rather, a story. Your crew are in every inn and tavern on these docks, being rather raucous, and they say you went beyond the Stormwall and killed Silvanus Lirr."

"I did not kill Silvanus Lirr."

"But you went beyond the Stormwall."

"If you intend to interrogate me, do buy me a drink," I suggested.

Forbara cocked her head to one side, examined my face for another moment, then nodded.

Soon after we were ensconced at a table in the corner of a tavern, a bottle of dark wine between us. Several patrons had saluted me on the way in, likely my own crewmembers, though I did not recall their faces. I hardly minded them seeing me in the company of a beautiful woman.

I surveyed my unexpected companion. Her expression was open and sharp, still lovely in that fathomless way. "What do you want?"

"I want to know about the Stormwall, and what is beyond it. There are shipwrecks there? How many?"

"Some," I said evasively. Demery and I had not agreed on many things, but protecting the wealth beyond the Stormwall was one. "As one might expect, considering how many ships have tried and failed to cross."

"Then there are many ghistings," she summarized.

"Ah." I reached for the bottle and filled our cups, but did not drink. "You are after ghistings, not riches."

She shrugged. "My people have no Wold. I wish to do something about it."

"The Cape has never had a Wold," I pointed out. "So why would you be the one to fix that? I mean no offense by that—you seem profoundly capable, along with being the most beautiful woman I ever encountered."

She pressed her lips together in a dry smile.

"Allow me to rephrase," I went on. "Why go to the trouble? Is this your commission? Do you expect some kind of reward?"

"I do it for the good of my people."

"Why? What good have they ever done for you?"

A line appeared between her brows. "They bore me and made me. They are my blood and my kin. They are my home."

Her words sank between us, stirring something in me that I did not look at too closely. She was clearly an idealist. Her first flaw.

"Was it also for the good of your people that you falsified your death?"

The expression on her face told me she was debating how much to divulge. Conversation flowed through the tavern, waxing and waning, and the warmth felt a little too close.

At last, the lines of her eased. She seemed to shirk a mask, and I realized that the version of her I had seen before was vastly different than the one I saw now.

"If I am honest, it was not," she admitted. "But I have since learned to think beyond myself. Rosser. I know of the *ghiseau*, and of the woman who planted a Mother Tree and reawakened the Northern Wold. I wish to find her."

She could not have learned that from my crew. I dropped a hand beneath the table, controlling an impulse to begin tapping agitatedly on my thigh.

"Curious," I said noncommittally.

The Capesh captain went on, watching me even more closely than before. "I have also heard of a powerful Sooth who tracked her across the Winter Sea. Your brother."

A discomforting blend of emotion struck me, one I had to guard with a more dangerous mask. "How do you know any of this?"

"Because ghistings are my business, Captain Rosser. But there is no need to be so defensive. I wish to hire your brother and his Stormsinger, not abduct them."

I relaxed marginally. "Why?"

"To find a ghisting," she said.

I finally took a sip of my wine, though I did not taste it. I would have to deal with Samuel and Mary eventually, given my brother's predilections—but if they were occupied with the Capesh, they would have less of a chance of waylaying me.

"Are you sure you do not intend to abduct them?" I inquired. "Because I have a proposal."

TWENTY-FOUR

Compass

BENEDICT

I took my time returning to the ship. Salvage was surprisingly quiet at the middling hours of the night, after the rowdier portion of the population gave way to the more sober, melancholy and wrathful drunkards. These were the ones who either stared past me with empty eyes, or hurled curses across the street for no discernable reason. Even the whores were less lively.

I spied a man perched on a mooring post where a longboat was tied to the dock. He had one foot tucked up and was smoking a pipe, smoke drifting up into the night.

I held up a coin to flash in the light of a nearby window. "I'm for that ship," I nodded out to *The Red Tempest.*

"Not for hire," the man said, without removing his pipe.

I glanced pointedly from his lackadaisical posture to the empty boat. Already, I began to summon Magni power, a casual pressure of compliance. "Indeed?"

The man's expression twitched. But before I could take hold of him, a breathless voice called, "Captain!"

I turned to see Moody peel from the darkness. She came up short a pace or two away, hands braced on her knees as she labored for breath. "Captain Rosser. He's… I had to…"

I pocketed my coin and abandoned the obstinate boatman. Taking Moody's arm, I pulled her into the shelter of a nearby warehouse, its large doors locked and its winch dangling against the night sky like a hangman's noose.

Moody battled to get her breath and despite the darkness, I noted smears on her face, and hands. Blood.

"Slow down," I instructed. I liked Moody. She was brunt and abrasive, and entirely competent. "Tell me what happened."

"Faucher stabbed Grant," she panted. "He's gone."

Alarm flashed through me. "Grant is gone? Grant is dead?"

"No, Faucher is gone, took off," Moody explained, shaking her head profusely. "Grant is bleeding out in a fucking alleyway, I carried him as far as I could, couldn't keep going."

"Where?" I demanded.

Moody pushed upright again and, by unspoken consent, we set off.

In a dark alley barely broad enough for my shoulders, Grant was crumpled against the wall, moaning and coughing blood.

"Charles." I dropped down beside him, pushing his hands away from his stomach to study the wound. "Damn it. Moody! Light!"

Footsteps ran off.

Grant made a little wheezing sound. "You called me Charles," he said fondly. "Never fear, Ben, the beasty will keep me on this side of the grave. Though if you could carry me back to the ship, I would greatly appreciate it. First day on my new legs, you see. Terribly uncoordinated."

"You still need a surgeon," I muttered. The fact that Charles's ghisting made him next to immortal failed to calm me, not when instinct and experience told me that a man this pale and this slathered with blood could not live out the night. "Moody!"

Light flooded the alleyway, washing over the downed man, and I felt the blood flee my own face. Grant's chest was a mess of blood, as was his head, his blond hair matted with scarlet.

"Faucher did this to you?" I demanded.

Grant squinted at me, his gaze uprooted, and more than a little confused. "Faucher? Oh, yes, yes, in a way. I intended to get him properly drunk, you see, and leave him tied up at an inn or some such thing 'til we were out of port. Did not… work out."

"Moody, find a surgeon and bring them to the docks. We are taking him back to *Tempest*," I instructed.

The woman vanished again without a word.

"He obviously fought back?" I asked, jerking off my coat and then my shirt, which I hastily wrapped around his midsection and tied tightly.

"Oh, thank you, I have been in desperate need of a hug," Grant murmured into my ear as I worked. I could feel him smiling inanely.

"Charles. Faucher. What happened?" My questions were about more than information, now. Grant was on the verge of passing out and with his head injury, I doubted that would be a positive step, ghisting or no.

"It was Alfwin!" Grant said with sudden revelation. "He hit my head. A few of the other fellows, they were drinking with Faucher and I, rather unintentional on my part, you see, given I intended to get him very drunk and leave him tied up in an inn or some such—"

"You said that," I said through gritted teeth. We staggered upright only to sag back into the wall of the alley. Grant's legs would not hold him.

"What do you mean?" I pressed as I picked him up like an infant, grunting with the effort.

"The lot of them attacked me when I refused to kill you," Grant said gravely. His eyes rounded in further revelation. "'Twas mutiny! Faucher wanted to kill you, thought I'd be amenable, given I am your prisoner. The nuances of our friendship are beyond him. I tried to leave… then… this."

I felt very, very cold. "Faucher tried to recruit you into a mutiny."

"Yes."

"And he already had others on his side?"

A more insistent, "Yes!"

"Why would members of my crew ally with a Mereish captain?"

"Money," Grant said gravely. "'Tis all anyone cares about, really. The poets say love is the driving force in the world, but then they are all very poor, are they not? Ben, I feel rather dramatic with you carrying me like this. Is it really necessary?"

"Can you move your toes?" I asked.

For some reason he gave a wheezing laugh, which descended into coughing. Blood flecked my face and the cold feeling in my chest became something darker, and harder.

I brushed at my power, easing it over his chest like a blanket. Calm. Peace. A numbing of pain.

I felt him relax.

"Stop bleeding. I am moving as fast as I can." I staggered under his weight, adjusted my grip, and pressed on. Several passersby gave us odd looks, others nervous ones. The darkness could not hide this much blood. "I would throw you over my shoulder, but your belly is full of holes."

He did not respond. Instead, his head bumped limply against my chest, and I realized he had passed out.

Moody ran up to me as soon as I came onto the docks. Behind her, the boatman on the mooring post still sat, pipesmoke drifting. Another figure stood next to him, a woman in a night shirt and a banyan with a bundle clutched to her chest.

"That's the surgeon, sir. But the boatman won't go. Someone's paid him off, and everyone else along this stretch."

I heard a growling sound and realized it was coming from my own throat. "Faucher."

Behind the surgeon, across the water, I could just see *The Red Tempest*'s masts amid the other ships, but the bulk of him was concealed.

"What do you know of this mutiny?" I demanded with a twist of Magni power.

The look Moody gave me was so shocked, I immediately discarded her as a conspirator.

"I'll deal with the boatman, sir," she said, strode back to the man, and punched him clear off the mooring post. He hit the water with a splash and a shout, which attracted far less attention than it might have in a more reputable port.

"Good work," I affirmed as I closed in.

The surgeon stared between the pair of us, but more in curiosity than fear.

"Should we not look for more of the crew?" Moody asked. "Or can we not trust them?"

"No, I will manage this. Help me with him."

We maneuvered Grant into the boat. I did not bother speaking to the surgeon—I compelled her to get to work at the same time as I took up an oar. Moody already had the other and was threatening to smack the flailing boatman with it if he drew close.

We set off for *The Red Tempest*, hauling in Magni-dictated unison. I did not have to think about my power, not when it kept Moody in time, not as it urged the surgeon to particular care and courage, nor noted the weak beating of Grant's heart.

That was a good thing indeed, for my mind was full to the brim with vengeance.

The Red Tempest was hidden behind a longer, lower ship. We skulked down its length and came into the clear a short distance away.

A cool breeze swept across the water, prickling at my bare chest beneath my coat.

The deck above was quiet, the lanterns burning strong. There were figures there, one just coming above, the other going to meet them. But before they had a chance to speak, my power took them. Both came to listless halts.

They still stood there, silent and staring at one another, when Moody and I came aboard. I quietly tied off the longboat with Grant and the surgeon—it was better they remain there for now—and strode towards the ensorcelled mutineers.

Moody followed me, surveying them cautiously. They were still, the whites of their eyes showing as they craned to see us.

I disarmed one, loading their pistol and drawing my own sword to match it. Moody did the same with the other, loading a pistol and taking a cutlass in hand. All the while, the only sounds were the creak of the ship, the brush of fabric and the tap of wood and steel.

We bound the mutineers to the shrouds and moved to the hatchway, pausing side by side.

The grating was open, the stair clear. Most of the crew would still be ashore, but I heard more voices than expected from below. They were heated and debating, occasionally overridden by Faucher's loud but indistinct tones.

Not everyone, it seemed, had capitulated.

I looked at Moody and, after a moment of thought, sheathed my sword. I retrieved the Magni talisman I had taken off Alamay from my pocket, careful not to let the talisman itself touch my bare skin, and held it out.

"Wear this, and stay behind me," I instructed. "I do not want you to be… swept along."

She nodded, eyes sharp and lips flat, and donned the talisman.

We descended. Magni power rippled ahead of us, snagging the first ranks of crewfolk and stilling them while their backs were turned. I took the next row, then the next, and forced them to part.

Moody and I strode down the empty center of the deck.

Faucher stood at the far end with a score of other figures—evidently allies. He looked up, eyes rounding as he saw my approach. But even as he opened his mouth to speak, my influence closed over him.

I held him still as I strode up, sword bare, and faced him.

I wanted to say something profound. I wanted him to understand, in great detail, how foolish and shortsighted he had been to wrong me. I wanted him to fear me, and to feel the pain he had inflicted upon Grant. But my power communicated the former without words, and my sword would do the latter.

I made to run him through.

Miaghis manifested in a burst of tentacles and ghisten light. Wood ruptured and splinters struck in with sudden, cracking force. I took them full in the side and staggered, my power momentarily fluctuating.

Several gunshots went off.

I advanced, ducking another spray of shards from Miaghis. He could not shatter the wood of the ship itself, but everything else was fair game. Sea chests. Chairs and tables. His barrage was indiscriminate, save when it came to Faucher. His captain, he sheltered.

I saw Alfwin flee towards the stern of the ship before several mutineers lunged between us with vengeful cries. I brought them up short with another push of power and turned them on one another.

One shot Faucher in the side. The other stumbled, slamming into another running figure. Moody. She dispatched her with a pistol butt to the face.

I grabbed the staggering Faucher by the collar and propelled him backwards, tossing him up against the trunk of the mainmast.

Miaghis's light rippled through the wood and the whole ship moaned.

I stabbed Faucher through the stomach. It was a quick, calculated thrust—I hardly wanted to lodge my sword in the mast itself, not when I intended to stab him several more times. I executed these swiftly, then stepped back.

Faucher toppled to the floor. Before Miaghis could assault me again I put the tip of my sword to the flesh of Faucher's throat, flicked aside his frantic hands with the tip of my sword, and severed the tender artery beneath his jaw.

Already soaked with his own blood—just as Grant was, back in the longboat—Faucher died rapidly.

Miaghis burst from the mast in a flood of tentacles and coiled over his staring corpse. I withstood his lashing, spectral tentacles no more than a breath across my skin. And when the creature's massive head loomed, overlaying the growing stillness of the gun deck and the staring crew, I did not back down.

"I am your captain," I stated calmly, looking from the beast to the crew all around. "Anyone who wishes otherwise had best get off my ship."

∽

I washed the blood from my hands and took my hammock from my sea chest. I strung it between the beams of my cabin and took a long, long drink of cool water directly from the pitcher on the sideboard. I slicked my hair back from my face and watching the lights of the port glisten through the gallery windows.

My mind was a quiet place, my bare chest rising and falling with steady, even breaths. Faucher was dead. Forbara and I had struck what I anticipated to be a profoundly useful accord, which would come to fruition soon. Grant was stitched and bandaged and being overseen by our new surgeon, Estia, who had yet to realize she had become a permanent member of my crew. Soon, we would continue on our way to Dreska Sank.

All was well, for the moment.

Faucher's face reappeared, unsummoned, before my mind's eye. He staggered against the mast. Once more Miaghis's tentacles exploded around him, the ghisting lunging from the wood. His translucent flesh obscured Faucher's expression, but the bloodlessness of his skin, the slow, resigned understanding of his coming death—I still saw it all.

My mind still retained that moment, hand in hand with my quietness of thoughts, as I pulled on a fresh shirt and descended to the hold.

Alamay awoke slowly.

"What do you want?" she whispered, not bothering to move. She was still heavily bandaged, and bundled against cold I did not feel.

"I shot you," I stated.

She gave me an exhausted stare.

"And I have killed Faucher. I feel no regret on either point."

She continued to stare, but her eyes contracted ever so slightly.

"Is this the way of our kind?" I asked. I kept my question light, factual, but there was a growing tension in my chest. "At the academy where I was trained, they insisted it was not, but life has led me to disagree. Do you feel regret when you kill? When you manipulate the wills of others?"

This did not seem to be the conversation she expected to have.

"I believe there is a certain… disconnect, in our nature," she admitted. "Because of your corruption you have experienced it far more than the rest of us. Have you felt a change since your healing?"

I gave this fitting consideration. "Yes. In being *that* I feel, though what I am feeling is often still beyond me. It is… exhausting. And baffling."

I was revealing too much, I reprimanded myself. But who else would I confide in? Who else could help me understand what it was to be a Magni? At least Alamay was within my control: a tool to be utilized, not a peer who would haunt me for years to come.

"So?" I prompted. "What do you do? How do you exist as one of us, and not become a monster?"

"Who says I am not?" She slowly sat up, her face pale with pain, and considered me as she caught her breath. "Our power can be used to kill and destroy. It can also be used to soothe and encourage. So can physical strength. So can words. So can intellect. We are all human, and we all have the potential for great violence, whether we are Magni or not."

I let that settle, momentarily. "How does that help me? I seek a practical solution, Alamay."

"The story is not about you."

"Pardon me?"

"Think of someone other than yourself. Step outside of your own skull, your own wants and desires. You are a captain, so choose what is best for your crew. You are a brother, so consider your brother. You are..." She trailed off, eyeing me. "Do you not have a daughter?"

I realized I had pushed off the wall and stood between her and the door.

"There," she said, pointing at my face. "There is your guidepost. There is your compass. Her."

My hackles rose. My hands began to tremor, a shuddering so deep I felt I could no longer breathe. There was little thought to the response, little rationality. I had a child, yes. That fact was years old and it was simply that—a fact. There was no emotion to it, no bond.

So why did the way Alamay spoke of that child, the suggestion of her inclusion in my motives, affect me so deeply?

I could not justify it. My reaction was senseless, a visceral intensity that erupted into a primal need—the need to either destroy the source of my discomfort or separate myself from it.

I put my hand on the latch and forced myself to step out.

"Enough. Enisca," I said, knuckles white on the latch. "We are bound for Dreska Sank. Tell me who you gave the documents to, and perhaps I will not have to learn regret by killing you."

NOSTA —*A creature adjacent to a cephalopod, which takes upon itself the great, shed shells of crustaceans. Though nosta groupings can travel vast distances across the warmer latitudes of the South Isles, the nature of the shells which they adopt may often be used to identify their particular spawning grounds. These grounds are divided by and fiercely guarded by females, who require extensive gifts of nourishment and novelties prior to permitting a male into her territory. Nosta young, it should be noted, are frequently and erroneously misclassified as blosquelle.*

—FROM BEASTS AND BEINGS: A SUMMONER'S
OBSERVATIONS IN THE SOUTH MEREISH ISLES,
BY SAMUEL I. ROSSER

TWENTY-FIVE

The Sea of Spires

SAMUEL

More rain blew in that night, coming in great sweeping sheets across the sea. It was warm and unexpectedly pleasant, and Athe did not bother waking Mary to disperse it.

I sat in Mary's and my small cabin, watching her hammock swing as rain drummed softly on the deck above. The woodstove was dormant, given the season, and the cabin was too dark to see her with my mortal eyes. But on the edge of the Other, the human world and the Dark Water coexisted. Her form was gently luminescent, rocking back and forth above a sheen of black waves.

Visions drifted past me in that half-formed place. I perused them as they passed, grasping and discarding them. Daily activities. Faces I did not recognize. I searched for whispers of a Ghistwold, the new Wold from which the ghisting stowed in our hold had been carved.

Mary and Demery had spoken of little else since the revelation of its existence, though in Mary's case I sensed the preoccupation largely came from Tane. Athe remained focused on finding Benedict, which I was grateful for.

But I, too, was distracted by the thought of a new, unclaimed Wold. If it fell into the hands of the Mereish—as seemed imminent, given that we had found the ghisting aboard a

Company vessel—they would become that much more powerful. Similarly, if the Aeadine or Usti took it.

But if the Capesh found it... that would mark a shift of power as momentous as Faucher's documents and the truth about the Usti.

The world, it seemed, was bound for change. And I was, once again, caught up in it.

A light flickered on the waves ahead of me in the Dark Water, a low Magni burn. A Sooth's forest green was there too, and a ghisting.

And...

Ben.

Ben was here. Ben had taken off his Sooth talisman. I sat bolt upright, focusing on the cluster of lights. The low Magni, that was Enisca Alamay. They were close together, along with the ghisting, Sooth, and... was that a grey haze? It was thin, nearly imperceptible. A *ghiseau*. Charles Grant?

"Mary," I breathed.

"No," she grumbled. "Whatever it is, no."

"I found *Red Tempest*. I can see Ben again. Perhaps Charles, too, and Enisca."

Hammock ropes squeaked and she dropped down next to me in a flash of long, pale legs and wash of indigo-grey aura.

"Is he close?" Mary asked, kneeling. I felt a fluctuation in the fabric between worlds and she appeared next to me in the Other—whole and physically present in her shift, no longer simply a glowing reflection.

I nodded, wordless on this side of the divide, and pointed her in the right direction.

Her eyes narrowed. She took a measured breath—her first breath of the permitted four, I counted—and Tane ignited in her eyes.

The Dark Water around us grew lighter, the water silvery.

A few curious fae dragonflies converged, tiny wings whirring. The lights of distant ships and beasts and mages somehow grew brighter at the same time.

I glanced at Tane's spectral flesh, marking, not for the first time, just how powerful she was. Not just that, but she was powerful in ways I could not begin to understand, and vastly older than Mary or I.

As if to reinforce my thoughts, Tane spoke. Her voice filled the air around us, disembodied and clear. *He is Adjacent, now. He looks like Silvanus Lirr—without Hoten, naturally. But he is Magni and Sooth.*

Mary's second breath came and went.

I looked closer. Tane was likely correct, though my recollection of Lirr's aura was muddied and opalescent. Ben clearly registered as both Magni and Sooth now, though the former outweighed the latter.

Mary's hand brushed my arm. There was no solidity to me, not in the way one would expect in the human world, but I felt her.

She pointed at something else. Something closer.

I followed her direction, noting more lights glimmering between Ben and us. The fact that there were lights was not abnormal—there were lights everywhere to varying degrees, stars cast across both sea and sky. Ghistings and ships, mages and beasts.

But there was an order to the lights Mary indicated. They were a burnt orange, tall and lanky. A forest of oddly shaped Otherborn beasts. Distance and space were difficult to gauge in the Dark Water, but these lights appeared to be converging on the collection of lights that was *The Red Tempest*.

I heard Mary take another breath, then another. Her physical form was replaced with her ethereal shadow, and I followed her back into the human world.

Mary was already speaking when I settled back into my bones. "You were always a Summoner. It makes sense, does it not? A Sooth's influence over the Other, and a dash of Magni compulsion? That makes a Summoner. But what has it made Ben? Something like Lirr, yes, but this is not the same. Lirr was no mirror twin, and Tane says he could not Summon. His influence remained over people alone."

"It is difficult to say. Perhaps Ben himself does not even know," I said. My legs were cramping and I rose, pushing my hair back from my face. "He was wearing a Sooth talisman until now, and it would have suppressed any new abilities. Either he took it off intentionally—perhaps so I *could* find him—or it was removed by accident."

"He may be setting a trap for us," Mary pointed out, getting to her feet too. "I'm going to warn Athe and Demery."

"I will go," I said, looking pointedly at her shift. The garment was loose and did little to conceal the soft curves of her hips and breasts. Nor the length of her calves. "You are indecent."

A dry smile flicked across her lips. "I enjoy being indecent."

"With me," I clarified. "In privacy."

She gave a distracting little shrug and waved at the door. "Go. I'll be right behind you. Properly domesticated," she added, that seriousness sharpening in her eyes. "And ready to end this."

∽

Rain still came down, steady and mild, as we approached the section of sea where Ben's light lingered. It was surrounded now by a haze of less familiar lights, predominantly Otherborn beasts like the orange forest beneath the waves.

We lit no lanterns and Mary nudged the rain into a foggier, thicker miasma to further obscure *Harpy*'s form. This shielded us from Ben and his probable trap, but meant that I was on constant alert to foresee threats, as was the crew.

I lingered on the edge of the Dark Water, monitoring visions and Otherborn lights.

"Forty-five fathoms," someone called from the stern.

"Easy, Brison," Athe murmured to the helmsman. She looked askance at Demery. "I do not enjoy springing traps."

Demery shrugged, scanning the sea ahead. "They cannot shoot what they cannot see. At least, not to any great effect."

Both former pirates were armed and the crew had gone to quarters, gun crews poised, marksmen lined up on the forecastle. Brid was among them, at ease with a long rifle and a distracted smirk as she spoke to one of her companions. I was pleased to see her so at ease—I still felt responsible for the woman, and the sight eased my burden.

Mary and I were also ready for conflict, she clad in trousers and a practical jacket, loose enough for easy movement and fitted enough not to be easily grabbed. There was a cutlass and knife at her hips, along with a pistol.

"Lanterns, Cap'n," one of the crew called. "Sou'-sou'-east."

"Forty fathoms," another added.

Ben was so very close. If we could end this tonight—what would that even mean? Would Benedict submit to Demery's plan, or would I be forced to do something unimaginable?

I narrowed my focus back into the Other. "Captain Kohlan, those lanterns appear to be *The Red Tempest*. If there are other ships out present, they have no ghistings. Otherborn beasts remain all around, however, and they are obscuring my sight to some extent."

Mary shifted at my side. She looked ill at ease, and there was more than a little Tane in her eyes. "What are they?"

A tapping, scraping sound echoed her words. A shiver ran through the deck of the ship and Harpy manifested from Demery's frame, only to vanish into the wood of the vessel beneath his shoes. Her and Demery's tether remained, smoke-like and indistinct.

"Only nosta," Demery concluded. "We are above a herd."

"What are those?" I inquired.

"A type of Otherborn squid," Athe replied.

"Fifteen fathoms!" called the sounder.

"Shallows ahead," I foresaw in the same instant. "Rocks to starboard."

For the next few moments the deck was overtaken with activity. Mary corralled the wind, Harpy rippled through the deck, and Brison took the wheel in steady hands.

That was when the warning shot came. It splashed into the water some distance away, a punch of sound followed by a heartbeat of silence. In that silence new lanterns unveiled, far closer than the original set. In fact, that set had vanished altogether.

A decoy.

Three ships surrounded us, all within or nearly within cannon range. Two Capesh oarships and one second-rate Aeadine ship of the line, at her ease with gunports open and scarlet sails.

Scarlet sails currently filling with a witchwind as the ship began to move away. The Capesh made no move to pursue—in fact, their only action was to fire another warning shot at *Harpy*.

Demery considered Athe briefly. "This is your ship now, Kohlan. Do we parlay and see what these Capesh want with us, or pursue *The Red Tempest*?"

Athe's reply, when it came, had lost all lightness. "We give chase. Mary."

Mary nodded and, with a rise and fall of her chest, began to sing.

"With her pistols loaded she went on board, by her side hung a glittering sword…"

Athe's commands rung out, the bosun's whistle piped, and the sails billowed with a coat-tossing, breath-stealing wind. The rain became nearly horizontal, blowing past me towards the fore of the ship.

Harpy rippled with ghisten light, not just from Harpy herself.

Mary and Athe both bled light as their ghistings manifested, surging to reinforce the wood of the ship as strains, scrapes and shudders momentarily overtook the vessel.

Harpy surged forward, cutting across the shallow sea as Capesh guns boomed.

"Not far they sail'd from the land, when a strange sail put them all to a stand…" Mary did not strain to be heard over the rain and guns and wind and waves, but her voice naturally wove through them all.

I stood vigil at her side, one foot in the Other. Still, when a string of islets rose before us, I had only moments of warning. I shouted, Brison threw his weight behind the wheel and the bosun's whistle peeled.

"And to her enemies, the witch did cry, but by my voice you all shall die, but by my voice you all shall—"

A whirling wail cut her off—bar shot. Mary and I instinctively ducked as the lines above were struck and tangled. Something snapped. Someone toppled from the rigging, just barely managing to grab the shrouds on the way down.

A scream. Another crack. I saw a vision of further shots striking the fore of the ship, momentarily overwhelming my senses.

I looked up just as the yard above us broke and, hinging, swung down with a tangle of torn sail and snapping lines.

"Mary!" I bellowed.

Blackness took me. My next crash of awareness—thick with fear, stabbed with confusion—was a tumbling blur as the deck tilted. There were hands in mine, Mary's hands, but no sooner had I felt them then they slipped away.

Water crashed over me. I struck out, reaching for Mary, for the ship, for a fallen rope—anything to anchor me as the sea began to draw me down.

Something brushed past my feet. I instinctively drew into a fetal curl and spun to look down—no, not down. Up. Through salt-burned eyes I glimpsed a ripple of ghisten light on waves and shadows retreated enough for me to see what had brushed me.

Slivers of silver flickered past. Fish. Just common fish, streaming past me in concerted eddies. They swirled on, rounding a seaweed-clad pillar—a mast from a shipwreck?—and vanished.

I struck out for the mast, intending to use it to propel myself upwards—my lungs burned now, my ears aching with pressure. My hands found its surface oddly smooth, nearly stony, and laden with velvety moss and trails of seaweed. Seaweed that trailed in an odd direction, alternate to the current.

I looked sharply down. There, just on the edge of the daylight, the mast ended in a fan of tentacles and a trio of craning, staring eyes.

Not a mast. A shell. A tall, tall pillar of shell.

I pushed off and floated free, only to find another pillar approaching from the murk, then another and another. As I drifted, suspended in the midnight sea, an army of creatures passed me by. Bearing their towering shells they walked upon masses of tentacles, devouring the bed of the shallow sea, while weeds streamed like banners.

A figure dove through the midst of them, bringing a flood of ghisten light. Mary, sheathed in Tane's light, her hair a wild cloud about her head. She reached for me and I grasped her forearm, pulling us together. For half a heartbeat we clung to one another, staring at the beasts, then we surged upwards.

We panted and coughed as we broke the surface. The rain had resumed its former driving, blinding form but I could make out *Harpy* close by, along with wreckage in the water. The yard that had been felled dragged behind her, slowing and straining the ship as sailors frantically hacked at lines.

Mary and I swam for the wreckage. Lines slithered past my legs and sailcloth bellied in our path, but I managed to swim around the bulk of it and grab a loose rope. With the other arm, I reached for Mary.

She bobbed out of my reach for half a breath, then took my hand. The other she slammed onto the hull. Tane's light rippled into the wood and, moments later, Athe appeared over the rail above.

Shouts and helping hands hauled us aboard as the wreckage was finally cut away. *Harpy* rocked at the release, nearly throwing us from our feet.

"Do they have a Stormsinger?" Mary shouted over the chaos. "Athe? Sam?"

"No!" Athe returned.

I shook my head, still breathless. "Are we fit to sail?"

"Fit not to sink, at any rate. If you've some witchery up your sleeve, I can get us away," Athe replied, hauling Mary to her feet. She looked to me. "But there will be no pursuing *The Red Tempest*."

My frustration was a dull thing, a background noise so familiar I no longer noted its coming and going.

"I will find him again," I vowed.

Mary lifted her voice and began to sing once more.

TWENTY-SIX

Isla Ascra

SAMUEL

"Your brother not only has gained the abilities of a Sooth, but has tried to deliver us into the hands of the Capesh for as yet unknown reasons," Demery summarized. "Tell me you have some insight."

I shook my head, lowering the mug I had just unceremoniously emptied of coffee. We were on the forecastle, where Athe and Demery were overseeing repairs.

"I do not," I admitted as the lanky, Whallish-pale cook refilled my mug. "Yet. I intend to return to the Other immediately."

"After you rest," Mary corrected. She lounged next to us on a crate, trouser-clad legs spread manfully, elbows braced on her knees. She looked pale and exhausted, and was nursing a cup of coffee thick with honey. "What would the Capesh want with us?"

"Benedict may simply have paid them to waylay us," I suggested.

"Well," Athe said. "My ship is in ruins, and we have enemies at every turn. I am sailing for Ascra."

Demery glanced at Mary, so casually I might have missed it.

"What is Ascra?" Mary asked, squinting tiredly. "I've heard the name, haven't I?"

"Yes." Athe's mouth cut a slanted, humorless smile. "It was Lirr's island."

I slipped an arm around Mary as the island emerged from a haze of fog. Isla Ascra lay within a forest of sea stacks, some as high as our masts, others barely more than wave-brushed caps lurking beneath the water. Here and there shoals stretched between the stacks, or stacks large enough to be called islets appeared. Trees clung to their heights and some of the stacks appeared to be populated, connected to one another via lofty, sturdy bridges of vine and moss-laden timber.

A fire ignited in the murk atop one stack, then another more distant light, and still another. They preceded us deep into the stacks.

"We have been sighted," I observed.

"And that appears to be our path," Mary murmured, peering at the way ahead.

Sure enough, the mist began to clear and a channel was revealed, marked on either side by flickering beacons. A song, too, came to our awareness, drifting from one of the larger seastacks— light, clear voice, dismissing the veil.

Harpy entered the channel. The rush of the open waves reduced to a ripple against the prow and the lapping of water against rock. The wind did not die but shifted, divided by the stacks and whistling, moaning in a great variance of tones. These backed the voice of the unseen Stormsinger, merging and harmonizing until the girl's voice faded, and the mist closed in, sealing the way behind us.

A shiver passed up my spine. "Has your mother ever spoken of Ascra?" I asked Mary.

She rested her elbows on the rail, letting my hand linger on her back. "Never. She doesn't talk about her time with Lirr, and I have never pressed. Sometimes the past is best left buried."

Footsteps sounded and Demery joined us, hands in the pockets of his overcoat and cocked hat upon his head. "Did you notice the guns?"

I slipped my hand from Mary's back as she straightened, and both of us followed his gaze to one of the nearby spires. At first the opening was little more than a darker patch of rock, but as we passed I saw depth, and the gleam of a long cannon.

Now that I knew what to look for, I saw multiple such cavities, and, upon closer inspection, the bridges or discrete landing places that accessed them—a squat, fortified door here, a rolled rope ladder there.

"No wonder Talys cannot uproot Idriss," Mary commented. "This is more than a fortress."

"A fortified labyrinth," I added.

Demery nodded. "Only one channel to the inner island—at least, one channel deep enough for anything more than a skiff. Combine that with the number of mages loyal to Idriss, and they are powerful."

"But they have no council seat," Mary pointed out. "Do the seats not go with the islands?"

"They often do," Demery affirmed. "But no one is giving a Stormsinger a seat. They conceded to Idriss's indenture laws, but only because there is little difference between indentures and slavery."

"An indenture instead of a slave. A mask instead of a gag," Mary murmured. I saw her fingers tighten on the rail. Harpy's light flickered through the wood in response, or perhaps consolation, and Tane's tones drifted into Mary's voice as she added, "At least with ghistings they do not bother to pretend."

Demery made an affirming sound. Looking between the two of them, I saw a similarity of expression, a grave solidarity.

"Whatever you do, do not mention the young ghisting in our hold to Idriss," Demery said. "Or the new Ghistwold."

Mary nodded, as if this were a given.

I also nodded, though more slowly. Matters were growing increasingly complex and, I sensed, the priorities of my companions beginning to skew.

But I had to remain focused, now more than ever.

Stop Ben. Evict him from my life. Find the documents.

And secure Mary's and my future upon the Winter Sea.

TWENTY-SEVEN

Hidden Places

MARY

Isla Ascra rose out of the calm waters, short cliffs laden with trees, spills of vegetation, and the outlines of stone buildings. Its highest point was a sprawling fortress, the forest cleared around fortified batteries situated atop the cliffs, along with bridges to nearby seastacks—these ones heftier and made of stone. The land itself was graced with lofty heights and shallow valleys, giving the buildings there a layered outlook of greys and whites, punctuated by ribbons of color which I could not identify at the distance, but reminded me of how the northern Mereish decorated their homes with psalms.

Three small ships lay at anchor, along with numerous boats drawn up onto a broad, flat beach at the foot of the cliffs. A cave yawned in the cliffs, blocked by a formidable and well-kept portcullis, while several staircases and paths visibly wound up the cliffs.

As we rowed ashore the portcullis rose and Idriss came out, followed by half a dozen other figures. She wore similar clothes to our first meeting and she was unarmed.

"Captain Kohlan, Lord Demery," she greeted, clasping their hands in turn and surveying Sam and I. "Mary Firth, if I recall. And not-Benedict Rosser."

Sam shook her hand with grudging good humor.

I took her hand last. "Idriss. Thank you for taking us in."

"Am I taking you in?" she asked, looking back at Athe and Demery. "Judging by *Harpy*'s condition, it seems I must."

"If you would be so kind," Demery said.

Idriss's expression said there was more to be discussed and negotiated, but she gestured us back up the beach.

Samuel strode close to me as we entered the tunnel and began to climb up a slow grade, similar to the entrance to the Sea Fort. The light shifted and swung, emanating from lanterns carried by Idriss's companions, and I noted that beyond the mouth of the cave, which had a natural texture, this path had been carefully carved and hewn. Doorways were set in the rock too, their peeked frames perfectly constructed and elevated from the main path with small, worn steps.

I had seen enough of the world now to note a particular style to those doorways, one not quite Mereish, or Usti, or Aeadine. This was made further clear as I picked out symbols and decorations, largely hidden by the shadows. They recalled to me an altar in a stone circle, on a barren, wave-washed shore.

"Lirr did not construct all this," I observed to Athe, who walked just ahead of Sam and I. "It was here when he took the island?"

"It was here," she affirmed. "He bought the island and its seat from the council and uprooted the alliance of petty pirates who had it at the time, but the structures pre-date even them. This," she waved at the next doorway we passed, "reminds me a little of home."

"Sunjai?"

Athe gave me a half smile, and there was something softer in her eyes. "Not quite. I was born in Opass, at the edge of the Far Sea, to a Sunjani mother, and an Opassi father. The symbols you see here and there? They're rooted in the mother-language of today's Opassi, Sunjai and Capesh."

Opass. I knew the name, but in the detached way that came with accessing Tane's memories, not my own.

There are still places in this world I have never heard of, I reflected to Tane. *History I never learned. Maps I have never seen.*

Tane's reply was a wash of memories, images of places *she* had seen. It was a gesture of kindness, a sharing of memory, but it was also an affirmation—I was small, and the world vast. And Tane had seen far more of it than I had.

There was a weight to that understanding, and even a flicker of guilt.

You went from your Wold to slavery, to me, I murmured in the quiet of our connection. *Where would you be, if you had the choice?*

I went to you willingly, she reminded me, but there was a feeling with her words, an overflow of want that had no beginning, only a forced, tight-willed end. *Now we are bound, and I would not change that. That is the way of things. We are one.*

There was more to be said on the topic, but just then the tunnel emptied into an open space within the settlement. The sky spread above us, the mist was gone, and we stood in the center of Isla Ascra.

Athe carried on as I slowed and gazed around, taking in more unfamiliar architecture along with a scattering of familiar sights. Mereish psalms painted under the overhangs of roofs, pale Usti colors lavished across plaster, carved Aeadine lintels. Memories of a world beyond the South Isles.

All seemed new, the colors bright, the paint fresh. The women of Isla Ascra claiming their home from beneath Lirr's long shadow.

Tane and I shared a wash of discomfort. Tane had left my mother before Anne had come here, but we were both struck by the reality that my mother had lived in this very place, under Lirr's control, for over a decade. The stones beneath us, the scents on the wind, the shapes of the buildings—they had been her prison. And the figures going about their day in the settlement around us, the women and men nodding their greetings and staring at me with blatant, clear recognition? They had known her, and evidently, saw her in me.

I realized Samuel was watching me. He did not speak, not with the others so close, but when our eyes met he offered me a concerned smile.

I slipped my arm through his, and he tucked me into his side.

A shadow crossed the courtyard, along with a stray, twining breeze. I looked up at the scudding clouds, cheek angled into that breeze, as a dozen other women did the same. Most had pale, pale eyes—the color of icebergs and winter skies, forget-me-nots and cornflowers. One was blinded, her closed, scarred eyelids glazed with ghisten light as she watched the sky. A *ghiseau*. A *ghiseau* who, evidently, felt no need to hide.

Someone began to sing, a sweet song in a language I didn't recognize. The breeze shifted, growing warmer. The clouds went on their way and once more, sun poured down upon the Stormsingers of Isla Ascra.

An entirely new sensation overtook me, one that made my hold on Samuel's arm relax. It was a sense of being one of many, of being innately understood. Of being known among strangers, and knowing in return.

Whatever this island had been, it was something else now.

A haven for Stormsingers.

∽

There was something of a feast that night in the central square of Ascra. Demery's crew mingled with the locals with an ease that indicated many had been here before, cheerful greetings and the rise and fall of conversation filling the waning day. Long tables of food were set out, both visitors and locals contributing, and a huge cask of wine was rolled out to a scattering of cheers and laughter.

I lingered with Samuel, sitting on a low wall as the sun disappeared beyond the tallest of the seastacks. The sky above the island remained clear but I could see the bank of the region's protective fog, hazing and swallowing the sun. Violet and orange transitioned to gold and grey, and torches flickered to life.

"This is not what I expected," Samuel murmured. He tracked a mob of children as they careened through the company, converging on woman with a lute and a man with a drum as they entered the square.

"What did you expect?" I asked, because I felt the same, but could not articulate my own thoughts.

"That Lirr's legacy would cast more of a pall," Samuel said, watching the children with a crinkling about the corners of his eyes. "More than half those children are his, and nearly all are mages."

I did not bother to ask how he knew. Several adults joined the children, organizing them into a circular, group dance. It was a jaunty, ridiculous thing which made the children laugh and tumble over one another.

"I can't see him. Not in them. Not like I saw it in Talys," I murmured. I forcibly shook myself and loosened my shoulders, leaning into him. "But I don't want to think of her or him."

He nodded his agreement. "Then may I distract you with an observation?"

He was very close, close enough to slowly, finally intrude on my preoccupation with the island.

"Idriss offered quarters ashore," he said. "Private quarters. I accepted on our behalf."

I looked to his mouth, then back up to the dark warmth of his eyes. "Private quarters, you say?"

"Yes," he affirmed, taking my hand and beginning to kiss my fingertips, one by one.

"But can we just... leave?" I whispered, though my mind was already careening away with a dozen images and impulses, many of which centered around climbing into Sam's lap. "I want to speak to Idriss, but..."

"We can return, later," he said, the movement of his lips on my fingers further stoking the heat in my belly. Capturing my hand, he started to rise. "But for now, I believe you need a distraction."

"I believe I do."

His fingers laced through mine and he began to lead me out of the square. My patience was thinning by the second, however, and I crowded him, urging him on as the music from the square chased us into the village.

At last Samuel's back hit a doorway—the doorway of a small house maybe, I could not see well in the dark and found I did not particularly care. The lantern beside the door was lit but low, casting more shadows than light on his handsome face.

At the same moment I leaned up, and he down. Our lips collided and he turned me into the frame of the door, plying me with kisses until I could barely breathe, let alone stand.

I vaguely fumbled for the doorhandle, trying to firm up my weak knees. His own knee provided an unexpected and rather firm seat, shoved between my legs, and I nearly smacked my head on the doorframe in sudden need.

"Sam… Open the door."

Instead his hands, which had been exploring delightfully, paused. "No, I mean—this is not it."

I recoiled. "Pardon me?"

"The lodgings Idriss showed me. I cannot remember…" He looked around rapidly, chagrin rapidly declining into a dark kind of frustration that made our lack of privacy and a large bed all the more maddening. He looked as though he might attack something.

I hoped it would be me.

"I have gotten us lost."

I slapped his chest in frustration and tried to disentangle myself. He remained unmovable, however, holding me in place as he considered the situation.

Then, suddenly, he stooped. Before I could cry out—in something that was not *quite* outrage—I found myself slung over his shoulder and carried off down an alley.

"Samuel!" I hissed, trying not to laugh.

In response a large hand slapped my backside and he adjusted his grip.

"Where are we going?"

"Leave that to me."

"Sam!"

Another turn and I scented moss and earth, and we passed into a ridge of forest. Sam stood for a moment, listening to the shadows, then set me on my feet.

"Tane?" Samuel requested.

I felt the ghisting's amusement as she manifested, her cool indigo light briefly illuminating our faces. Our spectral tether began to spool as she slipped off into the trees, giving me a meaningful glance in parting.

"She will keep watch," I told Samuel. His hands had begun to travel again, brushing stray hair from my face, my throat. His fingers trailed over my collarbones to the laces of my shirt, where they began to methodically unfasten and tug.

"Good," he said. He moved to kiss me, returning one hand to the back of my head, then paused. His eyes fell into mine, searching and assessing, slowing in a way that made my anticipation wind all the tighter.

It was a powerful thing, being the sole focus of Samuel Rosser's attention.

Reluctantly, I put a hand in the center of his chest and pushed him back slightly. "Sam. What is it?"

"I am wishing I could run away with you, this very night, and leave everything behind."

Something inside me faltered. There was absolute sincerity in his voice. For so long we had battled, for so long I had felt secondary to his ideals and obligations. But in that moment, I knew I had usurped their place.

The realization was heavy, weighty with responsibility.

"I wish we could, too," I admitted with a half-hearted smile and an ache in my chest. "But what I do not want is for you to lose yourself for me. And neither of us could truly run away, could we? We could not live with ourselves."

His expression flicked into discontent, then something quieter, something more opaque. "No. No, we could not."

"But we have this moment, alone," I reminded him, gentling my hand on his chest, skimming my fingers over the rise of muscle and bone beneath his shirt. "So let us make the most of it."

He removed my hand and inched closer, pressing us together and taking my jaw gently in one of his large, warm hands. His thumb skimmed my bottom lip and we watched one another for one more moment, assessing, searching. Assuring.

Then I captured his mouth with mine.

∞

Sometime later, I rested my head in Samuel's lap. He sat against a tree with his shirt still undone, running his fingers through my loose hair. Neither of us spoke, avoiding the reality that time was passing, as we should return to the village.

Languid as my mind was, eventually I felt a shift in the corner of my awareness and looked up. Trees, branches and dangling of moss waving in the breeze. Glimpses of starlight and moonlight, drawing out the curves and edges of root and stone, moss and trunk.

And there in the air before me, Tane's and my tether. It had thinned to near invisibility. No—it *was* invisible. Broken. Faded away, not a pace away from where it spooled from my chest.

I had only seen such a thing once before. When Demery, the Uknaras, Athe and our ghistings had separated Lirr from Hoten, right before we killed them.

The vulnerability of it struck me like a gale.

Tane!

I felt her respond like a distant voice across the sea, thin and distorted.

Samuel sat up, alerted either by his Sooth's sense or my sudden stiffness. "Mary?"

"Tane is gone," I said, the words feeling unreal on my tongue. "Can you see—"

"I see."

We climbed to our feet, he immediately wrapping his belt back about his hips and priming a pistol. I had not come ashore armed, trusting Tane and my sorcery, and fiercely regretted that.

Sam, Sooth to the core, pulled a sheathed dagger from his boot and held it out to me.

I took it with a grateful nod. "I can sense the direction she went. Can you see her?"

He shook his head and, handing me his pistol for half a moment, finished dressing.

"I cannot see her at all," he said. "Demery and Athe are back in the village. There are the other *ghiseau*, but no Tane."

The urge to panic swelled before me, but I shoved it aside. "Then let's go."

We moved together through the forest, staying close. There was little undergrowth but boughs rustled overhead and the forest night, rather than feeling sheltering as it had before, now felt riddled with threats.

We came out onto a clifftop, open and cool and laced with a damp breeze. Two paces out, a broad seastack rose out of the night, accessed by a narrow, rotting bridge.

"She is over there," I murmured.

The bridge complained as we crossed, choosing our steps carefully. As we went I brushed my fingers over the wood, instinctively searching for feeling or a memory, an inkling of ghisten life. Anything that might make Tane feel closer.

I felt a whisper in the wood.

"She went this way," I murmured to Sam. My feet sank into moss as we reached the top of the next stack, and I stopped. "I don't think the tether broke because of distance. It's rather... there's something in the way."

"Like Ess Noti magecraft?"

"Yes."

He surveyed the lofty little island, with its shadows and swaying trees. There was a taint to the air here, a thread of rotting mushrooms or stagnant water, and it turned my stomach.

"There is something ahead," Sam whispered. "Stay behind me."

Under any other circumstances I might have balked at the request, but under any other circumstances he would not have asked. I fell in behind his protective bulk as we advanced deeper into the island.

A building emerged from the darkness. I might have missed it entirely, but several fae dragonflies darted past my ear. They carried on through the low boughs and dark trunks and towards the shape of a low, broad stone structure.

Samuel and I came to its edge. The structure had six pillars and no walls, with a wooden roof. Inside was what might have been called a well. The dragonflies swirled down, joining a dozen fellows to skim over the surface of a layer of fetid, congealing water some half dozen paces below.

A staircase clung to the periphery of the well, leading to a shadowed alcove.

"A doorway," I murmured. "Tane is in there."

Samuel looked over at me, concern edging his eyes. "I would investigate alone, but I believe we are safer together."

I conjured a smile, beset by a sudden rush of fondness. "We are always safer together, Sam."

He held out his hand to me and we crept down into the darkness.

TWENTY-EIGHT

The Ghisten Three

SAMUEL

The steps were narrow, barely wide enough for me to set my feet next to one another. The dragonflies surged to join Mary and I, their pulsing gold and violet lights illuminating the way as we descended the slick, damp stair to the doorway.

I settled my boots on a broader landing and looked back at Mary. Golden and purple light played off her skin like twilight, and though she had wrestled her hair into a knot she was still gratifyingly disheveled.

I could not enjoy the sight, though. On the edge of the Other her normally strong aura had thinned and her tether to Tane, drifting in the air before her, was shorter than ever.

I steeled myself and turned on the door. The frame was tall, possessed of the same foreign architecture as the rest of the island's original structures. The door itself was banded with iron and beginning to rot at the bottom, though only slightly. Forgotten, I intuited, but not for more than a few winters.

I put a hand on the damp wood and pushed. The door swung open with a scrape and a crunch of freshly shattered wood—which, judging from the brackets to either side, were the remains of a hefty wooden bar.

"Tane must have done this," Mary whispered. Low as her voice was it echoed down a short tunnel. "Perhaps she expected us to follow?"

"Perhaps," I observed. I added to the dragonflies, "Ahead."

Half of them surged forward, streaking down the tunnel and illuminating a curve barely three paces on. Mary and I followed with the other half, leaving the damp and stink of the well and forging into the equally dank, but altogether staler, air of the underground world.

The tunnel turned into another, longer stair, then an echoing chamber with a floor so smooth, it glistened. No, I corrected myself. It was covered with a thin sheen of water, flowing inwards into a long narrow fissure in the floor. It looked like the Dark Water, particularly as the dragonflies skimmed across in streaks of gentle light.

My will shifted and dragonflies lifted off the surface of the water, spiraling off into every shadow, every corner, until the cave's secrets were revealed. There was a long, central fissure into which the water flowed. The water itself came from all sides, welling from cracks in the walls and rim of the floor, and even the ceiling. There was also an archway into another chamber.

I preceded Mary through. As I did, something momentarily slowed me. I reached out to caution Mary, but she had already stopped.

"There is something in this rock," I said, scanning the ceiling and walls. The chamber was man-made, walls reinforced with carefully hewn stone. Many of the stones were of a vaguely opal-escent black or grey. They latticed the ceiling and the doorframe, containing the chamber beyond.

The closest stones, beside Mary and I in the doorframe, seemed to hum. And as I stepped through, my connection to the Other dimmed.

"This is the barrier," Mary murmured. "Between Tane and I. It feels like a Mereish talisman."

I nodded, in the midst of another step. I had a sensation of my ears popping, then my Sooth's senses surged back, sharper and more focused than before.

Four ghisten lights bloomed. They were a surge of illumination in both the Dark Water and the waking world, filling the chamber and drowning out the dragonflies who alighted on their wooden bodies.

Three ghisten figureheads sat in the chamber, all in various stages of disrepair. One was an intricately carved horse, rearing through waves. The second a nude woman, her exaggerated figure clad in nothing more than a drape of gossamer. The third was a wolf, a snapping, leaping creature rendered in a startlingly lifelike style I marked as Aeadine.

The final presence was Tane. She coalesced before us and lingered for a breath, momentarily whole. Then between one blink and the next, she disassembled and flowed into Mary's frame.

Mary's eyes flickered closed for a moment, her skin sheathed in spectral power.

"This place belonged to Lirr and Hoten," Mary said slowly. She opened her eyes again, scanning the room in the brightening illumination. "This is where they made many of their *ghiseau*."

I swept the room with a sharper gaze. There was a pit in the floor, currently puddled with water, but I did not miss the blackness beneath, or the bits of old, charred wood scattered around. Pieces of old figureheads, I understood. Ghistings harvested and bonded.

My gaze dragged to the walls, and there I saw the chains. Manacles suspended from iron hooks embedded in the walls. One pair from the ceiling, just beside the fire pit.

"Children," Mary-Tane whispered.

The three ghistings in the figureheads manifested. The horse stepped down from its waves. The woman's bare feet alighted on the floor with graceful steps and the wolf prowled out, growing as he went until he was larger than the horse. He snarled and twitched his shoulders as a dragonfly landed upon him. The smaller creature took off in fright.

Mary listened for a moment, then looked to me, ghisten light reflected in the deep blue and pale grey of her eyes.

"They are showing me what they remember. No one has been here since Lirr left... but he made Talys here. He made his eldest children into *ghiseau*, and other people, besides. He burned the figureheads in there"—she indicated the pit—"and held his victims there." She pointed to the manacles suspended from the ceiling. She added more quietly, "Even the children."

"Pity we cannot kill him again."

"Mm. But there is more. The black stones act as a barrier, like Mereish talismans, but far stronger—that is what cut Tane and I off. Also... Lirr and Hoten did other work, down here."

I followed Mary as she moved away from the manifest ghistings. Tane stayed behind, still standing in the place Mary had vacated. She and the ghistings began to converse in their silent, unmoving way.

The tether between Mary and Tane, however, remained strong as Mary approached another region of the chamber.

There was a second room, accessed by another heavy door. As soon as I entered the air changed—it was sweet and fresh, backed by a distant whistling of wind through the shutters of several small, square windows. There was a stove, woodstack and a sitting area, and a long broad worktable where several of my dragonflies had alighted. Cases of moldering books clung to the walls between great swaths of maps, their edges curling with damp, or falling from their pegs. Lastly, there were chests of dozens of long, broad drawers.

"They were looking for something," Mary told me. "The ghistings remember that, but not *what*."

"Something more than you and Tane?" I asked her.

"Yes," Mary stared at the charts on the walls, her gaze drifting to the largest and most intact. It was painted on wood, a lavish and detailed rendition the South Mereish Isles complete with ornamental shipwrecks, monsters and gold-leaf.

As magnificent as the map was, it did not keep Mary's attention. She began to open drawers, sifting through more charts, letters and papers.

I examined the painted map a moment longer, noting an empty, almost unfinished portion at the bottom, before I joined her with an escort of dragonflies to illuminate her work.

In the first drawer I opened, I saw a star chart of exquisite design. Constellations were carefully traced out, though they looked little like the Aeadine arrangements I had grown up with and the language scrawled in all directions from a celestial heart was one that I did not recognize. Whatever sky this depicted, it was far beyond the Winter Sea.

Fascinated, I picked up a corner of the chart delicately and looked beneath it. There, beneath a dividing layer of dry, waxed onion paper, was another chart, and another and another. One was written in an old version of Aeadine, while another was modern Usti. One was long and narrow, made of pressed reed and delicately painted with Ismani symbols—the view of the horizon from the heart of Isman. All were in far better condition than those on the walls, thanks to pouches of desiccant.

A further drawer presented me with renditions of famous ports and cities, from the Usti Winter Palace to sweeping, high-pointed buildings surrounded by lush jungles. Most were rendered in simple ink—black, an occasional russet red or brown—but a third drawer proved to contain fully colored works. The styles, origins and ages of all varied widely, their only similarities being their foreign nature.

For the next few minutes, the space was filled with the rustling of aged paper as we searched—for what, I did not know, but my Dreamer's sense was growing, and Mary had intent written in every line of her body.

Tane eventually joined us, her gentle blue glow joining that of the dragonflies as she moved to the other side of the table, mirroring Mary in everything except her face, which was that unique melding of her, her mother, and a harsher, more elemental, woman.

"We saw this in the half-petrified ghisting's memories," Mary said. She traced her fingers across a mildewed map, identifying a series of three islands, rocky and barren. Two facing one another over a narrow passage.

The area was shown in two ways—one from above, Aeadine style, and one via a horizon, in Ismani style. Bold lines joined markers between both map styles, along with Ismani names in fluid, descending characters.

The map was rendered in a faded brown ink save for the trees. They sprouted here and there across the islands, outlined in halos of faded blue.

"Hoten and Lirr were looking for it too?" Mary muttered. I was unsure whether she spoke to me or Tane, or neither of us. "They certainly would have, if they heard rumors, but... did they find it?"

"What are you talking about?" I asked gently.

Mary took the chart in front of her and surveyed the maps on the wall with fresh eyes before striding over to the vast, painted map. She pointed to the uncharted region to the south, its emptiness occupied by a many-tentacled monster, a sunken ship and a saint in pious repose among lush clouds.

"Here," she said, pointing to the empty space, then raising the other chart she had gathered as if to fill in the space. "This is where the new Ghistwold is."

TWENTY-NINE

Forgotten in the Dark

MARY

Desperate for air, I tried to open one of the small, shuttered windows. The lock stuck. I shook it in frustration, all the burdens and unexpected turns of the night culminating in that lock.

Large hands intervened. Samuel pried up the stuck latch with a crack of salt-rusted iron and cool air rushed across my face.

"Take a moment," he advised.

I leaned against the wall and pinned my eyes closed. It was too much. Thoughts of Lirr, thoughts of my mother. The happiness, the momentary oblivion of tumbling with Samuel in the forest, crashing into the bewilderment of realizing Tane had been cut off from me.

The secret of a new Ghistwold that I now held in my hands.

Our hands, Tane reminded me. Her emphasis was clear, and I sensed the discussion she and I were bound for would not be a light one. But now was not the time.

"Do you think Idriss knows?" I asked Sam, rubbing at my face. "About this place? About the Wold? I can't see her sitting on an advantage like this, not when she is so determined to claim a seat at the council. Telling them of the Ghistwold would go a long way. Just possessing these three ghistings would be an advantage."

The breeze coming through the window was beginning to

feel too cold now, too indifferent. More of the black stones were embedded in the windows. My latent sorcery, it seemed, did not pass through.

Sam didn't speak right away, thoughts passing over his face.

Desperation rattled through me. "Saint… I can't think. Please say something."

Samuel glanced over the maps again. "The ghistings said no one had been down here since Lirr left."

I nodded.

"And neither Lirr, nor your mother, mentioned a South Mereish Ghistwold during our expedition over the Stormwall."

I took a moment to reflect on this, then nodded again. "Demery was as surprised as I when we took the half-stone ghisting aboard."

"Then I think it is safe to conclude that Lirr did not realize he already had the key to the new Wold," Samuel said. His voice was soothing, methodical. "You only recognized the landmarks because of what the petrified ghisting showed you."

"Yes," I breathed. I ground the heels of my hands into my eyes for a moment. "Yes, you're right. It's just… This place…"

"I feel it too," he finished for me. "Whatever is in these stones may be what the Ess Noti put in their talismans."

I pressed my hands harder into my eyes and groaned. "No. I can't think about them too."

"Let us go back to the village," Sam reasoned. "We can rest and decide what to do."

I need more time, Tane's voice interrupted. She had moved back into the other room without my noticing, which was unlike her, considering my current crisis.

What for?

These ghistings have been trapped here, alone and forgotten, for years, she replied. An odd distance remained in her voice, and I began to suspect it may not entirely be due to the dark stones. *They need me. They need to decide what they want to do.*

What the ghistings wanted to do? That took me aback. They had only three options, didn't they? Remain as they were, be burned, or be fitted to a ship. I supposed we could take them to a Ghistwold and leave them to sprout again, but that was... not relevant just then.

Are they why you didn't come back to me? I asked in sudden realization.

Yes, Tane replied simply. *You were with Samuel, and they needed me.*

I couldn't reply. Never had Tane so clearly prioritized herself, and I found myself at a loss for how to feel about it.

I realized I was staring at the door and Samuel was watching me quizzically.

"Tane needs more time," I said.

And so we waited. The clean air calmed me to some extent, and I began to work out the rest of my distraction by wandering the room. Samuel, noting my recovery, returned to where the map of the new Ghistwold lay, rolled it up, and shoved it under his coat. He gave me a small smile as he did so, one of sympathy and solidarity. Then he began a methodical search of a large desk and a series of cabinets.

I pulled a book off a bookcase and opened it. The pages were discolored and warped with damp, but it was still legible. It was written in a mixture of Aeadine, in one hand, and a language I had never seen before in another. There were dates, however, and each page had the structure of a logbook.

I glanced at the door, thinking to ask Tane her thoughts or at least access her knowledge, but she was still occupied. I could hear her conversation in the back of my mind, whispers and echoes that refused to form into words.

I shoved the notebook into my pocket and began to rifle through drawers. I almost immediately found a tarnished silver coin, considered it with raised brows, and shoved it into my pocket.

"Ms. Firth! Mr. Rosser!"

Sam and I both startled. I was unsure how much time had passed but the voice came through the window, and it was most certainly Demery's. It echoed bizarrely between the water and the sea stacks, and I realized it was carried on a Stormsung wind.

"They have noticed our disappearance," Samuel commented.

I hastened to the window, pockets clinking. Samuel glanced down at them.

"It's not theft," I stated. "It's reparations."

"I see. We should go meet them," Samuel glanced at the ghisten light in the doorway. "Though we needn't tell them where we were. Perhaps this is a secret best kept between we three, for now."

"Agreed."

∞

It took two days to repair *Harpy*. It was a tense time for Samuel, Tane and I, though it was also filled with stretches in which, under normal circumstances, I might have found peaceful. We sat together in the quarters we had been assigned by the light of loose, fae dragonflies and a single candle. Samuel poured over the logbook I had found, along with several other volumes he himself had confiscated from Lirr's lair. They produced another revelation—that the stone Lirr had used to hide his chamber contained gianeo, the very same ore that Voskin exported to Mere.

"It must be what the Mereish use to make their talismans," Samuel concluded. "But where is it found?"

The answer to that remained elusive.

Secondly, we studied the map of the Ghistwold and worked to discern its exact location in the southern reaches. Without more extensive charts we could not say for certain, but the general location was now known to us.

And with that, Tane and I faced our first great divide.

I sat on the clifftops, looking down on the harbor where *Harpy* was being repaired. Samuel was down there, lending his hands to the efforts with his shirtsleeves rolled up and his hair in a cursory knot. I admired the view through a spyglass as, in the silence of my skull, Tane whispered.

It was less of a conversation than a conversion, intertwined as we were. It came with all that she and the three ghistings in Lirr's lair had discussed. It came with Tane's lifetime of observations and experiences. Her suffering and theirs.

It came too with a great weight—the fate of a new Ghistwold, a sick Ghistwold, the location of which only she, I and Samuel knew.

The Ghistwold north of the Stormwall is safe, Tane concluded. *My children are safe. But this new Wold? Not only are they ill, but every power in the Winter Sea will seek to control them. Idriss, you and Samuel—you dream of a future for Stormsingers with no bonds, no indentures. Can ghistings not hope for the same? A future without being unwillingly bound to ships, torn from our roots. Forgotten in the dark.*

I watched the movement aboard *Harpy* without seeing it now, spyglass resting on my knees. *I don't know that there is hope for any of us.*

Tane turned us and, through the same eyes, we surveyed the island, the haven that Idris had made.

If I can choose to hope and labor for a better future, Tane said, *if Idriss and these women can after all Lirr did to them, surely you can, too.*

I closed my eyes, blocking out the settlement. I thought of my mother, my unborn sibling, and my own indenture. I thought of how tired I was of it all, and it left me feeling nothing but trapped.

I had no answer for her.

I still did not have one by the time *Harpy* was ready to depart. Samuel had sighted Ben's light on the horizon and our course was laid—we waited only for the morning tide, and Tane had a request.

I stood alone in Lirr's chamber, facing the three forgotten ghistings.

You are sure of your choice? I asked.

Yes, sister.

Together, Tane and I burned the ghistings. The act was not a quick one, though I sped it along with a barrel of oil I had confiscated from the storehouse where I pinched my lantern. Tane and I spent the entire night in the lair, barely communicating, our minds as much our own as they could be.

She watched the ghistings burn, standing manifest and unmoving in solidarity to their pain. I tried my best to ignore that suffering. I stared at Lirr's maps, the scent of smoke clinging to my clothing. I read his books and paced the chamber, and finally returned to the ghisten room, where I sat against the wall and watched the embers smolder.

Finally, as the last trails of smoke were swept up through windmoaning channels in the rock, ghisten light filled the chamber. Momentarily, the three newly freed ghistings manifested, whole and solid and eerie and free. Then they disassembled, as vaporous as the smoke and ethereal as moonlight. They rushed around Tane in a whirl of ghisten flesh, stirring her hair and skirts.

Then they surged off through the gaps in the rock, off to the Dark Water, to the sea and freedom.

Tane turned to me. Her sea-glass eyes looked harrowed, and exhausted and troubled as I was, my sympathy stirred in response.

I must ask you for something, Tane said. She came to kneel in front of me, the line of our connection a spectral umbilical between us. *When this matter with Benedict is settled, we will find the new Ghistwold, here in the South Isles. If an opportunity to visit it arises before matters with Benedict are settled, we take it.*

"I cannot leave Samuel," I said aloud. Speaking the words into the smoke-scented silence gave me some sense of independence, of separation of being, though of course it was a façade. "It's not that I don't care, Tane. You know that. You know… why do I even bother to speak my mind? You *know*. But my—our—own freedom is already on the line. I can't take the Ghistwold on my shoulders."

It is not time to hide, Mary.

"Hide?" Resentment flared, then extinguished, inside of me. I could not tell whether that feeling was hers or mine.

It has been over a year since I fully awakened, Tane said. Her sea-glass gaze still held mine, the sharp lines of her face tempered by a softness around her eyes. *In that time, I have cared for you and protected you as a mother. In the beginning we were alone, you and I, trying to survive. But now…*

She finished even more softly. *But you are no child and we are no longer alone, adrift in the world. And it is time we turn our eyes to something besides ourselves.*

I remained quiet, letting her feel the ebb and flow of my emotions. I knew what she was not saying—that she had always been selfless, while I remained entrenched in my own experiences and desires.

I felt a shift inside of me, the grinding of a great, heavy door. Beyond it I glimpsed a future of possibilities and responsibilities that left me with an ache in my skull and a weight in my soul.

But, perhaps, that weight was ballast, rather than burden. And that hollow ache was not the loss of my own desires, but a hollow where something newer, and harder, and better, could grow.

Do we tell Demery and Athe? I asked. *That we know where the Wold is?*

Not yet. Harpy is unpredictable, and Medved thinks of none but Athe and herself. They do not need to know until the time is right.

All right, I said to Tane. *After this matter with Ben is closed, we turn our attention to the Wold. And if the opportunity arises to do something in the meantime? We will take it.*

We drifted in the Lull for some days before we came upon the wreck. Its crew had long perished, with the marks of teeth upon their bones. Within the hold we found a most uncommon cargo—rough-hewn stones of black and grey which, when I neared them, altered my bond with the Other. I have put them to immediate and potent use. However, their source remains elusive.

—FROM THE WRITINGS OF SILVANUS LIRR
AND HOTEN MANIFEST, IN THE 13TH YEAR
OF QUEEN EDITH OF THE AEADINES, EQ.

THIRTY

Doldrums

SAMUEL

We sailed south from Isla Ascra, down the coast of a large island speckled with settlements and fortresses, and draped in lush fields.

"The Il Almere," Athe told me that first morning as I took a turn about deck, enjoying the cool before the dawn. There were dark shadows beneath her eyes from her turn on watch. "The breadbasket of the Mereish South Isles. You recall Lord Howell, Left Hand of the Council? This is his land. This part of the island, at least."

I eyed the vast stretch of land, greys and purples and blacks layered beneath the first, increasing blush of the rising sun. "Benedict is still heading south."

Athe nodded. "All that lies south now is empty ocean and islands outside the Council's control."

"The Usti exiles," I noted.

Athe nodded again. "Clean your pistols and sharpen your sword. Matters will only become more complex from here."

❧

We rounded the southern end of Il Almere on the third night. A storm blew in, heralded by rough waves and stifled sunset. It was not long before one of the crew came to summon Mary from her hammock.

"Sleep," she urged me as she dressed, and leaned up to plant a kiss on my cheek. I could feel alterations in the movement of the ship and hear it in the creak of the timbers, the rush of waves against the hull. "There's no need to play my shadow."

I relented, and slept. And awoke to an entirely new world.

The wind abandoned us as if we had been corked inside a bottle. I looked up at the sky as I came on deck, then turned full circle, taking in every part of the horizon I could see. Nothing uncommon presented itself, aside from the impossibly still mirror of the water, glassy and hushed.

When I moved to the side of the ship to look down, Mary joined me. We peered over the rail, only to see nothing but a perfect reflection of the ship, sky and our own curious faces.

"Saint. It's beautiful," Mary murmured. "What is this?"

"Doldrums," I said. "This is not your doing?"

Mary gave me an arch look. "I'm unsure whether to be offended or flattered. No. I did not. The storm last night was uncooperative; I napped in Athe's hammock and they only just called me back above."

Athe herself strode up to us, followed by Demery. Demery looked more than a little unhappy to be awake and scratched at his salt-and-pepper beard as he squinted out over the mirrored sea like a general over his army.

"Ill luck," he pronounced. "A Lull. We shouldn't be far enough south to hit them yet, but here we are."

"They are common in this region?" I asked.

Demery nodded. "Another reason why the council cares nothing for the world south of Almere. Mary, can you sing us out? The Other tends to thin in these latitudes but we may still make headway."

Mary's focus turned inwards. I did the same, reaching for the Other.

A sheen passed over the world, a thin shadow as if clouds had closed over the sun. But I did not sink into the Other world. Even its edge was hard to find, and visions scurried away from me like mice from a lantern.

Mary gathered her breath, but sang no more than a handful of notes before she trailed off, eyes widening.

"Damn," Demery muttered.

"Are we stuck?" Mary inquired.

"Perhaps?" Demery exchanged a look with Athe, who shrugged. "Consider the Stormwall, an endless, unnatural tempest sourcing its power from the Other. A Lull is the opposite. All contact with the Other is suppressed. Mary, even your connection with Tane may feel different."

"It does." She looked at me as she said it, and I caught a touch of anxiety in her eyes. "It's very unpleasant."

"Just how common are these phenomena?" I asked.

"I have never before encountered one," Athe said. "Neither of us have. I've had little reason to be so far south."

"The Lull may not last," Demery concluded. "For now, we wait."

∞

The next morning I came above as the sun crested the mirrored sea. We had, to all appearances, moved not an inch. Reflections danced across the deck as crewfolk sluiced buckets of water across the newly scrubbed wood, and there was not a peg or a line out of place. Athe presided over it all, a flask in one hand and her gaze on the horizon.

That horizon was, in all fairness, hard to look away from. The colors were richer than in the north, where pale pinks and oranges were the norm. Here, a bloody red ignited the motionless water in a fiery path, casting us all in its bloody glow. To the west, *Harpy's* shadow stretched long into violet murk.

Despite the crew's labors they were a hushed lot, and even the slosh of their buckets and the grate of holystones failed to shatter the peace.

"Mr. Rosser," Athe greeted me. "Have you had any sense of how long this will last?"

I shook my head. "I have not had so much as an inkling since yesterday."

She looked grim, but unsurprised. "I will send out the boats to pull the ship, today, but that may not work. We will need to send for help."

My Sooth's abilities might have been absent, but I caught her meaning. "A Sooth would have the best chance of locating you again."

She nodded. "Mary will need to remain here. If this lifts even slightly and there is any chance to summon a wind, she must be prompt."

"I understand," I said. "How many days of provisions do we have?"

"A week of water. Ten days of food."

"Then I had best not take more than a week."

"You'd best not."

Mary was less than pleased when I told her of my departure, but concluded, "I don't have to like it to understand it. Just be careful, Samuel. Take Brid with you."

"Brid?" I repeated, a little surprised.

"She is fiercely loyal and properly feral, and I like her very much," Mary said. She looked back to the hammock she had been pawing over, sketching lines on the fabric with a bit of charcoal. "Very little in these isles has been kind to us so far, but she has proven herself time and again. If I cannot be with you, take her."

THIRTY-ONE

The Balance of Power

MARY

"Oarship!" Someone bellowed from the maintop.

I shot to my feet, nearly sending my lap full of hammock and embroidery hoop toppling to the deck. I hastily set it on my chair and ran to the rail, following the gaze of the crew out across the glassy sea.

"Two oarships!" the watchman corrected.

"To quarters!" Athe commanded from the quarterdeck.

What followed was a chaos of action—bells ringing, whistles piping, Athe and the gunner and the bosun bellowing, then everyone fell silent.

I joined Demery and Athe as Demery lifted his spyglass, took a breath to assess the oncoming vessels, and passed the glass to Athe.

"Well, I doubt this is our rescue."

My heart jolted. "Are they the same ships who attacked us before?"

Athe assessed the view. "I would say so. Damn them to hell."

"Well, there will be no fleeing," I stated. "I still can't summon a wind."

"Fighting would be foolish," Athe said grimly. "It seems we will finally learn what our Capesh friends want. Let's have the flag of parlay!"

A flag of white and pale blue crosshatching soon joined us on the quarterdeck. With no wind to fill it the crew did not bother running it up the mast, but waved it attached to a long pole. A matching flag appeared on the deck of one of the Capesh ships and a ripple of relief traveled down the deck, though the gunners remained at their posts and the marksmen only shouldered their rifles.

"Greeting, James Demery!" A light female voice called across the water in Mereish, her voice amplified by the water as much as the speaking trumpet she held to her mouth. She was in her mid-thirties, wearing a deep purple frock coat of Capesh cut and a tricorn hat.

Demery accepted a speaking trumpet of his own from the steward.

"You have me at a disadvantage," he returned, not quite genially.

"Captain Wesna Forbara," the woman returned. "The edge of this Lull is four hours south today. Shall we tow you, while I come aboard and explain my business?"

"Would you not prefer to simply open fire from the dark of the night?" Demery inquired.

A moment's pause from Forbara. "Please accept my sincerest apologies on that front. I was advised to take a decisive approach. I see now that that was not only useless, given the qualities of your crew, but uncalled for."

"Did Benedict Rosser advise you of that?"

"He did."

"May I inquire as to why?"

"That is a conversation best had in privacy. I will come aboard, alone, as a show of good faith."

Demery lowered the horn and spoke to Athe, quickly and quietly. Then he relinquished the speaking horn to her, and she spoke across the water to the other woman.

"Send your boat, Forbara," Athe called. "And bring wine."

Forbara raised her trumpet in exaggerated solute, Athe did the same, and both captains turned back to their crew.

"Stand down but tell the crew to remain on alert," Athe instructed the bosun, lingering nearby, then turned to Demery. "We face her together."

Demery nodded and glanced to me. "Mary, keep a weather eye."

Keeping a weather eye involved returning to my chair and my embroidery, which I stared at in distraction for far too long before picking up my needle again and going to work. I watched the Capesh ships over the water between stitches, but there was little to see.

Finally, Athe's first officer exchanged words with the bosun. I set aside my work again as they joined with the Capesh to run lines between *Harpy* and the oarships. Clearly, Athe, Demery and Forbara had come to some kind of agreement.

The enterprise took over an hour, but then the shouts of the sailors changed. There was the clatter of oars, scraping out through their cradles and striking the surface of the waves. Then came a drumbeat, steady and measured. Two more drums joined in, one on each ship, and the oars began to move.

Harpy jerked as the lines went taut and the air stirred past in something I could almost fool myself was a breeze.

Despite the uncertainty of our situation, relieved voices rose all around me.

"Have we been captured?" I asked Demery lowly, after he had seen Forbara back to her boat.

"I believe we have, but we are all pretending to be amiable and polite, and that is a façade we should maintain," Demery replied, equally quietly. He stood conspiratorially close as he added, "The Capesh are looking for the new Ghistwold, and it seems Benedict has convinced them you and Samuel are the best duo to search it out."

The relevance of the observation caught me off guard. Had Samuel let something slip? Had Harpy glimpsed Tane's mind?

I looked at Demery askance.

"Mary," he nudged.

"James," I said evasively.

His eyebrows grew higher.

It's time we told him, I said to Tane in the quiet of my mind.

He is too pragmatic and Harpy too unpredictable, Tane reminded me. *He may simply give the location to the Capesh and be done with it.*

Surely, not.

I will not risk it.

"Do you have a plan?" I asked Demery. "This seems a rather more... complicated situation than usual."

"Not yet," he said, still watching me as if he suspected I'd intended to say something else. "For the time being, hold fast. And be polite."

THIRTY-TWO

Farland

SAMUEL

I slowly straightened, facing down some two dozen staring figures on the docks of a small port. They were a weathered lot, not a soft face among them, and a general lean towards the bloodlines of the central latitudes of the Winter Sea. Nearly all were pale-skinned beneath their tans and there was a certain unity of build and facial structure that made me suspect they were all related. This was no port of call—their attitudes, the lack of children or elders in sight, and the sprawling town's lack of a port mistress made that clear.

The island itself was low and wet, with the town built on one of its highest points. The proliferation of reed in everything from the thatch of roofs to the baskets on the women's backs spoke of marshes inland, and I caught a glimpse of a flat-bottomed pole boat leaning in the lee of one of the houses. Atop the house's roof, a kid goat stared at me with its head cocked.

There was not a scrap of wind. What trees were visible grew tall and perfectly straight, and the sea surrounded the island like a skirt of poured glass.

"Hello," I said, pulling my hat from my head and surveying the assembly. "My name is Samuel Rosser. Who speaks for you?"

One man stepped forward, his blue eyes capped by bushy grey eyebrows. He spoke, but had to repeat himself twice before I was able to navigate through his accent and understand the simple word, "Shipwrecked?"

He was speaking Aeadine, but an archaic dialect. It left me wondering how long these people had been isolated—or had isolated themselves—here.

"My vessel is trapped in a Lull," I returned, stepping up to meet him and offering my hand, which he slowly took. His grip was loose, but not through any lack of strength. "I would hire any boats and able-bodied rowers you have to pull her free. We will pay well."

The man shoved his hand back into the pocket of his worn coat and took in my clothing. "Seems you may. How far out is she?"

I proceeded to give what information I could. Some of the locals trickled away, while others crowded in and began to offer input in their thick, nearly untranslatable dialect.

"May I ask how long your people have been here?" I asked the town's spokesperson, whose name I had gathered—as he had not actually introduced himself—was Ichweny. "And—forgive me—what do you call your settlement?"

"Long enough. Farland," he answered each question perfunctorily, watching his kin begin to toss provisions into boats. Children and elders had begun to slowly filter back into town, the former staring at us while the latter took seats on benches in the shade, some dragging out reed baskets of wool for spinning or taking up the ever-necessary task of weaving nets.

Before the sun reached its zenith, we were back on the waveless sea. The stillness, however, finally broke in the form of a breeze, a timid exhalation from the north that served us not at all. But I felt my connection to the Other return in a prickling wave of half-formed images and intuitions.

I braced one hand on the side of the boat and bowed my head. The Dark Water erupted around me, dark and hushed and nearly devoid of lights. I immediately searched for Mary. I caught sight of her to the south, along with Demery's colors. But they were so faint I feared my eyes might be playing tricks on me. This feeling only solidified when I noted other, unfamiliar lights drifting around them.

"What do you see?" Brid asked.

"*Harpy* is no longer alone," I murmured, wary of my voice carrying over the water. "Perhaps she was rescued. Perhaps not."

Brid surveyed the little armada of boats around us. "Should we send them home?"

I contemplated this momentarily, then shook my head. "No. *Harpy* is not far, and these islanders may prove helpful. If not for their oars, for their number."

She looked at me. "Expecting violence, Mr. Rosser?"

"Prepared for it, Ms. Deeds."

MAGNI PRIMARY —*A subcategory of Adjacent Mage, Magni Primary originates in the abilities of a Magni and is thereafter augmented to extend into the powers of Sooth or Stormsinger. The most unpredictable of Adjacents, the varied abilities of Magni Primaries are difficult to categorize. Some maintain division between their two powers, while others merge into an array of lesser abilities, including Dreamwalking.*

—FROM A DEFINITIVE STUDY OF THE BLESSED;
MAGES AND MAGECRAFT OF THE MEREISH ISLES,
TRANSLATED INTO AEADINE BY SAMUEL I. ROSSER

THIRTY-THREE

The Dreamer's Wake

BENEDICT

I began to dream again on the voyage to Dreska Sank.

My dreams had stopped with the advent of my corruption. I had forgotten what it was to retain any sense of consciousness or experience once I closed my eyes to sleep. And I slept, as a rule, very, very well.

The first night I awoke inexplicably. I heard no sound of watch bells, no change in the movement of the ship that might have awakened me. There was no knock at the door of my cabin, no lurking Miaghis to creep his tentacles around the doorframe.

But as I lay in my hammock, I recalled a… sense. A feeling. It had no source and no substance, but I could not disregard it. It took me hours to return to slumber.

The second time, I became aware of the dream. This one was a sensual thing, a mixture of bare flesh and candlelight and the scent of rosewater. But as my awareness grew, the flesh became water and the candlelights drifted away, taking on varying colors and a steadier burn.

I resented the shift, but the harder I tried to reclaim the heady pleasure of the dream's first act, the more it slipped away from me.

I looked around myself, taking in the Other world Samuel had so often described. I still believed it to be a dream, or at least, suspected it was. I had been in the Other only twice, first on that fateful night when the Black Tide took me, and second on the night Enisca Alamay, Mary and Olsa Uknara healed me. But my dreamer's imagining felt remarkably real now.

I watched a deep purple dragonfly hover before my eyes, then skim away over the water towards a distant light of soft, pulsing red, so pale as to be invisible. A subtle Magni, less even than Enisca. Or an immature one.

That light lured me, drawing me towards a horizon I could not see. North, to Aeadine, to a doorstep, to a staircase, to a door to a small room. Children ran past that room, not in play but in urgency, and beyond the door, through the keyhole, I saw...

Do you not have a daughter? Alamay's voice whispered through the back of my mind.

I turned away from the door.

A woman stood not a pace away. She was a reflection of someone in the waking world, nude save for the obscuring glow of her Sooth's aura. She stood in the ankle-deep water, the light and shadows of fae dragonflies flickering about her.

Vachon watched me shamelessly, a question in her eyes. She began to move around me, scrutinizing me, then casting her eyes north towards where the pale light lay. However I sensed—I knew—that she could not see it as I did.

This was no dream. At least, not anymore.

I was bare and vulnerable in this world where I did not belong. I was wreathed in red Magni light, thick and dark, twined with the same Sooth's green as Vachon.

Vachon came to face me again, looking up into my face. She placed a hand on my chest—a hand I, unfortunately, could not feel—and pushed.

I stumbled back into my bones, into my hammock, in my cabin aboard *The Red Tempest*. I immediately dropped down to the deck with a whump of forgotten blankets, planting my feet like anchors and laboring to find my breath. I felt disoriented, even haunted, and my heart hammered in my skull.

Then I heard the brush of feet on the deck, the creak of a door, and Vachon stood in the doorway of my cabin. She wore her shift with her coat overtop, its shapelessness failing to cover the curves of her calves. Her hair too was uncovered, auburn curls thick about her face.

"You were in the Other," she stated, making no move to enter the room. She spoke in Mereish, but I found my understanding vastly improved. Or rather, I knew enough to intuit the gaps in my knowledge. "Watching me."

"Both were unintentional," I said, pushing my loose hair back from my face. I wore only my shirt, loose at the collar and falling to mid-thigh. The way Vachon was looking at me, however, made me feel as bare as I had been in the Dark Water.

It was a fleeting vulnerability. Once I discarded it, my tension loosened and my focus centered in upon her. We were alone, Vachon and I, in the dark. And surely she would not have placed herself in such a position if she did not want to be there.

I recalled the dream that had bled into the Dark Water, flesh and candlelight. I still felt somewhat outside myself, and the memory was a visceral, primal thing. A vision of the future, perhaps?

"Was that the first time you stepped into the Other?" Vachon asked. "Did you see any visions?"

"I saw you," I said.

She stiffened. "What did you see?"

"Why? Is there something you wish to hide?"

The hostility in her gaze made my blood run all the hotter, and I dropped my gaze meaningfully to her bare calves.

She reached for the doorhandle and started to pull it closed.

I grabbed the door and held it in place. She took a half step back to frown up at me, her gaze accusatory and warning. But she did not leave.

I pushed the door wide again with one and with the other, I clasped her jaw lightly. She startled but, once again, did not walk away. Instead, she watched me with calculation, and a growing... fascination.

I brushed a thumb across her lips, holding her gaze as I searched for the right words to bring her over that threshold and into the cabin. What could I say to turn that hostility and fascination into willingness and want, to convince her to join me in gentile debauchery in the dark until...

Until what? Until the sun rose, and she realized what she had done? Until she backed away from me, unable to trust her own feelings, her own mind, and fled?

Vachon blinked rapidly and, in one smooth step, pulled away. I let her go.

It was not until her footsteps faded that I realized I had not even considered using Magni influence. Part of me wondered if I regretted that.

The other part felt as though he had finally found foothold on a crumbling mountainside, and begun to climb.

FULGA —*Akin to the implings of the northern Winter Sea, fulga possess a passing likeness to a fetal human infant, though they are larger in size. They are treacherous and cunning, frequently luring human prey to their deaths by posing as drowning children.*

—FROM BEASTS AND BEINGS: A SUMMONER'S
OBSERVATIONS IN THE SOUTH MEREISH ISLES,
BY SAMUEL I. ROSSER

THIRTY-FOUR

Southern Cousins

MARY

Firelight filled a beach of reddish sand, capped by small, root-riddled bluffs and a towering forest whose floor was thick with ferns and other verdant undergrowth. It spilled out here and there in green tumbles, lining the numerous small, freshwater creeks that had brought us to the island.

Darkness was falling but sailors—both Capesh and Demery's—still rolled barrels to and fro between the creeks and the regiment of small boats at the waterline.

This is an island fit for a Ghistwold, Tane observed, a note of longing in her voice.

I murmured my agreement. This place was a shelter not only from the sea, but from the Lulls. A breeze stirred my hair and the leaves of the trees, soothing and familiar, and I could sense the presence of the Other close at hand.

A good island, I agreed.

All three ships anchored were offshore, but most of the crew was gathered around the bonfires. Polite niceties had, apparently, extended to pretending our rescue was some great victory, and worthy of celebration. Or, perhaps, the Capesh intended it as an apology for attacking us the week before.

I found all of it dubious and unsettling. But that did not mean I was about to pass by a feast.

Various game and fish roasted on spits and the Capesh had managed to erect an open-air kitchen in record time, filling the air with the scents of baking bread, roasting vegetables, sweet honey and an intoxicating combination of spices.

A handful of Athe's crew were already well into their cups, but the majority were cautious, withdrawn and watching the celebrants with skepticism.

None of them were armed.

I sat on the edge of it all, waiting for the hammer to fall and filling my belly in preparation for it.

There are Otherborn beings on this island, Tane told me as I leaned back against a fallen tree trunk. *A large concentration.* She added in answer to my unspoken question, *Not ghistings.*

I saw what she saw in the Dark Water. Lights speckled the island and the surrounding sea, clots and trails of them. But only here. Beyond, to nearly every side, there was utter emptiness. A Lull, as seen from the Other side.

There were other clusters of lights, but they were far distant. Other gaps between the Lulls?

They're fleeing the Lulls like us, I surmised, skin prickling. *Are they dangerous?*

They seem to be keeping their distance, Tane said, without truly answering the question.

"Would you like a drink?" The voice was vaguely familiar, and broke me from my conversation.

I looked up to see a young man. He was Capesh by his accent, holding a bottle of wine.

"What do you want?" I asked, anticipating a proposition and not in the mood to be polite about it.

"I am Atello," he supplied, a little sardonically. "You broke me out of prison. Though you did not mean to, perhaps."

I lowered my plate. "You were with Sam."

"I was, and I reunited with my ship," Atello said, nodding to the little armada. "May I sit? I have something to tell you. Or rather to show you, if I may."

I was intrigued enough to shift over and pat the sand next to me. It was bizarre to see him, but I sensed a potential ally in him—at least a not-enemy—and I was intrigued.

Atello sat and wedged the bottle into the sand between us. He listened to a musician ply the first few long, sweet notes from her fiddle before he reached out and took my hand.

Before I could rebuke him or pull away, I felt a tingle at the point of our contact.

Mother, a ghisting whispered.

I drew a sharp breath and clutched Atello's hand in return.

Child, Tane replied.

The rush of communication was momentary, but intense. I wavered, my senses overwhelmed, my human mind trying and failing to process the rush of ghisten conversation.

An expanse of rock and ice. Burning ships in the night. A man, his face full of firelight and benevolent malice. A shard of wood embedded in a beleaguered, dying heart.

Atello slowly released my hand. I stared at my fingers, then at his face.

"You're one of Lirr's *ghiseau*. The ones he made in the north."

He nodded. "I would have revealed myself before, but my ghisting advised against it. Only my captain knows what I am, though I believe Voskin suspected. I recognized Rosser in Voskin's pit, and you, when you arrived. From that night."

Again, I saw in my mind's eye a chaos of fire and snow, heard gunshots and felt Silvanus Lirr's hands on my shoulders, shoving me into hungry flames. I recalled too the host of faces that had watched me, willing and unwilling, ensorcelled and horrified, as I had stood in the shadow of Tane's great, sleeping ghisten tree.

Atello had been one of them.

"How... how did we not realize what you are?" I asked, more

myself than him. "Samuel must never have looked at you in the Other."

"No, and we never touched. Though I am not a mage, I understand that *ghiseau* auras are easy to miss. I have worked hard to keep my secrets, for the sake of my people. The Mereish recruit anyone with our… peculiarities."

I nodded, my shock finally giving way. "The Ess Noti?"

"You encountered them too?"

"I have."

"Oi, Capesh, do you dance?" One of Athe's crew stood over us, smiling at Atello with open invitation. Behind her, others were taking to an open stretch of sand to dance—or balter merrily, depending on how drunk they were.

"I do," Atello grinned. "The next song?"

She touched her forehead in salute, snagged the arm of another woman as she passed, and joined the celebrants.

"I am helping my people find a new Ghistwold," Atello said.

A cool breeze brushed past us, threaded with warmth from the fires and the scent of the coming feast.

He had said it. He had simply come out and said it, and I wished he had not. I was willing to lie to him: my hesitation was not in that.

I now knew something about Forbara and her crew that some would kill for. I might not be in chains, but I was most definitely a prisoner.

Tell him nothing, Tane said.

Of course not, I hissed back. *But if Atello is a ghiseau, he will be able to communicate with the ghisting in the hold. They will see what we saw, and find Lirr's papers if they search the ship.*

Then we need to go hide them.

I felt Atello's eyes upon me, waiting and assessing. "Mary?"

I decided to buy time. "What's in that bottle?"

Atello uncorked the stuff and let me sniff, though the

expression in his eyes told me he knew what I was about. Beneath the nip of alcohol, I smelled the molasses and spice of rum.

I held out my cup, and he dutifully poured me a knuckle. I sniffed at it slowly, brushing my nose across the rim of the cup as I surveyed the beach, the fires and the ships, with their bright lanterns and the vague outlines of masts against the night sky.

"Can you sense the new Wold?" Atello pressed. He leaned forward, close enough to touch again. I did not yield, holding my ground and meeting his gaze. He added respectfully, "Mother Tane."

"No," Tane replied to Atello through my lips. "The Mereish Trade Company ships are also searching for a new Wold. You and your captain ought to be more cautious."

"We know," he affirmed soberly. "All the more reason to help us find it first."

"Such a Wold should be left in peace," Tane said with a bitter wistfulness.

Atello's gaze was sad, and rimmed with ghisten light as he said, "If the world was fair and good, yes. But it is only a matter of time before someone takes that Wold, and I would rather it be my people. We would be good caretakers, I assure you."

As soon as he was out of sight I wedged the bottle into the sand, rose, and merged into the shadows.

Someone is going to stop us, I hissed to Tane as we strode towards the waves and the rows of beached longboats, giving pools of firelight a wide berth. A few stragglers or couples lingered out here in the darkness, but no one intervened.

When I was far enough to feel relatively alone, I tugged off my coat, stockings and shoes and raked my hair into a tight knot at the back of my head. Waves lapped at my bare feet.

This is useless, Tane. Atello will notice.

In response, she nudged me into the waves. I *tsk*ed in frustration, stomping out until the water lapped at my thighs. Then, I began to swim.

At first, the exercise was nearly pleasant, and my irritation waned. The water was cool and relatively still. I enjoyed swimming, and was certainly in want of a bath.

But I could not pretend to be out here for pleasure. Music and voices drifted from the beach, reminding me just how many eyes might pick me out of the water. The ships creaked, still surprisingly distant.

And then I saw the hands in the water. I thought them a trick of the eye, but no—someone was drowning, flailing and reaching, between myself and the closest ship.

All that remained was their hands. Their head was already submerged, a lonely figure, drowning alone in the dark.

The profound sadness of the sight struck me a fraction before I comprehended the reality of it. I started swimming frantically towards them.

I grabbed cold, limp fingers just as they slipped under the water. At the same moment, my toes touched bottom. The sea remained quite shallow here, barely deep enough to drown an adult. But the hand was small. Shockingly small.

A child?

The fingers cinched closed and I was jerked below the water.

Orange light erupted and a face loomed before me. Not the face of a desperate, drowning person, but an impling-like creature, feral and canine and possessed of giant eyes in the sides of its skull. It grinned a toothy little grin—its mouth was far too small for all its rows of teeth. Then it pulled my hand towards its face and bit down on one of my fingers.

Blood bloomed. I shrieked, but the water muffled the sound. I flailed and fought and burst into the air, screaming and trying desperately to reclaim my arm.

Tane ignited and rushed into the creature's face. It released me and, in a pop of shadow, vanished.

Tane's light dimmed. My toes bobbed onto the sand as I clutched my hand to my chest, conscious only of hot blood and a pulsing, thrumming, growing pain.

I pinned my eyes as wide as they could possibly go. *Where is it? Where did it go?*

Something brushed past my feet. I looked down just in time to see an orange light sweep by me beneath the waves. Then, in a splattering, shuddering chorus, a score of hands thrust up through the water all around me. Two score. Three.

Reaching. Waving. Shuddering.

The sea boiled orange, like rust and old blood and dying flames.

"Demery!" I screamed. "Athe!"

I heard shouts from shore, and from the ships.

I struck out wildly. *Keep them away from me!*

Small hands seized my feet and I kicked at the same time as Tane's light flared, sheathing me and surging outwards. The hands released.

But not before I felt the tearing of teeth. They were trying to bite off my toes. Trying to take little chunks from my calves, my thighs.

I swam. Tane fought. And when I slammed my hands against the hull of the nearest ship, shouting for help, I didn't care that it was Capesh hands who dropped a ladder and hauled me aboard. I tumbled onto the deck, only just managing to save my wounded hand from taking the brunt of my weight.

"What the hell were those?" I panted, clutching one of my rescuers. They had marvelously muscular arms, and if I couldn't have Samuel consoling me just then, by the Saint I would take those.

Another sailor arrived with a lantern, flooding us with warm, welcome, natural light.

"Implings," the man said, steadying me. For captors, they really were quite gentle-handed. "Of a kind. Fulga, in Capesh. Did they take any of your fingers?"

I raised my left hand. It was a mess of blood, pulsing and burning with increasing levels of pain, but my fingers were intact.

Why, then, did I feel as though I was about to pass out?

I squinted at my hand more intently. My fingers were multiplying, blurring. In fact the whole world had begun to feel oddly distant, sound distorting and the drip of water and the feel of the breeze becoming numb.

"Please catch me," I requested of my rescuers, and collapsed.

THIRTY-FIVE

The Mirrored Deep

MARY

I awoke to find myself lying on a cot in a steady glow of ghisten light. Demery sat next to me on another cot with barely a foot between us. We were surrounded on three sides by crosshatching iron bars, with our backs to the hull.

Beyond the bars, a ship's hold was draped in darkness. A cat's glowing eyes blinked at us, once, then the feline vanished.

Eyes in the dark. Eyes in a ghastly face with too many teeth and too small a mouth.

Memory chased me into full consciousness. I threw up my left hand, finding it carefully bandaged and smelling of camphor.

"Demery?" I breathed. "What happened?"

"We are prisoners," He informed me, his tone pragmatic. "I would like to blame you, but I suppose it was inevitable. Do you remember the fulga?"

"The implings in the water?" I pressed my hand to my chest. "Saint. Yes. Are my fingers still—"

"All accounted for, along with your toes," he said, managing to sound not remotely consoling. "However fulga, unlike their northern cousins, are venomous. You are very lucky you made it to the ship before you collapsed. Tane would likely have saved you, I am sure, but in what state? I cannot say. Being torn to shreds by fulga may be rather too close to immolation for a *ghiseau* to endure."

I put my unbandaged hand to my forehead, which ached fiercely. My feet did too, and my legs, and I could not bear to imagine the tears and bites more bandages concealed.

I reached instinctively for Tane. She felt distant again, in the same way as she had in the Lull. It was, I realized with sudden clarity, very close to the feeling I had had on Isla Ascra, when she had been in Lirr's cavern.

I could not contemplate that just then, however.

For as my awareness expanded, I realized that the sounds of the ship were different than *Harpy*'s. I heard a steady grinding I supposed must be oars, and the pounding of a drum.

"We are back in a Lull?" I pressed. "We left the island?"

"You and I and the Capesh have," Demery said. "*Harpy* was disabled and left behind with Athe and the crew. You and I are prisoners, as the Capesh are convinced you know where the new Ghistwold is." When he looked at me now, there was accusation in his eyes. "They discovered a stash of maps and journals, and notes in yours and Samuel's hands. No—no excuses. Tane has explained it all to me. And she has given the Capesh a heading."

I reached instinctively for Tane, searching for her reasoning, but our connection remained dampened.

"Forgive me, but why are *you* here?" I asked, squinting at him. "They only need me."

"An ill-timed fit of valor," he replied. "Forbara is an admirable woman, and I would like to think the best of her, but she is single-minded in her pursuit of the Wold. So I determined I had best accompany you."

"You came with me voluntarily," I translated, my heart doing something odd and embarrassing in my chest.

"Also, if you *did* die, unlikely as that was, Forbara determined I was the next best thing," Demery added.

I let out a huff of a laugh and sagged back onto my cot. It occurred to me to be frightened, but circumstances had moved too rapidly for proper fear. Besides, Samuel was still out there, and he would be looking for me. *Harpy* was safe, provided none of the crew decided to swim with the fulga.

And Tane was very likely headed to her Ghistwold. That, I realized, despite the thinness of our connection, was a great source of consolation.

But why had she suddenly elected to include Forbara in her quest? What had changed?

The answer was already there in my mind, sifted through from Tane's consciousness and as part of me as my own memories.

I looked over at Demery and he looked back at me, arms laced over his chest. "Exactly what heading did Tane give them?"

∽

The ship gave a long, low moan. Tane's presence came into full focus as the Lull passed, and her light filled my eyes.

Demery too climbed to his feet, ghisten light bleeding from his eyes.

We did not speak but stepped up to the bars, side by side. Side by side we took hold of them as, with a bleed of ghisten flesh, Tane and Harpy sank into the wood into which the bars were affixed. It began to crack and flake and crumble.

Demery and I threw our weight against our prison. The barrier shook and a bolt clattered down, but did not yield.

"If this doesn't work," I grunted. "Tell me you have another plan?"

Three objects punched through the hull of the ship behind us. Demery and I froze, staring at the long, stained and glistening lengths of three enormous teeth.

The teeth ground, the deck rattled, and the entire ship tilted. I slammed into the hull, barely avoiding being impaled by a giant tooth. The I slammed back into the bars with a sudden, blinding crack.

My next awareness was of aches, a slosh of cold water and the cracking of wood, the clatter of oars and the screams of sailors. Then, a roar.

I thought it was the beast, for an instant. Then more water gushed over me. I realized the roar was the ocean itself, surging through the gouges where the teeth had been. Where the back wall of our prison had been. Where the *hull* had been.

Demery staggered to his feet, battered by rising water. There was another series of cracks, the ship rocked, and the water closed over us.

Darkness did, too. It was terrifying, the darkness, and the force of the water. It blasted my hair back from my face, pried into my nose and mouth and eyes, bitter with cold and thick with salt.

Demery's form loomed in the churning darkness. A grey-blue ghisten glow seeped from his skin, brightest around his eyes, and Tane responded. My skin ignited and the shadows flew back.

I saw the rift in the hull, a splinter-toothed maw of ocean murk. I saw the swirling rush of water that prevented us from escaping, laced with sand and algae and threads of Otherworldly light.

But the flow of water was slowing. My clothing tugged less and Demery's loose hair began to float back around his cheeks.

I met the man's gaze and we pushed off. He seized the side of the rupture and pushed me out first, untangling my skirts from the splinters. On the other side, in the cold, open vastness of the deep, I spun around and planted my boots on the hull, then reached back. He grasped my arm and I pulled him through, his broader body raking splinters in blooms of blood.

I saw no tentacles, no teeth in the water around us. But pale illumination began to gather below our feet, turning Demery's face skeletal and casting our shadows upwards in beams of spectral white light.

Morgories.

I felt an absurd flash of relief—*just* morgories, not some new terror. At least I would be eaten by something familiar.

But it certainly had not been morgories who bit a massive hole in the side of Forbara's now sinking ship.

Demery grabbed my arm and together we surged upwards, fighting the pressure of the water and pull of the current. The morgory light pursued us. I saw the creatures swirling below, hundreds upon hundreds. But after the first few meters of pursuit, the ghisten light deterred them and they diverted, swarming the sinking ship instead.

The sound as they began to devour the vessel was one that I would never forget. It was a churring and a cracking, like a strong wind through the driest of autumn leaves, backed by the assault of hail on a wooden roof. The water should have muffled it but instead, it transformed it into a physical feeling, a constant ripple of gooseflesh on my skin.

Distracted as I was, I never saw the tentacle, only felt a lungful of water burst from my lips as it cinched. My world spun. I scrambled for Demery but my hands found smooth, scaly flesh instead—flesh with the barest Otherworldly glow. More tentacles wrapped around my wrist, then arm, with serpentine snaps. The pressure was intense, so much so that I cried out in a stream of water. Dozens of small, sucking mouths closed over my skin and clothing.

Tane's light flared, as did the creature's. I reared back, jerking at my arm and staring at my captor. A pair of narrow, vertical eyes looked back at me for half a heartbeat, then a forest of tentacles rose around us. A dozen. A hundred.

As one they slapped down and the beast shot off through the water like a cannonball. I felt my shoulder pop and every muscle, every joint in my body strain as I was hauled through the crushing deep.

My last glimpse of the ship was a broken hull and tangles of sail, sinking in a mesmerizing confusion of currents and debris, the bubbles streaming behind me, and an endless assault of Otherworldly lights. Demery was lost in the melee.

Then, I saw *it*. A beast so massive, I could not see the edges of it. But I saw the arc of its teeth, rising up towards the sinking belly of the Capesh ship, ready to swallow it whole.

Then I was too far away. Water and darkness closed in. The ship was gone. Demery was gone. My consciousness fractured and all I knew was the rush of water and the crush of tentacles.

Finally, I drifted to a slow, bumping stop against an unseen barrier. Sand plumed around me, soft and slow.

I squinted upwards. There, for the first time, I saw my captor whole. It was an octopus or a squid, but with more tentacles than one could reasonably ascribe to one being. A great pillar of a shell rose above it, overgrown with barnacles and seaweeds. Its soft, burned orange light fluctuated as it gusted away, abandoning me on the sandy shelf and confronting another orange light. Another nosta. I had a sense of a battle, beast against beast in a silent rush of water, though my eyes struggled to focus. I saw only the light, the sand, movement and whirls of tentacles and teeth.

I retreated further, my body no longer demanding air, relying instead upon Tane and her connection to the Other to sustain us.

Her connection to the Other. Saint, if we drifted into another Lull, if that connection was cut off while I was surrounded by the crushing deep—

I began to swim frantically for the surface. Gradually, the pressure on my ears eased. The water warmed, ever so slightly.

Air caressed my skin, and I drifted until my feet touched a hidden sandbar. I crawled up until I could kneel, waist deep in the water, and then began to retch.

When my lungs were full of salty air instead of salty water, I sank back onto my bottom and stared out across the black waves. Tane materialized before me, prowling atop the still surface of the water in a smoky, half-formed rendition of herself.

We're on the edge of another Lull, I observed, even my internal voice somehow feeling hoarse and haggard.

We are. Her light pooled on the mirror of the water, casting an eerie, nearly perfect reflection that made me feel disoriented and nauseous all over again. Which image was the ghisting? What was water, and what was sky? Or were we simply in the Dark Water?

Tane cocked her head to one side and circled me, staring out at our surroundings.

Is anything else going to try to eat us?

That nosta would not have eaten you, Tane corrected absently. *You were a gift for its mate.*

I recalled the second nosta and cringed. Perhaps that had not been battle I was witnessing.

So, the mate would have eaten me, I said.

And used your defecated bones to structure its nest. But I would not have let her.

I tried to moan, coughed and spat up another pleasant stew of seawater, bile and spittle. It preceded to drift around me in viscous chunks and I moved wearily away. My entire body felt bruised, riddled with ridges where the tentacles had stuck to me. Not to mention the stinging pain of fulga bites.

Can you sense Demery? I asked, though I feared the answer.

Distantly, she said to my relief. Tane looked around, her form solidifying here, and disintegrating a bit more there. *They should be able to find us. Do you feel that?*

I turned to follow her gaze, splashing away a drift of my own bile, and squinted into the endless dark. My human senses roiled at the lack of input—no light, no texture, not even a star in the sky.

But there. I did sense something. It felt like the last strains of a sound, waking a sleeper from a dream.

Tane sensed my affirmation. *That is a Ghistwold.*

THIRTY-SIX

The Stone Forest

MARY

The sandbar on which I walked broadened here and narrowed there, joining with other unseen paths and turning the sea into a labyrinth. As time stretched on and I forced worn muscles into one slogging step after another, it became clearer to me why the Ghistwold had remained so protected. Between the Lulls and the sandbars, only the shallowest, oared vessels might be able to cross this area. Vessels like the Capesh sailed.

Despite the fact the Capesh had abducted us, I could find no will within me to celebrate the sinking of Forbara's ship or my supposed freedom. Captivity had been far more comfortable than slogging through the night in my shift and stays, shoulders burdened with damp petticoats and hair caked into knots and tufts.

But when the sun began to rise, all self-pitying thoughts were quelled. A warm wind blew across the crystalline surface of the sea, stirring patterns of delicate ripples. Soon those ripples caught the growing light of the sun, and the water around me ignited in a blush of violet, pink and gold. I no longer walked through shallow, gloomy waters; I stood upon the finest of stained glass, with the sun the flame of a candle of light.

I stopped moving, my own ripples gentling and fading into the wind's broader flow. The sensation of the Ghistwold came on that wind. I followed its pull and saw, closer than I could have imagined in the dark of the night, a series of islands rising out of the sea. I knew the shape of them, their ledges and arches, and a thrill of discovery shot through me.

I began to move more quickly. I had to swim the final stretch to land, but I hardly cared once my feet touched solid rock. I immediately stripped what remained of my outer clothes, boots and stockings and all, until I wore only my shift. Then I collapsed onto my back, splayed like a starfish left behind by the tide, and closed my eyes.

The sun was a balm, warming me through. And beneath me, within the rock, I felt a presence—ghistings.

Their presence did not allow me to rest for long. Soon I was dressed again and moving, now slightly drier, and with every step I took, my sense of the ghistings increased.

Then as I crested a rise, it wavered. The wind died too, leaving me back in the familiar, deadening presence of a Lull.

The island dropped steeply down into a series of lagoons or little lakes, some deeper than others, and many patched with trees. Some had their branches reaching above the water— dead branches, sun-bleached branches. Others were entirely submerged, their presences only hinted at by shadows in the water and a feeling in my bones. More islands rose all around, marked here and there with rock arches and swaths of scrub, but very few trees grew on the land. Some of them were normal trees, uninhabited by ghistings. But all of them, at least in part, were petrified.

From this height I could see patterns in the bare rock of the island, striations of a black and grey that swirled and thinned and broadened and faded. Where it was most prominent, the ghisten trees were entirely stone. Where it thinned, half-petrified trees huddled.

I turned, looking back towards the open sea and the sandbars

I'd just come across. I saw wave-pummeled threads of darker sand threading through lighter stretches, a mixture which, presumably, carried on across the sea floor.

I made for the nearest tree, marking shifts in my connection with Tane and the Other as I strode over ribbons of black. Sure enough, our bond came and went in proximity to those ribbons. Just like the stones in Lirr's lair. The effect was nauseating.

But my concern for the Wold was stronger.

The nearest tree was not large, an immature cedar of some variety with red bark that shed threads under my touch. Its branches were clear of leaves and petrification climbed up one side like rot. The source of that petrification seemed not the be the rock immediately below the tree, however, but the water of the pool into which the tree's roots had stretched. Its stone bowl was shot through with black rock.

Water seems to amplify the effect, I noted.

Or the water is simply saturated with it, Tane returned.

We delved further into the strange, watery Wold. I walked ridges of rock between the lagoons, careful not to touch the water, and gradually I became aware that I had begun to drift in a singular direction. It was as if pulled there by an unseen thread, a dreamer's instinct like a Sooth. I squinted ahead.

There, I saw a collection of stumps. There were several smaller ones, some of the least petrified wood in the entire Wold. But on a little island of its own, a larger stump languished. It was crudely hacked, working around roots thick with petrification, and the type of tree that had stood there was unidentifiable. But what type of ghisting had inhabited it was clear.

Her. Tane murmured in the quiet of my mind, her horror a whisper and a thrum in my chest. *That was their Mother Tree.*

∞

"Miss Firth."

I turned from where I sat against a rock, the back of my outer skirt raised over my head against the sun like a shepherdess, and peered up.

Demery descended the rise towards me, surveying our surroundings. He looked startlingly put together, his hair tied back with a fragment of cloth and his clothing dry, if salt-caked. He was also slung about with a musket, a satchel and a flask of water, which bounced against his flank as he reached the bottom of the hill, skirted the dead Mother Tree, and made his way towards me.

"Is that fresh water?" I asked, my voice appropriately raspy. I pointed at the pools. "This eventually turns one to stone, apparently."

"Intriguing." He disentangled the flask and handed it to me. It was large, and he helped me steady it as I took my first greedy drink, then a slower second one. When I was less feral, he unloaded the rest of his supplies and pointed to the satchel. "There is food in there."

I dug in, only bothering to wonder where the supplies had come from once a chunk of flat bread and a long twist of salted beef was on its way to my stomach.

"Only Forbara's flagship sank," Demery explained. He continued to study the Ghistwold as he spoke, and I suspected silent communication between him and Harpy. "I and other survivors were rescued by the other ship as a new Lull blew in. Harpy had some sense of where you'd gone, however, so I stole a boat and provisions and left in the chaos."

"They let you just row away?"

Demery gave me an arch look. "I am a pirate, Miss Firth. I have a certain array of skills."

"Or they let you go to follow you."

"Perhaps," he admitted. "However, darkness was my close companion, and they certainly did not see which way I went."

I decided I was too hungry to care. I tore into a wedge of cheese, dipped it in some kind of fruit preserve, and pushed it between my dry lips. By the time I chased it down with more water, Demery had focused on the petrified, butchered stump of the Mother Tree.

"Is any of her left?" he asked.

I shook my head. "Not that we've sensed. Either she went willingly or what remains of her roots were not enough to hold her in our world. It's the stone, Demery."

Quickly, I explained my observations of the black rock. I told him of Lirr's lair too, and of the connection to the ore Voskin dealt in.

"You kept all this from me." Demery said in disapproval. I knew he did not speak just to me, but to Tane as well. "Do you realize what this means? The true value of this place," he threw out a hand to encompass the Wold and islands, "is *not* ghistings, not primarily. It's the ore. Saints, there's enough of it here to... the possibilities are limitless. Forging talismans will be nothing compared to what the Mereish could do with this."

"Perhaps if the ore was mined, the land and the water could recover, and the Ghistwold could grow," I added, Tane's thoughts still firmly entrenched in the ghisten side of it all. "Or the trees could be harvested and moved to a new island, one more habitable. Tane could heal them and give them a new Mother Tree."

Together we surveyed the Wold again, and my eyes lingered particularly long on the petrified trees beneath the water.

"There are many possibilities. But for now, we need a better vantage from which to make a proper assessment," Demery concluded. "That, and I am ill at ease without a clear view."

Gathering my resolve, I thrust out a hand and he hauled me to my feet.

Together we began to climb, first out of the low area where the lagoons lay, then up onto the surrounding ridgeline and higher, towards one of the arches. It was unexpectedly easy to climb, broad and with numerous footholds, and soon the retired pirate and I stood looking down at a remarkable view of the region. Expanses of pink and grey and black rock, baked by the sun and patched with modest growth. Pools of clear water, rivers of seawater, inlets and tidal pools and lagoons. It stretched on and on, until the still, flat horizon swallowed it into obscurity.

"I see no settlements," I remarked. "No ruins."

"Indeed." Demery scratched his forehead and turned full circle. He looked about to speak, but abruptly cut himself off and swung back, eyes pinned to the north and the open sea. "However, I do see ships."

THIRTY-SEVEN

The Shadows of Saints

SAMUEL

Mary sprinted towards me down a barely submerged sandbar, bare feet splashing, skirts tucked up into her belt. Another figure strode behind her at a steadier pace, his posture and gate identifying him as Demery.

Harpy's absence was a pressing concern, but the sight of Mary dashing pell-mell towards me was all I could think of.

I splashed out of Ichweny's boat into thigh-deep water and strode onto the sandbar. I caught Mary as she flung her arms around me, staggering under the strength of her embrace.

"Are you fleeing something, or simply glad to see me?" I asked, peering over her shoulder.

Demery, still some distance off, waved his hat in perfunctory greeting. I raised a hand in return.

Mary dropped back down. "You're not dead," she said, taking my face between her hands and kissing me thoroughly.

"Thank the Saint," I said through her lips, and she laughed.

When we disentangled, it was to Ichweny calling from the boat, "Where is your ship, Mr. Rosser?"

"We are castaways, I fear," Demery replied. He was nearly with us, and his voice carried across the water and distance, as Ichweny's did. "Who are you?"

We made our introductions. Demery was notably cautious of

the Farlanders, but that was not unexpected nor unwarranted. My Sooth's abilities might be quiet here in a Lull, but I still had eyes. I did not miss the change in the Farlander's expressions when they realized *Harpy* truly was not present, and my suspicions about their intentions firmed into conviction.

But Mary was with me once more, whole and well save some bandages, and was in exceptionally good cheer. Though there was a strained edge to her merriment, I was buoyed.

Even if the day ended with gunshots and stabbing, Mary was tight to my side, warm and firm under my hand. All would be well.

I would ensure it.

"This is… quite the rescue," she murmured behind the smile. "Very rustic. Likely better than the ones we found, though."

The sun beat upon us and the waveless sea glistened, disturbed only by the movement of the little armada. Mary scanned the boats, noting Brid and smiling.

"What happened?" I pressed.

"The Capesh, but I doubt we will encounter them again," Mary said, patting my chest and slipping from my grip. The look she gave me was complex, a mix of regret and practicality, and promised a more detailed explanation to come.

"If you are amenable, my ship was bound for a particular island before we were attacked by beasts, and my companion and I were so unfortunately washed away. If I describe it to you, could you locate it?" Demery asked, looking to Ichweny. He nodded back to the low, rocky islands. "Presuming this is a rescue, of course, and you do not intend to leave us here on this Saint-forsaken rock."

"This is no place for anyone to linger," Ichweny replied. He surveyed the sandbars through narrowed eyes. "This whole place is cursed."

"You will hear no protest from me." I knew Demery well enough to see the flicker of relief in his expression. I glanced back to Mary, but her face revealed nothing.

Demery added, "Permission to come aboard?"

Ichweny beckoned and soon after, the Farlanders had us moving at steady pace away from the islands. Mary situated herself between Brid and I and, when Brid discretely slipped a knife into Mary's hands, she took it without a word.

∞

The journey to *Harpy* was long and laborious. Everyone took turns at the oars save Mary, who pled her wounded hand and stared over the glassy sea, clearly preoccupied. I labored at my oar and silently vowed to learn the truth of what had befallen her and Demery as soon as I could.

Darkness began to fall, chasing the sun over the horizon in a bloody bloom of scarlet and orange and gold. The Farlanders put in at a scrubby island, built fires and set to fishing, singing a rhythmic chant that echoed and built off one another until schools of fish churned in the water around them.

If it were not for the weight of the Lull, I would have called it sorcery.

My rescue party and I took to a fire with Demery and Mary, hunkering against the eerie still of the night. With no breeze, the fire burned straight towards the star-cast sky, even its sparks subdued.

Discretely, Demery told us what had befallen *Harpy*, but his description of the barren islands he and Mary had been found on was still vague.

I was forced to wait until everyone else had gone to sleep, bundled around the fire, before my questions were answered.

"A full Ghistwold," I mused. I watched the remaining Farlanders as they too turned in for the night, overturning their boats on the dry sand and crawling beneath them with goodnight calls in their ancient Aeadine. "That is momentous."

"It is," Mary said, voice so low I barely heard it. While I watched our dubious allies she glanced at Demery, who lay with his hat over his face and one arm behind his head. "But we have more pressing concerns. Like how long it will be before these islanders gut us, or chain us to oars. At least they will not have much use for Stormsingers and Sooths, living in the Lulls."

"I think they will simply attempt to take *Harpy* and leave us naked on the nearest rock," I speculated.

"Well, there are worse seasons to be left naked in."

I considered her, every soft curve and windblown lock of hair. "I would rather you remain clothed, given our mixed company. I may become irrational and jealous, and lose all dignity."

She grinned broadly, eyes flashing in the firelight. "Would you now?"

Stalwartly resisting a grin of my own, I reached over to tug her skirt down over her calves.

She slyly slid it back out again, wiggling her bare toes in the sand, and despite the circumstances, I could not help but laugh.

"Saint, I love you," I said.

"I love you, too," she said, and leaned into my side.

For that moment, all was right in the world—the fire warm and the night cool, the sand soft and Mary softer. But when I looked down at her face, it was not simply the firelight that reflected in her eyes.

There was a ghisten glow.

∽

Before dawn crested the horizon, the Farlanders floated their boats. Our party was distributed more broadly than the day before, under the banner of allocating able bodies to the oars. But the look Demery and I exchanged told me that he, too, recognized this as a ploy.

Still the Farlanders would not be dissuaded, and short of enacting violence then and there, where we stood no chance of success. There was naught to be done.

We set off, Mary, Brid and I in Ichweny's head boat, Demery in another, and so on.

We endured another long session at the oars, broken only by the Farlander's chanting work songs. By noon, a large, lush island emerged from the sea with *Harpy* anchored offshore. A soft breeze blew and, with its gentle brush across my hot, sweaty skin, the Other returned to me.

The lights of beasts prickled to life at the edges of my senses.

The Farlanders also noted the breeze, but without relief. Given the lights I could see and what Mary had told me of beasts sheltering between Lulls, they had likely learned to fear the wind.

Some Farlanders rose to their feet, balancing with spears in hand, eyes fixed on the water. The sight of those spears only added to the rising tension as we drew closer. I began to breathe more deeply, slowing my oarwork to conserve strength.

The Farlanders produced a worn, sun-bleached flag of parlay and ran it up the mast of Ichweny's head boat, where the breeze flapped it over our heads.

Athe appeared on *Harpy's* deck, along with a great portion of her crew. They had wisely gone to quarters, and did not stand down as our boat bobbed close.

"James," Athe called down to Demery. "Who are your friends?"

"The good people of Farland," Demery called back, his tone a touch theatrical. "They have very kindly rescued Mary and I and offered to pull us into a wind, but fortune seems to be with us and that will not be necessary."

Ichweny coughed and scratched at his beard and, glancing around at his little armada, nodded towards *Harpy*.

An arm laced around my neck. My Sooth's senses warned me and I ducked, grabbing the arm instead and hurling the attacker

right over the side of the boat. At the same moment Mary leveled
a knife at another Farlander's throat, forcing the man to back off,
hands in the air.

Another figure lunged at Mary from behind. My attempt
to intervene met with a pistol to the face, but Brid delivered the
attacker such a punch that a tooth struck my face, leaving a trail of
blood. The offending Farlander toppled into the water.

Mary leapt onto the rail, sending the boat rocking and water
sloshing. She tottered, very nearly toppled into the sea herself, and
leapt for the fore of the boat. There was a small platform there and
she took to it like a stage, looking back down the boat at Ichweny.

Tane manifested. At first she was a sheen across Mary's skin.
Then she began to expand, growing out from Mary until she
was three times the woman's size, ethereal and billowing in the
breeze.

Behind and beneath her, Mary stilled, her eyes pits of ghisten
light, her aspect somehow older and darker, less of this world. Her
appearance chilled me and, in the same breath, stirred something
I could not name. It was a feeling that recalled cathedrals and
mountains, tempests and moonlight on ice. It was deep forests
and the vastness of the horizon.

And it was *Mary*.

Demery was also on his feet on his boat, the Farlanders
cowering back as Harpy prowled around him, flicking through
her masks. He had something of the look that Mary had, but if she
was the sun, he was a shadow.

Both boats had shuddered to a halt in the water, as did all in
proximity. The crackle of wood filled the air as oars began to
shatter; masts began to moan as Tane and Harpy took control.

Beneath the water, the lights of Otherborn beasts began to
converge.

The Farlanders that had gone overboard lurched back aboard
with desperate speed, helped along by their comrades.

My gaze wanted to return to Mary, but I did not permit it. Instead, I recalled my own part to play and took my own opportunity.

"To me," I called.

Grotesque faces and reaching, shuddering hands erupted through the waves. Tentacles crept over gunnels and, deep in the forest on the island, trees shuddered as winged Otherborn beasts erupted in great, bellow-like clouds.

Ichweny was still in the center of our boat, a pistol in one hand. He stared from me to Mary to Demery, to the ghistings and the monsters all around, and shot straight into the air.

With that, the Farlanders lowered their weapons.

I sent the monsters back beneath the waves with a push of will.

Ichweny brushed the back of one hand across his forehead, still holding the pistol loosely in his fingers, and looked back at Mary.

"We have no dealings with saints," he said. "We want no dealings with saints. Let us be on our way, and we'll let you on yours."

Tane nodded with all the gravity of a true saint and, beneath her, Mary moved in a perfect, fluid unison.

∽

Demery was the last to board *Harpy*, the ship's namesake ghisting finally sifting out of sight. He joined Athe, Mary, Brid and I and a dozen other crewmembers all along the rail, many with rifles in their arms.

Together, we watched the Farlanders leave.

"Well, that was a near thing," Athe said at last. She continued wryly, "We had best be on our way before the Lull ebbs and you are reduced to mere mortals once more. To Dreska Sank?"

Demery saluted and strode away off the deck. "To Dreska Sank. But for now, I intend to use your bath."

[illegible] *story was told to me from the lips [of] those hapless survivors: then did a ship hove into sight, a single gun deck, three masts and a square rig and Mereish lettering upon her. [illegible] say: "Set upon us without regard for life nor for the condition of [their] prize; no, their sole goal seemed to shatter us [illegible] as the sea was quite still, their voices upon the air. Not Mereish, but Usti, did [we] hear."*

—RECONSTRUCTED FROM THE LOGBOOKS
OF ERMINA MABB, AS CITED IN THE
FAUCHER DOCUMENTS

THIRTY-EIGHT

Yissik Ocho

BENEDICT

I stood before my cabin windows, watching *The Red Tempest*'s wake froth and turn in upon itself. Cays lined the channel into Dreska Sank, each one ornamented with gibbets. Some held living prisoners, others little more than bones dangling from desiccated skin and sinew. The latter clacked and clattered, while the former reached desperate hands towards us, or simply stared hopelessly at the cloud-heavy sky.

Grant looked up from the book he was reading at the table, a cooling mug of coffee before him. Between the admirable effects of his ghisting and the attentions of our new surgeon, he was recovering quickly from his confrontation with the mutineers. Something in the way he sat, however, told me he was still in pain.

"Stop looking at them, Ben," he chided.

I slid my gaze over the nearest gibbet, where a man battered the bars with the jawbone of his predecessor and screeched at us. Either the waves and the distance stole his voice, or he had lost it.

"I find I cannot," I said.

"The horror is mesmerizing, yes." He turned a page. "And nauseating, and depressing. To spend one's final days in such a state, watching the sun rise and set, waiting for death. One's mind steadily collapsing into terror over the approach of the dubious beyond. And—Saint." He put his book over his face and groaned.

"Now I've gone existential, Ben, do not do this to me. You know how morose I become."

"I simply feel that someone ought to acknowledge them," I stated, surprising myself at the words. "It is a matter of solidarity."

Grant removed the book and sat up. "Are you quite serious?"

I reflected on my words, and nodded. "I am."

"Ben, that is called compassion."

I rolled my eyes. "I am hardly overwrought." I turned away from the window, giving the nearest gibbet one last look, then headed for the door. "Come ashore with me, once the boats are ready."

"Of course," he said, his tone distracted. I felt his eyes upon me, and was relieved when I closed the door.

I made for the hold, and Enisca Alamay.

"We are in Dreska Sank," I told her as I closed the cabin door behind me. "Now is when we end this dance, you and I. Tell me who you gave the documents to. I will retrieve them and set you ashore with enough funds to see you through the rest of your convalescence."

"I am only convalescing because you shot me." She sat at a desk over a stack of paper and pen and ink, her posture still stiff with injury, but she was clothed and relatively clear-eyed.

I moved to the desk and took the topmost paper. It said much to Alamay's state that she did not try to stop me, neither physically or with her Magni power.

The page was written in Usti. I scanned the text, picking out enough to recognize it as a personal letter, and handed it back.

"Did you send them to an Artan?" I inquired. From the texts Grant had acquired in Salvage, I had gained a comprehensive, if ten years out of date, understanding of the exiled Usti royals in the region. "Elesi Artan?"

She discarded her pen in frustration. Ink splattered and trailed across a fresh, clean page.

"Keeping the documents from people like Elesi Artan is precisely what I hoped to do. In the hands of the exiles, they will lead to an Usti civil war and further instability on the Winter Sea."

"Then you should have destroyed the documents altogether," I informed her, leaning against the wall. "Not entrusted them to…"

"A friend," she snapped. She rubbed her eyes and nudged her chair around so that she could squint at me. "Or someone I hope is a friend. Saints, there is no point to this. I am so fucking tired."

I was quiet, waiting for her to go on.

"I did *not* send them to Elesi. I intended for my friend to simply hold them for me, while I set the board."

"Set the board for what?"

"Peace."

I very nearly rolled my eyes. "You are not that naïve."

"No, I am not," she replied icily.

"How can *you* create peace?" I asked.

She gave a thin, half laugh. "By selling it to the Capesh. My friend was to bring the documents here, while I found the Capesh ambassador to the Isles and brought him south."

"Did you find the ambassador?"

Enisca shook her head. "You abducted me before we could meet."

"But you were in contact with him."

Enisca nodded. "It is with the Capesh that our hopes for peace should lie. I spent months in the heart of the Ess Noti, listening and reading and searching. I know more of this world's secrets than anyone was meant to, and I know the intricacies of the Capesh and Mereish alliance. If the Capesh gain enough strength to break from the Mereish, the Mereish *must* become less militant. They will simply be unable to maintain their current ways. And if the Capesh use the documents to gain sway with the Usti? They will have power."

"You are suggesting the Capesh blackmail the Usti?" I clarified.

"That is a tactless way of putting it, but yes," she said.

"You are still putting your faith in powers who will betray you." I did not bother trying to hide my scorn. "Any 'peace' you forge will not last, not when the world is run by cowards and hypocrites, navies with mages in chains and queens with golden pisspots. Would you not rather see it all burn?"

"Fire is indiscriminate, Captain Rosser. It will burn you, it will burn me. It will burn the guilty and the innocent, together."

I watched her face in the flickering light of the candle. I remembered Scn, aflame, the screams and the laughter and the bewilderment in the eyes of those I puppeteered.

"I do not want the world to burn," Alamay filled the silence. There was passion in her voice, conviction and *want* so forceful I was almost taken in by it.

But, more importantly, a passion that distracted her to such an extent, she did not notice when the threads of my power began to saturate the air around her.

I saw my opportunity.

"I do not want to see whores and slaves suffer for the avarice of the queens and navies," she went on. "But the queens and navies, they are another matter."

I made a contemplative sound. I nudged her will, ever so slightly. It was the flick of a painter's brush—deft, subtle and transformative. "You left a lover in the Ess Noti, did you not?"

"I did," she admitted. Her emotion was becoming rawer, the rhythm of her heart a little more erratic.

"You must miss them very much."

Her gaze was daggers. "At least I have someone worth missing. Someone to fight for."

"You speak as if I do not," I observed. The move was tactful, but also unexpectedly compulsive. "I do. Though not a lover, nothing so temporary."

A flash in her eyes at that.

"You know I have a daughter," I reminded her. "The question is whether she would have me. Her mother thought I was Samuel, you see. She was in love with him."

"You bastard."

I gave a half-shrug. I kept my expression neutral, but found it harder than I anticipated. Now that I was speaking of her, thoughts—and visions—of the girl became sharper, burrowing into my skin. It took a force of will to keep my magecraft moving, infiltrating.

"I took what was on offer. She was lovely and married to a fool and oh, very, very willing." I smiled nostalgically. "I had her in her husband's bed."

Alamay shook her head in disgust.

Without faltering I continued in the same tone, "What is your friend's name?"

"Miko Solov," Alamay replied without noticing, her mind evidently still on her lover. Elation shot through me but I contained myself, nudging further, encouraging her to continue. My magic thickened, heady in the air now.

"The priest of Yissik Ocho—" Her eyes snapped wide in realization. She surged to her feet, sending the chair tumbling in the confined space.

The pen, still bloodied with ink, stabbed towards my eye.

I grabbed her wrist. It took little effort—simply standing so quickly left her unsteady.

"Thank you," I said, propelling her backwards onto the edge of the cot and kicking at her feet. She sat hard, gasping with pain, and I pried the pen away. "Think of how much frustration and suffering we might have avoided if you had told me that weeks ago."

"You have no soul," she spat, but over her rage and shock, I saw a more vulnerable emotion, one bright with frustrated tears.

I smiled, but my satisfaction was a hollow thing.

∽∞∾

I took a moment to breathe as I came above decks. The air was not what might be called clean, not this close to port, but it was better than the close quarters below deck and the ghost of Alamay's betrayed gaze.

The crew were subdued at their posts, eyeing the gibbets and the port ahead. Vachon and Charles lingered near the fore, speaking quietly to one another.

As I came into sight, the Sooth turned to look down the length of the ship at me. The memory of our encounter in the Dark Water, and her subsequent rejection, passed over me. As unpleasant as it was, I welcomed it. It buried Alamay.

I leveled my shoulders and joined them.

"Have you seen anything of use?" I asked the Sooth in Aeadine. "Anything of Yissik Ocho?"

"The saint?" Vachon replied in Mereish, she seemingly unaffected by the memories that continued to flicker through my head. "I've seen a great many things, most of which I wish I had not. But yes, I saw the many-faced ghisting."

"Where?"

She nodded vaguely ahead. "In the city. I can take you there, I think. It is hard to see in the Other, among so many ships."

"Very well," I said. "The two of you will come ashore with me, along with Barrat and Moody. We will do this as quietly as possible."

Soon, we dropped anchor just beyond the reach of Dreska Sank's chaos of docks. We were immediately assaulted by boatloads of brazen hawkers and enterprising whores, the wares of both parties well on display to the crew leaning out of gunports and over the rails.

"Keep those women off my ship," I instructed Ms. Olles

pointing to a particularly rowdy boat of whores. "No one steps foot aboard this vessel until I return."

"What of the men?" Olles asked archly.

I followed her gaze and noted more than a few men mixed in among the ladies of the night. That made me look all the more closer at the lot of them, and I began to pick out faces far too young for such clothes and paint.

One girl, little more than a child, watched the ship with a vacant, practiced smile.

"No one," I repeated.

My chosen company and I rowed ashore, fording the melee of boats and ships. None neared us, beat back by my will, but as soon as I passed out of range they forged back in, berating *The Red Tempest* and every other ship in the harbor.

Dreska Sank's dockside and streets were even more disordered than her waters, but it was not the sound or lack of space that struck me most—it was the smell. Fish guts, night buckets and mold proved to be the port's signature aroma, threaded through with stale sweat and thick perfumes. Even baking bread and roasting meat could not combat the stench and my stomach turned with every shift of tepid air.

Then, of course, there were the bodies. For the gibbets had not ended with the channel; they lined the docks, swinging listlessly. Birds swarmed them, the buildings, docks and ships alike, adding their chatter and shit to the miasma.

There were no soldiers, no guards, no agents of a port mistress. No one approached or even acknowledged us, though more than a few passersby eyed us with calculation.

Vachon inserted herself into the center of our band, hands in the pockets of her overlarge coat and her hair hidden beneath a tricorn hat. She looked for all the world like a pretty young man, though no effort could entirely disguise the roll of her hips.

"I may be able to see more clearly once we leave the docks," she said, mistaking my attention. She nodded up a central road. "That way."

We set off. Within moments Charles grunted and stopped, holding the hand of a young boy aloft. He pried his purse from the pickpocket's vice-like fingers and sent the child skittering back into the crowd with a cursory flick to the ear.

"That was foolish," Vachon commented.

"Agreed, that pickpocketing was grossly substandard," Charles wrinkled his nose after the thief.

"No, you," she clarified. "Keeping money in your pocket, in a place like this."

Charles, rather than look offended, grinned. "I tend to be a fool in the company of beautiful women."

Vachon gave him a jaded look. I anticipated—hoped for—some dry comment or rebuke, but before she could speak, something else snared her attention.

The Sooth looked sharply behind us, brows furrowing. "Benedict."

Her use of my first name took me off guard. "What?"

"The many faces."

We halted, turning as one to survey the street behind us. It was packed with people, churning and weaving around the steps of a large building. Its façade was in surprisingly good repair, plastered and painted a mixture of cream and light blue.

Over the pointed doorway, seven busts sat in recessed alcoves. One had no face, smooth and vague. The other six held clearly rendered likenesses—some men, some women, some animal-like.

"Yissik Ocho," Vachon said, following my gaze. "That is a sanctuary."

I looked at Barrat and Moody. "Stay out here and keep watch."

The two split off, leaving Charles, Vachon and I to climb the stairs and enter a long, candle-lit vestibule.

The noise of the street immediately muffled, but thankfully so did the stench. It was replaced by drifts of incense, the scents of beeswax and old wood.

With the scent came memories of the last sanctuary I had been in. Dedicated to the ghisten saint Adalia Day in her carved tree, that visit had ended in ample violence.

I grabbed Vachon's wrist as she tried to pass me. "Stay behind me."

She searched my face, the pulse of her blood warm under my thumb. Whatever she saw must have convinced her, because she nodded and gave way.

Through a set of double doors lay the sanctuary. Heavily carved wooden pillars ran along each wall, supporting a vaulted ceiling. Alcoves with benches lay to either side, curtains in various stages of concealment. I glimpsed supplicants and carved, painted icons.

A figure approached, robed in a dull grey fabric. Around his neck was a leather cord with an exquisitely carved wooden face on a medallion—an old man with gold-painted eyes.

"I am looking for Miko Solov," I said in carefully constructed Usti.

The priest nodded and, without a single question or caution, led us to an alcove and gestured for us to sit. He pulled the curtain and his footsteps retreated, loud in the pious hush.

Grant fidgeted, looking up at the alcove's décor. There was a recessed little altar, its arched top decorated with seven faces, as the doorway outside had been. The central one was faceless, same as the one outside, but the others were different and had a decidedly animalistic lean; bear-men, fox-children and wolf-women.

"I dislike this," Grant said, eyeing a leering fox-child.

Vachon shrugged, appraising the face of the bear-man with interest.

"Ghisten saints are dangerous," Grant insisted, clearly perturbed by her casualness. "Adalia Day would have murdered both Ben and I, back in Mere."

"Why? What did you do?" Vachon asked, swiveling her pointed gaze to him.

Grant frowned. "*I* did nothing save be a good, loyal friend."

"And steal several horses," I put in. "Or am I remembering that wrong?"

Grant blinked, as if he too could not quite recall.

The curtain opened to reveal a man. He opened his mouth to speak, presumably something pious and empty, but hesitated at the sight of us. He looked from our weapons to our faces and frowned.

"I am Miko Solov," he said. "Who are you?"

I leveled a pistol at his face. Grant leaned forward and tugged him inside, sitting him down forcefully against the wall. Vachon, still calm as always, pulled the curtain closed and settled back on the stone bench.

"Grant, check him for a talisman," I said.

Grant complied, revealing the priest's chest. He wore no talismans save a carved medallion like the other priest, his depicting a woman with a scarred face. He was also heavily tattooed in traditional Usti motifs. I recognized a stylized rendition of St. Helga, bare-breasted as she rode into battle upon an ice-bear, bracketed by interlocking, geometric patterns.

Grant fixed the man's clothing with a thin smile and a pat on the collar.

"Now," I lowered my pistol, seizing Solov with magic instead. "Give us Enisca Alamay's documents."

THIRTY-NINE

Elesi Artan

SAMUEL

I had anticipated a foothold of disposed Usti royalty to possess something of Hesten's regal, organized air. But Dreska Sank was Whallum after a riot and a hurricane, and everything about it set me on guard.

"If I requested you remain on board the ship today, you would protest?" I asked Mary as we surveyed the warren of docks from the forecastle of *Harpy.*

Mary started to say something, paused, and made a face. "I have no desire to be stabbed, robbed or otherwise accosted," she said, absently tapping her still-bandaged hand on her stomach. "I suspect this may be one of the worst places on the sea to be a Stormsinger."

I nodded. "It would put me at ease if you stayed here. Even if you only accompanied Demery and I, we have no notion what kind of man this Elesi Artan is, other than the fact that he lets his port exist in chaos and shambles."

"I shall stay aboard," Mary said with a gracious air. She leaned up and kissed my cheek. "Just return to me whole, if you please."

I smiled down at her and pulled her into a lingering embrace. "That I can do."

We parted an hour later. Demery had managed to threaten and bribe our way onto the last dock and as soon as we stepped off the makeshift gangplank, the crew hauled it back in again.

"Well," Athe called, leaning on the rail next to Mary. "If I see either of you in a gibbet by the end of the day, I will attempt to rescue you, but can make no promises."

"I will try harder," Mary added, soothingly.

"How kind," Demery saluted, and turned to me. "Come now, the day is wasting."

❦

Where Dreska Sank itself was nothing like I had expected, Elesi Artan's home was everything and more. It lay in an elevated region of the city, atop a flat rise that displayed his lavish three-story stone house, stables, kennels and various other outbuildings like a crown. His was not the only house in the area—more stone and plaster buildings clustered on the hilltop, a decadent topping on a cake of murder and disease.

We were met at the end of a steep road by guards, at which point Demery flashed a ring with a seal I had not seen before.

We were admitted straight into the shadows of the kennels, where Elesi Artan cradled a small, whimpering lump in his arms.

"A fine bitch, strong pups," he declared with a broad smile. He could not have been a day over twenty, with smooth, handsome features. His hair was black and curling, tucked into the nape of his neck, and he wore his lavish clothing with the comfortable disregard of one raised in extreme wealth.

He held out the lump. "See? Fine creature. Who are you?"

"Lord James Demery," Demery said. When he did not take the puppy, I stepped forward and rescued the poor, dangling creature.

I settled it in the crook of my arm, where it promptly shoved its little snout under my shoulder and let out a tiny, mewling sigh.

I scratched it gently behind the ears.

Demery went on. "This is Samuel Rosser."

"A pleasure." Artan stooped to pick up another puppy. There

were at least a half dozen of them in the hay, fumbling into the side of their exhausted mother. "I am Elesi Artan, scorned heir to the Usti Empire, and this"—he hoisted the puppy and looked between its legs—"is Miria, I should think. After the saint. Go on, name that one."

An odd ritual, I decided, but it seemed prudent to play along. I looked down at the creature in my arms, small and soft, with a mottled black and tan coat.

"Ocho," I pronounced.

"Ah," said Artan with a knowing smile. He settled the newly christened Miria back with her siblings. "You know he is my patron saint, and you are pandering. I do not mind. Why have you come? Did you come seeking my late father, and are disappointed to find me in his stead?"

"Not at all," Demery placated. "Perhaps we could speak somewhere more comfortable?"

"I am quite comfortable. Mr. Rosser?"

"Entirely comfortable," I replied.

Artan stepped away from the pups and accepted a cup of wine from a servant who had appeared, seemingly, out of nowhere. None was offered to us.

"Go on," he said.

I exchanged a look with Demery. We had discussed possible tactics to take with Elesi, but he was not what either of us had expected. Despite his youth and arrogance, there was an incisiveness in his eyes that warned me to tread carefully.

"This may be an odd question," I said, "But did you recognize me, when we entered?"

Elesi's eyebrows rose. "I did not."

"Then we have not come too late. My twin is the captain of a ship called *The Red Tempest*. We have been sent by the Council of Lords to apprehend him, and we believe he is here in Dreska Sank."

"I know of *The Red Tempest*," Artan said, nose slightly

upturned. "An upstart pirate. Why would he be a threat to me?"

"He is searching for an Usti document," I said, obscuring just how much we knew. "Given your family's connections, your power and influence in the region, we thought it prudent to come to you. He may, too. If you have heard anything of this document, we would be grateful for your aid."

Artan showed not a single flicker of recognition, but he did not need to. My Sooth's senses were heightened, my spirit toeing the edge of the Other, and I felt what he did not show.

He knew precisely what I was speaking of. I could not intuit whether the documents were in his possession, but if they were not, they soon would be.

"Tell my steward where you are staying, or where your ship is docked," Artan declared. "If I learn anything, I will send for you."

"An honor," Demery said. "Thank you, Your Highness."

I relinquished Ocho back to its mother, with not a little regret as the creature gave a soft mewl of protest. "Your Highness."

Artan's mouth quirked at our use of the title and left us without a word.

In the courtyard outside, we awaited the steward. It had begun to rain: misty, dank rain that made the short wait interminable.

Eventually the steward appeared, looking as irritated by the rain as I was. Demery spoke to the man while I waited off to the side, in a scrap of shelter beside the gate.

As I watched, a boy ran up to the guards, said something quickly, and was permitted to leave through a smaller door in the larger barrier just as Demery joined me again. We ducked through the gate, and caught sight of the child again as they reached the bottom of the road.

They waited for a cart to rumble past, then ducked right and vanished into the crowd.

"I suspect our visit has set something in motion," I murmured to Demery. "We need to follow that boy."

ORMNA —*A variety of sea serpent possessed of multiple sets of wings. Similar to a sea moth, these wings function as both a means of propulsion and camouflage, and differentiate it from its more traditionally serpentine cousins. Ormna prefer the shallower waters near land and are known to hibernate through the Bitter Moons, locked in sea ice. This vulnerability has led to the gross exploit of Ormna bones, scales and various other body parts, believed to retain the creature's power and connection to the Other.*

—FROM BEASTS AND BEINGS: A SUMMONER'S
OBSERVATIONS IN THE SOUTH MEREISH ISLES,
BY SAMUEL I. ROSSER

FORTY

Thieves and Brigands and Brothers-in-Law

MARY

I had intended to remain aboard the ship, truly. It was not a trial, particularly once I began to pass the time with a steady commentary on the unsavory figures who I spied on the docks, guessing at their favorite crimes and debaucheries, where they were from and how long they would last in a battle against a nosta, or a huden, or an impling.

Brid proved a competent companion in this; before the passage of a quarter hour, I had learned a half dozen new insults and nearly as many profanities.

Then, the tolling of bells drew our attention east. There, a pair of massive frigates were being towed out of harbor and, as they departed, the ship that had been lying behind them came into sight.

"My eyes are not playing tricks on me," I said to Brid. "That *is* his ship."

Brid nodded. She wore trousers and a sailor's short coat, with a slim cudgel at one hip and a knife at the other. "That's *The Red Tempest*."

I quickly stood, shouting down the deck, "Athe! We've company!"

The captain joined us. She took the news with a little surprise and considered *The Red Tempest* through her spyglass. "Mary, can Tane sense where Demery is?"

"She can," I affirmed.

"Then take Brid and go warn him," Athe said, spyglass still to her eye as she slowly surveyed the length of *The Red Tempest*. "If you move quickly and keep your head down, you're as safe on shore as you are here."

"Why is that?" I asked, though even as I spoke, I saw the flash of a spyglass out across the water, in *The Red Tempest*'s direction.

"Because we are being watched," Athe said. "And if I were Benedict, I would already have a party headed this way."

"They won't attack us in port," I protested.

Brid made an unconvinced sound and muttered something that did not bear repeating.

"This is Dreska Sank," Athe smiled dryly. "No one and nothing is safe."

∞

The riot and press closed in about Brid and me, along with a miserable trickle of rain. I steeled myself, kept my head down, and moved with intent through the crowd in the direction of Demery and Sam.

They were a beacon on the edge of Tane's senses. A thousand other beacons, however, stood between us: mages and ghistings, and a shocking number of Otherborn beasts.

Are beasts concentrated here because of the ships and mages? I wondered to Tane. *Like in Ostchen, when the fleet was gathering? Or are they just displaced by the Lulls?*

Before Tane could reply, I walked into someone. I stepped back, opening my mouth to apologize to the woman who I had nearly trampled, and trod on a foot. A fist connected with my kidney in recompense and I sagged, wheezing.

Brid grabbed my arm and hauled me, less than gently, up against the nearest wall. I spluttered and slipped in mud, still half-blind with pain.

"Stop it!" I slapped Brid away. "What are you doing? You're not helping!"

"You can't walk into people," she scolded. "You're lucky you weren't stabbed. What's wrong with you?"

"Saint, you're not gentle, are you?"

"This place is not gentle," she retorted.

I pinned my eyes shut, waiting for the pain—and my indignation—to subside. Then, setting aside my questions and observations, I gave Brid a bracing smile and stepped back into the street.

Slowly, I began to adjust to the chaos. I was far from comfortable, but I began to see the patterns in the crowds, the currents and the eddies. I began to peel through the hubbub and see the individual, instead of the whole. The good and the bad.

I saw a mother proudly showing her baby to a hawker under an awning, who laughed and tickled the infant's toes with gentle fingers. I saw an old man, slumped motionless in the muddy mouth of an alleyway. I saw a young woman, laughing merrily as she led along an equally young, bashful man. I saw a child steal a loaf of bread, and the baker who watched it happen with a tight, saddened look in his eyes.

Then we came to the market. The buildings did not draw back but rather clustered in, hunching lower over the masses of people. Open-fronted shops vied for space with hawkers and tinkers and temporary stalls, parked wagons and, of course, the crowds.

Eventually we spilled out into a slightly more open area. My relief, however, was short-lived. A great howl split the air and the crowd parted to allow a procession of white-clad mourners through. The mourners keened and wailed, dragging at their hair and clothing with such grief and vehemence that I physically recoiled.

Brid did too, and we stepped between the pungent barrier of a manure cart and the heat of an ironsmith.

The procession passed slowly. I caught sight of a litter decorated with endless tassels of grey and white, a shrouded corpse lying atop. The litter bearers, both men and women, were stripped to the waist, but there was no sensuality to them, despite bared breasts and muscular chests. They were streaked with ash and dirt, cut through by trickles of misty rain and their rigid postures, combined with the blood-curdling keening of their companions, turned my stomach.

Their faces were concealed by black masks, each one unique and yet familiar. A hard-faced warrior woman. A sly fox.

They were Harpy's faces.

"Who the fuck are they?" Brid hissed. Or rather, shouted in my ear.

"Priests of Yissik Ocho," Tane replied through my lips.

Tane, Harpy is not Yissik Ocho, is she? I asked silently.

Tane's response was the closest to a laugh she had ever made.

Fine, I said. *Just take us to Samuel.*

Brid and I took advantage of the temporary gap in the crowd to gain ground. We picked up our pace, weaving between people and animals, gesturing shopkeepers and obstinate drunks.

Finally, the crowd thinned. I rounded a stall selling bones with vaguely Otherborn glows and slowed, feeling as though I was being watched.

"Brid," I said.

The woman was gone. I turned sharply, in one direction then the other. Brid had completely vanished, and in her place, Benedict Rosser watched me.

The crowd did not press against him. They rounded him like a river breaking around a rock as he stared me down, his long brown coat open to reveal his weapons and his jaw clad in a careless beard. He did not seem to notice the misty rain, nor care for the mud that splattered his legs to the knee.

I did not run. I meant to, just as I had meant to stay aboard the ship. Instead, a trail of Magni influence tugged me towards my future brother-in-law.

I fought it. I even managed to stop for half a moment. But Ben's power felt more potent than ever, more fixed and adept, and I could not break free—not taken so off guard, nor surrounded by the chaos and distraction of the market.

"Mary," he said, took my arm and propelled me away into the warren of Dreska Sank.

FORTY-ONE

Comrades and Captives

BENEDICT

I pulled Mary closer to me as we walked, Moody leading the way with Miko Solov at the point of a discrete pistol. Not that Solov had any chance of running, not with the lion's share of my power focused on him. The rest was divided between urging the crowd out of our way and Mary.

"I have many questions," I muttered to her. "But now is not the time. Is Sam here? Demery? I will know if you are lying."

"They are." She tugged on the arm I held, just enough to show her obstinacy, but not enough to break free. She caught sight of Grant behind us as she did, and startled. "Charles?"

"Mary," Charles said warmly, touching the brim of his dripping hat. "It has been too long."

"Where is Samuel?" I cut in.

"If I knew, I wouldn't be searching the streets alone now, would I?" she returned. She craned to see Charles again. "You look pale. What has he done to you?"

Charles waved a dismissive hand. "I was stabbed, but no matter. The beasty has seen to me."

"Mary." I tightened my grasp. "You lost Samuel?"

She shot me a frigid look. The grey rims on her irises were particularly evident just then, looking up from a handspan away. I had forgotten how tall Mary was, and how eerie her regard could be.

"When did you last see him?" I pressed.

"This morning." A fist of Magni influence made her add, "He was with Demery. They went to Elesi Artan, looking for the documents."

At the name, Miko Solov looked back at us sharply. He asked something in rapid Usti, repeating Artan's name, and got a pistol prod in the ribs for his trouble.

"He doesn't speak Aeadine but recognizes the name," Mary said to me. "Is your Usti still terrible?"

I ignored that. "Mary, I know you to be pragmatic, so let me speak plainly. I know where the documents are. I am on my way to retrieve them. Short of killing you or leaving you trussed in an alley, where someone else is likely to kill you, I have little choice but to bring you along."

"You could let me go," she pointed out.

I took in the bustle and stink of the port in another, rapid sweep. "Alone? Here? I am not that callous. And you are not that foolish."

Even as I said the words, their truth prickled at me. Profoundly rural as Mary was, she was not naïve, nor was she stupid.

She would not be out here alone unless she had no other choice, meaning either Samuel *was* in need of finding—

Or she was not actually alone.

"Who are you with?" I demanded.

"Just you and members of your crew," she said. It felt like truth.

"Fine," I said, blocking out my growing tension. "Mary, I propose a temporary alliance. Help me recover the documents. I do not care if you try to steal them from me afterwards—you will fail, regardless."

"Aww," she said, looking up at me through round, falsely gentle eyes. Her smile, though, was wholly sly, and a little dangerous. "You don't want me to die trussed up in an alleyway. You care."

"It would be a waste," I stated. We turned down a narrow side street, scattering damp feral cats from the corpse of what might have been a goat, lain out on a stone slab under a lording statue of some militant Usti saint.

Up the way, a bent old man saw us coming and scuffled away.

"A waste of a good sister-in-law," she affirmed, raising her free hand to pat my chest, then wrap it around my arm. It turned my hold into something more companionable than forceful.

Something inside me… slipped. It was not due to the meaning of her words—my mind had not seen fit to process them. I was fixated on her touch. It was firm and a little possessive, perhaps a little warning. It held no fear, despite the complexity of our history, and perhaps even sought some consolation—particularly as the stink of the dead goat wafted across us.

But none of that was what truly struck me. It was the *familiarity* of her touch.

Women did not touch me like this. They did not touch me as if they had some attachment to me, or claim over me or need of me, beyond the coins in my pocket. Perhaps my mother had, once, but she—my mind flatly refused to contemplate *her*.

"Pardon me," I said, belatedly. The stink of the place was making my eyes water unpleasantly. "What did you say?"

Miko made his move. I felt him break free of my sorcery at the same moment as he seized Moody's head and smashed it off a stone wall. The woman slipped in mud and crumpled without so much as a cry. Miko drew her sword as she fell and spun towards me into a fluid, long stab.

Grant shouted a warning.

I thrust Mary aside. The sword passed through the air between us and I seized Miko's wrist as it came abreast. I jerked him off balance.

He managed not to fall—an admirable thing in the muck and mire. Instead, he turned the momentum into a tumble, back past the disgusting altar and onto his feet again. He leveled the sword, and in the other he raised Moody's Magni talisman.

I glimpsed Grant, dragging Moody away from the melee.

Miko swiped rain from his eyes and started to say something in Usti, very likely a threat.

He cut off as a half-rotting, stinking goat leg flew at his face. Mary shouted in disgust as she lobbed the limb at Miko, following it with half a rib cage. Saint. The skull went too. She threw the goat skull at him, its shredded tongue lolling and its eyes pulpy smears.

Even I nearly retched as rotting goat splattered the priest of Yissik Ocho. Behind us, I heard Charles swear.

As for Miko, he moved to knock the projectiles from the air before they struck him.

Mary saw the opening at the same time as I. She lunged. I lunged. Almost too late I realized our imminent collision and sent a pulse of sorcery to redirect her.

I took Miko down in a rib-cracking thud—quite literally, as the goat's ribcage was partially pinned between us and the ground. I knocked aside the priest's sword arm, smashing it off the wall as he had Moody's head.

Mary joined me to tackle Miko's other arm and pried away the Magni talisman.

My power flooded back over Miko, and I did not hold back. I poured the whole of it into him, enough power to turn a port in upon itself and make a hardened soldier fall on his own sword.

The Usti went limp beneath us, staring up at the narrow slice of sky above through suddenly vacant eyes.

"Saint, you are savage," I grunted to Mary. I sat back, disentangling myself from Miko. "Please see to my companion while I deal with him? And arm yourself with her sword."

Mary glanced at me, possibly at my use of 'please', but complied. I watched her join Grant and crouch next to Moody, speaking gently. Only once I saw the other woman move did I look back to Miko and his unsettlingly blank, staring face.

I did not look into those eyes as I stood, and forced him to do the same. He staggered upright, oblivious to the rot and offal on his clothing, not to mention dark smears of mud from the alley floor. I directed him ahead of us and, trailing behind, came abreast of Grant, Mary and Moody.

Grant had an arm under Moody's shoulders and she leaned heavily into him.

"Are you well enough to continue?" I asked, peering at her face. There was no blood, but I knew that meant little as far as head injuries went.

"I had a good lie down," she said, waving an absent hand at the spot where she had crumpled. She was pale with pain and covered with mud. "I'll not be left behind, regardless, Cap'n."

I pulled a thread of my power off Miko, delivering it to Moody instead to dull her pain and monitor the flow of her blood and the rhythm of her breath. She visibly rallied, though still leaned on Grant, and cracked me a smile.

"How much further?" I asked Miko.

He blinked at me, still lost in my thrall, and pointed.

There, behind the statue and the altar, was another little alley. It turned off into darkness someway in, but I could just make out the frame of a door.

"That looks ominous," Mary observed.

I prodded Miko ahead of us. "Lead the way."

Miko unlocked the door and directed us into a darkened interior.

Grant glanced from the doorway to the street, with its misty rain and growing puddles. "We will keep watch," he said.

Moody moved to sit down on a stone bench beside the door, looking as though she were about to vomit.

Mary and I proceeded inside with Miko. The rain gave way, but the dampness did not.

The room was long and narrow with a gradual decline to a broad-slabbed stone floor, as if the building had been built on much older and much decayed foundations. There was little furniture save a side table, which had been overturned. Books were scattered across the floor along with previously folded, clean linens and a slew of candles. The far end of the room was too thick with shadows to see.

Miko stood still, oblivious to it all.

Mary hesitated, looking around in sudden comprehension. "This is a shrine."

Immediately my senses were on high guard. "Is there a ghisting?"

A pause, then a relieved: "No."

"Benedict Rosser," a smooth Usti voice drifted to us. A young man strode out of the shadows with a dozen figures behind him.

I drew my sword and Mary raised Moody's.

"Or I presume you are Benedict," the skulker continued. "You cut a different figure than your brother, I see. A touch wirier. A touch more harried. Like a whipped dog." He smiled with a belittling affection, all the more infuriating for his youth. Eminently slappable. "I do not whip dogs. Have no fear. Who are your companions?"

"Crewfolk," I said dismissively, hoping Grant and Moody had the good sense to stay outside and Mary to stay quiet—and not reveal herself as a Stormsinger or *ghiseau*. We needed no further complications. "What do you want?"

"I am Elesi Artan," the young man continued, a shadow crossing his brows at my breach of etiquette.

Mary made a small sound that might have been a warning.

"I don't care about your fucking name," I snapped. "What do you want?"

"Several documents, which Mr. Solov intended to auction," Artan stated. His eyes had a dead quality which, combined with their current stare, made the hair on the back of my neck rise. "Release him or compel him to retrieve the documents from their hiding place—I do not care what you do. But I will leave with them, and you will not."

"Ben…" Mary whispered.

I shushed her with a curl of power. My attention flicked around the room, to the scattered books and toppled table, and otherwise a lack of adornment. Where would Miko have hidden the documents? Presumably nowhere low and damp—these ports always had a habit of flooding.

I purposefully did not look up at the strong beams of the ceiling.

Mary drew up to my side, ignoring my influence. In the low light, I saw something clutched in her opposite hand. Broken leather ties. Moody's Magni talisman, which she'd taken off Miko in the fight.

Elesi gave her a head-to-toe glance that did not, in any way, disguise the baseness of his thoughts.

One of his people stepped up and murmured in his ear.

"Do you remember the guardsmen at Fort Gat?" Mary asked quietly. "What I did to them?"

Elesi said something to his company, clearly growing tired of the standoff, and they began to surround us.

"Mary—" I started.

"Hold your breath," she said, and began to hum.

I cut off my protests by raking in a deep bellyful of air. She sang no words but I heard the lyrics running in my head, running, circling. Pulling me back to another dark, cool room.

The fox is in the bushes. The wolf is in the wood.

There was a rush of air. Hair and clothing stirred, wind whistled through the gaps in shuttered windows and around the door. It took half a heartbeat. Then the air began to grow thick.

Artan's people began to stagger.

The deer is in the meadow, but John is in the well.

I blinked slow, heavy eyes. My lungs began to burn.

Elesi braced on his knees, his gaze fixed on Mary. He made a rough sound and pointed at her.

His closest companion shouldered a musket.

Mary, bless her, stepped behind me. I found I could not fault her for that. I could not do much of anything, actually. Even blinking was laborious.

Miko slipped from my sorcerous grasp.

The hen is in her roost, Mama, but John is in the well.

Artan's companion fired at Mary. She toppled over at the same moment, however, and the shot passed by my ear so closely that I felt its heat.

My mind was a languid thing now. I felt no surprise, certainly no fear. Darkness closed in around my vision and I realized that I was putting a great deal of effort into standing. Surely if I just... knelt down...

The door smashed open. Light and clean air burst into the chamber, along with moving figures. I heard Mary shout in frustration, heard the end of Charles's distant warning, then there was wind. Everywhere. Wind in my eyes, wind in my lungs.

I was still half out of myself when I felt Miko again. I had instinctively reached for his heartbeat and found it in the shadows, beyond the light from the door and the melee of clashing figures.

I stumbled towards him. I saw shadows against shadows, blurs of grey against darker black. The flashes from several deafening gunshots.

Miko was reaching up to a beam.

Elesi Artan stabbed a knife into his back. He did not bother to retrieve the blade but dropped it with Miko's paralyzed body, plucking a packet of waxed, tightly bound leather from the priest's hand.

I loomed. I was gratified to see a flicker of intimidation in the younger man's eyes and reached out to take the documents with an open, meaningful palm.

Something struck me over the back of the head.

FORTY-TWO

The Market

SAMUEL

I grabbed Elesi Artan by the shirt as he sprinted past, tossing him into a toppled table. He tripped but did not fall and, when he straightened, looked all the more enraged for the embarrassment.

Demery made to shove him against the wall and put his sword to the boy's throat, but one of the many unfamiliar figures in the room—Artan's people—intervened with a flurry of flashy and entirely inefficient swordwork. Demery was momentary taken aback, then sidestepped the display and, in one quick movement, caught the enemy's blade and slit open his wrist with a flick.

"Sam!" Mary's voice cut through the melee.

Artan darted past me. He plunged through a knot of people and straight out the door. His guards flooded after him, guarding his retreat. Mary and Demery set off in pursuit but before I could follow, a moan pulled my gaze to the back of the room.

Was that... Ben? For an instant I froze, torn between pursuing Artan and the documents and my obviously wounded brother. He was what I had come for, was he not? So why was the urge to ignore him so appealing?

Because if I found him, I would have to face him. And if I faced him, I also had to face the reality that he might reject Demery's offer of a new identity and new life, and then... and then my options became much more grim.

A figure stumbled from the shadows and unfolded slowly, painstakingly. Ben glowered at me in the rapidly accumulating quiet of the shrine, one hand clasped to the back of his head.

In the silence before he spoke I heard the sounds of someone dying, water dripping—or perhaps blood.

"Well?" Ben asked. Blood trickled down his neck from beneath his hand. "Are we going to stand here and let Artan escape with the documents?"

The question made my fingers twitch. "I came for you, not a stack of papers."

Something obscure moved through his eyes. He seemed to push it forcefully aside. "Come now. Would you really choose *me* over the future of the world? That shitsmear of a royal will do nothing good with those documents, I assure you."

"Demery and Mary can manage him," I stated, both to him and myself.

"Mary? Mary would rather burn them, she's nearly as selfish as I am," Ben scoffed. "And Demery... well... He's a pirate, Sam."

I did not yield. "As are you, apparently. Come with me back to *Harpy*, Ben. We will find a way forward."

Ben stooped, picking up a fallen sword, and looked it over. "I think not. If you do not intend to behead me, I will resume my previous business."

He started to walk past me. I leveled my sword at him.

"Sam," he chided down the curve of my blade. "Are you truly going to fight me when your wife is chasing Usti exiles through the streets?"

Wife? Clearly there had been some communication between Mary and him, even if our exact matrimonial status was skewed.

"Ah, Charles," Ben said with a smile in his voice.

I turned as a bedraggled Charles Grant slipped in through the battered door, a pistol in hand. A woman leaned on the doorframe behind him, features obscured in silhouette.

Outside, the rain had stopped.

"Samuel, now you must fight the pair of us, and even injured as I am we shall certainly waste a great deal of time bleeding one another as Artan escapes," Ben said. "Let us pursue the documents together, then hash out this matter like gentlemen."

I knew the last part was certainly a lie, but there was a rigidity to Grant's expression that warned me Ben's threat was no bluff. Either he had ceased to be Ben's prisoner, or his cooperation was ensorcelled.

I lowered my sword. "Did you see what direction they ran?" I asked Charles.

"East." Charles looked at Ben. "I can join you or see Moody back to the ship."

"Go with Moody," Ben said, striding past me without a care for my bared sword. He regarded my face. "Shall we, brother?"

His use of the familiar term was, as always, a weapon. I fought back a frustrated snarl and waved my sword at the door. "Go."

A moment later, we followed a path of disruption through the streets. As we ducked and wove and shouldered our way through the crowds I reached for Mary in the Other, sighting her light ahead. The Other was nearly as chaotic as the human world, with lights and mages and creatures condensed on both sides of the border.

Until, without warning, they all muted. The sky opened and we ran into an open, flat area—a market, but unlike the one Demery and I had trailed the messenger boy through not long ago.

Ben and I came up short at a wall of cages. Huden and implings leered out at us, a dittama shrieked, and some burly monstrosity between a wolf and a badger battered the bars of its cage. Ghistings were here aplenty, too—stolen figureheads with raw, hacked edges, their carven faces weathered and chipped and frozen. Others were freshly hewn, the scent of pine and cedar and birch still upon them.

Then there were the mages. Beyond the creatures, rows of three-sided cells, fronted with tight-knit bars, housed clusters of men and women, adults and children. I knew what they were, intuited it, though their lights in the Other were dim.

The sight was horrific, a waking nightmare, a terrible menagerie of Otherworldly beings.

Furthermore, the place should have been blinding in the Other, but instead the lights of mage and beast flickered like fire behind charred glass.

A presentient whisper drew my gaze down to our feet. There, amid the cobblestones, between muddles and trampled paths of mud, I saw blocks of black and dark grey stone. Gianeo.

No wonder Elesi Artan had run here. These mages could not fight. The ghistings could not manifest. The door to the Other was closed. Ben and I would be rendered powerless over the border of those stones, as would Mary.

Mary. I glimpsed her streak past a line of carved ghistings, each flickering in her wake as if they fought to manifest. Artan's people pursued her with pounding boots and coordinating shouts. Demery was nowhere to be seen.

Ben said something I did not hear. My head was full of the understanding that not just Mary's power would be dampened on those stones, but also her protective connection to Tane.

All thoughts of documents and indentures and Dreska Sank's seemingly limitless immorality fled, chased away by the threat of the stones and the ripple of enemy footfalls.

"Ben." I grabbed my brother's arm but there was no time, no real thoughts in my head. My grasp was instinctive—a farewell and a plea and everything in between.

For an instant his eyes strayed between me, the market and Mary's fleeing form. I followed his gaze as Elesi Artan himself stepped from the crowd, directly in Mary's path, and lowered a pistol.

Ben and I moved as one, charging over the barrier of gianeo stones and into the sorcery-killing mire of the market.

A chorus of gunshots assailed us. Ben jerked me to one side, saving me from a peppering of lead balls. These lodged into a carven ghisting, a wave of crows in flight which shuddered under the impact.

Ahead at the mage cells, Mary charged Artan. He fired. She ducked, turned and tackled him into the bars of the mage cells. Hands burst from between the bars to seize the pair of them and guards converged, swallowing them from sight.

Ben and I stumbled to a halt beside a murky canal. It divided the market in half, previously hidden from sight.

"Mary!" I shouted.

I glimpsed her through the melee, though only for an instant. She had freed herself from the reaching hands and, in the small space between a barrier of legs and shoulders and glinting weapons, I saw her wrestle something from Artan.

A heavy leather envelope.

I nearly laughed, but the sound was more of a choke. Mary vanished again, and hounds began to bay.

"Sam." Ben dragged at my arm. It was unclear whether he had seen Mary and Artan—his gaze was fixed down the canal where more of Artan's guards rushed us, releasing the leashes of massive, slathering hunting dogs as they came.

I had just enough time to recall the innocent pups in the kennel, the tiny creature burrowing its face under my arm, before Ben dragged me away.

We sprinted through alleyways and streets. The market fell behind, Mary's light burst into sight again, ahead in the Other. But the dogs came on and Artan's people flowed out of sidestreets and buildings like cockroaches.

"*Harpy!*" I panted. "Mary will be making for *Harpy*!"

"*Tempest* is closer!" Ben panted. He reached for a wall as we turned a corner, supporting himself for half a moment before hastening on.

We hit the docks in a thunder of boots. I cast a look across the water. Ben was right—*The Red Tempest* was three times closer than *Harpy*'s smaller form. As distant as she was, I could not miss the fighting on the docks leading up to her, nor the movement on her deck. Athe was ready to depart, the conflict moving closer. How long would she wait?

That was when Ben stumbled. I grabbed his arm, hauling him back up. No new injuries, but a renewed stream of blood trickled down the back of his neck and coat. Whatever strength had propelled him thus far had run its course.

My brother squinted up as if, for a moment, he did not recognize me.

I cast my gaze to where Mary fled for *Harpy*, and felt as though my chest were being cracked open. No. I could not consider this. I should abandon Ben, take my chances alone sprinting towards *Harpy*.

But I would never make it. Not with the crowds and the converging guards and baying dogs. Not with Athe already preparing to make way.

"Fuck," I bit out, and dragged Ben towards his ship.

FORTY-THREE

The Blockade

MARY

The rain came again, thick and stifling and sweeping down the inlet from the sea. It battered the docks of Dreska Sank as *Harpy* began to slip out, heading slowly for freedom via the combined influence of three ghistings in her wood.

I leaned against the main mast, letting blood and mud wash from my skin as I tried to gather breath to sing. I didn't mind the rain itself—it was cool now and I was so very hot, my skin flushed and clothes plastered to me.

But my lungs burned and my muscles trembled. Even the weight of my sodden clothes felt too heavy, especially with Tane's focus on maneuvering *Harpy* out of Dreska Sank's warren-like docks without a proper wind.

I sunk down on the deck and closed my eyes. I needed to find Sam and Brid and Demery. I needed to sing. But first, I needed to breathe.

"Mary." Athe loomed over me, water dripping from the brim of her hat. "If you're not dying, I need you to find us a wind. This storm is not natural."

My wheezing glare must have been eloquent. She cursed and started off, shouting for the bosun over the patter of the rain.

Moments flicked by, too fast and too slow all at once. Crewfolk moved around me. Warning bells clanged throughout Dreska

Sank, chasing us down the inlet towards the sea. Ships moved through the rain and the voices of other Stormsingers awoke as Dreskan vessels made to give chase.

Clearly, Elesi Artan was not about to let us sail away.

In the meantime Tane was quiet. What I could sense of her, beyond her influence upon *Harpy*, reeled from what we had seen in the market. Mages. Ghistings. Beasts. All trapped by the iron and wood and the stone beneath their feet.

I was as shaken by the sight as she. We knew the world was harsh. We knew there was cruelty and brutality on every side— told and untold, blatant and hidden. We had been bought and sold and stolen. We had experienced much of it and I lived in the legacy of it, passed down from my mother.

But until I had seen that market, humans and ghistings casually sold alongside one another on such an organized scale, I had not fully known how far humanity could fall. How much deeper the depravity ran.

I sensed, more than saw, when the last gnarled arm of Dreska Sank's docks gave way to the broad mouth of the inlet. The movement of the ship changed beneath my feet as the waves turned to chop and a natural wind, feral and full of the scent of the open sea, gusted across it.

I drank the fresh air as I finally found my feet again. I prepared to summon a witchwind, using the time to scan the deck for Samuel. He should be in sight, playing the Sooth—guiding us through the docks and other ships in concert with the ghistings.

I did not see him. Was he below, then? Injured? That would explain why he hadn't come to check in on me.

Out across the water, right on our heels, *The Red Tempest* sailed. The voice of her male Stormsinger came to my attention, lifting from the general clamor and rush in a lament to the sky.

"Mary!" Athe bellowed. She pointed ahead to what should have been open sea but now, instead, was a veil of rain and a growing line of ships. Small, quick vessels passed us on the way out of Dreska Sank, joining up with an existing blockade of four large vessels. "Find your voice now, or we are finished!"

I raced to join her and Demery on the quarterdeck, grimness and resolve strengthening my steps as I went.

"That is Voskin's *Dominion*," Demery observed as I joined them. "And that is Talys Lirr's *Windwarden*. The third…"

"Not a clue." Athe muttered something in Sunjani and hissed through her teeth. "What are they doing here?"

"They may have come for Ben," Demery said. "Or it is an ill-fated coincidence."

Suspicions tickled at the back of my mind, pieces of a puzzle scattered across a table. First were the black and grey stones in the market, their ties to Lirr and Voskin and the Ess Noti. Then I recalled Artan's words to Ben, in the dark of the shrine.

What do you want?

Several documents, which Mr. Solov intended to auction.

I put a hand to my chest, to the fitted structure of my stays, and the thick pouch tucked beneath. Could it be that Voskin had come not for Ben, but for a stack of papers that could upend the world?

I opened my mouth to say as much to my companions, but hesitated. Samuel's long-ago caution about telling Demery of the documents returned to me, and I bit my tongue.

Perhaps I should keep this secret close. Just until Samuel and I could decide what to do and how to proceed.

Or perhaps I should just burn them, I muttered to Tane. *End this madness myself.*

She did not disagree.

"It has been some time since we ran a blockade," Demery remarked to Athe. The retired pirate looked up at the masts, the sails, the lines, then the crew hastening to quarters as efficiently as rain and wet powder would permit. Rain sheeted past his face, and the soft grey of his eyes was flinty.

Athe shrugged. "No help for it. Mary, give us full sails."

I nodded and took a deep breath, tracing the ache and burn all the way to the bottom of my lungs. I glanced back towards *Red Tempest*, tracing the voice of his Stormsinger to a masculine form on the quarterdeck.

Tempest would be running the blockade too, and in that, Benedict's Stormsinger and I were united.

I began to hum along with the other Stormsinger's song. Words came to me, fragments of Aeadine lullabies and laments, woven together into an intricate melody.

I began to sing in harmony.

The wind came, arcing and turning until it found the path I wished for it, and filled our unfurling sails. Benedict's Stormsinger grew all the louder, sensing my comradery, and our two vessels plowed towards the blockade.

The unity of our voices brought a rush of Otherworldly power. It was heady and novel, something I had felt few times before— when I sang in concert with my mother, and more recently, at the battle at the Anchorage. It erased the events of the day, smothering even the persistent worry of where Samuel was.

But *Tempest*'s witch and I were not the only weather mages on the waves. Distant voices surged, rising and falling into gusts and eddies. The wind tried to tear away from us, but we stayed our course.

Directly into cannon range.

Guns boomed.

"Bow chasers, a warning shot!" Athe shouted. "Pass the word, prepare and hold!"

Shouts were repeated down to the gun deck, and the pair of guns foremost on *Harpy*'s forecastle thundered in close succession. The shriek, whine, scream and howl of shot joined the rain and the wind and the drums and the waves.

The Red Tempest hit the line first, cutting between *Dominion* and one of the unfamiliar ships.

Rain—heavy, driving rain—struck my face. I lost sight of *Tempest* and braced against the rock of the ship as we, too, crossed the line.

Gunsmoke. A grating and a crack. The thunder of guns and the conflict of winds. I sang on in a timeless void, my only thoughts my breath, my voice, and the wind in my face.

The sea opened before us. I looked down the line and saw *The Red Tempest* erupt into freedom, her guns smoking, sails billowing, and her tentacle-wrapped prow cutting through rain and wave. I fancied I could still see Ben's Stormsinger on the quarterdeck, standing in place as gunners ran and muskets fired and topmen clambered overhead.

"Nor-nor-west, Mr. Brison!" Athe bellowed. Demery cut her off and there was a moment of conflict, but Athe pushed him aside and affirmed, "Do it!"

"Nor-nor-west!" Mr. Brison affirmed, his words echoed by the bosun a moment later, who followed it with a stream of instructions and a shrill of their whistle.

The Red Tempest fell in behind us, chasing or in convoy, I couldn't tell.

I pressed a hand to my chest again, feeling the press of the documents, and wondered what in the Saint's fiery hell I intended to do with them.

FORTY-FOUR

Mirror Twin

BENEDICT

The sails of our pursuers clung to the horizon, blurred by steadily retreating rainclouds. I stood in the cold and wind of the balcony beyond my cabin windows, nails digging into the rail. I was still wet from the rain, chilled to the bone, and did not care in the slightest.

"Ben." Samuel's voice was unsettlingly calm. He stood in the balcony door, his torn and bloodied coat hanging open, his hair in a rough-raked tuft.

"Shut up." I bit off my next words as a tremor of wrath and frustration shuddered across my jaw, up my cheek, and drove like nails into my forehead. "You. You—I have nothing to say to you."

He ignored me, looming at my side. "You cannot blame me for losing the documents to Artan."

"You complicated matters," I snapped. "I had the matter in hand. I had the priest. You alerted Artan and blew the whole encounter out of the water."

He turned and stood beside me, staring back at our pursuers. I saw his posture relent, though the breath he exhaled was lost to the churn of *The Red Tempest*'s wake.

"You are correct," he said, lifting his voice to be heard. "Demery and I miscalculated."

Something inside me was assuaged at his admission, but I

ignored it. I turned to lean on the rail, watching him. "Did you truly intend to give Voskin my head?"

"You speak as if that is no longer an option," he replied, still calm.

"They shot at both ships, Sam. *Tempest* and *Harpy*. I believe your little deal with Voskin is over and done with. If he ever intended to honor it at all, which I doubt."

"I had little choice."

"Yes, yes, Mary's indenture, your crew, your ghisting," I rattled off, rolling my eyes. "Just put a bullet between the man's eyes, Sam. If you cannot stomach that for the sake of your wife, you do not deserve her."

"We are not yet married," he said distractedly. "How... I am still unclear as to how Mary ended up in your company."

"She was looking for you and found me," I said smoothly. "Not the first time that has happened."

He refused to rise to the bait, and I found myself passingly grateful. As soon as the words left my lips, they had lost their shine.

"Why is she not Mary Rosser yet, then?" I prodded.

"Why do you care?" He asked the question not as if it were a threat, which I anticipated, but as if he truly could not fathom the answer.

"I would find it uncomfortable and impractical, such a state of half-belonging," I replied. "Close the matter before she changes her mind."

"Ah," he said, as if I had confirmed some suspicion of his. But instead of continuing the topic, he caught me broadside with a blunt: "You burned down an entire port, Ben."

I felt as though my lungs were growing smaller. *It was a mistake*, I thought, but did not speak it aloud.

"I did," I said levelly.

Samuel studied me. His gaze was different than before, somehow immensely heavy. "I feared I would find you a mad dog. In answer to your question, yes, I considered I might have to kill you."

The admission was colder than the wind in my rain-soaked clothing.

"Go on," I prompted.

"But Demery and I intended to offer you an alternative. You leave the Mereish South Isles, and we will falsify your death." Sam cleared his throat and glanced down at his hands, or perhaps beyond them into the churning sea. "That is still on the table. I doubt this will end well."

"'This' being the fact that we are hunted by an alliance of Voskin and Elesi Artan?"

"Among others," Samuel nodded out towards the ships, the same gesture I had made moments before. Saint, I had forgotten what it was to look at him, to see myself so clearly in another human being.

I feared I would find you a mad dog.

"I do not recognize three of the ships that blockaded us, but I sense one at least sails under Talys Lirr," he went on.

I considered I might have to kill you.

My gaze dropped to the empty scabbard at his hip, his sword lost in the chase. His pistols were gone too.

"Talys Lirr," I repeated. "Daughter of Silvanus Lirr?"

"Indeed."

"I suppose there is not much good in hoping she is nothing like her father," I said. The words seemed to linger in my mind, sticky and viscous. Like her father, a Sooth and Magni. A pirate and monster.

I saw a little girl hiding behind a closed door, as other children thundered past.

"Fuck." I snapped myself out of the image, walling the whole of it away—fathers and daughters and monsters all. "I need a drink."

Expression inscrutable, Samuel followed me back into the cabin.

∞

Sometime later, after we had warmed ourselves with drink and I had tossed dry clothes at my brother's head, we sat together at the table. Moody had made it back to the ship with Charles but was recovering in her hammock, and another crewman brought us hot coffee and a serviceable meal.

"Do you still believe you have a chance to recover the documents?" Samuel asked, sitting at his ease across the table from me. Plates were scattered between us, fish and potatoes, bread and butter and slices of fruit. Just because we were being chased did not mean we could not eat well, after all.

I sat at the other end, flicking fishbones onto the tabletop with studied disinterest.

"Or," Samuel was still talking, "will you abandon this madness and consider Demery's proposal?"

"Tomorrow's troubles, Sam. Our first concern is to evade our pursuers. Where is *Harpy* leading us?"

"Isla Ascra, I assume."

"That is?"

"A safe harbor, allies of Demery. Two days north."

"Two days," I repeated, flicking another bone onto the table. It bounced and tapped off his mug, earning a frown of distaste. "Shameful if we have not lost our pursuers before then."

"If we do," he began with a note of caution. My interest rose. "Am I free to return to *Harpy* and Mary?"

"She made it aboard?"

He nodded. "I can see her there, in the Other."

The impulse to tell him of my Sooth's abilities welled. I regarded that impulse, held it at a distance and discarded it. It seemed a useful card to tuck up my sleeve. Besides, my focus should be on my anger just then, wrath at his meddling and my delayed plans.

"You are not much use to me as a prisoner," I noted. "You will only question my every decision, and pepper me with guilt at every spare moment."

"I will," he affirmed. "I will be incorrigible."

"Then it is best for both of us if you leave as soon as the opportunity arises. Oddly, it seems I am the more principled brother now, because it has not once crossed my mind to kill you."

Samuel lifted his coffee in salute, though the smile he painted across his lips was humorless. "I will remain aboard until we reach Isla Ascra, then."

"I have no intention of making port at an ally of Demery's," I said. "Once darkness falls we shall cut our lanterns and go our own way. I will drop you at the first neutral port."

Samuel regarded me for a very long, very quiet moment. That new Sooth's sense of mine prickled, warning me of something I could not identify.

"That would be foolish," my twin said, draining his coffee and setting down the mug a little too firmly. The fish bone I had flicked at it earlier cracked. "Because Demery has Enisca's documents."

I watched the subtle movements of his face. "You are lying. Have you not learned better?"

"Mary has them," he admitted. "I saw her take them from Artan."

I rocked my chair onto its back two legs and sifted through my thoughts. My choices were narrowing, but my anticipation rising. It would be far simpler, and faster, to take the documents from Mary and *Harpy* than Elesi Artan in the heart of his power.

That being said, with *The Red Tempest*'s current depleted complement and the nearness of our pursuers, I did not like our odds of attacking *Harpy* at open sea.

"Then we shall go to Isla Ascra, parlay with James Demery, and make our final stand." I lifted my cup to the stern windows, and the pursuing ships beyond. "And there decide the fate of the Winter Sea."

FORTY-FIVE

Return to Isla Ascra

SAMUEL

Isla Ascra's stone forest took shape on the horizon, layer upon layer of spires coming into view in varied shades of purples and greys and deep, smoky green.

Harpy reached the forest first, passing into safety and a whirl of conjured fog. For a short time, *The Red Tempest* was alone upon the waves between the isle and our ever-encroaching tail of ships—now settled into six distinct vessels.

Yesterday, the four ships that had formed the blockade had been joined by two more. These newcomers were swift sloops and had soon taken the lead, bringing the warbanners of the House of Artan into sight of the naked eye.

Now, Benedict and I stood on the quarterdeck as we came within cannon range of the seastacks. Benedict stood with his hands braced wide on the rail while I lingered just behind him with Charles Grant.

"Will they fire upon us?" Grant asked, including me and Ben's Mereish Sooth, Elise Vachon, in the query.

"There will be a battle, but not today," Vachon said in her own language. She stood on Grant's other side in a long, loose coat and a cocked hat. She cast her calm gaze to me. "What do you see?"

"Blood in the water and smoke on the wind," I replied. "Nothing of substance."

Ben made a derisive sound and surprised me by speaking in Mereish. His command of the language had improved remarkably, even if his tone was droll with impatience. "Enough, Saint. The witches will not fire upon us."

"Why? What did *you* see?" Vachon asked Ben curiously.

Ben, seeing? Her choice of words gave me pause. Naturally certain changes in Ben's aura had not escaped my attention, but this was my first hint that he had begun to utilize any Sooth abilities.

"Mary would not allow it," Ben replied, looking at me with a note of challenge in his voice. It was unclear whether this was due to the hint at his new power or his statement itself.

"Furthermore," I added, "they have all the power. *The Red Tempest* makes a better prize than an enemy. He does not pose a threat to Isla Ascra."

"Our stalkers will, however," Ben pushed off the rail and straightened. "So, let us be timely allies."

Several crewmembers cast him looks, but any doubt in their eyes was overridden by unseen sorcery. Unease rooted in my stomach and my conflict over my brother's condition compounded.

A gun boomed ahead of us. A cannonball splashed into the water well away from us and, on the foremost seastack, a sequence of flags were raised. Combined with the warning shot, the meaning was clear—proceed with caution. Two fires ignited, one on either side of the safe channel heading inland.

Tension rippled across the ship, followed by a sorcerous wave of Magni calm. I did not fight that particular influence of Ben's, standing a little easier as the fog wrapped around us and our pursuers were blocked from sight.

Guiding beacons continued to ignite ahead of us, one by one by one. The breathy flicker of their burning was the only sound other than that of the ship and the slosh of water.

But unlike the first time I was at Isla Ascra, this time I saw figures everywhere. They moved in silence, the passage of their feet over rock and moss and bridges muffled by tactful applications of wind. Smaller boats slipped between the stacks, all heading towards the sea, and their oars were equally noiseless.

Even the songs of the Stormsingers who conjured that hush were little more than whispers, hisses and echoes that made the fine hair rise on the back of my neck. So too were the witches whose voices provided our own, tactful wind.

"There are hidden fortifications," Benedict observed to me lowly. There was a look of respect in his eye, even a hint of disgruntled intimidation.

I nodded. "Yes. This is not the first time Talys Lirr has attacked Isla Ascra. I have little doubt she will take this as another opportunity to reclaim it from Idriss."

"But Talys is not a mage as her father was," Benedict stated, glancing at me for confirmation. "And she must be young, very young."

"Her age matters little. Her father made her *ghiseau*, and her ghisting is old, and from what I have gathered and seen, cunning."

Ben's expression darkened. "Fucking *ghiseau*."

"We are everywhere now," Grant quipped easily. "Like a plague."

My brother looked at him and almost, *almost*, smiled.

"Well," he said, turning to regard our path once more. "We will soon meet our hosts. Let us make ourselves presentable."

∽

The cliffs of the main island were lined with Stormsingers as we dropped anchor off the main beach. *Harpy* was already there, her boats on the beach, and I saw Mary among the figures waiting on the sand.

The gate to the tunnel and the heart of the island, however, remained closed. That did not bode well, but I could not begrudge the Stormsingers their caution.

Mary met us at the waterline. I leapt out into the knee-deep water, gathering her into my arms without a word. Her breath escaped in an endearing huff as I carried her back to shore, one arm bearing her weight, the other hand buried in her hair.

I found my footing in the dry sand and lingered for a moment, breathing her and feeling her body against mine—the curve of her breasts, the rapid rise and fall of her breaths beneath the stiffness of her stays.

No, there was something more to that last feeling. Something that yielded less than her stays and did not match the evenness of their structure.

Something roughly the size of a pouch of documents.

I opened my mouth to accuse—no, ask her—when she tugged her head back and asked, "Where is Charles? Did he not come ashore?"

Either she had no idea I had felt the documents, or was brazening her way past it.

"He will," I said. "He elected to wait with Ben's Sooth. She is quite pretty."

"Is she now?" Mary looked past me at *The Red Tempest*. "Well, good for him. Sam, your arm is shaking."

"It is."

"I have gotten heavier," she diagnosed.

"Then I shall become stronger."

Her mouth twisted in a wry smile. She went on, ignoring what I was sure was a tense standoff behind us as Demery, Athe, Ben and Idriss met. I should be part of that meeting, but I could not look away from Mary's face.

"It's the stress of all this," Mary continued, her tone forcefully light. "I am ravenous, and growing ever so lazy, unless I am being chased, of course. But I cannot say I dislike what it has done to my breasts."

She looked pointedly down at her chest, where the rise of her breasts was undeniably plump atop the line of her stays, beneath a worn linen shirt.

I realized I was staring and set her on her feet, clearing my throat. "Let us pick up this thread again, later?"

"Will there be a later?" she asked, snaking her hand into mine. She lost some of her lightness, "Dusk is only hours away. Surely they will attack with the tide."

I tightened my fingers around hers and, together, we headed for the confrontation.

"...lend my aid," Benedict was saying as we arrived. There was not a trace of Magni power in the air, and he stood in his most practiced, respectable-Naval-officer stance. "Captain Kohlan, Lord Demery and I may have a complex history, but you and I, Ms. Idriss, may begin with a clean slate. I am a powerful Magni. My crew are proficient and my ship one of the finest."

"What of your Stormsinger?" Idriss asked, her tone neutral.

"He is yours," Ben said. "I freed him from the Mereish Navy, but he has not thrived under my command. Take him, as a sign of my goodwill. Though in order to engage the enemy, I will need the services of another weatherwitch. Mary, perhaps, as we have an established rapport."

"Do we?" Mary asked archly.

"We are family." He matched her expression before he looked back at the others.

My fingers twitched in Mary's grip and my thoughts flicked to the documents stuffed down her stays. If Ben realized she had them on her at that very moment, if Ben *saw* it, what would he do? Enthrall the lot of us and leave?

Benedict, meanwhile, went on. "Also, I do not possess a full complement of crew. Captain Kohlan, if our crews were to combine aboard *The Red Tempest*, we could make a much better show of things. And Idriss, if you have experienced gunners to spare? I dare say *Tempest* could hold that channel indefinitely."

"I've little doubt he could. I agree, that would be the best position for him. However…" Idriss glanced up at the clifftops where her people watched, sitting or standing, coming and going. "It is not the channel I am concerned about. There are other routes in by longboat, many of which Talys is aware of and has tried to utilize in the past. She may not have intended to attack Ascra today—but she will certainly take advantage of the opportunity. We will be spread thin."

"How many such routes are there?" I asked.

"Six, seven that will need to be watched," Idriss replied.

"Idriss," Demery said. "May we lay our plans somewhere other than the open air? We have been two days harried and I believe we can all agree that none of our pursuers will make a move until cover of dark and high tide. And if they do? Your mages will give us fair warning."

Idriss looked to the cliffs and raised a hand. Several silhouettes vanished and moments later, the grating was raised.

Mary's expression was thoughtful as all this unfolded. I gave her a prompting look, but she shook her head and, giving my hand one last squeeze, hastened her step to fall in with Charles Grant.

I, meanwhile, fell into step beside my brother.

"Is she carrying the documents with her?" he asked under his breath, without looking at me.

"Do not touch her," I replied, matching his tone, and keeping my eyes ahead. "We can settle the matter of the documents when this is over."

He finally looked at me, taking me in with a depth of perception that was wholly new and unfamiliar.

"Swear to me you will do nothing," I said. "Ben."

"I suppose I owe you that," he murmured, and strode ahead of me into the shadows.

STRANGER —*In the context of the Other, a Stranger is one of the oldest known terms for a ghisting or ghisting-like being, preceding even the ancient title of Wood-Wight. Once thought to be a primeval predecessor of modern ghistings, greater in power and independence of will, they are now understood to be the immensely rare equivalent of a Mother Ghisting—a ghisten sire, though as the nature of ghisten genesis is unknown, one may only speculate as the functionality of such a title. See also:* GHISTING, WOOD-WAITH

—*FROM THE* WORDBOOK ALPHABETICA:
A NEW WORDBOOK OF THE AEADINES

FORTY-SIX

The Stranger

MARY

Four hours after our arrival at Isla Ascra, the first shots were exchanged on the edge of the seastacks. The inner island, already a hive of tense activity, erupted into action and, as the afternoon waned and the tide came in, I kissed Samuel, stepped onto one of the bridges leading into the seastacks, and left in the company of a dozen allies.

Trees. Rock. Yawning stretches of water, here choppy, here still. The ethereal songs of Stormsingers rising and falling, calling in fog and tricking the ears. Rickety stairs and shoulders of rubble, then hidden passageways and the bones of a great whale, cast between the stacks by a long-ago hurricane.

I slowed on the top of a particularly broad stone tower, boots on a worn path between the trees and their mossy, bubbling roots. Ferns and mushrooms spilled here and there; more moss dangled from the branches, wispy beards of pale green bleached even paler in the dusky light.

For a moment I lingered in the scent and feel of the forest and let the tension building at the base of my skull dispel.

Samuel had been assigned to *The Red Tempest* with Benedict, to hold the main channel. But I, as *ghiseau* with particular skills, had been released to the seastacks in one of multiple parties of Ascra's mages and assorted allies.

I did not allow my thoughts to linger on Samuel's and my separation. I did not allow myself to wonder if or when or in what state I would see him again. He and I had already weathered too many storms together.

A low whistle caught my attention. I resumed a steady, jogging run and caught up with my detachment on a narrow bridge to the next stack.

Charles Grant fell into step beside me, musket across his back, handsome face still more than a little gaunt from what I understood to be a recent brush with murder.

"You could have stayed in the village," I told him. "You look terrible."

"And miss the opportunity to venture out with you, sallying forth unto glory and that sort of thing?" He scoffed. "I think not."

"What about the Sooth?" I pried.

"What Sooth?"

"The pretty one."

"Samuel is a fine-looking fellow, but I would not call him pretty," Charles huffed, though it was clear he knew exactly who I was speaking of. "Now I was pretty in my day, in an eminently masculine fashion of course. Before Kaspin and these scars, and the various trials and travails you have put me through."

"Benedict's Mereish Sooth," I prodded. Such topics were far easier to contemplate than our approach to the periphery of the stone forest and the likelihood of battle. "The short one?"

We passed over another seastack, this one so small it acted as a mere landing between the bridge and a rickety stair, which wound down to a section of fallen stacks and tumbled trees. The wood was weatherworn but had been hacked relatively flat. It served as an efficient pathway through the rubble and onto a surreptitious boardwalk.

"Oh, Vachon," Charles said as he slipped on a slick patch of wood. "Whatever you have heard was certainly in error. Benedict has his eye on her."

That nearly made me slip too.

"Hush," one of the Stormsingers called from up ahead.

Grant and I picked our way along for a time, neither speaking. But he was clearly as distracted as I, and the intentional lightness that had buoyed us along was fractured.

"I am glad you're here," I told him as he offered me a hand with jumping over a pace of open water and into the shadow of a seastack. "I worried for you. Off with Ben."

He smiled and squeezed my hand before releasing it again. "Likewise, my friend."

Nearby, something fell into the water.

Everyone stopped. The world hushed, leaving little more than the prickle of mist on skin, the wash of waves and the occasional creak of wood.

Then, a gunshot.

Our nearest ally, who had just stepped out from behind the seastack that sheltered Charles and I, fell. He did so slowly, collapsing backwards off the boardwalk and into the water without a cry.

I was close enough, however, to hear the crack of his bone and feel a warm splatter of blood.

Only experience kept me from crying out, but I flinched, still breathing, still staring.

The smell of iron filled my senses. I felt Charles's hand on my arm, and together we eased closer to the seastack. The musket across my back clattered softly against cold, wet stone.

A witchwind roared past us. I staggered and barely caught a voice as it shouted, "Firth! Grant!"

Keeping low, Charles and I bolted after our companions. Lead balls sang by and we dove into the shelter of the next stack, thundering around a curve in the boardwalk and up a set of stairs.

A tunnel swallowed us and we caught up with one of our companions in the dark, an Ascra Stormsinger. An old woman with white hair and dark skin, she held a finger across her lips and prodded me not towards the tunnel exit on the other side of the stack, but through a nearly imperceptible crack in the wall.

I barely managed to wedge myself through, musket in hand. Charles came after, grunting with the effort, and we popped out at the top of a hidden staircase. The rest of our company were clustered there in the light of a single dragonfly, contained in a glass orb in one of the mage's hands.

"Any hope for Kerill?" someone asked me, their gaze sliding over the blood on my face.

The dead man. They meant the dead man.

"None," I replied.

The person who had asked blinked slowly, obviously in shock, and a nearby woman took their arm, whispering something in their ear.

The old woman appeared, glanced over the company with a matriarchal air, and nodded. "Onward."

Down, down, down the stair we went and into a long, half-flooded tunnel.

"Keep your powder dry," the old woman said, her voice echoing over the slosh of water.

I waded in slowly, all too aware of the water creeping up my calves, my thighs, and to my hips.

The documents in my stays pressed tight to my ribcage. They were well wrapped and their pouch waxed, but would they survive a dunking?

Saint. I needed to find somewhere to hide them. More than that, I needed to confer with Samuel and decide what was to be done.

The water rose no higher than my hips, but I did not breathe easily until we ascended again.

We climbed a slippery, steep staircase—closer to a ladder than a stair—and emerged through a trapdoor atop another spire.

We moved stealthily. I leaned against a tree to pour the water from my boots as Charles eased himself down beside me, panting. Several of our companions bellied up to the edge of the stack and peered out.

"There," someone whispered.

I glanced at Charles, who waved me on to join the others.

This stack was taller than many, and close enough to several others to nearly form an island of their own. A wooden ladder led down to the top of the next stack over an armspan's gap of sloshing seawater. Bridges fanned out from there, lacing off into the most extensive network of paths I had yet seen. Several buildings were here, too, mostly ruins threaded with mist and enterprising greenery. One, however, was whole and tall and appeared to be something of a lighthouse. One of the beacons along the main channel?

There was no sign of our pursuers, at least not from my current vantage. But if Talys or her people were among them, they might very well know of the tunnel.

Am I truly hoping its Voskin's people shooting at us?

He is not a Lirr or an outright slaver, Tane murmured. *He has become the lesser evil.*

"Hold," the old woman commanded. She murmured to two of our companions, who slipped down the ladder and darted off with spyglasses.

Cannons boomed in the distance. One, two, then a cacophony. Light bloomed over the channel, billowing under the mist like lightning beneath a distant storm.

Mary!

Tane drew my gaze down, down through the crevice between the stacks. I lay fully on my stomach and peered down through rock and root and a drape of moss.

A ghisting looked back up at me, his neck grotesquely twisted.

Though he was human in shape, there was so little human about him that my mind struggled to rationalize the two facts. His features were too small in his jagged face. His hair was a cloud of seaweed, lifting and bobbing on water that was not there, and he did not wear even the suggestion of clothing. But he had no distinguishing markers of gender, only an ever-shifting sheen of ghisten glow.

He—That—He is not right, Tane warned, her usually calm tones sharp with sudden realization. *He's—*

The roots beneath me roiled, the ground crumbled, and I toppled forward. I cried out, twisting to grab at something, anything. But the roots fled my grasp and—

A hand seized mine. Charles braced on a boulder, his skin alight with his own ghisting's glow, and hauled me back up.

I toppled into him, clutching him first for stability, then out of sudden protectiveness as every tree on the top of the stack began to moan and tremble. I heard cracks, like sap exploding in the deep winter. Leaves and needles and droplets of water began to rain down, along with insects and chunks of dangling moss.

Tane was in the trees. Charles's ghisting was in the trees. And so was the stranger.

Stranger. That was what he was called, I sensed. A stranger. *The* Stranger.

Charles abruptly bundled my head into his chest.

A trunk fell right next to us. The ground shook and I screamed into Charles's shoulder, less out of fear than a need to do something, anything, to give voice to the blank-minded pressure inside of me.

But no shards stabbed into us. No branches fell on our heads. Moss and leaves and needles and beetles and ants rained, but Tane and Nosewise—that was his name now, I sensed through unspoken bonds—turned all else aside.

A momentary hush fell. Charles and I pulled apart, surveying our surroundings.

The remnants of our company stood with us, staring in shock. Not one had fallen, thanks to Tane and Nosewise, but some had fled. I saw them regrouping on the next stack, unshouldering muskets and rifles and calling back to us. Pointing at the sky and shouting in warning.

A deep, bruised purple light caught my eye. A familiar flying beast of bone and taut Otherworldly flesh moved above the fog, visible one moment, a mere light in the next.

It took position to the west, beyond the beacon marking the channel, and roared.

"Is that not…" Charles breathed.

"Inis Hae's beast," I replied.

"Then Voskin's new allies are—"

"The Ess Noti." I spoke the words quietly, beset by a surge of responsibility, drive and fear.

If the Ess Noti was here, if Inis Hae was here, Samuel would be his first target.

I looked west towards the beacon and the channel.

"Move!" someone shouted, and I realized our entire party was abandoning us. They leapt the gap between stacks—the ladder was gone—and one lone woman looked back at Charles and I as the others sprinted away.

Charles and I shared a flicker of silent, ghisten communication and we moved as one. We clambered over the toppled, crumbling tree next to us and ran the last three paces towards the edge of the spire.

I jumped the armspan gap where I had seen the Stranger a moment before and dropped onto the top of the next tower. I landed hard enough to send a spasm through my knees and tumbled forward, smacking my shins off rocks and narrowly avoiding taking the spear-like end of a shattered branch to the eye.

Charles landed with more grace. He seemed as surprised by this as I was and, briefly, grinned.

The world erupted into noise. New figures burst onto the top of the stack, clambering up with what appeared to be inhuman skill until I saw the ghisten glow of manipulated wood. Ladders of roots and vines grew everywhere, and from everywhere, attackers came.

Charles dropped into the shelter of a rocky outcropping and a toppled tree, priming his musket with quick fingers. I crouched next to him, unslinging my own weapon.

Tane, where is that thing? I asked as I staggered to my feet. *Stranger?*

I am not sure yet, Tane replied and fell back into vigilant silence.

"How many are there?" Charles asked, shoving his ready musket into my hands and taking mine, priming it too. He was the one who had taught me to shoot—he knew I was slow at priming but a fair shot. "Go, go, I've got this."

I put the musket to my shoulder, sighted over the tree, and fired.

I missed my running target in a swirl of mist, but attracted two shots in return. Figures flitted through the boulders, wind-bent trees and deadfall.

I ducked back into shelter. "Too many," I said, switching muskets again and settling my shoulders.

"The creature?"

"Lurking," Tane's voice replied through my lips.

I fired again. This time one of the enemies, vulnerable at the top of a ladder, toppled backwards with a startled yell.

I ducked back down as more shots peppered our shelter.

A Stormsinger's song rose as Charles once more traded rifles with me. I tracked their song as I fired again and again, monitoring their melody and intent as more voices joined from all sides.

The fog thickened. Shots rang out and someone screamed in pain, a wailing, keening pain that tore at my nerves.

I could no longer see my targets, but neither could they see us. Or rather, I could not *quite* see my targets. Tane could sense several mages, mostly our allies, whose auras she marked with familiarity.

But several were not familiar. I focused on one of those.

There was a Sooth with a grey edge to his aura. Near him was another aura, this one more... silver than grey. With a heart of brooding, dark indigo.

If that was not Talys, I would give the documents to Ben.

I sighted, low on the silver-wreathed figure, and fired. I could not kill her, not with her ghisting present. But I could certainly slow her down.

My shot landed, but Talys did not so much as flinch. But she did turn, slowly, as a gap materialized in the fog.

The Stranger regarded me, his face overlaying the youthful features of Talys Lirr. Then he—she, the pair of them—smiled an open-mouthed smile in perfect unison, and charged.

BRITTLEWING —*Among one of the largest and rarest Otherborn beasts, the Brittlewing is an avian creature with bat-like wings. Only three references to Brittlewings entering the human world have ever been recorded, the most recent being at the Battle at the Aeadine Anchorage where a Brittlewing, in the thrall of a Mereish Summoner Adjacent, fought against the Aeadine Fleet.*

—FROM BEASTS AND BEINGS: A SUMMONER'S
OBSERVATIONS IN THE SOUTH MEREISH ISLES,
BY SAMUEL I. ROSSER

FORTY-SEVEN

The Collared Beast

BENEDICT

Grappling hooks clattered over the rails. I seized a hatchet from a dead sailor and ran along the rail, hacking ropes as I went. Wood gouged as the hatchet bit; ropes snapped and whipped away. Someone screamed as they dropped back into the water while another plunged straight down onto a rocky shoreline. I fancied I heard the crack of bone.

The deck rumbled beneath me as cannons boomed.

The Red Tempest lay angled across the mouth of the main channel, full broadside brought to bear against anyone daring to sail inland. Only the two small sloops had tried, coming as far in as they could before we blew one out of the water. The other ran aground and attackers dispersed, swimming, taking to longboats or attacking the warren of tunnels, bastions, stairs and bridges along the channel.

There were a great many longboats, however, and despite the maneuverability of our canons and the quick actions of swivel guns on the rails, we were now surrounded.

"Benedict Rosser!" a voice bellowed. "Face me!"

I saw a man standing on my quarterdeck, shoulders hunched with rage, coat torn open and smallsword in hand. He advanced towards me, cutting down a charging sailor with a deft, careless thrust.

"Who the fuck is that?" I asked Sam as he appeared at my side. "Voskin?"

"That is Voskin," Sam affirmed.

My lack of an immediate response seemed to enrage Voskin all the more. He descended the quarterdeck stairs. "Speak, you coward!"

"Do you intend to play this fairly?" Sam asked lowly.

"Saint, no," I returned.

I expected a glower of disapproval but saw only resignation. "Then you will not mind it I interfere, if the opportunity…"

"Please."

"Rosser!"

"Apologies," I shouted to Voskin. I waved my sword and gave a theatrical chuckle. "I forgot who you were! So sorry. Come, come."

What little control Voskin retained broke. He hurtled across the deck towards me and attacked in a flurry of impassioned blows. Samuel sidestepped and was immediately engaged by more boarders, but I spared him no more attention.

I could not. Despite his blinding rage Voskin was clearly well trained, his muscles repeating what his rage-addled mind could not. I deflected several blows, sidestepped or retreated from others, and led him out to the center of the deck.

Realizing what I was doing, Voskin slowed. He kept his sword up in a long guard as he began to circle, panting and spitting off to one side.

The moment stretched inordinately long in my mind; the longer he glared, the more the coy indifference I'd felt when faced with his rage faded. In its place there was a void where other thoughts began to seed. Memories of Port Sen. Of the fire and distant eyes of enthralled locals.

That little girl with fire all around.

I was not using my power. The realization was a shock, as if I had suddenly discovered I was not breathing, or had ceased to remember to blink.

I looked down to see the hilt of a throwing knife protruding from my side, rife with a dulled Magni glow.

A woman advanced. I had no memory of her, but she was clearly with Voskin, and she readied another throwing knife.

"Sam?" I shouted, suddenly very aware that my brother was not beside me. I moved to jerk the knife out, but hesitated, fingers crooked over the hilt in hesitation. I'd no desire to bleed out. "Sam!"

Voskin darted in with a long thrust. I deflected and twisted, but the movement was stiff. I took the tip of his sword straight to the bicep. My hand reflexively dropped my sword and I cursed, my own temper breaking free.

I barreled him over in a tumble of fists. A knee in my gut. My arm across his throat. I felt the knife slide from my side on a gush of blood and scrambled for it, but it was too slick to hold.

Voskin's face smashed into mine. I reeled, blinded, and struck out wildly. Teeth tore my knuckles open. A boot hit my chest.

Voskin scrambled upright again. The knife-throwing woman passed him his sword—no, *my* sword—and stood back.

"My people have justice," Voskin panted. He was covered with blood and his voice was rough. That was a comfort. At least I would not die without having made my mark.

My thoughts came up short. No. Why was I thinking this? Why was I capitulating already to this monster? I would not die. I would not yield.

But I longed to. I blinked, long and slow, and finally recognized what was happening.

Magni influence.

I caught sight of Enisca Alamay leaning against the door of the main cabin, her dark-rimmed, hollow eyes meeting mine before the world upended.

The Red Tempest tilted as if some great hand had seized his mast and pulled down. No—as if a great Otherborn beast plunged from the sky and landed upon it, bone-and-seaweed wings shuddering, shrieking a soundless screech of wrath.

Ghisten light shuddered across the deck as the beast began to drag *The Red Tempest* into the seastacks. Miaghis erupted, tentacles hurtling, body massing as he lunged at the beast.

The bulk of a stone spire reared above us, as high as the captive mast. Wood grated and cracked.

The winged monster released under Miaghis's assault. The deck righted with a chorus of shouts and screams, a great splash and clatter and groan. The monster took to wing, leaping to the nearest stack in two great shudders of its wings, and roared vengefully back at Miaghis.

As it did, its neck stretched and I saw the collar about its throat.

"Sam!" I bellowed. Too many threats, from too many sides. I needed my brother. I needed—

There was no response. I searched across the rocking deck, but Sam was nowhere to be seen. Nor was Enisca, or Voskin's knife-throwing compatriot. Only scattered crew, fighting and dying.

Voskin lunged at me. There was no move waiting, no hesitation. He stabbed towards my chest.

A woman grabbed him from behind and discharged a pistol under his jaw. His skull ruptured in a spray of teeth and blood, bone and brain matter.

I watched in stunned fascination as he fell. It was a remarkably grotesque end, yet it was not the repugnance of the moment that struck me. It was that, as he fell, he revealed his killer. Vachon.

The ship rocked violently, sending us both staggering. The winged beast had latched onto the mast again, wings thundering as it dragged us from the channel.

Vachon dropped into a crouch, maintaining her balance as the ship shuddered and bucked. I was less graceful—the fault of my wounds, naturally—and staggered back into the mast as the ship ground into a seastack. Rock toppled, clattering onto the deck and striking cannons with resounding gongs. Wood shrieked and protested. People fell and slid and grabbed one another, the heat of combat abandoned in face of this greater threat.

Miaghis surged again and the beast flapped away, but the damage was done. I could feel it. The ship was aground, rock continued to fall, and the channel was exposed.

Atop a nearby spire, one of the beacons lit.

"Their ships will come now," Vachon said, slowly rising.

I peered at her, squinting through the fog that had begun to waft past us.

Smoke. Not gunsmoke, but woodsmoke, thick and pungent with tar. It came from the quarterdeck. From the belly of *The Red Tempest*.

Vachon glanced at the nearest billowing hatch, but showed no surprise. Yes—that felt right. My Sooth's senses understood her casual regard of the smoke, and subsequently the fire that would consume my ship.

Because she had done it.

"What did you do?" I still asked, because I needed to hear it, needed to confirm what this new, traitorous sense insisted.

She gave me a half smile, neither satisfied nor sorry. "I wanted to burn my indenture, but I could not find it. So I burned your cabin." She raised the pistol she had used to kill Voskin to her forehead in a salute. "I hope you survive, Benedict. Do not waste my kindness."

"Your what?" The words burst out of me on tide of disbelieving, crimson rage. *The Red Tempest* was on fire. My ship was on fire and Vachon, Vachon had—

I stepped towards her and swayed. My knees hit the deck, skidding in blood and gore from Voskin's execution. His body was crumpled against the rail to one side with half a dozen others, his mangled head twisted.

I felt a heady, tremulous rush. My blood was too light in my veins. This was not battle fever. My thoughts ran and churned, too fast, too complex.

We were overrun. *The Red Tempest* was on fire and under attack from the Other. Mary had the documents, somewhere off in the seastacks—likely getting captured or killed. Samuel was out of sight, Alamay had escaped and Vachon had betrayed me.

Betrayed. I considered the word as the smoke thickened and the ship's bell clanged, its normally pure sound distorted by damage. No, betrayal implied there had been trust and loyalty to be broken.

I had never had that from Vachon. I had had a piece of paper that forced her compliance, and she had destroyed my ship to burn it.

"Fire's spreading too fast, Captain!" Ms. Olles shouted. I squinted at her—she had appeared seemingly out of nowhere. But then, my perception of the world was narrowing, lined with crimson and black. "There's no saving him, not as put upon as we are!"

I blinked, languidly. Vachon had vanished. Only Ms. Olles stood before me now, not offering to help me up, simply looking down at me with barely concealed contempt.

She took an instant longer to consider me, then turned back to the crew.

"Abandon ship!" she bellowed.

Thoughts of Vachon evaporated. I stared at Ms. Olles as she waved the crew towards the lowest angle of the deck and the seastack onto which we had been dragged. There, the first crew-members dropped out of sight, presumably scrambling down rocks to a beach below.

No.

My power flared. No longer was the knife in my side, dampening my power. No longer was Alamay lurking in the quarterdeck door, manipulating me. No longer was Vachon clouding my thoughts.

Ms. Olles stilled. The crew stilled. As black smoke billowed around us, thick and choking, they moved no further.

"You will not abandon ship," I stated. "Pumps and buckets."

Off in the fog, drums beat and guns thundered.

"We are aflame and the enemy is coming," Ms. Olles stated. She was resisting me, and shockingly well. Slowly, she raised a hand to show the Magni-dampening knife that had been embedded in my side. In the other, she leveled a pistol.

Suddenly, I was roaring. "I will *not* lose my ship!"

"Then you will lose your ship and your crew!" she shouted back and cocked the gun.

"Mutiny," I spat. "You're fucking mutineers! Cowards! Faithless, ungrateful—"

The force of my rage was too much for my bleeding body. I staggered, the world blurred and dipped, and I knew no more.

BLOSQUELLE —*A variety of miniature jellyfish with a red aura, these creatures drift across the sea floor in spherical form before unfurling to attack their prey or defend themselves. They are considered an ill-omen in many places across the Isles, with the notable exception of Indry, whose shallow, warm waters house what is believed to be their only breeding ground outside of the Other. In Indry, the gathering of blosquelle therefore marks a change in seasons, and their presence is both a point of pride and a mark of strength among the Indry's people.*

—FROM BEASTS AND BEINGS: A SUMMONER'S
OBSERVATIONS IN THE SOUTH MEREISH ISLES,
BY SAMUEL I. ROSSER

FORTY-EIGHT

Old Faces, New Threats

SAMUEL

I climbed back over the rail and dropped onto *The Red Tempest*'s deck, sopping wet and aching. "Ben!"

No one replied. A few figures ran across the deck, obscured by smoke billowing out from the hatches. Down the channel, the bruised light that was Hae's beast moved and the punch of cannon fire continued as the core of the battle slipped out of sight.

I found Ben moaning in the middle of the deck. As I hastened towards him he tried to find his feet, staggered and rounded on me—a pistol in hand.

"Fuck, it's you," he panted, lowering the weapon again. It dropped fully from his fingers to the deck but he did not seem to care, merely frowning at it before he lifted his leaden eyes back up to mine. "My ship is burning."

I pulled one of his arms across my shoulders. He leaned into me more heavily than I expected and I staggered, then found my feet and started for the side of the ship.

"What are you doing?" Ben asked dully.

"Throwing you overboard."

That put some life back into him. "Sam—"

I shoved Benedict over the side. Then I climbed up and jumped.

Water rushed into my ears. I hit the bottom faster than I expected, plunging right past Benedict's flailing form.

I spluttered onto the narrow shoulder of a seastack a moment later. I hauled Benedict—now coughing and groaning—half out of the water and knelt beside him.

I pulled the knife from my belt and reached forward.

He seized my arm, eyes suddenly wide with near maddened accusation. "Sam—"

"I am cutting off your shirt to bandage you with," I snapped.

"Use your own shirt!"

"No." I pried his hand away—it was unsettlingly easy—and went to work. "Hold still and this will be over faster."

He gave a choking, bitter laugh. "Over. It *is* over. I lost my ship. I lost them. I lost…"

I sensed his next word, *her*, but he did not speak it.

"You must have gotten the documents from Mary," he said. "Where did you put them?"

I ignored him.

"Sam. Where are they? They are all I have left, all that's left of this entire sordid fucking enterpri—" He cut off in a gasp of pain as I tightened the bandage over his wound.

I started to stand.

He grabbed my ankle. He looked hollowed out, pale, stripped of his dignities there upon the rock. He did not seem to hear the distant guns or shouts of combatants, though they reverberated through the seastacks from every direction.

"Sam," he said, sounding pleading now. "Sam. You have to want it too, you *have* to want to see them fall. Think of what they did to Mary. They betrayed us! They deserve—"

I jerked my ankle away. "I am going to leave you here. The situation grows dire and there is little I can do burdened by you, not with Inis Hae and the Ess Noti involved. Stay here and stay quiet. Please."

The words struck him harder than I anticipated. Hurt gored through his expression, followed by rage. His power billowed over me, but I had spent a lifetime resisting him, and he was weak with injury. I stepped away.

"Sam!" he shouted. "Samuel!"

I rounded the seastack and eyed a stretch of water between it and the next pillar. I would have to swim. But the twisted Sooth's aura that was Inis Hae was close, and drawing closer with the light of a ghisten ship and a distant, threading Stormsinger's song.

"Sam!" Ben's voice broke. "Let me help you!"

Slowly, I walked back around the spire. Ben met me halfway, clutching his side, face bleached pale and his expression shuddering between determined and beseeching.

"You will slow me down," I pointed out, walling off the tide of conflict I felt at his obvious pain.

"I will not." He rasped, coughed and spat blood on the stones. "I can still shoot. You're falling back to the island? Find a boat and I will be your gunner. Or are you going after Mary? My offer stands."

"I am going to manage Inis Hae."

"Who?" He squinted.

"The mage who shot me at the Anchorage? Who chased us across Mere?"

"Ah, that Inis Hae," Ben sucked at his teeth and spat again, this time less bloodily. "The Ess Noti is simply another reason to stay together. Where *is* Mary?"

I slipped over the edge of the Other, letting a cast of lights overlay the dusky human world.

"On the edge of the stone forest," I said, more than a little surprised. Less surprising was the plethora of other lights threatening to blur her from my sight—mages, ghistings and Otherborn beasts. The latter had increased in number, and I had no doubt Hae was part of that.

"That was not the plan," Ben murmured, stepping closer to me. Rock clattered, drawing my attention back to the human world and the sounds in the night. Or rather, the lack thereof.

There were no more cannons. Only a few shouts and gunshots came now, along with the songs of distant Stormsingers, the backdrop of sloshing water and the blaze and crumble of *The Red Tempest*.

Two ships came into sight, one behind the other in the channel. The farthest was *Dominion*, Voskin's vessel. Their Stormsinger abandoned her song and the wind that had propelled them up the channel died. The vessel loomed, gunports open, light pouring out around cannons, banners lifting on eddies of witchwinds.

The closer ship, meanwhile, was one of the nameless vessels who had held the line with Voskin and Talys. Elesi Artan stood at the forecastle, conferring with another young man and the familiar figure of Inis Hae.

The first time I had seen the dark-haired man was on the streets of Hesten where, with one brush of his hand on the street, he had ensured he could track me from Tithe to Mere, to the battle at the Aeadine Anchorage.

The last time I had seen him, he put a bullet in my chest.

If I had had an Usti long rifle, I could have done the same to him, then and there. But all that remained to me was my sword.

A flicker beneath the water broke me from my vengeful thoughts. At first I thought the fresh, reddish light was a reflection of the flames consuming *The Red Tempest*, but they moved with Hae's ship.

The lights of Otherborn beasts surged around his vessel in shades of red, orange, gold and bronze. As the ship slowed they pooled, spreading out among the seastacks, creeping closer to the flames, and carrying their unearthly light with them.

Ben and I held perfectly still as the water around our stack filled with drifting, red orbs.

"Samuel," my brother murmured to me, still clutching his side. "What are those?"

"Blosquelle," I murmured in reply. "Jellyfish, of a kind."

"Is that Mereish?"

"For 'fountains of blood'."

"I hate this place."

"We should be grateful," I replied, looking back to the ship, which had now drifted past and was, to all appearances, waiting for the wreckage of The Red Tempest to burn itself from their path. "I suspect they are the only reason Hae has not spotted us."

"They are also the reason we are now trapped," Ben bit back. He looked down at himself, opening the bloody hand he had pinned to his bandages. "I will not slow you down, as I said. But blood in the water…"

"Is unlikely to be helpful," I finished. I eyed the creatures, now interspersed with other lights, more obscure and less identifiable. "If all these are under Hae's thrall, which I believe they are… any interference on my part will alert him."

"Mr. Rosser," a voice hissed across the water.

A longboat drifted into sight off in the stacks, illuminated from below by the drifts of Otherborn beasts. Several people were in the boat, though I could not identify them from here.

The voice came again, this time recognizable. Brid. "We'll put in for you, sir."

Several tense moments later, the longboat bumped up onto our shore. I risked one step in the water, bracing Benedict as he climbed in.

"Brid," I said, giving her a meaningful look.

Ben appeared not to recognize the woman, offering a tight nod of thanks and focusing instead on a woman with an oar in her hand.

"Moody," he said, giving her shoulder a familiar thump. "Glad to see you."

"Sir," she said. The woman looked worse for wear, a mix of old injuries and new, but apathetic to them all.

I had the impulse to remind Benedict of who Brid was, but now was not the time.

"We should retreat," I said. "Rejoin with the forces at the main island. The wreck will hold the larger ships back for some time, but not forever."

"We can't slow them?" the woman Moody asked.

I hesitated, then shook my head. "No, not with any great effectiveness, and not without cost. We *must* get back to Demery and warn him that the Ess Noti are here."

"What about Mary?" Ben asked, brows furrowed at me.

"I must trust her and Tane," I said, affirming this to myself even as every part of me longed to go after her, to warn her first. I added with a half-hearted smile, "Besides, she does have Charles with her."

FORTY-NINE

Unexpected Allies

MARY

Charles and I clattered over a rocky shore and around the wreckage of a ship, pinned between two stacks on the edge of the stone forest.

The sea yawned ahead of us, vast and riddled with whitecaps beneath a cloud-choked moon. Waves crashed against the perimeter stacks, unchallenged and unchecked, and stirred to new violence by clashing witchwinds.

Spray blasted over Charles and I and foam chased us deeper into the rubble. So did a flurry of gunshots. They struck wood and pinged off stone as I threw myself behind a chunk of decking.

"Mary," Charles panted, plastered at my side. "I do not say this lightly, but I believe we should surrender. That *thing*..."

"Wood will not stop her. It." I agreed. My heart trammeled painfully in my chest and my mind refused to order itself. I was all instinct, and instinct agreed with Charles.

The wreckage around us crackled with ghisten light. Tane surged to meet it and ethereal illumination burst across the waves and down the stacks.

"Tane." Talys Lirr appeared—manifested—beside me. I had only a brief understanding of the fact that she had Otherwalked through the shipwreck before Stranger overwrote her features and leered at me, his grin once again passively echoed by Talys's youthful face.

A second *ghiseau*, the Sooth I had noted earlier, rounded the spire. He led an entourage of seven armsmen and women who, at a flick of his hand, leveled muskets at us.

Talys's voice was a croon, and it sent shivers up my spine. "Come, let us speak. You cannot easily die, but you can be incapacitated, and I will not hesitate to do so. So, cease your flight. It is shortsighted."

The wind picked up and water sloshed over our ankles.

"What are your intentions with us?" Charles asked.

"At the moment? Keeping you from causing further trouble, but after that there are possibilities. Hoten spoke of you at such lengths," Talys—Stranger, because there was nothing human left in the girl's voice—said, continuing to address Tane. "The Mother who planted the great Wold beyond the Stormwall. The one who turned a common Stormsinger into the Fleetbreaker. Oh, how he wanted you for his favorite daughter. But then he found me, of course."

Stranger smiled again, all teeth and inhuman features. Tane's unease met mine, thick and clotting.

"Our melding turned out, very, very well," Stranger added in a chill-inducing whisper. Then he straightened and beckoned to his minions.

The Sooth ghiseau came closer. As the light fell across him, the familiar lines of his face came into relief. Familiar not because I knew him—I certainly did not—but because he was clearly also one of Lirr's offspring.

The armsmen moved to bind us.

Tane, I roiled. *There must be—*

"There is no escape," Stranger said through Talys, perhaps reading my expression. "Your best option is to begin to earn my goodwill. Understood?"

A sound prodded at the back of my mind. I looked out to sea, ignoring Stranger.

Drums. They beat a steady rhythm, as if setting pace. *Boom, boom, boom.*

The pace of oars.

The Capesh, Tane and I realized as one. But who? Forbara aboard her remaining ship, still bent on forcing me to take her to the Wold?

I didn't care. I decided then and there that I would join with whoever sailed into sight, barring the Mereish Navy, or Lirr resurrected.

"Silvan," Stranger prompted, speaking to the young man.

"Those ships are not ours," Lirr's Sooth offspring, evidently named for his father, said.

Stranger's gaze returned to my face. "You know who they are."

"From those drums I would say they are Capesh oarships," Tane said through me. "But I am no Sooth."

Stranger flicked a hand at their people, and Charles and I were immediately set upon.

The impulse to Otherwalk, to try to flee again despite its uselessness, assailed me. They grabbed, and tied, and shoved. But I could not bring myself to leave Charles, not when I knew how little chance of escape I truly had.

We allowed ourselves to be led away, back into the fog and the seastacks.

FIFTY

Ice Bound

BENEDICT

Thunder rolled as we rowed in near silence through the seast-acks. At first I attributed it to cannon fire—perhaps *Harpy* coming to take up *The Red Tempest*'s mantle and guard the main channel. I reflected on this with intense bitterness, interspersed with a deathly sort of calm, one that turned my rage and pain at the loss of my ship into an empty void.

But this thunder did not pause. It continued to roll, transitioning into a storm of unnatural darkness and intensity. It swept over the seastacks on a winter-edged witchwind, and the fog began to freeze.

It froze in my beard and atop my collar. It froze to our clothes and lashes and wind-tossed hair. It froze to the oars and rock and began to crystallize in the seawater.

"They are calling winter in midsummer," I murmured to Samuel. I saw him from below, as he was seated over me at an oar, rubbing shoulders with Moody. I had given up my bench to him and sat cross-wise in the bottom of the boat, freezing water sloshing beneath my knees. "No Stormsinger is that powerful."

"This is not a matter of a single Stormsinger," Samuel replied, rowing steadily. "Nor even a chorus, as in the fleets. Isla Ascra has a hundred witches."

"Witches working in concert to protect their home, not the

ship on which they are captive," I added.

Samuel glanced down at me, his expression hidden by the angle and the murk. "Indeed. It is a powerful thing, fighting for something that is yours. Something to which you belong."

His words—and the resulting train of my thoughts—fed that hollowness inside me. I suspected that was his goal, reminding me that I now had nothing to which I belonged—my ship burned, my crew mutinied, my reputation soiled from one edge of the Winter Sea to the other.

It should have enraged me. But my emptiness was all-consuming now.

"I suppose it is," I murmured, and settled my head back into the bulwark. My gaze drifted up to the open sky, interspersed with the darker lines of sea stacks and trees. I glimpsed a few lights out in the night, in the sky and on the sea stacks, and at the periphery of my senses, but they were no stars. Just Otherborn beasts on the prowl.

I wrapped my arms across my chest, careful of my wound and bandages, and closed my eyes. "Wake me when someone comes to kill us."

Rain abruptly splattered my face. It was shockingly cold, already more sleet than rain, and I groaned. I cracked open an eye again and scowled up at the sky.

Samuel tossed his hat onto my chest without a word, exposing his own head to the downpour, and continued wordlessly at his labors.

I slowly took the hat, tented it over my face, and closed my eyes again.

I must have slept or passed out, for the next thing I was aware of was a bitter, bone-chilling ache. I sat up, my clothes crackling, and saw the cliffs of Isla Ascra's main island looming above us. They glistened with ice in a steady, passive light, and an odd sound filled the air. The creak of oars, and the musical, tinkling clatter of ice in the water.

At least the cold numbed my wound. Still I braced on the hull as I took my weight on my arms and looked out into the sea stacks.

It was dawn, or near to. Red, orange and gold light cut through the spires under a belly of cloud, a summer sunrise for a frigid world. Hoarfrost coated everything in sight, save for the surface of the water, which had turned to thick flows of frazil and emitted clouds of drifting mist, which only lent more moisture to the arctic air.

Harpy was coved with ice, too. She lay nearby, bowsprit and the bare-breasted, shrieking figurehead facing down the main channel to the island. Figures moved on her deck, stovepipes pumped woodsmoke into the dawn, and her lines glistened with ice.

There was a steady wind, blowing in a circular current around Isla Ascra. This was evident from the swirl of the clouds overhead, a great cyclone of cloud spreading out across the stone forest and keeping Ascra within a bubble of sorcery.

Then there was the singing. It seemed to come from every corner of the island, echoing and turning and reverberating, melodic and unspeakably eerie. The Stormsingers maintaining their spell.

It was strangely peaceful. But it was also false. I had awakened in a deceptive lull, for a moment later *Harpy's* bow chasers erupted, firing off into the stacks and out of sight. All along the cliffs, more guns fired. And a moment later, the unseen replied.

We landed on the beach around the same time as Voskin's *Dominion* emerged from the channel and rammed *Harpy*. The smaller vessel shuddered and rocked.

Samuel stood for a moment on the ice-slick beach, staring out at Demery's ship. Then I took his arm, he tore his eyes away, and we ran for the tunnel.

The portcullis was already half closed, ready to fall at a moment's notice. Someone saluted Samuel and waves us hurriedly on, away from the light of the beach and up into the village of Ascra.

The air was gentler here. Sunlight beamed down on a central square, but there was no comfort to be found in its warmth.

The village was in a state of organized confusion. Wounded lay in rows under makeshift shelters and fires burned everywhere, surrounded by clots of exhausted combatants.

Most of them were my crew. I met Ms. Olles's warding gaze as words like *betrayal* and *murder* and *revenge* passed through my mind.

But I only nodded in reply. She was clearly in command now. And I had other things to do.

"Every able body to the cliffs!" someone bellowed. "They're making landfall! If you can hold a gun, on your feet!"

"Go," Samuel urged our companions from the longboat.

Moody gave me a bland, tired look but started off. "Get stitched up!" she shouted at me.

I saluted crookedly.

"Yes, go to the healers," Samuel agreed. "I will find you later."

Before I could answer, he sprinted off. As he went I heard him shout to a brown-skinned woman, "Idriss! Has Mary returned?"

An explosion shook the ground, sending him staggering, and screams arose here and there.

Mary. The thought of her took hold, along with the knowledge of what she carried.

I had lost my ship. I had lost my crew. But I had not yet lost the reason for which I'd come to the South Isles.

"They're on the beach!" someone said.

Well, then. This might all be over rather soon, and I had an erstwhile sister-in-law to find.

I rubbed at my face and hobbled towards the healers.

"You," I said to the first blood-splattered, competent-looking individual to meet my eyes. I used my power and their attention focused wholly on me, even as shouts continued to echo around the courtyard and guns boomed on the cliffs.

"Stitch me up, quickly," I said, taking off my coat, untying my makeshift bandage and tossing it on the ground. Blood slowly started to ooze from my side as the cold raised gooseflesh on my bare skin. "And someone find me a rifle."

FIFTY-ONE

In the Well

MARY

I watched the deck of Talys's ship as the sounds of battle waned, transitioning into whoops and howls, cries of victory and determination. There was a chaotic, celebratory firing of guns and a repetitive stomping on the deck, followed by a chanting, triumphal song.

"I take that to mean they have made landfall," Charles said, staring up at the deck above with his manacled hands in his lap.

I was also manacled, but not only that. There was a band on my forearm of thick, rough iron. It left me with a terrible feeling of claustrophobia that had nothing to do with the closeness below decks.

There was no air. Or rather, the air was impassive to me.

Legs appeared on the stairs and Silvan followed two large men into the hold. The Sooth watched as Charles and I were unlocked and propelled up on deck.

A sense of profound disassociation overtook me as I saw the cliffs and beach of Isla Ascra to one side, *Harpy* to another, and the sea stacks all around—all sheathed in ice. Storm clouds circled overhead and the air was frigid, turning lines to ice and making the deck slippery beneath my feet, despite a layer of scattered sand.

If the witches of Ascra had done this, it was a staggering feat. But a sheath of ice had not been enough to stop their invaders.

Already the beach was swarming with figures and boats. The portcullis was mangled upon the sand, surrounded by a blossom of char marks from explosions.

Charles and I were loaded into a boat and ferried ashore. We joined a flow of enemies up through the tunnel and into the heart of Isla Ascra, where rows of prisoners were on their knees in the square. I saw faces from Athe's crew, but Athe and Demery themselves were not present. Nor were Sam, Ben, or Idriss.

That brought me some hope, until Talys met us. Stranger still glistened in her eyes and there was an air of profound satisfaction about the creature.

That satisfaction, however, flickered as Elesi Artan stormed up and grabbed me by the arm.

"Where are they, you bitch?" he demanded, shaking me.

Charles tried to jerk from his captors and Tane flared across my skin as I leaned away from him.

"Pardon me?" I asked.

Stranger's voice was too level, too calm. "What are you doing?"

Artan considered the creature with a marked disdain. "Talys," he said, intentionally cutting Stranger out. "This is the woman who stole the documents from Solov, the one we needed to find."

I glanced between the Usti and Stranger. Clearly, there were dynamics at play that I was not privy to. But I would not be cowed, not when my friends were still free and hope remained. Unless they were dead, in which case I would likely be joining them soon anyway. That left me with a terrible feeling not of fear, but of sadness.

There were fates worse than death on the Winter Sea, but I had looked death in the face many times now, and we shared a familiarity I no longer feared.

"No, I stole them from *you*," I said, seeing an opportunity to divide my enemies. "After you stole them from Solov and murdered him. You little twat."

"That is a lie," Artan spat, shaking a finger in my face. "I will gut you, woman."

I considered the finger, then looked around Artan to Talys. "Solov invited you to his auction, didn't he? You, Voskin. The Ess Noti."

Artan moved to strike me across the face.

Inis Hae seized the younger man's arm and hauled him unceremoniously aside. Artan raged, berating Hae and spouting threats at both Stranger and I.

Hae kicked him to the ground. Artan landed on his hands and knees on the stone of the courtyard and then, only then, did he seem to grasp his situation.

"How dare you!" he raged, his eyes filling with a dreadful fear.

Artan's people rushed forward. Others—loyal to Stranger and Hae, I assumed—met them with a wall of pistols, muskets and swords.

Hae planted a boot in the middle of Artan's chest, holding him down.

I heard Charles mutter under his breath. He knew where this was going as well as I did.

"Solov invited us south, indeed," Stranger told me, watching casually as Hae issued an order to a soldier and returned to lording over Artan. "He sent out a number of invitations, and Voskin and I set out together with Mr. Hae. Mr. Hae, who had fortuitously come to Voskin with a fascinating tale of the Rosser twins and the Fleetbreaker's daughter, and the profoundly valuable documents they fled Ostchen with."

The fact that Enisca had stolen the documents, not us, seemed unnecessary to point out. I had already admitted to having them.

Yes, what is your plan now? Tane asked in the quiet of my skull.

I could not answer quite yet. There was something profoundly terrifying, and mesmerizing, about the way Stranger considered Artan.

"I am glad I did not kill you immediately," the ghisting said. "You were a timely and adequate ally."

From the twitch in Artan's expression, he understood precisely what Stranger meant.

"You would not dare," he spat again. He twisted, looking to his perimeter of armsmen. "What are you doing, you fools? Help me!"

"If you do, you will die," Stranger said. Where Artan seemed careless and disdainful towards the ghisting, his people were not. Several lowered weapons. Others shuffled back. "If you wish to live, join me as Voskin's people have."

Voskin is dead? I whispered to Tane. It should have been a relief. I was free, the pressure to apprehend Benedict alleviated, and whatever my mother had promised Voskin—or threatened him with—nullified. But it all seemed small in the face of Hae's presence and Lirr's legacy. Voskin had forced us into this mire, but we were far too deep now for his death to free us.

Hae leaned down and took Artan by the hair. The young man struggled, a burst of indigence fading to bewildered fury, then desperation.

All faded into gargling as Hae, grunting with effort, slit the other man's throat and stepped back.

Artan tried to get up. His hands slipped in the growing pool of his own blood and he collapsed, staring, over the crimson puddle. Stray hairs over his mouth twitched with the short, bubbling gasps of his final breaths.

Around us Artan's people abruptly retreated, their expressions showing varying degrees of shock and uncertainty.

An officer in Mereish uniform began to shout over them and gradually the square cleared.

I was left with Charles, Stranger, Hae, two guards and Artan's twitching corpse.

The young Usti's little finger drummed manically in his cooling blood.

I became aware of Stranger speaking to me. "Now, the documents? Then I will see you to some place comfortable."

My lips parted—to say what, I had no idea.

"The documents are aboard *Harpy*," Charles leapt in. "Captain Kohlan put them with her papers. She can tell you where those are better than Mary."

"I doubt that is true, but why not? We have time." Stranger looked to Hae, and for the first time I noted their dynamic. Stranger maintained his air of superiority but he did not order Hae about, did not speak to him disdainfully. Hae, and perhaps by extension the Ess Noti, was someone he either needed or actually respected.

"I will have my people search *Harpy* and interrogate the crew," Hae conceded. He pointed his bloody knife at me. "However, I have the Rosser twins to hunt."

Sam. Saint, last time he had faced Hae, he had been shot and nearly died.

I did feel fear then, but not for myself.

Hae was still talking. "She is my key to finding them."

Stranger nodded, the movement mimicked by Talys beneath his spectral shell. "I will personally see her secured."

Hae left, and Stranger conferred with several of Talys's people before he led Charles and I out of the village. More guards joined us, highly alert and well armed.

"We may yet expect a rescue," Charles nudged me, scanning our escort and the surrounding trees. The ice had begun to melt, leaving the world glistening with dripping meltwater. "Clearly the island is not secured."

Any hope of rescue became thinner the deeper we went into the forest. I had no sense of what direction we went—the last time I had been in this forest was at night with Samuel, and my thoughts had been on Tane, not the path we took. But a suspicion began to grow.

Now, the forest looked vastly different. Ice and snow melted on the trees, glinting in the sunlight as the storm the mages of Isla Ascra had woven gave way. It was beautiful and chill, with drifts of clarifying cold from the shadows and the scent of damp earth in my lungs.

I drew a deep, calming breath.

Talys turned on me. Stranger manifested, overlaying her face as he had before, billowing and shuddering and leering.

"Why have you not tried to escape?" he asked, shoving his face into mine. "I speak to you, Tane, not this human shell. I was led to think more of you, expect more. Do you bow to *her*?"

There was a heartbeat of silence, then he seized the sides of my head. Talys's hands were cold and bony, a set of short nails and trembling grip overwhelmed by Stranger's longer, thinner, larger hands. His grip, however, was absolutely steady.

Ghisten communication crashed over me. The flood was always overwhelming, but this was more. This was a winter wind scouring through the heart of me, a violation I could not stop, a grasp I had no hope of breaking.

Tane erupted. She burst from my mouth, my eyes, my shuddering chest, and the trees around us swayed and shuddered and cracked.

Stranger released me but I still felt fingers gouging my flesh, and my skin burned.

He raised a hand and the trees stilled, but it was a tremulous silence, the forest caught between the wills of two opposing powers.

Tane stood before me like a shield, our bodies linked by thick cords of spectral flesh.

There you are, Stranger crooned. He said nothing else—everything he might have said was all already there in my mind, left by the scouring deluge from our contact.

I saw Hoten and Lirr in a hundred settings—at sea, in this wood, in storms and sunlight, pouring over documents and taking a young, fragile Talys by the hand. I saw burning ghistings. So, so many burning ghistings. I saw Stranger manifest for the first time, overwhelming the bewilderment in Talys's eyes. I saw further back, to the wreck Stranger had been salvaged from by Lirr. A ship of unfamiliar, ancient construction, with high curved prow and stern, rows of oars and generations of bronze-skinned, black-haired sailors.

There too were glimpses of a future which Stranger intended to carve, one of increasing power across the Winter Sea with Talys as his docile host, his human allies bowing to and revering him.

It was familiar, and yet it was new. It was Lirr and Hoten. It was the Mereish and the Aeadine. It was Ben and the Navy. It was another quest of greed and want, another endless hunger and clawing for power.

It left me profoundly weary. This, then, was the inevitable pattern of the world. Greed. Violence. Power.

All I wanted was a Wold. The steady strength of ancient trees, and the shelter of their branches. The soft cushion of moss. The hush of falling snow among white-blanketed bows.

You have seen it?

The last whisper caught me off guard. Stranger stared into Tane's eyes, and I knew that he had seen the Southern Ghistwold in my memories. Not only that, but he had known of it before, from Hoten and Lirr's searching years ago.

I felt a presence at my back and realized it was Charles, his bound hands on my back, bolstering me with the presence of another, gentler ghisting. Nosewise.

Stranger did not interfere. In fact he watched the exchange with calculation, one that I was sure did not bode well for Charles.

Stranger set off with decisive steps. The guards jabbed Charles and I into movement again, but a mere half a dozen paces on, Stranger slowed, glanced about, and seemed to... settle.

"Here we are," he said, pushed aside a veil of greenery, and revealed the yawning, darkened maw of Lirr's well.

FIFTY-TWO

Even Ground

MARY

We emerged into the cavern I had discovered with Samuel. The thin sheet of water continued to pour across the floor, uninterrupted and smooth except for where our footsteps splashed.

We traversed the room, entered the passage and stepped into Lirr's chambers. The numbing power of the black stones struck me like a blow, redoubling the effects of the cuff on my arm. Charles visibly flinched.

"Idriss and her witches have been here," Stranger spat, surveying the empty first chamber and peering through the door to the study. Frustration, which had overcome him at the sight of the crumbled door, redoubled. "Well, whatever they have taken can be recovered. Suspend him here, and fasten her to the wall."

My stomach turned as Charles was wrestled into the manacles beside the burn pit. The threat to the act was clear, and given how little Stranger seemed to know of Charles or acknowledge his existence, I suspected the message was solely for my benefit.

If I did not comply, Charles would burn.

I was prodded into the wall and the manacles fastened around my wrists. When that was done, Stranger-Talys crouched to fit a key in the lock of my Stormsinger's cuff. It came away with a stiff click, revealing sweaty, reddened skin.

No power returned to me. Not here, in this place.

"I will finish conquering this island," Stranger told me, pocketing the cuff and key. "I will deliver Hae his documents. Then I will return to you, and we will discuss the future. It may take several days, so take this time to consider what part you would like to play in that future." He nodded back to Charles. "And who you would like to share it with."

With that, Stranger and his people left. I listened to their footsteps fade, sure that their departure was a trick. They were not leaving us here, alone? There had to be a guard, someone left behind to watch us.

But then again, what could we do? We had no weapons and I had no magecraft. There was not a scrap of wood in sight for the ghistings to manipulate, and the furniture in the library was beyond another arch of stone and its invisible barrier.

Charles's boots scuffed the char of the pit and he grunted in discomfort.

"I suppose they intend to kill me," he observed. "Immolation, and all that. But Sam will find us. If not Ben! I hate to brag, but he has grown rather fond of me."

"Ben wouldn't know where to look."

"No, no," Charles said. "He has the Sight now, like Sam. Very convenient. Or inconvenient, depending on how he feels towards you, but as I said, I am favored. As are you, occasionally."

"Neither of them will be able to see us," I said. "The black stones block the Other. It's the same substance the Ess Noti use in their talismans. Lirr was doing more than searching for me, when he lived on Ascra."

"I take that to mean you also cannot Otherwalk out of these restraints."

I shook my head. The helplessness of that admission overtook me, leaving me breathless. Here, I was no *ghiseau*. I was no Stormsinger. I had no Samuel, no weapons. I could barely move.

I barely even had Tane.

A figure stepped into the chamber, long rifle in hand. He looked up sharply, perhaps noticing the effect of the stones, and surveyed Charles and I.

"Ben!" Charles laughed. "See, Mary, I told you."

Benedict's mouth twitched at that, but the expression lost its life before it reached his eyes. "What is this place?"

"Lirr's torture pit. Unlock us, quickly," Charles urged.

Ben crossed the room, peering into the library, before he turned back to us. He kept one arm a little tighter to his torso, and I noticed a thick bandage around his side. Blood was already seeping through, and his face was paler than usual.

His gaze locked on me and any hope I'd had that this was a rescue evaporated. "Where are the documents, Mary?"

I felt something break inside of me, though I hadn't known I had anything to break when it came to Ben.

I considered lying. Ben's power was as stifled here as mine; he could not tell truth from lie, nor compel me to the truth. But what would it accomplish?

"You will release us if I tell you?" I asked.

"Ben," Charles broke in. "What are you doing? Let us go and we can discuss—"

Ben put up a silencing hand and approached me, slinging his rifle over his back and dropping into a crouch just out of reach. "Well?"

Charles watched us with a wary, increasingly more caged expression. It reminded me that, for all his jesting and frippery, he had survived in this cutthroat world for longer than I had.

I released a long, weary exhale and reached down my stays. I pulled out the packet of documents, hot and sweat-slicked from my skin, and tossed them at Ben's feet.

Without a word Ben picked up the pouch, untied and unrolled it, and pulled out a stack of papers, envelopes and missives. They were damp along the top edges, but intact. "Thank you."

The words sounded, of all things, heartfelt.

"I am not simply doing this for vengeance," he said, rising to his feet—trying to hide a wince—and stuffing the envelope inside his own jacket. "I was in the beginning, I admit that. But I have seen beyond that selfish horizon. I am doing this for you. For captive mages and pressed sailors and everyone else whose lives were torn apart by Usti treachery. Perhaps I will end the war. Perhaps I will start a new one. But the truth will be known."

"Ah, so that is how it is now," Grant muttered. "Nicely palatable."

I gave a bitter little laugh and discovered tears in my eyes. "Ben, I don't care."

Interest flicked in his eyes. "Why?"

"Because the fate of nations is not something I want on my shoulders," I said simply. "It's not my burden to bear, not my right to decide. I am only one person. Saint, I have enough obligations as it is."

"Ben," Charles cut in. "Release us."

"Not your right?" Ben repeated, still ignoring Charles. "Then who has the right?"

I threw up my bound hands with a clink of chains. "I don't know, Ben! Not me!"

"Philosophy later!" Charles shouted. "Go look for keys!"

Ben raised placating hands and vanished into the other room. After several nerve-tearing moments of clattering and rustling, he reappeared with a set of keys.

He dropped them on the floor just out of reach of my toes. "Tell Sam not to follow me this time," he said. "Please."

With that, he began to walk towards the door. I stared after him. I had thought there was no more space in me for feeling, numb and overwrought as I was. But I still managed to feel somehow hurt by his abandonment.

"Ben," Charles shouted, exhibiting an emotion I had rarely seen in him before—anger. "Ben! You cannot leave us here!"

"If I do not, you will try and stop me. Besides," he added. "The Capesh have arrived. The island will be freed, and Forbara is a decent woman."

"You cannot know that," Charles insisted. "Do not delude yourself, Ben."

I leapt in. "Please don't leave us."

Ben stopped in his tracks. He looked back at me and there, in his eyes that looked so much like Samuel's, I saw conflict.

But it did not stop him from turning away and striding out the door.

FALSE MORGORY —*Similar to the aquatic morgory, this feline creature is found solely in the southern half of the Mereish South Isles. Powerfully muscled and possessing a crushing bite, it lacks the sea-dwelling morgory's signature mane, along with any predilection for devouring wood. Instead, they freely hunt flesh, whether that be human, beast, or various Otherborn creatures.*

—FROM BEASTS AND BEINGS: A SUMMONER'S
OBSERVATIONS IN THE SOUTH MEREISH ISLES,
BY SAMUEL I. ROSSER

FIFTY-THREE

Two Summoners

BENEDICT

I paused, back in the sunlight, under the dripping trees, and caught my breath.

Please don't leave us.

My blood moved too fast. My wound ached and my head spun. I stepped behind the trunk of a towering cedar, blocking off my view of the well, and clutched at my chest. I felt the documents there, beneath my jacket. I had them. I *had* them. I held the fate of the Winter Sea between my fist and my hammering heart, above the bloody stain of my bandages.

The thought filled me with triumph, but it was an oddly tilted thing, as if I stood on the deck of a ship about to be swamped.

Charles and Mary had spoiled my victory. I should not have had to take the documents from them, with their accusing eyes and their chains in the dark. It should have been Miko Solov or Elesi Artan. Someone whose eyes I could look into and not have to swallow... whatever unpleasant sensation was currently souring my stomach.

I started walking, forcing one foot in front of the other towards the village. I was in pain, but I needed to reach the beach, board one of the ships, and ensorcel a crew. Then I could leave all of this behind. Preferably, before Forbara and her Capesh overran the island and someone had the time and presence of mind to stop me.

"Rosser!"

A gun cracked. I foresaw the shot, the figure materializing from the forest, and dodged.

Inis Hae stood behind me, trading a spent pistol for a primed one.

I started to raise my own weapon, then realized I had not loaded it. No help for that. Hae had already leveled his pistol at me anew, and we were in a standoff.

"This is Magni shot," Hae informed me. He spoke just loud enough for his voice to carry and, in that, I sensed something close to... distraction. As if his mind were divided. "You are injured, and I am warded against you."

My Sooth's senses plucked at me and I felt something—many somethings—closing in.

"Also, your musket is not primed," the Ess Noti added.

Ah. Well, as long as he did not see I had the documents.

"I nearly mistook you for your brother, you know. Your auras are remarkably changed since we last met."

The somethings were drawing closer and I picked out the flicker of Otherborn lights. There were dozens of them, all converging on Hae.

"I will give you one offer. One." Hae went on. A creature skulked from the brush to weave past his legs in greeting, then began to prowl towards me. It was feline and twisted like a morgory, but larger and seemingly adapted to the land, with the powerful muscles, wide face and slavering jaws of something much, much stranger.

"There is a place in the Ess Noti for someone with your skills. But there is no place outside, and I will not do myself the disservice of underestimating the trouble you could cause on a voyage back to Mere."

I barely heard Hae anymore. There were so many of the creatures, all hung about with a bronzed, orange light. They were in the trees, in the brush. Closing in to block off any escape.

"So surrender, or—"

I did not hear the rest. I turned and ran.

I pounded through the trees, over roots and loam and moss and rock. I found a path and swerved onto it, blinking a red haze of pain and fatigue from my eyes.

One of the things leapt at me. Any hope I had that they were not wholly present in the human world—and thus, unable to tear me limb from limb—evaporated as jaws closed on my collarbone.

I shouted and tore the creature off, stumbling as I did. I found my feet and ran on.

Beasts converged from every side. Not just the small, twisted cat creatures, but a great presence above, one with a rattling shriek I heard in my bones.

I exploded into the village with the horde of Otherborn beasts on my tail. I dashed through wafts of gunsmoke, narrowly avoided a sword to the face and ducked an outthrust arm. Pain made me stagger.

Sam. I saw him in the heart of the village square with a score of allies, including Athe. He fought with cutlass and a swinging, spent pistol, stabbing and bludgeoning with abandon, avoiding thrusts and shots with an effectiveness that I marked, in some corner of my mind, as admirable.

"Sam!" I shouted. There was panic in my voice, but to hell with that. "Sam!"

I burst in with my escort of horrific beasts.

Sam grabbed me and shoved me behind his back. He shouted something I did not hear—someone discharged a musket beside my ear at that very moment, leaving my ears ringing. I coughed gunsmoke from my lungs, stole the sword from the belt of the ill-timed musketeer, and stepped shoulder-to-shoulder with my brother.

The beasts broke around us like a tide, most fleeing from the bedlam, others leaping at more hapless combatants.

The winged monstrosity that had attacked *The Red Tempest* and tormented the Aeadine fleet plunged out of the sky.

A winged woman met the creature. Harpy, her face a mask of fury, bare-breasted and spouting three sets of glorious, spectral wings, drove a very real spear of wood into the chest of the creature, which shuddered and shrieked.

A shot clipped my arm and I turned to see Hae shouldering through the melee. He glared at the pair of us, his gaze never breaking as his beast crashed into the roof of a nearby building, caving it in. Its wings and limbs flailed as Harpy plunged after it, stabbing again and again.

Samuel raised his musket. I leveled my sword, moving to stand half in front of him—a physical barrier as he took the shot.

Hae staggered. The tide of Otherborn beasts around him seemed to pause, wavering with his control.

One of the morgory-like creatures advanced, neatly avoiding running steps and falling combatants. Samuel made a sound, a command, and the beast leapt.

Hae went down with the creature latched to his throat. There was a horrific, gargling scream. The tide of the battle moved, another beast came, then another—some shaking, some snarling, one by one breaking free of Hae's hold.

And turning upon him. By the time Samuel shouted his next command of "Flee!", Hae's body was still.

Every Otherborn beast in the courtyard took flight save Hae's winged beast, which was now limp on the wreckage of the house. Harpy hovered over the ruins of wood and bone and thatch and spectral flesh like an avenging Saint, and I felt gooseflesh ripple up my arms.

Then she reached to her belt, chose a new mask—a grinning vixen—placed it over her face. She vanished into thin air.

"Mary," Samuel seized my arm, panting. "Have you seen Mary?"

I stared at him as the battle waxed and waned and, from the mouth of the tunnel leading to the beast, a stream of Capesh sailors emerged. They were led by the lovely, vengeful form of Forbara and a bronze-skinned man I vaguely recognized from Demery's study, back on Oranmur.

The moment of my decision was short. One beat of the heart, one crack of a musket, one flash of sunlight in my eyes. I glimpsed the ship I would steal, sail out on with the documents in my possession, ready to make the world fall at my feet.

And then I saw Samuel's eyes, desperate in their intensity.

Please don't leave us.

FIFTY-FOUR

Regret

MARY

There was a scrape and echo in the dark. I flinched and Charles spun in his manacles, toes tapping on the stone.

"Hurry!" Charles hissed.

I fumbled the keys, shoving another one into the lock of my manacles. "I've tried them all!"

The scuff of boots, echoing down a corridor, and reverberating voices.

"Try them again!"

I dropped the keys with a clatter and cursed. "They're not right, Charles!"

I heard running footsteps, then the barrel of a musket came through the door and swept the room. As if time had folded back in on itself Benedict stepped back into the room, followed by Samuel.

"You bastard!" Charles shouted. He kicked at Ben as the other man strode over to him. "You are the absolute worst fucking person I know, you are, I swear it."

Ben, one arm tight over the wound to his side, surveyed Charles with a resigned kind of helplessness.

"Mary, are you all right?" Samuel asked, crouching before me and taking up the keys.

I gave a breathy, hysterical laugh. "I am now."

Sam considered the keys, then selected one and fitted it into the lock. "What is Charles raging about?"

"Ben didn't tell you?" The manacles fell away and I rubbed my wrists. "Ben's the one who left us here."

Samuel paused, a dangerous light in his eyes. With gentle hands he helped me to stand, then he turned on his brother.

"You left them here?"

"I did," Ben said. That resigned look was still in his eyes—a gallows look. "I had a crisis of conscience over it and would have returned, if not for Hae. But I still did it. I stole the documents and left them here."

Samuel took one step, closing the space between them, and punched Benedict across the face. Ben toppled into the burn pit but Samuel was not done. He followed the first blow with another, grabbing his brother's collar to jerk him up just enough to punch back down again.

Benedict did not fight back. His coat fell open, revealing blood-soaked bandages as he collapsed into the coals. He looked up at Sam through half-dazed, half-deadened eyes. "I would have come back."

The rage seemed to flee Samuel. I abandoned my manacles and quietly came over, giving the brothers what space I could while I reached up to unfasten Charles.

He dropped down with visible relief and came to stand beside me, watching the twins.

Wincing, Benedict reached into his coat. He took out the document envelope and threw it at Samuel's feet, then started to get up.

Samuel did not move, neither to take the documents nor help Ben rise. It was painful to watch—the instinct to help him even passed through me—but not one of us moved.

Ben found his feet and looked between us. "I am sorry," he said, and limped from the room.

Together, we listened to his footsteps grow more distant. Samuel's expression was too calm, too smooth—I did not dare to take his hand. Charles looked more incredulous than anything else, still clasping his raw wrists.

I stooped and picked up the documents, tucking them back into my stays. What I felt for Benedict then was not forgiveness, nor was it worry. But it was, in some way, mercy. "I will go after him, if neither of you will."

Samuel cast me a half-seeing look. There was gratitude in his eyes, and a growing resolve.

"No," he said. "Leave him to me."

FIFTY-FIVE

Tempest Choir

SAMUEL

We found Benedict on the edge of the island. I gestured for Mary and Charles to keep watch, just out of sight, and approached on my own.

My twin sat against a tree at the top of one of Ascra's cliffs, coat discarded, blood-soaked bandages exposed. His gaze was directed away from me down the coast, and it was not until I neared that I saw what he looked at. A many-tentacled ghisting.

Miaghis had been freed by the burning of *The Red Tempest*. There was a substance to his form and a clarity to his eyes, no longer sea-glass but sharp and clear as the noonday sun.

He massed before Benedict on the edge of the cliff. The tree behind my brother quivered. Roots rippled. But Ben simply stared at the beast with the same soulless regard he had given us before he left Lirr's well.

I drew breath to shout for Mary, but Miaghis began to fade. I felt a rushing in the fabric of the world as the ghisting slipped back into the Dark Water and faded from sight. He seemed to relax as he went, tentacles no longer coiling and flicking. A moment later, he was gone.

Benedict stared briefly at the space where the creature had been. Then he cast his gaze down the coast once more, towards a drift of thick black smoke and the beginnings of a Stormsinger's eerie, growing chorus.

One of the large ships was burning as she drifted down the rim of the island. Hae's ship, I recalled from the channel. It was a reminder of the battle still raging, even if all we heard were occasional gunshots and the distant song of Idriss's army.

Clouds gathered in, dark as slate.

Benedict spared me a sideways squint as I closed in, his expression unchanging beneath wind-tossed shanks of hair. He opened his mouth to say something, then cut himself off with a disgusted sound and turned back to the burning ship.

As I had so often before, I felt the weight of years as I looked down at him, the burden of memory and obligation, of an endless cycle of conflict and hope and disappointment.

Here I was again. One last time.

"I have no intention of throwing myself off this cliff, if that is what concerns you," Benedict said without inflection. "That is too easy an escape."

"An escape from?" I asked.

"Restitution." He finally raised his eye to mine, leaning his head back against the tree as if he lacked the strength to hold it up. "That is my only road forward, is it not? That is what you would advise me."

An old hope, unwanted and untrustworthy, tightened my chest. "It is. But you will not do that sitting morosely beneath a tree."

"I have been stabbed," he reminded me. He added with a pointed glance at my fists, "And beaten."

"I will help you," I said. The words felt too meaningful on my tongue, discomforting and vulnerable. "Besides, the island is still at war—you should not be alone."

He made a dry little sound. "I felt better when you were striking me."

We both came to alert as a sorcerous wind swept down the coast. The trees swayed and the voices of dozens of Stormsingers came to us in eerie, contrasting harmonies, berating and building off one another. They were drawing closer.

I offered him a hand. "I can do that again later, if it makes you feel better."

"You are too kind," Ben muttered, glowering at my fingers. He seemed to deflate and finally, reached up to grasp my hand. "Fuck, I am pathetic."

"Sam!" Mary's voice hurtled towards us from the trees. "Ben!"

She and Charles burst into sight, Charles taking up shouting and waving while Mary sprinted pell-mell.

A mass of figures pursued them, running and shooting and roaring, with Talys Lirr at their center.

"Run!" Charles yelled.

Ben seized my hand, I hauled him upright, and we ran.

We had barely made it fifty paces, down the coast and into an arm of the forest, before a Stormsung wind swept us into a frigid embrace. Mary slowed at the suddenness of it and turned as if on unseen strings, throwing her own voice into the fray as the forest around us filled with Stormsingers.

They did not run. They did not dodge into cover or coordinate with shouts. They did not use weapons of steel, though they bore them at their hips and carried them in their arms. They strode through the forest instead, singing as they came, woman after woman, voice after voice. Here and there a male Stormsinger walked with them, deep rumbles backing the higher, lighter, softer, strains of the women. I saw Benedict's weatherwitch too, shoulders level, his voice the richest of them all.

The Capesh came behind them, muskets cradled, strides cautious—yielding to the Stormsinger's lead. A female captain I assumed must be Forbara was there, as were Emre Solla and Atello. Demery and Athe accompanied them, along with a ragtag band of Aeadine and Mereish and Usti sailors, their swords and bayonets already wet with blood.

Stranger shouted something over the wind, his ghisten form manifest and far larger than Talys. She lingered, small and desolate, in his shadow.

His people opened fire. The Stormsinger's song split and the wind blasted ahead of us, tossing trees and undergrowth. At the same time Tane's light bloomed from Mary in a hundred threads, wending into branch and root. Another ghisting joined her, then another and another as every *ghiseau*, from Demery to Charles to Atello, ignited.

Roots twisted up towards the enemy. Branches fell upon them. They snatched at ankles and interrupted musketballs, any eruptions of splinters promptly hurled back upon our enemies.

No shots reached Ben and I, rebuffed by wind and wood. Forbara gave Benedict a brief look as the Capesh advance surrounded us, she nodded to a place at her side, and we shouldered our way to her.

"Is this a rescue," I inquired, "Or a second attack?"

"A rescue," Emre replied, nodding his greeting and passing me a pistol.

"A rescue with a price," Forbara replied at the same time.

I had little doubt what that price would be, but that was a challenge for another day.

Stranger struck. I knew it was him, though I could not see the creature himself. His influence rippled through the earth beneath us, his light visibly bypassing the contrary lights of Tane and Harpy and other allies.

"Down!" I shouted and pulled Ben to the ground.

Not a moment too soon. A massive cedar in the heart of the Capesh forces exploded. Shards hurtled in every direction, tearing through flesh and embedding in bone. A gale heeled back upon us, rushing and swirling so fast I could not see or breathe.

Then, the wind was gone. Leaves and debris drifted down as Ben and I raised our heads.

I could not see Mary. The Other was blinding with mage and ghisten light, and the human world a disaster of storm-ravaged woods. Ghisten lights faded here, retreating back towards their hosts.

A prescient whisper propelled me forward, first at a walk, then a run. I did not have to ask Ben to come with me—he was already at my side, weaving through the chaos.

We found Charles just as Mary and Idriss approached the toppled form of Talys. The enemy fled their coming, retreating through the rain with gunshots and cries. But Lirr's daughter remained, along with dozens of bodies.

Stranger's spectral form and light was nowhere to be seen; the girl's eyes were blank, fixed on something none of us could see. She did not even seem aware of the series of long shards buried in her flesh—stomach, chest, thigh, shoulder. She was a puppet with cut strings, and there seemed little life left in her.

"He left her," Charles said. His eyes had a lingering ghisten glow and he appeared windblown and sharp. As he continued, there was little satisfaction in his voice. Only pity. "She is dying, and he left her."

"I did not think that possible," Ben said. "Would that not kill him?"

"It may yet," Tane's voice broke in, carrying uncannily on an ensorcelled wind. She spoke through Mary's lips, her light in Mary's eyes. The intensity of Mary's appearance recalled me to the boats and the Farlanders, and a chill slid up my spine. "But for the time being, Stranger has fled to the sea."

FIFTY-SIX

The Indifference of Empires

SAMUEL

I t took another day and night of hunting to rid Isla Ascra and the stone forest of lingering enemies. Stranger truly had disappeared, to the sea and on to death or the Dark Water, we could not say. Talys, dying and listless, had been delivered into the care of her brother, the Sooth called Silvan, but within captivity. Lirr had extensive dungeons below the village, and it was to these they were entrusted.

They were joined by the remnants of Voskin's, Artan's, the Lirrs', and Ess Noti combatants, including Voskin's woman Osso.

On the second day, the gathered prisoners were transferred into the belly of several of their ships in preparation for Idriss's immediate departure.

"I will go to the Sea Fort and drop this rabble at Howell's feet," Idriss said, obviously savoring the thought. We were gathered in the courtyard as bonfires burned and the remnants of a communal meal were put away, leaving Idriss, Demery, Athe, Emre and Forbara, Mary, Charles and I under an awning. The man Atello was there too, with Brid, and the two of them sat off to the side. They were halfway through a bottle of wine as Atello spoke of his own time on Ascra.

Ben, as had frequently been the case since the final battle, was absent.

"Multiple council laws were broken in the assault and if they think I will sit by, they are sorely mistaken," Idriss went on. "Voskin is dead. Talys might as well be, and the Lirrs were already radicals in the eyes of the council. By the time I have finished, Talys's seat will be mine and I will have reparations."

"They will discard you again," Forbara warned. She had inserted herself into the heart of things over the past days and now lounged companionably beside Solla, who, I gathered, was an old friend.

The Capesh woman had yet to demand her price for our rescue, but now that the waves had settled, I had little doubt it would be forthcoming.

Forbara continued, "You need more leverage than being wronged."

"Use the documents," a voice said.

Enisca Alamay stepped into the light of our lantern, with Benedict in her shadow. She held open the sides of her coat, showing she was unarmed, and surveyed the lot of us.

Ben moved to lean against a post and watch the proceedings with tired eyes. He looked as though he had not slept in several days.

"What documents? Also, who are you?" Forbara inquired. She glanced around, noting the expressions of everyone else. "It seems I am the only one unenlightened."

"Where have you been?" Mary asked the Usti woman. "We thought you were dead again. And you." She glared at Ben. "You did not come back last night. I strongly considered worrying about you."

"I did worry about you," Charles offered over the rim of his wine.

Ben's mouth quirked. "Apologies. I was soul-searching. And apologizing."

Alamay gave him a lingering look. "A skill which requires some improvement."

He conceded with a shrug.

"Personal grievances must be set aside, regardless." Alamay turned to the rest of us. "May I have a drink?"

Forbara leaned to take her own cup from the table, half full of wine, and handed it to Alamay. She gave Ben a questioning look, but he shook his head and remained leaning against the post.

"Here," Forbara said to Enisca. "Sit. What documents?"

Enisca sat. She took a short sip of wine, rallied, and began to speak. "My name is Anessa Voron, and I was an Usti spy in Mere under the name Enisca Alamay. This spring I stole documents from a Mereish officer which prove that the Usti have been manipulating Mere and Aeadine to continued war. Letters. Ship's logs. The like."

Alamay considered us all calmly, even as we all began to openly stare—save for Ben, who had noted Brid and wore a disconcerted expression.

Alamay—Voron?—went on. "I entrusted those documents into the care of an old colleague, Miko Solov, and reached out to Emre Solla with the intent on handing them over to the Cape to assist in their bid for independence."

Solla cleared his throat. "That had not been aired yet."

"It must be," Alamay replied practically. "Because those documents remain the best hope for the Cape—and for you, Uma Idriss."

"Go on," Idriss prompted.

Across the table, Demery hooked his pipe over a bowl and delivered the whole of his focus to Alamay. Ben, meanwhile, had begun regarding his boots, expression obscured by the fall of his hair.

"Ally yourselves," Alamay said, gesturing her glass between Idriss, and Emre and Forbara. "The Cape will need Stormsingers, not to mention a solid footing in the South Isles and a voice on the council. The documents will be your leverage against the Usti."

"You intend to blackmail the Usti?" Demery clarified.

"Tactfully," Solla interjected. "And in doing so, stop their manipulations. The war between Aeadine and Mere will not end, not quickly—hostilities run too deep and are too complex—but, in time, there will be peace."

"We would need ghistings, too," Forbara put in, resting her gaze upon Mary. "A Ghistwold of our own. A fair price, I would say, for a timely rescue?"

"A rescue made possible because you were hunting us down," Mary replied, her expression less than warm. "I will not give you a forest of slaves, Forbara. Even if the cause is just."

"The ghistings of this Wold would be allies," Solla clarified. "No ghisting will serve aboard a Capesh ship without their consent, just as no Stormsinger would. We have seen similar bargains succeed in places like Tithe—this will be our example. The Cape would be guardians of the new Ghistwold, not owners."

Ghisten light dusted around the edges of Mary's eyes, and I sensed unspoken communication. I saw her hand rest on the table and noted that Grant, Demery and Athe were also all in contact with the wood.

"How can you guarantee this?" Demery asked. "If the matter were based solely on you, Solla, I would not doubt it. But when nations and empires are at stake… I need not elaborate."

"It will not happen overnight, as I said," Emre acknowledged with a nod. "But my people have spent centuries navigating the shoals of Winter Sea politics. We are prepared. Not only that, but we know what it is to be used."

"So, unite," Alamay finished. "Go forward, together."

The conversation continued from there. As critical as the discussion was, Mary was more central than I. When Ben abruptly strode over to Brid, I followed him.

"I know you," Ben said to Brid, who watched him with guarded eyes. "I left you behind in Port Sen, along with several others."

The frankness of his admission startled her as much as I. Atello, meanwhile, watched over the rim of his cup.

"The others are dead," Brid informed him. "Killed in prison."

"The prison where Brid saved my life after Voskin arrested me," I added, lowly, in my brother's ear. "She thought I was you, too."

Ben did not speak again for a long moment. His silence had stretched into awkwardness by the time he finally said, "I see. If you require anything, any funds or aid, only say so."

It was not quite an apology, but there was sincerity in his voice.

Brid inclined her head. "I may, that. One day."

Ben's eyes passed between the three of us again, then he cleared his throat, gave a nod of farewell, and strode away.

I offered Brid and Atello an apologetic look and caught up with Ben near the opposite side of the courtyard, where the pools of light from lanterns and fires ended and the shadows concealed us.

"My Sooth... the woman Vachon, she has not reappeared?" he asked me. "I cannot see her in the Other."

I shook my head slowly. "No. But more than a few longboats escaped. You have learned how to see into the Other?"

"Learned, no. Happen to every now and again, yes." Ben worked his jaw for a moment, then said without further preamble, "I need a ship. That sloop of Artan's will do, along with a small crew. I will pay them well and leave the Isles."

The fact that he had not already done so, without permission, was a mark in his favor.

"I will see what I can do," I promised.

Ben nodded, looking as though great weight had settled upon him. "I must leave, Sam. Even with Voskin dead, we cannot predict what the council will do with me. I could continue as a pirate, I suppose, but I found the life... In some says it suited me too well, in others, not at all. I did not like who that life allowed me to be. I cannot allow Port Sen to be repeated."

Any reply I might have given faded at the last. His words collided with my uncertainty surrounding *Reckoning*, the recovery of Hart and my crew, and the loss of Mr. Penn. But Ben could not change the past. I would go to Sen. I would recover them.

"Nor continue to endanger you and Mary and your future," Ben added solemnly. "Like it or not, I am bound to others in this world. I must begin to live as such."

My eyes began to burn. There were a thousand things to say and at the same time, none at all. I settled for a simple, "Thank you."

He nodded.

"Where will you go?"

"Back to Aeadine," he said. "There I am only disgraced, instead of being a criminal, and I suppose that is the best I can hope for. As I said before… I have reparations to make."

I wanted to ask what he intended those reparations to be, but my dreamer's sense had an inkling, and I feared his decision was still too delicate to touch.

"I may turn up at Rosser House," he went on. "You can write me there."

"I see."

He bumped his shoulder into mine. "Now, get your crew back, and get married," he charged me. "Make some more dutiful sons and feral daughters."

I had started to smile, but at his phrasing, I hesitated. "More?"

"You are the Sooth," he said, nodding across the courtyard to Mary. "Take a good, long look at that woman."

With that, he strode away. I was left staring at Mary and her light, on the edge of the Other. Stormsinger blue. Ghisten teal. Ghiseau Grey.

And, cradled in the gentle arc of her belly, a new, glistening spark.

FIFTY-SEVEN

A Fitting Gift

MARY

Autumn in Oranmur brought a blissful end to the warmth of the southern summer. I languished in a chair on the stoop of the house Demery had given Samuel and I at the edge of the village, halfway up the spur. From here I could see the sea and distant islands, Demery's house and the entirety of the settlement.

So it was that I saw Emre Solla's ship and *Reckoning* sail in together. I was still languishing when, several hours later, my mother climbed the path from the village with the girl Poverly in tow and my half-sister in a wrap across her chest.

The child was well and properly asleep, her face turned to one side, lips puckered in steady, unconscious suckling. She had her father's black curls, already thick, but I saw my mother in her little face and, by extension, myself.

The sight made my heart ache and some of my discomfort fade. My exhaustion did not seem so heavy a weight with her in sight.

"Mary!" Poverly greeted brightly, lowering a heavy basket and a satchel. "Captain will be along soon. He sends this, and told me to tell you the Uknaras are coming up too."

Digging into the satchel, Poverly pulled out a string-wrapped box, which I opened with growing suspicion.

"Toffee," I beamed.

"She didn't eat a single one," my mother put in, swaying slightly with one hand on her second daughter's back.

Poverly rolled her eyes, following the box with a stack of letters. "Also, there are these."

I recognized Idriss's hand on the top letter and tucked the bundle into the pocket of my skirts. Poverly disappeared into the house with the basket and I sat back down, opening the toffee box and eyeing my mother.

"So?" I prompted. "What word from the Cape?"

"Emre has set the wheels in motion," my mother said, sitting down in a second chair and placing a gentle kiss on the infant's forehead as she stirred in her sleep. "There are good people there, Mary. I've hope. What of the Wold?"

"Forbara was through last week," I said, offering her a toffee, which she fortunately refused, as I intended to eat every one of them. "Every ghisten tree has been harvested, healed and settled on the Otherborn island. The ghisting we saved from the Company has been returned and the new Mother Tree Tane planted is strong and healthy. And Hart has rooted well and thrives as a guardian of the young Wold. It will take time, but the entire Wold will re-root and be all the healthier for it."

"How did you manage, in your condition?" my mother pressed.

"I vomited on Forbara once. She took it well." We grinned at one another for a moment then I went on, "I am exhausted, and glad to be home. I'll not leave again for a long while."

"So this is home?" she said. There was an edge to her voice, a thread of hope I did not want to snap. She and Emre had made their home here, too, as much as their traveling between Cape and Oranmur allowed for one.

I rested a hand on my swelling belly. "I've promised my aid to Idriss, and Tane has promised hers to the Wold. Samuel has been more than happy with his work for Demery and the council. You are here. Charles is here."

I trailed off, my thoughts coalescing, and spoke again into the cool wind and the autumn sun. As I did, I heard my own voice strengthen, and I considered how deeply I meant my words. "We will not let this child be born into a world of slaves and indentures. She is our compass, now."

"She?" my mother repeated, something very, very soft in her eyes.

"Tane has told me," I said, finding my smile tremulous on my lips. The winds swept up to me, bringing with them the warmth of sun on rock and the promise of snow over the horizon. It also brought the sound of footsteps.

Samuel was climbing the hill. He was not alone, the large figure of Illya Uknara at his back, and the smaller of Olsa. Since their rescue the pair had been working with Mr. Maren, the talisman maker, under Demery's employ. They had a new path ahead of them, just as we did—one intent on leveling the divide between Mereish magecrafts and that of other nations.

"Has there been any word from Benedict?" my mother asked, her gaze too straying to the approaching company.

I shook my head. "No. But Samuel says he is in Aeadine. He can still see him in the Other."

"What is he doing there?"

I rose as Samuel crested the hill, his face breaking into a smile of greeting so warm and so raw that my chest ached and my eyes felt too damp.

"Finding his compass."

FIFTY-EIGHT

Josephine

BENEDICT

I stood before a door. The latch turned easily under my hand and I pushed it open, keeping the toes of my boots on the outside of the threshold.

A little girl sat on the floor beneath the window, between a chair and a narrow bed. Her hair, soft blonde like her mother's, caught the light off the winter's first blanket of snow. Her sock-clad feet were just beneath her skirts.

She had been staring at a doll in her lap, whispering something to the toy's blankly smiling face, but now she raised her eyes to me. Eyes that were, though wide in the soft face of a child, mine. Sam's. Ours.

We watched one another for a long, long moment. I meant to speak. I had had six weeks of agonizing over this moment, of what I would say, of how I would apologize, if I should apologize, if she would even understand.

"Are you my father?" She asked the question while considering her doll again, poking at its narrow chest. "You look like me."

I found my voice, though it was quiet and thick. "I... am."

She stood up, tucked the doll under her arm, and crossed the room to stand within arm's reach. The simplicity of her approach, her lack of fear, struck me almost as deeply as the sight of her or the sound of her little voice.

"Mama said she would send you to get me," the girl said. She was right—I had found a stack of letters from her mother at Samuel's lodgings in Ismoathe, all of them addressed to me under Samuel's care. All of them requests for help.

My husband has sent the girl away, Benedict.

She is your responsibility, Benedict.

She is yours.

"Did she tell you my name?" The girl asked.

"Josephine," I rasped. I crouched down and put a hand on the doorframe, losing faith in my legs to hold me up. "You are Josephine."

She nodded, smiling shyly, and held up her doll. "This is Beth."

I nodded, unable to take my eyes from her face.

"You should say hello to Beth," Josephine instructed.

"That's—" I cleared my throat again and nodded. "Hello, Beth. Josephine…"

She watched me, waiting for me to go on.

I wanted to say that, in that moment, I knew what fear was. When I saw her standing before me, heard her acknowledge me as her father, seeing her approach as if I were no true stranger—something within me had crumbled, and behind it there was only terror.

Terror of the unknown. Terror of failure. Terror of the intensity of feeling that constricted my chest and pulled the air from my lungs. Terror that I could not be what this child deserved, or that I would destroy her, and she was better off without me.

Then I saw the room again, the narrow bed and the foggy window, and a child alone. And in my heart, I found another feeling, new and possibly even more terrifying.

It was a well of want, a need and a drive and a desperation to be what that small figure, that familiar little stranger with her eyes like mine, needed me to be.

"Josephine," I began again. "I would like you to come with me. I've spoken to the mistress, and put everything in order. We can go to Rosser House, where I grew up." I added the last with marked hesitation, "If you want to go. You do not know me and—"

She cut me off: "A house? Your house?" Something tremulous entered her eyes.

I nodded, unable to speak again. But I found the strength to hold out an open hand.

She considered the hand for a long moment, then shuffled her doll under one arm.

She laid her fingers in mine.

The snow comes, heavy and hushed. It shrouds the branches of the trees and rests to unseasonable leaves, nestles into the hollows between roots and clings to the eyelashes of the Woman from the Wold.

Hart considers her from beneath the spreading branches of his towering oak. She approaches through the veil of white. There is a child on her hip and a familiar man at her side, and the ever-present Mother Ghisting in her bones.

Hart meets them at the edges of his roots. The snow does not gather on his massive antlers, ethereal as they are, nor do his hooves leave tracks in the growing blanket on the ground. He huffs, and considers the man.

He lowers his head towards Samuel. There is no hostility in his spectral regard. If anything, there is a certain affection, a gratitude and mutual respect for this mortal he once guarded from threats both of this world, and the Other.

Then he lowers his head a little more, to peer into the eyes of the girl on the woman's hip. His gaze is gentler then, and when she reaches out to place a hand on his nose, it is a true contact. Flesh to flesh.

The child smiles.

Sister, murmurs Hart.

SONGS REFERENCED

"Pibroch of Donald Dhu" by Sir Walter Scott

"The Female Smuggler," a traditional English ballad

"The Fox is in the Bushes," a traditional song

"The Rime of the Ancient Mariner" by Samuel Taylor Coleridge

ACKNOWLEDGMENTS

It's an honor and privilege to be sitting here at my keyboard, closing off my second series.

A most sincere and heartfelt thanks to my editor George Sandison for all his patience and insight, as well as the entire Titan team. You have always made me feel like a person in what can often be a painfully impersonal industry, and you are all so wonderful to work with.

To my mother, GG, my husband, and my father—this book truly would not have happened without you. Thank you for all your sacrifices providing childcare and love for our little boy, and allowing me to continue the career I worked so hard for, even into this new chapter of life.

Thank you to all my author friends for standing with me through the struggles and triumphs. Thank you to my agent, Naomi Davis, for your skills at negotiation and optimistic outlook.

And thank you, my readers, for your enthusiasm and love for Mary, Sam, Charles, Demery and even Ben.

May there be many more stories to come.

ABOUT THE AUTHOR

H.M. LONG is a Canadian author who inhabits a ramshackle cabin in Ontario, Canada, with her family. However, she can often be spotted snooping about museums or wandering the Alps. She is the author of *Hall of Smoke, Temple of No God, Barrow of Winter* and *Pillar of Ash*, along with *Dark Water Daughter* and *Black Tide Son*.

For more fantastic fiction, author events,
exclusive excerpts, competitions, limited editions and more

VISIT OUR WEBSITE
titanbooks.com

LIKE US ON FACEBOOK
facebook.com/titanbooks

FOLLOW US ON TWITTER AND INSTAGRAM
@TitanBooks

EMAIL US
readerfeedback@titanemail.com